A DAWN OF DRAGONFIRE

A DAWN OF DRAGONFIRE

DRAGONLORE, BOOK ONE

DANIEL ARENSON

ISBN: 978-0-9878864-9-1

CRESCENT
ISLE

FIDELIUM

NOVA VITA

REQUIEM

CASTELLUM
LUNA

OSANNA

GILNOR

TIRANOR

MORI

Mori was standing on the fortress walls when she saw the phoenix rise.

A bird of fire, it soared from the snowy horizon, wings outstretched like sunrays. It must have been huge--the size of a dragon or larger. Mori gasped and shivered. The wind whipped her cloak, scented of fire, too hot for winter. She grasped her little finger behind her back, the sixth finger on her left hand, her *luck* finger. Her pet mouse clutched her shoulder; he too had seen the creature of flame.

"Orin!" Mori whispered, lips trembling. She wanted to cry out louder, to sound the alarm, to summon her brother and all his guards... but her fear froze her lips like the frost upon the endless forest before her.

The phoenix coiled in the distance, soaring higher, a creature of grace and beauty. It seemed woven of nothing but fire, and a wake of sparks like stars trailed below it. Mori could hear its distant call, caws like a southern bird of many colors.

Mori wanted to flee. She remembered all those stories her brothers would tell her, terrible stories of griffins attacking Requiem and killing a million of her people. *Even when we took dragon form, we could not stop them,* her brothers would say and squawk like griffins, making Mori run and weep and hide.

"But that was a long time ago," Mori whispered, fingers shaking, even her luck finger. It had been hundreds of years since griffins had attacked, and Requiem was strong now, so powerful no enemy could harm her. Fifty thousand Vir Requis lived in Nova Vita, fair city of the north, and each could grow scales and wings, take flight as a dragon, and defend her.

Still, she reminded herself, Nova Vita lay far north--so many leagues away, she could not count them. Here in the south, in cold and lonely Castellum Luna, only fifty Vir Requis dwelled. Her brother Orin. A few soldiers. And her... the princess Mori, an eighteen-year-old girl with one finger too many, a pet mouse, and enough fear to drown her.

She squinted at the horizon. The phoenix was undulating skyward like a candle's flame torn free from the wick. Its song carried on the wind. Her mouse twitched his whiskers, scurried down Mori's gown, and entered her pocket. Mori envied her pet; she often wished she too could hide so easily.

"Maybe it's good," she whispered. "Maybe it won't hurt us, Pip."

Without Pip, her dear mouse, she would have gone mad down here, she thought. It was just so *lonely* in this southern hinterland. So... so cold and distant and everything frightened her. Mori missed Nova Vita. She missed the city's marble columns that rose between the birches, so beautiful, not like the rough bricks of this outpost. She missed her father the king, her friend the Lady Lyana, and all the minstrels and priests and jugglers and storytellers. Most of all, she missed the library of Nova Vita, a towering chamber with so many books she could read for a lifetime.

Why did Father have to send her here? Why did Requiem even need another settlement? Nova Vita was good enough. Mori had tried to tell Father that, but he only spoke of Requiem recovering from the griffins, and expanding to her old borders, and how the southern air would put some courage into her, and... Mori wanted to weep. None of it made sense to her, and nothing so far had made her any braver. If anything, her fear only grew upon these cold stone walls, staring into this frosted forest, and watching this bird of fire.

As she stood frozen in fear, the horizon kindled. An orange glow rose from distant mist, spreading tendrils across the white sky; it was like sunrise from the south. The snowy forest turned red, and the smell of fire filled Mori's nostrils, spinning her head. Flames crackled and finally she found her voice.

"Orin!" she shouted from the walls. "Fire, Orin! The forest is burning!"

But no, this was no forest fire, she saw. These were no earthly flames. Countless more phoenixes spread wings. Countless wakes of fire rose like comets. The horizon blazed with an army of firebirds, eagles of sound and fury. Their shrieks rose, cries of war. The clouds themselves burned and the forest shook, its frost melting, its trees crackling.

"Orin!" Mori cried. She wanted to use her magic, the magic of Requiem. She wanted to grow scales and wings, breathe fire, and fly as a dragon. But she could only stand upon these walls, a girl with tears in her eyes, a lucky finger, and fear that froze her.

Armor clanked, swords hissed, and boots thumped. Orin ran up the wall, his men behind him. They formed ranks upon the battlements, and their scent filled Mori's nostrils: the smell of oil, leather, sweat, and safety. Her brother clasped her shoulder, staring at the flaming birds that rose in the south. He was a tall man, ten years her senior. His hair was brown like hers and his eyes the same gray, but his face was so much harder, his soul so much stronger. His armor was thick and his sword heavy, and Mori clung to him. He was Orin Aeternum, Son of Olasar, Prince of Requiem, and he was the strongest man she knew.

"What are they, Orin?" she whispered.

His men leaned over the parapets, frowning, each burly and bedecked in steel. Their breath plumed and frost covered their beards. They were the finest warriors of Requiem, sent here to guard this southern fort, this border, and her. Their hands clutched the hilts of their swords. Orin stared with them, frown deepening.

"I don't know," he said softly. "But we're going to find out." His voice rose. "Men of Requiem! We fly!"

He tossed back his head, outstretched his arms, and drew his magic, the magic of Requiem's stars. Silver scales flowed across him. Wings unfurled from his back, claws sprang from his fingers, and fangs grew in his mouth. Soon he roared upon the walls, a silver dragon, fifty feet long and blowing fire. His men shifted around him. They too grew wings and scales, and soon fifty dragons took flight, their fire crackling.

Mori took a deep breath and prepared to shift too. She could not become a burly, powerful dragon like these soldiers, but her scales were still hard, her breath hot, her wings fast. Many called her the fastest dragon in Requiem. Yet Orin, flying from the wall, looked over his shoulder and glared.

"Stay here, sister!" he called, wings churning the falling snow. "Go into the hall, bar the door, and do not emerge until I return."

With that, he roared flame and soared, howls ringing in Mori's ears. His fellow dragons flew at his sides, scales glimmering and breath flaming. Mori watched them, clutching her eleventh finger behind her back.

Help them, luck finger, she prayed. In the distance, the phoenixes screeched, moving closer.

She could see the birds clearly now. Their bodies were woven of molten fire, coiling like storms upon the sun. Their beaks were white and blazing, their eyes swirling stars. With every flap, their wings sprayed fire. Their heat crashed against Mori, even from this distance. The forest wept beneath them, melted snow running in rivulets toward the fort Mori stood upon. Ten thousand firebirds flew there, maybe more. The fifty dragons seemed so small before them--specks of dust flying into a furnace.

"Fly back, beasts of fire!" Orin cried to them, voice thundering. His wings fanned their flame. "Turn from our border."

The phoenixes screeched and swooped toward him.

Mori watched in horror, clutching her finger so tightly she thought she might rip it off. The phoenixes reached out claws of white fire. Flames swirled around their wings and their eyes blazed like stars. The firebirds crashed against the dragons, engulfing them with flame.

"*Orin!*" Mori shouted. She could barely see him, only the fire and smoke... but she heard him. She heard him scream.

What could she do? He'd told her to hide in the fortress, but... they were killing him! She stared, biting her lip so hard she tasted blood. The dragons were howling, kicking, and clawing. She glimpsed their lashing tails, their scales, their maws crying in agony. They tried to fight. Their fangs bit only fire, and their tails only scattered sparks. A few dragons were blowing flames, but that only stoked the phoenix fire.

"Orin, come back!" Mori cried, tears in her eyes. The heat blazed against her, drenching her with sweat. Her gown clung to her body, and her damp hair stuck to her face. She coughed, struggling for breath.

His roars tore at her, cries of pain. Mori wanted to fly to him. She wanted to hide. She could barely breathe, and she knew the phoenixes saw her; their eyes blazed against her. One dragon cried in agony, a sound like tearing flesh. A phoenix claw slashed him, and Requiem's magic left him. Where a dragon had flown, a man now fell, blazing, and thudded dead against the trees. Three more dragons burned, and in the pain of death, their magic vanished. Three more bodies tumbled.

"Mori!" her brother cried from the inferno. Flames engulfed him, white around his silver scales. His wings churned the fire, showering sparks like exploding suns. "Mori, run! Hide!"

"Orin...," she whispered, trembling, clutching her hands behind her back.

"Mori, run!" he cried as the phoenixes tore into him. Their beaks thrust, woven of hardened fire. Their claws dug into him. Their flames surrounded him. Orin Aeternum, Son of Olasar, Prince of Requiem... lost his magic, turned from dragon to burning man, and fell from the sky.

Something tore inside Mori. Her heart shattered. A pain splintered in her chest and shot through her. A cry fled her lips, and before she knew it, she had shifted into a dragon. Golden scales clinked across her, her wings flapped, and she flew into the southern fire.

"Orin, where are you?" she cried, swooping through flame. The fire blazed around her, so hot she could only squint, and her scales felt ready to melt. Three phoenixes dived toward her, each larger than her. Their shrieks tore at her ears. They clawed at her scales, and Mori screamed, tumbled, flapped her wings, and howled. She soared, knocked by them, and rose through an inferno of heat and sound and rage. Everywhere she looked were blazing eyes, beaks of fire, talons that lashed her. She soared higher, burst between them, and swooped again. She had to find her brother. She had to find her Orin, her dear Orin, her hero, her only chance for life. She knocked between phoenixes and falling dragons, crashed toward the earth, and saw him lying in snow.

His clothes smoked. Singed black, they clung to his melted flesh. Half his face was a burnt ruin, red and black and blistering. His skin peeled. He gazed at her with one good eye, and his lips worked, trying to whisper, trying to call to her.

"Oh, Orin," she whispered, horror pounding through her. He was alive. She could still save him. She lifted him with her claws, as gently as she could, but he cried hoarsely and his eyes rolled back.

Was he dead? Had she killed him? She had no time to check. The phoenixes swooped down, an army of wrath, and Mori took flight. Fire bathed her. She shot through flames, wings churning smoke.

I'm the fastest dragon in Requiem, Orin always said so, I can do this. She screamed and emerged from the flames, her brother's limp human form in her claws. The phoenix army on her tail, she flew over the walls of Castellum Luna, down into the courtyard, and landed by the doors of their hall.

They cannot enter, she told herself. *They're too big.* She placed Orin upon the flagstones, shifted back into a human girl, and pushed the doors. They creaked open, revealing a hall full of trestle tables, tapestries, and spears.

The phoenixes shrieked behind her. Their heat blasted her. Mori raced into the hall, dragged her brother inside, and saw countless phoenixes descending into the courtyard. She slammed the doors shut as they landed, sealing their fire outside.

"Mori...," Orin whispered, voice hoarse. "Mori, leave me... fly north. Fly to Nova Vita."

Mori pulled a lever, dropping the doors' bar into the brackets. She stood panting. Could the phoenixes break the doors? They were thick and banded in iron, built to withstand fire and axe. And what of the other dragons? Stars, were any still alive, and had she doomed them to death? She trembled.

The phoenixes screeched outside. Their light glowed under the doors, and tongues of fire reached around the frames. They began slamming at the doors, howling. Mori whimpered with every jolt.

I must go deeper, she thought. *Into the dungeon. The door there is small, too small for them.*

She leaned over Orin, and her breath left her. Tears filled her eyes. Half his face was gone, melted away. Half his body was a wound of welts, smoke, and seared cloth clinging to flesh. Mori gagged, for a moment able to do nothing else. Then she steeled herself. The phoenixes were lashing at the doors. She had to save her brother.

She looked at the eastern wall. A small door stood open there, revealing a staircase that plunged into shadow. Mori tightened her lips. The dungeon of Castellum Luna lay down those stairs. The place had always frightened her--she would imagine ghosts lurking in its shadows--but today she would seek safety there.

"Come on, Orin!" she said, placed her arms around him, and tugged. She grunted, grinding her heels against the floor. "Come on, Orin, get up! On your feet!"

He managed to rise to his knees, coughing, breath like a saw. With strength she had not known was in her, Mori pulled him to his feet. He leaned against her, twice her weight. She thought she would collapse, but she walked, step by step, and helped Orin onto the staircase. She pulled the door shut and began walking downstairs, Orin leaning against her. As the phoenixes howled, and the fortress doors creaked, they descended with blood and tears.

Finally Mori found herself in the dungeon of Castellum Luna, a cold place of shadows, sacks of wheat, barrels of wine, and now the stench of burnt flesh. An oil lamp glowed upon a table, painting the room red. Panting, Mori lay her brother on the floor and touched his hair. His breath wheezed and his flesh still smoked.

Upstairs, she heard the fortress doors shatter. She started. Great eagle cries echoed. Even here in the dungeon, Mori felt the phoenix heat as they stormed into the hall.

"We'll be all right, Orin," she whispered and held his hot, sticky body. "They can't fit down here. The staircase is too small for them. We're safe here. We're safe. I'm going to take care of you."

He only groaned, and she felt his blood upon her, staining her gown, and she held him tight. They trembled together. Above in the hall, she heard the phoenix cries; they seemed to shake the fort, cries of hatred, rage, and bloodlust. *This must be how the griffins sounded when they toppled our halls of old.*

"Mori..." Orin spoke hoarsely, barely able to speak at all. "Mori, you must fly north. You are fast. You..."

He could say no more. Mori held him tight. How could she fly north? How could she escape so many phoenixes, an army of flame? Her head spun. Perhaps she should not have entered this fort, but... Orin had told her to hide here! And now he wanted her to flee? What was she to do? Her head spun, and she shook it violently.

"Rest, Orin," she whispered. "Please. Rest."

She would have to take care of things now. She would have to make the decisions. His life depended on her. *Be calm, Mori,* she told herself. She forced herself to take slow, deep breaths, to steady her trembling limbs.

"We'll wait here until the phoenixes leave," she whispered. "They have to leave sometime. They *have* to. They can't fit down here. When they go away, we'll fly north. I'll take you to the temples, to healers, Orin. They can heal you. They can... they can fix your..."

Your ravaged face, she wanted to say. *Your flesh that melted off. The ruin of your left side, a wound of blood and bone.* Yet could anyone save him now? And could anyone save her?

Gently she pulled back from him; their bodies parted with a sickly, sticky sound like a bandage pulled off a wet wound. In the darkness, Mori crept upstairs toward the dungeon door. Firelight burned behind it. The phoenixes stood in the main hall. She heard their cawing, the crackle of their fire. Squinting against the heat and light, Mori knelt and peeked through the keyhole.

Two phoenixes moved through the hall. Their flames torched the tapestries and trestle tables. One tossed back its head and screeched, and Mori covered her ears. She thought that screech could tear her eardrums and shatter her ribs.

Please go away, she prayed. *Please please leave this place, fly away from here, and let this only be a nightmare.* She clutched her luck finger behind her back, praying to it. *Please send them away. Please let me just wake up and be in Nova Vita again, with Lady Lyana and Father and everyone else.*

Yet the phoenixes in the hall remained. They sniffed, stirring wisps of fire upon their beaks. *Stars, can they smell me?* The firebirds turned toward the door where Mori hid, cawed, and stepped toward it. Their claws rained sparks. Mori caught her breath, too frightened to even flee.

They can't hurt me, she told herself. *They're too big to enter the doorway. Even if they burn the door, they can't enter. And they can't burn the stone walls of the dungeon.* She forced herself to breathe. *We're safe here.*

As she watched through the keyhole, her breath died.

The phoenixes tossed back their heads, cried so loudly that they shook the hall, and outstretched their wings. Their flames rose in fury. They seemed to... not to shrink, Mori thought, but to... fold in upon themselves. Their fire twisted, darkened, shaped new forms. Suddenly the creatures appeared almost human to her, their limbs long and fiery, their heads burning. The flames coalesced, forming a man and woman of liquid fire. The lava hardened. Last wisps of flame clung to the figures, then pulled into crystals they wore around their necks. Finally all the phoenix fire glowed inside the amulets--two small, blazing lights.

Mori gasped and whimpered. She reached into her pocket and clutched Pip so tightly the mouse bit her.

The two figures stood in the hall, smoke still rising from them. Both wore armor of pale steel, gilded helmets, and curved swords upon their waists. Their hair was platinum blond, so pale it was almost white. *They have ghost hair.* Mori trembled to see it.

The man stood facing her, staring at the dungeon door. He was tall and broad, with a face like beaten leather. His eyes were small, blue, and mean. A golden sun was embedded into his breastplate. Mori recognized the emblem--the Golden Sun of Tiranor.

Tirans! she thought. She had heard many tales of them; they were a cruel, warlike people from southern deserts beyond mountain, lake, and swamp.

The woman stood with her back toward the door. She was tall and slender, and her hair was long and smooth. Two sabres hung from her belt, shaped like the beaks of cranes, their pommels golden. Slowly, the woman turned toward the door. Her eyes were blue, her face golden and strewn with bright freckles like stars in sunset. A scar, as from an old fire, ran across her face from head to chin, then snaked down her neck into her breastplate.

Mori gasped.

She knew this woman.

"Solina," she whispered.

Some of her fear left her. Solina was her friend! A princess of Tiranor, her parents slain, she had grown up in Requiem. Mori remembered many nights of sitting in Solina's lap, listening to her tell stories of Tiranor--its white towers rising from the desert, capped with gold; its oases of lush palms, warm pools, and birds of paradise; its proud people of golden skin, bright hair that shone, and blue eyes that saw far.

Solina won't hurt me, Mori thought, breathing shakily. *Solina will realize this was a mistake, once she sees me, once she realizes it's me, Mori. I was like a sister to her.*

And yet... Mori hesitated. She stayed frozen. That scar that ran down Solina's face... could it be from that night? The night

Solina had attacked Father with a blade, and Orin burned her? Mori shuddered. *No, it can't be!* But she knew it was true; that was the scar of dragonfire.

She remembered, Mori realized, and tears filled her eyes. *And now she's here to burn us too.*

The tall, stately woman took a step toward the door, and those blue eyes stared right at the keyhole, right at Mori. Solina's lips curled into a smile.

She saw me! Mori leaped back from the door, heart pounding. She heard footfalls move toward her, and Mori scrambled downstairs. She knelt in the shadows by Orin. He was moaning, body hot, burnt, stinking with death. She clutched his hand.

"Don't be scared, Orin," she whispered as the door above shook. "I'll protect you."

Splinters flew. The door shattered, and firelight bathed the dungeon.

Mori wanted to shift into a dragon. She wanted to let scales cover her, let flame blow from her maw. Yet she dared not. The dungeon was so small, a mere ten feet wide. If she shifted, her girth would fill the chamber, would crush Orin dead. Instead she clutched the hilt of her brother's sword, steeled herself, and drew the blade. It hissed and caught the light.

Solina walked downstairs, hands on her own swords' hilts. Her breastplate sported a golden sun. Around her neck, her crystal of fire crackled, painting her face orange and red. The burly man walked behind her, eyes blazing and teeth bared.

"Stand back!" Mori said, holding her brother's sword before her. Her voice trembled, and the sword wavered. She added her left hand to the hilt, the hand with six fingers, her *luck* hand. *Bring me luck today,* she prayed to it.

Solina approached her. The scar that halved her face tweaked her lips; she was either smirking, or her scar locked her lips in eternal mockery. She seemed inhuman to Mori--her skin made of gold, her hair of platinum, her eyes of sapphire. She was more statue than flesh and blood.

"Why, if it isn't little Mori!" she said, and this time Mori knew that she was smiling. Those scarred lips parted, revealing dazzling white teeth. "Last time I saw you, you were but a girl, a slight thing with no breasts and skinned knees. You've become a woman!"

Mori stood, holding her sword in trembling hands, her brother groaning behind her.

"Stand back, devil!" Tears rolled down her cheeks. "Stand back, or my father the king will hear of this, and he will kill you!"

Solina's face softened--the face of a woman who saw a cute, angry puppy that melted her heart. The man at her side, however, seemed not to share her amusement. He stared at Mori hungrily; she felt his small, mean eyes undress her.

"Oh, dear dear, frightened sweetling," Solina said and clucked her tongue. "But we were such good friends once, were we not? We were as sisters. I remember holding you on my lap, mussing your hair, and reading to you stories of romance and adventure. I promise not to hurt you, my little sparrow... but please, do not stand between me and your brother, or Lord Acribus here will hurt you. And he will hurt you greatly, little sparrow. More than anyone ever has."

The tall man with the golden, leathery face licked his lips. His tongue was freakishly long--it nearly reached his eyes--and white as bone. It looked like a snake emerging from his mouth. His eyes dripped lust, both for flesh and blood.

An hour ago, if somebody had told Mori this would happen, she would have expected to faint, weep, even die of fright. Now she found herself snarling. Her love for Orin, and her fear for him, swelled over fear for herself. Teeth bared, she swung her sword before her, slicing the air.

"Stand back!" she said. "You will not touch him."

Solina sighed. "My sweetling." She ran a finger down her scar, from forehead, to chin, and down her neck. She kept tracing her fingers along her breastplate and finally down her thigh. "Do you see this scar, Mori? I call it my line of fire. It runs from my head to my toe. Your brother gave me this scar. He deformed me. Surely you of all people, with your freakish left hand, know about being deformed." She looked at the burnt, groaning Orin. "So I burned him too. But I am not done with him. He will feel so *much* more pain before I let him die. But you, Mori, need not feel the same pain. You were as a sister to me; I want to spare you this agony. Step aside... or I will give you to my pet. You will scream and beg me for death before he's done with you."

Mori was scared, so scared that she couldn't breathe, and cold sweat drenched her, and her heart seemed ready to crack. She thought of her brother Orin, so handsome and strong, now this ruin of a man. She thought of her other brother, the wise Elethor, who lived up north among the birches.

It's up to me now, Mori knew. *Me, the younger sister, the slim girl who is always so fast to cry, so fast to hide.* She took a shuddering breath. *For years my older brothers protected me; now it's my turn to fight for them.*

With a wordless cry, she swung her blade at Solina.

So fast Mori barely saw her move, Solina drew her left sword. The blade was curved, glimmering with white steel and gold. The two blades clashed, one a northern blade kissed with starlight, the other a desert shard of fire. Sparks flew, and before Mori realized what had happened, Solina's blade flew again, nicked her hand, and blood splashed.

Mori's sword fell and clanged against the floor.

Nearly as fast as Solina's blade, her companion, the snarling Lord Acribus, moved forward. He looked to Mori more beast than man, a wild dog of rabid fangs, cruel eyes, and an appetite for flesh. She screamed when he caught her arms, digging his fingers into her; she thought those fingers could break her bones.

"Solina!" she cried. "Solina, please! How could you do this? We... we raised you as family. You... my brother Elethor loved you, I..."

But her words failed her. Solina stared at her with those cold blue eyes. They were as chips of ice in a golden mask. There was no humanity to them, no compassion, nothing but cruelty.

"Lord Acribus," the woman said, "make her watch."

The lord's fingers dug so deep into Mori's arms, blood trickled to her elbows. "She will watch, my queen, if I must cut off her eyelids."

She shook in his grasp, a tiny mouse caught in a vulture's talons; she was shorter than his shoulders. She watched, trembling, as Solina approached the wounded prince of Requiem.

"Please," Mori whispered, but Solina ignored her.

Orin groaned upon the floor, scorched and convulsing. Somehow he managed to rise to his elbows. Sweat and blood drenched him.

"Sol... Solina," he managed, so hoarse Mori could barely make out the word.

Solina stood above him, sabre drawn, eyes cold. If Orin was a wounded beast, a twisted creature, Solina was a queen of beauty, a statue of gold and steel and ice.

"Hello, Orin," she said softly. "So you remember me too. Perhaps you know me by the scar you gave me." She caressed it. "My line of fire. It is a strange thing, is it not? I used to fear fire. When I lived in Requiem, among you beasts of scales and wings, I feared it." She laughed mirthlessly. "Imagine it! A young, frightened girl from Tiranor, snatched from her home. You could all turn into dragons--noble, ancient children of Requiem, flaunting your magic of starlight. Yes, I feared this fire I could never wield. And I screamed, Orin. I screamed when you burned me."

"You..." He moaned and shivered. His peeling skin hung from him. "You attacked my father, you..."

Again her bitter laugh pierced the air. "I attacked King Olasar, yes. I attacked the man who murdered my parents. Who enslaved me. Who would banish me only because I dared to love Elethor, your brother, the dearest man I've known. Did I ever stand a chance, Orin? Could I ever dream of reaching him with my dagger, when you were there to burn me? The pain of your fire nearly drove me mad; you feel this pain now. So I left, Orin. And I tamed fire." She snarled like a wild beast, and her voice rose. "I wrestled it, and made it my own, until I could become a thing of flame itself. And I burned you. And I will watch you die in agony."

Her sword lashed.

Mori screamed.

Acribus laughed.

With a whistle, Solina's curved, glittering blade sliced Orin's belly and splattered blood across the wall. Mori shut her eyes, whimpering, but Acribus pulled her eyelids open with rough fingers. She tried to turn her head away, but he held it, forcing her to look, forcing her to see it. *Stars, no... no, please, stars, no....* Her tears fell.

Orin screamed. He clutched his wound, trying to stop it, to stop the spilling of it, the glistening, bloody, pink horror of it. Half-burnt and cut open, he cried for Requiem. He cried for their mother. Mori wept.

"Please, Solina, please, please, please...," she whispered.

But Solina only stood frozen, staring down at the dying man, and still no emotion filled her eyes, not a glimmer of pity nor disgust nor even delight.

"You can make it end, Orin," she said softly. Blood sluiced around her boots. "Tell me of Olasar's forces. Tell me how many dragons in his brigades, where they are stationed, who leads them. Tell me everything... and I will plunge my sword into your heart, and I will end your pain. If you do not speak, well... I can stand here for hours. It will take you hours to die without my mercy, do not doubt it. Maybe even days." She smiled softly. "As long as it takes."

He screamed. And he spoke. And he told her everything as he writhed and begged for the pain to end.

Mori trembled, kicked, tried to look away, tried to break free, tried to do anything but see this ruin of her brother, hear his screams, see his blood and entrails spill upon the floor until finally, finally after ages and ages of it, Solina drove her blade into his chest. Finally some emotion filled the queen's eyes. Pleasure. Deep, horrible, hot pleasure. She twisted the blade, and Orin's breath caught, and his scream died... and his pain ended. It was over.

Thank the stars, it's over, Mori thought as she sobbed and shook.

But it was not over. Not for her.

"My queen?" Acribus asked, voice like gravel, breath hot and stinking against Mori.

She looked at him, eyebrow raised, and nodded. "Have your treat, dog."

Now Mori did try to shift into a dragon, even if her girth would slam against the walls, and the dungeon would crush her. She tried to clutch her magic, to grow scales, grow fangs, grow talons that could slash Acribus. But her pain was too great.

When she thought she could grasp her magic, his fingers clutched her neck, and it was all she could do to even breathe.

He tore her gown. He shoved her across the table. She felt her mouse flutter against her breast, trapped in her pocket, throbbing like a heart. Shadow covered her world and her eyes rolled back. Pain and blood filled the dungeon, and Solina smiled.

Fire.

Floating stars.

Darkness underground.

Outside, the phoenixes shrieked. Myriads of flaming wings rose, showering heat and light and fire. The forests of Requiem burned, and smoke veiled the sky, red and black. A single fortress rose from the inferno, hiding its shame underground. Deer fled burning, trees toppled, and ash fell like burning tears. The land wept. Her soul tore.

When he was done with her, he shoved her aside. Mori slammed against the dungeon floor, bloodying her elbow. She wept and shook, stars before her eyes. Her mouse lay still in her pocket, a dead heart, crushed under her weight.

"Get up," Acribus told her in disgust. He spat onto her. "You're coming with us. You will be mine every night until we find and kill your father."

She lay on the bloodied floor, her face an inch from Orin's. His right eye stared at her, huge and pained in the dripping, red wound of his face. Mori gasped for breath. She could not rise. She could barely see. Pain dug through her like a cold iron bar. She closed her eyes, so ashamed, praying for death. *Please, Solina, please kill me too, stab your sword into my heart and end this.*

"Stand up, sweet little mouse," Solina spoke above, voice distant as from miles away. "Stand up now, or he will hurt you again."

Mori looked at her brother's body. She forced herself to look. He was no longer Orin, she realized, the hero she had loved, the prince of Requiem. He was nothing but flesh now, a charred and emptied shell. *Your soul now dines in the starlit halls of our fathers,* she thought. *You rest now among the Draco stars, and I know you watch over me.*

The dragonclaw pommel of a dagger rose from Orin's boot. Mori had always feared this dagger, thinking its pommel a true dragon's claw, but today was all about shattering fears. Acribus grabbed her hair, twisted, and pulled. Mori had always been the fastest dragon in Requiem. Fast as she could, she drew her brother's dagger, leaped up, and thrust the blade.

The dagger gleamed in her hand, her *luck* hand. Mori screamed. The dagger scraped against Acribus's breastplate and drove under his arm. He wore only chainmail there, thinner than his breastplate of steel; it was no match to the starlit dagger of a Requiem prince. The blade tore through the mail, blood showered Mori, and Acribus howled.

I'm sorry, Orin, she thought as she ran, tears on her cheeks, blood on her thighs. *I'm so sorry.*

She left him there, racing upstairs. Solina shouted and tried to grab her, but Mori was too fast. Blood pounded in her ears. Every step shot pain through her; it felt like demon spawn had invaded her womb and clawed inside her. And yet she ran, burst out of the dungeon, and raced across the hall. She had always been so fast. *You always said how fast I was, Orin, whenever we'd race through the pure, blue skies over King's Forest.*

Now the sky was red, full of smoke and fire. Mori burst into the courtyard, shifted into a dragon, and soared into the flame. Ten thousand phoenixes roared above her, an inferno; it looked like the sun had engulfed the world. Mori screamed, a hoarse cry that consumed her--for her pain, her rage, the death of her brother. She sounded her howl, a dragon's howl, the howl of a frightened girl who will never more feel joy under this sky. She soared through fire, wings roiling smoke and heat, and shot into the north.

She flew, a thin golden dragon, wings beating, eyes narrowed and wet. The wind roared around her. Behind her, ten thousand phoenixes screeched.

When Mori looked over her shoulder, she saw them following, an army of sunfire. Did Solina fly among them, the woman who had killed her brother? Did Acribus fly there, the man who had... Mori gritted her teeth, shame burning across her. He had done something to her, broken something inside her, taken something she could never retrieve. She ached for it. She wanted to die, to never more feel this impurity, but still she flew.

She still had a second brother in Requiem. She still had a father. *I have to warn them. I have to survive. Whatever more happens, however more they hurt me, I must live.*

She flew north with tears and ice, the fury and heat of Tiranor on her tail.

ELETHOR

He stood in his workshop, white columns rising around him, and stared at the statue. The woman was carved of marble, skin smoothed, body nude and flowing. Elethor had spent hours gently chiseling her full lips, her straight nose, her hair that cascaded like silk. And yet, for all his effort, he thought the statue fell from the true grace of Solina.

If only you were still here, Elethor thought, hammer and chisel in his hands. *If only I could see your true beauty again, not content myself with this cold marble. If only I could caress your soft skin, and kiss your lips, and hold you one last time.*

He sighed, laid his tools on the table, and sat on a bench. Around his workshop, six more statues of Solina stood, some nude, others clad in flowing gowns of stone, all beautiful and all painful for him to see. And yet he kept carving her, laboring for months on each effigy.

I will create one every year until I see you again, he thought. Seven statues. Seven years. Seven lost hopes of seeing his love again.

The sun was setting, he noticed; he had been working all day without sensing the time pass. He rose, lit an oil lamp, then stood between the columns of his workshop. The house rose upon a hill, commanding a view of Nova Vita. Elethor often stood here, between these columns, gazing upon the leagues of birches, the houses of white marble, and the herds of dragons that flew above. The city was still beautiful to him, even if sadness had dwelled here since Solina departed.

Soon the sun dipped below the horizon, and the stars emerged. The Draco constellation glittered before him, the stars of his forefathers, the light of his people. He was a prince of Requiem. Those stars blessed him, and the people of this city served him, yet Elethor would forfeit both for the touch of a hand, a breath on his neck, a whisper of her voice.

"Solina," he whispered. A woman of sunlight and a prince of stars. *Solina.* The fire of his night. The pain that coiled forever in his soul.

As he watched the night, he saw a slim, sapphire dragon flying toward the hill. The starlight glimmered on the dragon's scales. Elethor heaved a sigh.

"Perfect," he muttered. "A visit from Lyana. Just what I need."

The blue dragon glided through the night, fire flickering in her maw. Soon Lyana landed upon the hill beyond the columns, her claws kicking up grass and dirt. She gave her wings a last flap, tilted her head, and regarded Elethor.

"You were missed at dinner," she told him, baring her fangs. "Your father is upset."

"I wasn't hungry," he said flatly.

Lyana spat a flicker of disdainful fire. With a growl, she shifted. Her wings pulled into her back. Her fangs and claws retracted. Her scales faded. Soon she stood before him as a young woman. She wore silvery armor engraved with dragons-- the armor of the bellators, Requiem's ancient order of knighthood. A sword and a dagger, their pommels shaped as dragonclaws, hung from her belt.

Elethor hated the sight of her. He hated that upturned nose. He hated those green eyes that always seemed so haughty. He even hated her curly red hair, if only because he knew she was so vain about it.

"Not bloody hungry?" the young knight demanded, chin raised. She was a slight girl, a good foot shorter than him, but always strutted around like a giant. "Elethor, I don't give a damn if you just ate a walrus. You are Prince of Requiem. With your older brother in the south, it's your duty to sit at court. Lord Deramon asked for you, and--"

Elethor groaned. "Lyana! I don't want to hear any more of your lectures."

The girl was insufferable; she had been especially bad since betrothing Orin last summer. If before she had boasted of her knighthood--which was bad enough--Lyana was now set to be a princess, then a queen someday. It had inflated her pride to intolerable levels. She was perhaps shorter than Elethor, and five years younger, but she still acted like she was his mother and he was an errant boy.

She marched up toward him, tightened her lips, and raised her chin so high, Elethor thought her head might fall off. She snorted--a loud sound of pure disdain.

"Oh, I see," she said, hands on her hips. "Maybe you think that because I'm a girl, and because I'm young, that I should just be quiet and pretty. Is that it?"

Elethor sighed. "Here we go again."

He turned and headed back into his workshop, but Lyana followed him, ran around him, and faced him again. She glared.

"Well, I have news for you, Prince Elethor Aeternum. I *will* lecture you, as often as I like. And you will listen to me. I am engaged to your older brother, remember that. I'll be his wife this summer and queen consort when he's crowned, and if you think I will be quiet and subservient to you, well... you better think again. Do you understand me?"

"I understand perfectly," he said.

Her eyes narrowed, shards of green fire. "Do you?"

He nodded. "I understand that you are an intolerable, overbearing, supercilious--"

"Watch it, Elethor!" She raised her hand, prepared to strike him. "You forget that in addition to being intolerable, overbearing, and supercilious, I am also a knight in Requiem's army. And I can kick your backside across this forest if I must."

He snorted. "Yes, you are a soldier. A soldier like my brother Orin. You two are brave, strong heroes of Requiem. And I suppose you think I'm but a lowly sculptor, so weak to your noble eyes."

Her face flushed. "Don't put words in my mouth, Elethor. I don't think you must be a soldier like your brother, but damn it, do *something* with your life. Do something more than stargaze, chisel, and bloody mope all day."

He roared with rage, fingers trembling. "My life is my own to live! Not yours. Not my father's." He raised his fist; it shook with anger. "I'm so sorry, Lyana. I'm so sorry I can't live a life you approve of, that I'm such a failure to everyone. Maybe I should go to court and talk of battles and politics and ancient histories; you and Orin would love that, wouldn't you? Maybe I can grow a couple inches taller, until I *look* more like Orin too. Is that what you want to hear?" He glared at her. "But I'm not him, Lyana. I'm very sorry that I can't be tall like Orin, handsome like Orin, brave or strong like Orin. Maybe *I* should have gone south to Castellum Luna, and Requiem's favorite son could have stayed among you instead of poor, weak Elethor."

He was speaking from anger. He knew that. He knew he'd regret those words later. And yet he could not stop it; Lyana always brought this out from him. He turned his back to her, fuming. He liked to think of himself as a calm man. He was an artist. A scholar. A poet. He was not some hot-headed brute. And yet whenever Lyana was around, he wanted to beat his fists against the walls... or strangle her. Whenever she scolded him, he felt like an angry, hysterical child. He forced himself to take slow, deep breaths and count silently to ten. He stared at his new statue, letting Solina's marble beauty soothe him.

I miss you, Solina, he thought, remembering how they would run through the forest, hide in caves, whisper and laugh about Lyana and Lord Deramon and all the others. *I am a ruined man without you.*

Behind him, he heard Lyana sigh.

"You've carved another one," she said softly.

The sadness in her voice stoked Elethor's anger. He spun toward her, fists clenching.

"That is none of your business. This is my workshop and I will sculpt what I please."

He expected her to shout, to rail, maybe even to strike him. But Lyana only seemed so sad, and somehow that was a thousand times worse. She touched his cheek.

"El, I worry about you," she said, eyes soft. "We all do. Since she left, you... spend all your time here in your workshop. Sculpting her. Whispering her name as you sleep. Gazing at the stars all night as if she glowed among them. When will you let her go?"

Elethor shut his eyes. They stung, but he would shed no tears around Lyana.

"I love her," he whispered.

"And your family loves you!" Lyana said, voice more emphatic. "*I* love you. I know you don't believe me, but it's true. Look at me, Elethor. Open your eyes and look at me, and look at the world you live in. Those days are gone."

He did open his eyes. He looked at his brother's betrothed, this young woman of green eyes and red hair and words that cut him.

"You cannot know what it's like," he said, voice choking. "You did not lose somebody you love."

She sighed, and before he could stop her, Lyana embraced him. She laid her head against his shoulder, arms around him.

"No," she said softly. "But... if I were to lose Orin, I don't know how I would live. I love your brother. I love him like the stars, like the sun after night, like spring after frost. If he were to leave, I would be as a shattered jug." She looked into his eyes, hand against his cheek. "But it's been seven years, El. It's time to return to your family. You must let the past remain what it is--the past. Your future lies ahead, Elethor, if you dare walk down its path."

He turned away from her, almost violently, freeing himself from her embrace. She stared at him with huge, damp eyes, mouth open. Elethor stormed away, leaving her among the statues, until he stood outside in the night. Under the stars he shifted, took flight, and soared as a brass dragon. He roared and blew fire in the darkness, fueling it with his rage.

Once you and I would have laughed at Lyana, he thought. *Do you remember, Solina? You used to imitate her, walking around with nose upturned, scolding the plants for growing, berating the sun for turning, and calling yourself the Lady Know-It-All.*

Now such jokes had lost their humor. Now it seemed life itself had lost its light. Orin had burned Solina and betrothed Lyana, and now Elethor remained here, trapped and lost, his love gone into deserts beyond immeasurable wastelands.

Cold air streamed around him, scented of snow. He circled over Nova Vita, so high that the air thinned, making him heady. Whenever he could, he flew this high, far above the herds, higher than his father flew, or Lyana, or anyone else. He used to tell Solina, *Come, ride on my back and we'll explore the skies.*

But she would never ride him or anyone. *I am a proud child of Tiranor,* she would say. *We do not become dragons, and we are no poorer for it; I walk where I must go.*

Elethor looked over Nova Vita, the heart of Requiem, the only home he'd ever known. The palace stood ahead, white columns rising like pillars of moonlight, and near it rose the Temple of Stars, its dome carved from polished silver. Around these great halls rolled hills covered with birches, the trees rustling and sweetly scented in the night. From the foliage peeked homes of white stone, workshops, and squares full of statues and fountains. Three white archways led to underground tunnels where Requiem stored its treasures: ancient books, magical artifacts, and sacks of golden grain for winter. Finally, two great forts bookended the city, their bricks craggy and their banners thudding: Castra Murus, a squat garrison housing the City Guard; and Castra Draco, its four towers housing the Royal Army.

The structures--even the two forts--seemed part of the landscape to Elethor, blending with the forest as naturally as boulders or rivers. It was a beautiful home--he had always thought so--but for Solina it had been a prison. A place of exile. Of pain.

Once, he knew, a million dragons had flown here, and Requiem had been a wonder for the world. It had been three hundred years since the griffins burned this place, killing all but seven dragons. Today fifty thousand Vir Requis lived here, descendants of the Living Seven--a small light, a whisper after the great song of the glory days. *Yet we are rebuilding,* Elethor thought. *We are making a new age of glory.* His father carried the torch of Requiem now; Orin and Lyana would follow. Elethor was second in line, and he would not sit upon the throne, for which he was grateful. He wanted nothing more than a life of reflection, sculpture, and stargazing.

"And a life with you, Solina," he whispered. "I pray every night that you return to us someday... that you return to me."

A cry pierced the night.

Elethor frowned and stared south. A lone dragon flew there, wobbling, wings shaking. She was a slim dragon, female, with golden scales. She cried again, a cry of anguish and fear.

Elethor's breath caught.

"Mori," he whispered.

He flapped his wings, narrowed his eyes, and dived toward her. His sister blew weak flame, cried again, and began tumbling toward the forest. Elethor swooped, fear twisting his gut. Air whistled around him. Mori spun toward the distant trees, wings limp, sparks flying from her maw. Elethor caught her ten feet above the ground, wrapping his claws under her. She was so thin, so light in his grip. He lowered her gently onto the snow.

"Mori!" he said. "Mori, can you hear me?"

Birches rose around them, naked and icy. His younger sister blinked at him, thinner than he'd ever seen her. Her wings splayed out around her, and her tail flapped weakly.

"Elethor," she whispered.

His breath caught. Mori had always been a timid thing, but there was new fear in her eyes, a haunting pain that tore through him.

They shifted into human forms. Mori lay in his arms, gazing up with huge gray eyes. Her gown was torn and bloody, her face pale, her lips trembling. Dried blood filled her brown hair.

"What happened, Mori?" Elethor whispered, feeling as if snow filled his belly.

She held him, staring up into his eyes. Her shaky breath frosted.

"They killed him, Elethor," she whispered. Her fingers dug into his back. "They killed him. And they're coming here."

ADIA

Mother Adia, High Priestess of Requiem, stood above the grave of her daughter.

It had been thirteen years since Noela had died--a cherubic child of dark eyes and darker hair. In those thirteen years, Adia had watched her other children grow into adulthood, watched white invade her hair, watched her husband turn from loving man to cold warrior... and yet the pain still lingered.

"I still feel like you only just left me," she whispered to the grave.

She smiled to remember the softness of Noela's hair, the sweetness of her smile, the warmth of her little fingers. Adia's two other children looked like their father. Bayrin and Lyana had the red hair, the green eyes, the fiery temper. But Noela...

"You were like me," Adia whispered. "You had black hair like mine. Soft brown eyes like mine. A sweet sadness like the one that lingers inside me. You wouldn't have been a warrior... you would have been a priestess like me."

A cold wind blew through the night, scented of fire. The wick of her lamp danced. Adia wrapped her white robes around her. *The people are lighting bonfires,* she thought. It was the Night of Seven, a night to remember the seven Vir Requis who had survived the Destruction three hundred years ago, the seven who gave birth to this nation of fifty thousand. Across the hills of Requiem, people would be lighting bonfires of memory, and this midnight Adia would walk through the temples, light incense, and praise the stars for their blessings.

*But I'll be thinking of you, Noela. Today we remember the Seven...
and today is the day you left me.*

Thirteen years. A lifetime of memory and grief.

"Adia."

The voice spoke behind her, deep but soft. Adia turned to
see Deramon, her husband, walk between the snowy graves.
Frost covered his plate armor, sheathed sword, and red beard.
His eyes, deep green, stared at her from under bushy brows. In
his left hand he held a lamp; in his right, an axe.

"Why do you bring steel to this place?" Adia whispered.
"This is a place of rest. Of beauty. A place for Noela to forever
sleep under starlight. Why do you bring axe and sword to the
grave of our daughter?"

She saw the pain that caused him. His eyes darkened, his
mouth twisted, his knuckles whitened. She had loved him once,
Adia thought. Thirteen years ago. Before her world had
crumbled. Did she love him still?

Maybe, she thought. *But how can I love another? How can I love
anyone when my Noela awaits me in the starlit halls of our ancestors?*

"I am Captain of the City Guard," Deramon said. His voice
was gruff, but she heard its pain. "I am sworn to defend this city,
my king, and my people. My weapons stay with me... at my post,
in my bed, even at the grave of our child. You know this, Adia.
You are a priestess; forever the light of stars glows around you. I
am a warrior. Forever steel shines with me."

Adia looked away. She looked at the grave, her throat
tightened, and her eyes stung with tears. She felt one roll down
her cheek.

"She would have been a priestess too," she whispered. "I
gave birth to three of your children, Deramon. Two look like
you, with red hair and green eyes and steel in their hands. They
are warriors. They are proud. And I love them. But Noela..."

She trembled. "She was like a young me. A sad, reflective child. Why did she leave me?"

Deramon growled, a low sound like a bear in his cave. He placed his lamp down by the grave. "Noela died in her cradle, Adia. She was not yet two years old. We do not know the woman she might have become."

She spun toward him, glaring. "I knew!" she hissed. Her eyes blurred with tears. "I knew her soul, and her heart, and--"

Deramon grabbed her arm. "Adia," he whispered. His eyes narrowed, drowning in pain. "Adia, I loved her too. More than you can imagine. But I also love Bayrin and Lyana--who still live, who still need us. And I love *you*. We still have a family to protect."

She closed her eyes. "A family to protect. A king to protect. A city to protect. You protect everyone, Deramon, but who protected her?" She opened her eyes. "We were not there for her, Deramon. We didn't even *know* until the morning!" Her voice rose, torn in pain. "She lay dead in the cradle all night, as we slept, and it was dawn before we--"

Deramon howled. "Enough!"

He tossed his axe aside; it thumped into the snow. He held her with both hands. She struggled, but he pulled her into his embrace, and Adia found herself weeping against his shoulder. She shivered against him, and he held her tight and smoothed her hair. She stood with arms at her sides, but then slowly reached around him and embraced him.

Yes, she thought. *I love him. I love Deramon, though he has changed, and I have changed, and joy has left our lives. But I still love him.*

She looked aside at the grave, at the marble tombstone, at the place of all her sorrow and memory.

And I love you, Noela. Always. I will see you again in our starlit halls.

Wings thudded behind her. A dragon's roar pierced the air. Adia spun around to see a blue dragon spiraling down toward the graveyard.

Lyana. My daughter.

The young dragon's wings roiled the falling snow. Smoke plumed from between her teeth, and the moon glimmered against her blue scales. She landed, claws digging into mounds of snow, and shifted into human form. Lyana stood before her parents, her cheeks flushed, her eyes wide and frightened. Frost whitened her armor.

She is like a young Deramon, Adia thought again. *A warrior like him, angry and proud like him, clad in steel and honor.* Mother and daughter--fire and water.

"Mother!" the young woman said, panting. "Quick, to the temple. Princess Mori is hurt."

Adia frowned. "Mori is far south in Castellum Luna. The king sent her to--"

"She's back," said Lyana. She shifted back into a dragon and took flight. Her voice roared. "Follow me! She needs your healing."

Adia's head spun. She took a deep breath and summoned her magic. White scales flowed across her, clinking and glimmering. Leathern wings sprouted from her back, and fire tickled her mouth. She took flight as a long dragon, white as snow. Her husband shifted too, and soon Deramon flew at her side, a burly dragon with clanking, coppery scales.

Parents followed daughter. The three dragons flew over the graveyard, over city streets, and toward Requiem's palace of white marble.

Again the Night of Seven comes to Requiem, Adia thought, *and again sorrow falls.* It had always been a night of destruction.

As she flew over the city, she looked south; the horizon glowed red. Distant fires blazed.

LYANA

Lyana Eleison, a knight of Requiem, stood in the hall of her king. She wore chain mail, a breastplate, and a helmet of steel. She clutched her sword so tightly her knuckles were white.

I will be strong, she told herself, struggling to calm her racing heart. *I am a bellator of Requiem. Whatever evil befell my princess, I will fight it.*

The palace's columns rose around her, pale as moonlight, their capitals shaped as dragons. Braziers stood among them, crackling with embers, filling the hall with warmth and light. Yet no fire could warm Lyana today; her chill gripped her from her belly, sending icy fingers through her.

People filled the hall around her: Lyana's father, the burly Lord Deramon; Lyana's mother, the willowy priestess Adia; King Olasar upon his throne, a crown of gilded oak roots upon his head; Prince Elethor, his eyes dark; a dozen guards with spears and shields. All eyes stared at the young Princess Mori who stood trembling upon the palace's marble tiles.

"Hush, child, you're safe now," whispered Adia. The priestess stepped forward, white robes fluttering, and embraced Mori. "Nobody will hurt you here."

Lyana looked at the two--her mother and her princess--and her throat tightened. *I am a knight of Requiem,* she thought. *I am betrothed to a prince. Yet now I too want to weep into a warm embrace. Now I wish my mother held me, her daughter, the way she holds our princess.*

"You're safe now, Mori," whispered Adia. "You're safe."

The princess wept, a blanket wrapped around her shoulders. Blood caked her hair and tears etched lines down her ashy face. She whimpered and clung to Adia, digging her fingers into the priestess's robes.

"I'm scared," she whispered.

Adia raised her eyes and looked over the weeping girl's head. She stared at the Oak Throne of Requiem, which stood upon a marble dais engraved with gilded leaves.

"Please, Your Highness," the priestess said, "let me take her to the temple. I will tend to her there."

King Olasar sat upon his throne of twisting oak roots. His brows were heavy and black, his beard snowy white. A tall man clad in dark green and steel, he held a sword on his lap--Stella Lumen, ancient blade of the legendary Lacrimosa, the queen who had fought the tyrant Dies Irae and reigned over ruins. He was a wise king, Lyana thought, and a brave warrior. She loved him like a second father.

"Not yet, Adia," the king said, eyes dark. "Let my daughter speak. Mori, look at me. Tell me what happened. Tell me everything."

Still clinging to Adia, the princess looked up at her father. Tears spiked her lashes and her lips trembled.

"They killed him," she whispered. "They killed Orin, Father! They killed him."

Lyana stared.

Her heart shattered inside her.

Orin. My betrothed. No. No...

Tears filled her eyes. Pain gripped her heart and squeezed. She looked up at her mother with burning eyes, at her father who stood by the throne, at Prince Elethor who gasped. Tears blurred her vision and the world spun around her.

Orin. Dead.

The grief swelled through the hall. Lyana found herself clinging to Elethor, digging her fingers into his back. He held her, tears in his eyes, his breath heavy. King Olasar rose to his feet, his chest heaved, and even this great ruler's eyes filled with tears. Lord Deramon gritted his teeth and clutched his axe, and the warriors who served him, guards of the throne, cried in grief.

He's gone. Stars, he's gone. My betrothed. My love. My Orin.

Lyana trembled as the world crashed around her. If the columns of this palace fell and King's Forest burned, she'd have felt no less grief and shock.

Her father spoke first. Captain of the City Guard, Deramon raised his voice above the cries of grief; it boomed across the hall.

"Who killed the prince?" he demanded. He was perhaps the greatest warrior in Requiem, a gruff man of muscle and grit, but even his eyes shone with tears. "Who killed Prince Orin?"

Mori dared not look at Deramon; she had always feared the lord's fiery beard, booming voice, and blazing eyes. Face pale, the princess ran to her father. She clung to the king. For the first time, Lyana noticed that blood slicked the princess's thighs, and an iciness seized her. She shivered. *They killed Orin, and stars, what did they do to Mori?*

"Tirans," Mori whispered, voice so soft, Lyana barely heard. "They bore the sun of Tiranor on their armor. Their swords were curved and gilded; they looked like beaks. They had golden skin, and blue eyes, and hair like platinum. I... they could fly, Father! They flew as firebirds, great beasts of flame. They are coming. They will be here soon. They burned him! And they will burn us. Father... they are coming, they..."

Mori's eyes rolled back, and she fell limp in the king's arms.

Lyana wanted to faint too. She forced herself to breathe, to focus her eyes, to clutch her sword. Tiranor attacking Requiem? She clenched her jaw. Tiranor had not attacked Requiem since the war nearly thirty years ago, a decade before Lyana's birth. She knew little of Tirans, only that they were proud, tall, and fair--a beautiful and cruel desert people with sapphire eyes and blades that thirsted for blood. Why would they attack Requiem?

But of course Lyana knew. She whispered the answer through cold lips.

"It's Solina."

Solina. The orphaned princess of Tiranor, taken captive to Requiem after the devastating war. Solina, who loved Elethor, who had attacked the king, who had fled burnt to her desert home.

Lyana snarled, pulled back from Elethor's embrace, and drew her sword.

"It's Solina!" she repeated, louder this time, loud enough for the hall to hear. "She killed Orin. And I will kill her."

The hall erupted in cries. Father and his men, warriors clad in steel, called for vengeance. Mother called for calm. Only Elethor stood silent, face pale and mouth open.

King Olasar stood, his unconscious daughter in his arms, and raised his voice.

"Silence!" he thundered. Pain filled his eyes, but he narrowed them and stared upon the hall. Mori hung in his arms, head tilted back, blood trickling. The hall fell silent; all eyes stared at the king. Lyana stood panting, sword drawn, grief like a talon clutching her.

The king turned his dark eyes toward Lyana's mother. The priestess stared back, blood smearing her white robes, her eyes huge and haunted.

"Adia," said King Olasar, "take my daughter to the temple. Heal her. Let her sleep. And Adia... prepare the temple for wounded. Many wounded." His jaw was tight. "And for the dead."

Adia nodded, face pale but strong. She walked forward and took Mori from the king's arms. Carrying the girl, she left the hall, robes sweeping behind her. Lyana watched the two leave,

throat tight. She knew what this blood meant, this tremble in
Mori's voice, the shame in her eyes.

They raped her. They will do the same to me if they can. Her eyes
stung and her throat felt so tight she could barely breathe.

Next King Olasar turned to Lyana's father. Deramon
stared back, eyes dark under his bushy red brows, his heavy hands
upon his weapons. He stood clad in steel and leather, every inch a
warrior, but Lyana saw the fear and pain that lurked behind his
scowl. *Father is as scared as I am,* she knew.

"Lord Deramon," said the king, "prepare the City Guard.
Summon every last man from your barracks, all one thousand.
Man the walls and patrol the skies. Protect Nova Vita."

Deramon bowed, one hand on his sword's hilt, the other
on his axe. His armor creaked.

"My king," he said gruffly. "It will be done."

With that, Deramon turned and marched out of the hall.
His soldiers followed, armor clanking. Soon Lyana heard them
shift outside--their wings thudded, and their howls shook the
palace. She saw them take flight outside the windows, great
dragons blowing fire.

Only Lyana and Elethor now remained before the king.
The young prince had not spoken yet. He was pale and his fists
shook at his sides. Lyana knew what he was thinking. He was
thinking of *her.* The woman he loved. The woman whose parents
King Olasar had slain. The woman who, Lyana knew, now
marched against them. *Solina, bane of Requiem, forever a curse upon this
place.*

She knew Olasar was thinking the same thing. The king
was staring at his son, the younger prince, now heir to his throne.

"Elethor," the king said, and for the first time his voice
was strangely soft. "Sit upon this throne until I return. You rule
in Nova Vita in my absence."

Still pale and silent, Elethor nodded. As the king walked across the hall, Elethor approached the throne and sat, eyes staring at nothing, fists still clenched at his sides. A tear streamed down his cheek.

"My king!" Lyana said as Olasar walked by her. "How shall I serve you?"

Olasar paused and stared at her, and Lyana lost her breath. She saw such pain in Olasar's eyes, such grief and rage and terror, reflections of her own turmoil. Olasar's lips trembled only slightly, and his brow remained strong, his jaw squared.

"You will fly at my side, Lady Lyana," he said, voice soft. "We call the banners. We summon the Royal Army. And we fly south. We fly to war."

Lyana sucked in her breath. Not since the war thirty years ago had the Royal Army--five thousand warriors led by the king and his knights--flown to war.

Orin. My love. My eternal prince. Tears stung her eyes, but she bowed her head. She gritted her teeth, grief and rage like ice and fire crashing inside her.

"To war," she whispered.

They marched across the hall, boots echoing against the tiles. Around them between the columns, Lyana saw thousands of dragon wings and blasts of flame. When they reached the hall's end, the gatekeepers bowed and opened the doors, revealing Nova Vita. Deramon's guardsmen ran between the birches, shifted into dragons, and took flight.

King Olasar marched into the courtyard and shifted. His wings thudded, and he flew as a great black dragon, flames seeking the sky. Lyana was prepared to shift too, but paused and looked back over her shoulder.

Elethor sat upon the throne across the hall, staring at her. He looked so small in the empty palace, nearly lost in the grip of the twisting Oak Throne.

"Lyana," he said and stood up. In the empty hall, his voice echoed and flowed to her. "Lyana, I'm sorry. Be careful tonight."

For the first time, Lyana realized that by the law of Requiem, she was now betrothed to Elethor. *His older brother is dead; he inherited the right of succession, and he inherited me.*

Lyana nodded, silent, jaw clenched. She turned and left the palace, leaving him among the marble columns. The dragons of Olasar's army, five thousand warriors, were taking flight, following their king to the south. Already Lyana saw a fiery glow upon that horizon, sending red claws toward their home. She shifted, flew to join her king, and roared her flame.

A wall of fire rose ahead, shimmering with sound and heat.

OLASAR

A fire rose in the south. From the inferno flew the phoenixes, beasts woven of flame, large as dragons and cruel as wildfire. Thousands shrieked and beat blazing wings, showering sparks. Their cries seemed to shake the world.

"The sun herself has hatched," King Olasar whispered, "and given birth to countless birds of prey."

The enemy soared, lighting the night with fury. The clouds themselves seemed to burn, roiling and raining ash. The phoenix army swallowed the sky and stormed forward; they would reach him soon.

Olasar flapped his wings and blew fire. He roared, a dragon roar that could shatter men's ears. Behind him, his army answered his call. Five thousand dragons howled, a song of rage and fire.

He turned to face them, his wings churning the falling snow. They flew in phalanxes, each lead by a bellator with gilded horns, each a terror of a hundred dragons. Fifty knights and thousands of hardened warriors; they all roared in the night. Their jets of flame rose like pillars of a burning cathedral, blazing against their scales. Their fangs shone like whetted daggers.

"Dragons of Requiem!" King Olasar called to them. "Show the enemy no quarter. Defend our land. Destroy these beasts of unholy fire!"

Their cries shattered the night. The falling snow flurried and steamed around them. Olasar turned back toward the enemy, the countless phoenixes that had swallowed their southern lands,

slain his son, and now flew toward Nova Vita itself. The firebirds
screeched and burned with the fury of the sun.

"To war!" Olasar shouted and flew toward them.

"To war!" cried five thousand voices behind him.

Their wings thudded. Their flames roared. Thousands of
dragons, warriors of Requiem, soared through wind and darkness.
Their cries rose in the night--for war, for fire, and for glory. The
smell of smoke and fear filled Olasar's nostrils, and he bared his
fangs.

*As my forefathers fought for Requiem, I will fight too. For the
memory of my son. For the eternal light of our people. I will not let Requiem
fall again.*

The phoenixes flew toward them, a mile away, then a
hundred yards. Their heat blazed. Olasar had never felt such
heat; it stung his eyes and throat. The firebirds soared and
swooped, their cries thudded in his ears... and then they were
upon him.

Roaring, Olasar blew a jet of fire. It crackled, spun, and
slammed into a phoenix. The great bird tossed back its head and
screeched. The dragonfire only seemed to fuel the creature; it
grew larger, and its talons lashed.

The claws slammed into Olasar, and he howled. The fire
roared across his chest, raising welts. The heat consumed him,
and all around, countless other phoenixes flew. He swung his
claws, tearing into one. It was like clawing a campfire; there was
no flesh to cut. The phoenix roared, a sound like an erupting
volcano, and thrust its beak.

Fire blasted Olasar and raced across his scales. He reared
and beat his wings, trying to scatter the phoenix flames; it only
fanned the fire, making the bird larger, hotter, crueler. Its eyes
crackled, white pools like smelters.

Olasar bared his teeth and soared higher. The phoenix
chased him through the clouds. All around, he saw dragons

battling more phoenixes. The flames and clouds roiled, and cries shook the sky.

"We cannot kill them, my lord!" cried a dragon to his left.

"The demons cannot be burned or cut!" shouted another dragon.

Everywhere he looked, Olasar saw dragons burning. Their wings flamed and they howled in the night. They fell around him. In death, Requiem's magic left them, and they took human forms. The bodies of men and women fell like comets.

"They must not reach Nova Vita!" Olasar shouted. Thousands of his people dwelled there--women, children, the elderly. He howled. "Dragons, hold them back!"

Five phoenixes soared toward him, a shower of flame. Their wings battered him. Their claws burned him. Their beaks of fire dug into his flesh. He roared, flapping his wings, beating them back. When he scattered their fire, they reformed. When he cut their bodies, the flames only burned his claws.

"We must retreat!" cried a slim blue dragon beside him. Her gilded horns shone in the firelight--a bellator's horns.

"Lyana!" Olasar cried to her. "Lyana, fly to Nova Vita! Get everyone into the tunnels and seal them! We will hold them back. Go underground!"

The young blue dragon howled. She blew flame at a swooping phoenix but could not stop its dive. It slammed into her, knocking her into a spin.

"I will not leave you, my king!" she cried, dodging the phoenix claws. "I will not leave my men!"

"Fly!" he cried to her. "Save those that you still can. Lead the city into the tunnels, Lyana! That is my command."

Three phoenixes crashed into him, and Olasar howled in pain. Welts rose across his belly. The scales covering his back blazed; he felt that they would soon melt. He could barely see; smoke and flame filled the night.

"Fly, Lyana!" he shouted.

He thought he glimpsed a flash of blue scales shooting into the distance. *I must only hold the phoenixes back long enough,* he thought. *Long enough for Lyana to evacuate the city underground, to save herself and my living son.* He gritted his teeth. *I will hold them back.*

"Dragons of Requiem!" he shouted into the inferno. "Cut them with claws, scatter their flames, do not let them fly forward! Hold them back!"

The phoenix beaks bit. Their wings slammed into him like fountains of lava. All around he saw dragons blazing, shouting, and turning into men who burned and fell. The smoke filled Olasar's lungs. He could not breathe. Soon he could no longer see; he seemed to fly inside the sun.

Will Requiem fall again? Will it fall like in the days of King Benedictus, when the griffins toppled our halls?

A great howl rose before him, a sound of collapsing mountains, of primal rage, of shattering kingdoms.

The smoke parted. The flames rose in a wall. From the holocaust soared a phoenix, brighter than the others, slender and graceful. Its eyes were molten stars, blazing white. Its wings stretched out, red and orange, tapestries of inferno. It was the most beautiful creature Olasar had ever seen, a deity of punishment and brimstone.

The great firebird soared toward him. Its claws were shards of purest white, hotter than forge fire. They slammed into him, and the world burned, and white light flooded him.

Olasar the First, King of Requiem, fell from the sky.

He crashed through the clouds, tore through burning trees, and slammed into the snow. The shock and pain tore his magic from him. His wings pulled into his body, his claws and fangs retracted, and his scales vanished. He lay as a man, burnt and cut, dying. When he looked around him, he saw the bodies of slain soldiers; they too were only men now, their magic extinguished, their bodies seared red and black.

Olasar looked above him. The phoenix army covered the sky; he could see no end to them. They were flying north, heading to Nova Vita, the capital where forty-five thousand of his people still dwelled.

"Save them, Lyana," he whispered, feverish and trembling. Smoke rose from him. "Save our people."

The great, beautiful phoenix descended toward him, burning with the fire of the sun. *So graceful,* Olasar thought in a haze. *So beautiful. How could something so beautiful be so cruel?*

The phoenix landed in the snow before him. It regarded him for a moment, and then its fires flared, twisted, pulled inward. It shrank and reformed, taking the shape of a human. It was a woman, he realized--a woman with platinum hair, a golden mask, and sabres at her hips. She walked toward him as the sky burned. A crystal hung around her neck, a flame dancing inside it.

"Who are you?" Olasar whispered, staring up at her.

She came to stand above him, staring down through her golden mask. In one hand, she held a sack. Her other hand rested on the pommel of her sword.

"Olasar," she said to him, her voice itself like caressing flame. "Hello again."

He squinted, staring up at her; she stood dark before the wall of fire. Her golden mask glimmered. He tried to rise but could not. Welts rose across him, seeping. The pain spun his head and sweat drenched him.

"Show yourself," he managed to say, reaching for his sword with charred fingers.

Slowly, the woman removed her golden mask... and Olasar snarled.

You were right, Lyana. Stars bless us.

"Solina," he whispered hoarsely.

Her face was golden, her eyes blue, her lips cruel. A burn mark ran across her face, from forehead to chin and down her neck. She traced the scar with her fingers.

"My line of fire," Solina said softly. "You remember how your son, the great Prince Orin, burned me." She opened her sack and held it upside down. A severed head rolled out. Half the head was burned into pulpy, red flesh. The other half was locked in a cry of anguish.

"No," Olasar whispered, then howled in the night. "My son! My son." Tears filled her eyes.

Solina nodded, smiling softly. "He burned me... and so I burned him. And so I will burn all of you."

Olasar shook his head. Though the pain suffused him, he managed to rise to his feet. He drew Stella Lumen, his ancient sword. The fire of the phoenix army blazed against the blade.

"I took you into my court," he said, voice trembling but still strong. "I raised you as a daughter. I--"

"You lie!" Solina screamed. Suddenly her eyes blazed, and her fury twisted her face. "I was no daughter to you. I know, Olasar. I know what happened to my true parents. I know that you killed them." She laughed and touched the crystal at her neck; the flame inside it danced. "But I am strong now; I have the strength of the Sun God. As you killed my parents with steel, so will I kill you. Goodbye, tyrant. May your soul forever burn in the court of my lord."

She drew her sword. It crackled with fire and she drove it forward. Olasar parried, sparks showered, and his blade shattered. Shards of steel flew.

Solina snarled and her blade thrust. It drove into Olasar's chest, burning, blazing, twisting inside him.

He fell. Solina laughed above him, and all Olasar saw was the thousands of firebirds flowing north, burning all in their path, heading to the heart of his realm... and then the flames flooded his world, and he saw nothing else.

LYANA

"No," she whispered, eyes stinging. Her breath died within her. "Stars, please, no... Stars, no."

The image seared her. Orin's head, severed and charred, rolling from a sack. It stared up at her from below, hundreds of yards away, but dragon eyes were sharp, and she knew it was him. Tears blurred Lyana's vision.

"Orin, stars... my Orin."

My love. My betrothed. My prince.

She watched as Solina pulled her sword free from the king's body, this woman who had once been like an older sister to her. Smirking, Solina sheathed her blade, leaped into the air, and flames engulfed her. She spread fiery wings and took flight as a phoenix, a flaming beast the size of a dragon. Her shrieks tore the air.

"Kill every last dragon!" Her voice stormed through her beak of fire. "Soon we fly to Nova Vita."

Lyana had heard enough. She had to warn them. The king had commanded her. Growling, she spun around and began flying north. *I will warn them. I will save our city.*

She shot through the battle, eyes narrowed. Around her, dragons were still dying, burned in the grip of phoenix talons. Three of the firebirds dived toward her, leaving trails of flame. Lyana flew sideways, dodging them, and flashed around them. She soared, jaw clenched.

You will not have died in vain, Orin, she vowed. *I will save our people.*

She had always been fast--not as fast as Mori, perhaps, but faster than anyone else she knew. Her body was slim, her scales smooth, her wings strong. She burst through walls of fire, howling, and shot into the clouds.

Snow flurried and filled her maw. Its ice stung the welts that covered her wings. She flew higher and higher until her eyes burned, her lungs ached, and she could barely see or breathe. She straightened, glided forward, and looked down.

The battle raged below, hidden under the clouds. She saw bursts of light where phoenixes flared. She heard their shrieks and the death cries of dragons. When she looked north, she saw only darkness, but she knew Nova Vita lay ahead across lake and mountain. Capital of Requiem. Home to thousands of Vir Requis she had to save.

The shame of leaving her phalanx--a hundred soldiers sworn to serve her in battle--dug through her chest. She was a knight, a leader of warriors... and she was leaving them to die. She gritted her teeth and fire flared inside her.

Yet I will obey my king. I will save the people of Nova Vita. I will do what I must.

She flew toward the city. She cut through the night, the cold air stinging.

Shrieks sounded behind her, moving closer. When she looked over her shoulder, she cursed. Three phoenixes emerged from the clouds, flames blazing, and flew toward her.

"Damn it!" Lyana gritted her teeth and flew faster. She could not let these beasts follow her home. She dived, plunging into the cloud cover. The snow slammed against her and the wind screamed.

The phoenix cries rose behind her. She turned her head and saw blazes of light through the clouds, like three suns chasing her. She flapped her wings mightily.

Even three could destroy our city, she thought. *I can't let these ones reach Nova Vita before I evacuate everyone into the tunnels.*

She kept flying. They kept chasing, orbs of light inside the clouds. *They will not leave me.* Lyana swerved sideways and flew east, cursing the delay; every moment she lingered could mean another life lost. When she looked back, she saw the flames follow, blazing among the clouds.

Stars! How could they keep following her? The clouds were surely too thick to see a slim, blue dragon who blew no fire. *I must be leaving a wake through the clouds... that, or they can smell dragons.*

She flew up and down, left and right, but the phoenixes followed. Their shrieks grew closer. The clouds began to thin, and Lyana cursed under her breath. Soon the flurries of snow died, and only wisps of clouds raced across her scales. Sky burst open before her, black and tainted with the orange glow of distant fire. Smoke billowed above, umber and gray. Behind her, a wall of fire rose from the battle, casting red light like blood across the land.

The phoenixes cried behind her. Lyana glanced back and cursed. They tore through the last clouds, comets of fury, blazing toward her. Their wings burned red and yellow. Their beaks opened, revealing gullets like flowing lava. Their eyes flared, collapsing stars. They left wakes of flame as they soared toward her. Though the night was black, their light filled it; they saw her, and they cried with bloodlust.

What unholy magic had created these beings? Lyana growled and swooped. She had seen one turn into Solina, adopted sister to her fallen betrothed. *These are no demons,* she thought. *They are men and women with magic similar to ours. We can turn into dragons; they turn into these creatures.*

She could not fight fire. If she could face them in their humans forms, she could kill them.

She dived toward Aranath Mountains below, chunks of black rock in the night. The phoenix light blazed against them, racing across the black stone and patches of snow. Lyana would come to these mountains with Orin--sweet, handsome Prince Orin--and they would walk through caves, whispering, holding hands, stealing kisses. *If I must die today, let these caves be my place of eternal rest.*

"Come on, you bastards!" she shouted over her shoulder. She blew a jet of fire back toward the three chasing phoenixes. "You killed him. You killed my love. Now come face me."

She swooped, claws extended. She knew these mountains better than anyone in Requiem. Wind whistled around her, and the phoenixes cried so loudly, snow cascaded and melted below. She saw the cave there, *her* cave, hers and Orin's, its mouth round and five feet tall, short enough that she'd always had to stoop to enter.

She landed outside the cave. As soon as her claws hit the ground, she shifted into human form. Her wings pulled into her back. Her fangs and claws retracted. Instead of scales, steel armor covered her body. Her sword--as much a part of her as her arm--still hung on her belt. She ran into the cave, hand on its hilt.

She spun around, the cave walls close around her, and saw an inferno.

Damn them. This delay shot fear through her. She needed to reach Nova Vita quickly. Mori had fainted after only a vague warning and might still be sleeping. Did the city know of this phoenix fire? Did they know they could not fight, only hide? Lyana had to warn them. She had to fly now. She had to kill these beasts quickly, or it would be too late.

The phoenixes landed outside the cave. Snow melted and fell like rain around them. Wings thrashing, they reached into the tunnel with claws of fire. The flames blazed. Lyana leaped back;

the heat blasted her armor, and she felt like her eyeballs could melt. She retreated into the darkness.

The first time we made love was here, sweet Orin, she thought, eyes stinging and throat burning. The image kept playing before her eyes--his head rolling from the sack, burnt and grimacing--even now as these beasts of sunfire clawed outside.

"Come in and face me!" she cried. "You are like us children of Requiem. You have human forms; I have seen it. Come face me, or are you such cowards that you dare not face one woman?"

They howled and flared. Their heat drenched Lyana with sweat; locks of her damp, red hair stuck to her face. She snarled, holding her sword before her. With her left hand, she drew her dagger, its blade shaped as a dragonclaw. The heat of battle raged over her loss of Orin, simmering over her grief.

"Be with me, stars of Requiem," she prayed. "May your light shine upon my blades."

With cries of fury, the phoenixes outside shifted.

Their fire pulled into them, twisting and coiling into human shapes. The flames darkened and hardened, like lava cooling into stone, until they became flesh. They stared at her, eyes still burning like coals. They wore breastplates of steel emblazoned with the golden Sun of Tiranor, and swords hung at their sides. Their hair was a blond so pale, it was almost white. Their skin was golden, their eyes blue and cold. Each wore a chain holding a crystal glimmering with fire. Two were men, their faces bearded and cruel. The third was a woman holding a sabre and a spear. The sides of her head were shaven, revealing sun tattoos, and her lips were pierced with rings.

"See how she cowers in darkness," said the woman to her companions. Her voice was cold, her eyes ruthless. "When the dragons burned our homeland, they howled with their pride, their bloodlust, their cruelty. See what pathetic creatures they've become." She snarled and her voice rose to a shout. "Hail the Sun God, destroyer of Requiem!"

"Tirans," Lyana said, eyes narrowing. "Return to your homeland that we burned. Leave Requiem, or we will kill you on our mountains, like we killed you in your deserts."

The female Tiran smirked. Her armor was bright, and her blades glimmered like shards of light, flames racing across them.

"You may call me Phira of the Two Blades," she said, raising her sword and spear. "Do you see them? They will cut your tongue from your mouth, weredragon." She spat out the last word in disgust.

Lyana snarled. *Weredragon.* It was a dirty word, an ugly curse. She was Vir Requis, a proud daughter of Requiem, descended from the hero Terra Eleison himself. Hers was old blood, proud and pure. Like every child of Requiem, she could grow wings and scales, breathe fire, and take flight as a dragon. It was a magic old and noble, kissed with starlight. *Weredragon* meant a reptile, a filthy beast.

"And you may call me Lady Lyana Eleison, a knight of Requiem, daughter of Lord Deramon and Mother Adia," she said. "May the stars burn your souls."

She ran toward them.

The two men ran to meet her. Lyana lashed her sword and dagger. The soldiers parried. Flames leaped from their swords and burned her sleeve. She screamed, swung her sword, and blades clashed again. She raised her dagger, parrying a thrust. Flames hit the cave walls and steel rang.

"Requiem!" she cried. "May our wings forever find your sky."

The words of her fathers. The words of battle, of death, of blood and hope.

Her blades swung and thrust, glowing bright. She knocked one sword against the wall, thrust her blade, and pierced the man's neck. The second Tiran swung down his sword, and she raised her dagger. The blades sparked. The blow nearly dislocated her arm, and she screamed, but pulled her sword free and swung low.

Her blade slashed the leg before her, and the second man fell. She leaped back, dodging his sabre, and thrust. Her sword slammed into his mouth, muffling his scream. Blood spurted and he fell. More blood painted the cave walls and floor, congealing in the heat of fire.

Two men lay dead, sabres still crackling.

Phira, the Tiran woman, snarled. She stepped over the bodies and raised her blades. Fire wreathed her, glittering upon the rings piercing her lips. The suns tattooed onto her head seemed to burn with real fire, but her eyes were cold, chips of ice. There was no humanity in them, only hunger and cruel amusement.

"Very good, girl," she said and licked those pierced lips. "Not bad for a weredragon. But now you will taste true steel."

Phira thrust her spear.

Her arms ached, but Lyana parried. The blades clanged. Phira's sabre swung next, and Lyana barely checked the blow.

Phira was strong, stronger than Lyana had expected. She cried in pain. Her sword nearly flew from her arm, and her bone felt like it could snap. The sabre swung. Lyana parried with her dagger. Phira's spear sliced her hip, and she cried.

"Do you like the taste of my steel?" Phira asked, smirking. She thrust her blades again. Lyana parried, grunting in pain. Sweat dripped into her eyes. The spear sliced a lock of her hair, and the Tiran laughed.

"Yes, groan for me, weredragon," she said and spat. "That's how I like to hear reptiles die."

Lyana screamed and thrust her sword. Phira parried, caught her wrist, and bent her hand back. *Fight her!* Lyana cried to herself. *You are a knight of Requiem!*

Phira clutched her right wrist, twisting, her strength almost unreal. Lyana felt like her bones could shatter. As her fingers uncurled and her sword fell, she thrust her dagger. She aimed for Phira's neck, but the Tiran moved aside, and Lyana's dagger scraped across her pauldron. Sparks flew. Phira laughed and punched, slamming her fist into Lyana's face.

Light blazed. Blood filled her mouth. Lyana fell, hit the ground, and tried to rise. Phira kicked her chest, knocking her onto her back. Her boot stepped onto Lyana's left wrist, and she yanked her dagger free. Stars floated before Lyana's eyes.

Up! Up, daughter of Requiem! She growled and tried to rise, but the boot crushed her hand. Phira's second boot pressed down on her neck. Lyana couldn't breathe, couldn't even scream. She groped for her weapons, but couldn't reach them.

Phira smirked above her. "You must be that Lyana the Weredragon Prince spoke of," she said. "The troops speak of this Prince Orin. When my queen tortured him, he cried your name. *Lyana, Lyana!* All the while as Queen Solina's blade cut him, he shouted for you." Phira laughed. "He cried like a girl, they say, and squealed like a pig when my queen finally ran him through."

No. No, stars, it can't be. Tears blurred Lyana's eyes. She wanted to see him again, to hold her Orin, kiss him, heal him. *But he's dead now, dead like the king, like so many upon the battlefield.*

The smirk never leaving her face, Phira knelt. Her knee drove into Lyana. She gasped in pain, and Phira's hand clutched her throat. Lyana struggled, and Phira backhanded her, rattling her jaw. She spat blood and coughed, gasping for breath.

"We shall see," the Tiran said, "if I can make you squeal and beg for death too."

She kept one hand on Lyana's throat. Her second hand drew a serrated knife from her belt. Despite the heat that still lingered, her hand was icy. Lyana kicked the air, trying to hurt her, trying to break free. She could not. She could see only stars, the Tiran's snarl, her cold eyes. Her knife ran down Lyana's cheek, drawing blood.

"Filthy weredragon," Phira said in disgust. "Will you beg for death too before I pull you entrails from your body?"

Lyana clenched her fists. She was a bellator, a knight of Requiem. *I will not die today.*

With a howl, she grabbed Phira's wrist, twisted, and shoved the knife up.

The blade slammed into the Tiran's neck. Blood gushed, showering onto Lyana's face. Screaming, she twisted the blade.

For an instant, Phira stared in shock, eyes wide, spittle on her lips. Then she screamed, a gurgling sound. Lyana shoved the woman off, rose to her feet, and lifted her fallen sword.

Phira convulsed on the ground, knife still buried in her neck. Fear flooded her eyes. Lyana looked down at her, dripping sword in hand. With her other hand, she wiped the blood off her face.

"Will you beg for death?" she whispered.

Phira stared up at her, eyes blazing.

I didn't think so.

Lyana drove her sword down, blood splashed, and it was over.

She turned, ran out the cave, and stood upon the snowy mountainside. Screeches and howls rose in the night. Lyana was slick with blood, her eyes stung, and her knees shook. She had never killed before; tonight she had taken three lives.

No, she told herself and forced a deep, shuddering breath. *There's no time for horror now.* She allowed herself to count to five.

That was all. *One. Two. Three.* She trembled, forced another breath, and clenched her jaw. *Four. Five.*

She leaped and shifted into a dragon.

I must save Requiem. I can feel no fear. No pain. Not now. Not yet. There will be time for pain later. A blue dragon, she flew north, heading toward the city of Nova Vita. *I will warn them. I will save them, even if I can no longer save those left behind.*

She shot through the night. Behind her, flames rose and all the horrors of the world seemed to cry for her blood.

ELETHOR

My brother is dead.

The thought clutched him like claws of ice. Fear for his father, his sister, and his friends filled him too, but all drowned under the flood of grief. *Orin. My brother. My pillar of strength. Gone.*

He stood in Gloriae's Tomb, a towering hall of marble, its ceiling domed, columns lining its walls. There were many places Elethor could have gone this night. He could have gone to the temples and sat by Mori's side. He could have stayed on the Oak Throne, gazing upon an empty hall. He could have flown over the city with Lord Deramon, waiting for danger in the dark. But he had come here, to this place of shadows and solitude, to think and to pray.

The statue of Gloriae towered above him. Carved of marble, the legendary Queen of Requiem rose fifty feet tall. She held a sword of stone, and her hair was gilded. Her stone eyes stared forward, brave and determined. Elethor stood before the monolith, gazing upon the queen who had defeated Dies Irae, rebuilt Requiem from ruin, and founded this city of Nova Vita.

"I am descended from you, my queen," Elethor said softly to the statue. "But I lack your strength." He lowered his head. "In the stories you are always strong, brave, and noble. Even when Dies Irae murdered your parents, you fought with fire and defeated your enemies. Lend me strength now."

The statue was silent, staring into the shadows of the hall, eyes forever strong, sword forever drawn. The true Gloriae was entombed beneath the statue, Elethor knew, her bones resting eternally in the earth of the city she'd built. Would her city now fall?

He clutched the hilt of his sword, seeking strength from the leather grip. Ferus was an old longsword, forged in dragonfire a century ago. Its blade was three feet long, pale and grooved. Its crossguard and pommel were dark, unadorned steel. Many lords of the court wore decorative blades, pieces of art that glittered with gold and jewels. Today Elethor had chosen a simple sword; a weapon meant for battle, not ceremony. He had trained with Ferus for years--every prince of Requiem learned swordplay from childhood--but had never swung it in battle.

Orin was the warrior. He should be the one standing here, preparing for war.

Elethor clenched his fists and lowered his head. The pain constricted his throat, and his eyes stung.

"My brother is dead. My father flew to war. Tiranor attacks, and... what if Solina is among them? What if the woman I love returns with fire and death?" His chest felt tight, and he could barely see the floor's tiles. "What do I do now, Gloriae? Give me advice, my queen."

A voice rose in the temple, speaking in exaggerated falsetto.

"Well, first thing, my lad, I advise getting a haircut and a shave. You look like a bloody sheepdog. I don't know whether to help you or pat you."

Elethor raised his head and frowned. From between the columns stepped Bayrin Eleison, a gangly young guard with large ears, a head of orange hair, and mocking green eyes. An impish smile split his wide, freckled face. He wore a steel breastplate engraved with the Draco constellation. A sword, its pommel shaped as a dragonclaw, hung at his side.

"Bayrin!" Elethor said and grimaced. "How could you joke in a place like this, in a time like this?"

The young man shrugged. "The world is burning, my friend. What better time to joke?"

Eldest of Lord Deramon's children, Bayrin was nothing like his fiery sister Lyana. When Lyana would lecture, Bayrin would joke. When Lyana would drill with sword and dagger, Bayrin would sneak into the armory and draw rude pictures on shields. Lyana was a warrior, Bayrin a prankster. Ostensibly a city guardsman in his father's force, Bayrin spent less time patrolling the streets, and more time singing hoarsely in alehouses.

He's just as insufferable as his sister, Elethor reflected with a sigh. *But he's also my best friend.*

"Bayrin, you think every time is best for joking."

The young man gasped. "Me? Never in the bedroom. No, Elethor. That is all serious business in there." He looked around him. "But unless you plan on bedding a fifty-foot statue of a dead queen, I think we're safe." He stepped forward, and now his smile did vanish, and his eyes turned somber. He clasped Elethor's shoulder. "But I'm also sorry, my friend. Deeply and truly. I heard about your brother."

Elethor nodded and looked away, blinking. He did not want to cry in front of Bayrin, his friend who seemed to live for laughter, but couldn't help a tear from falling.

"I can't stop thinking that... that *she* did it. Solina." He looked back at his friend. "When Orin burned her, she swore that she'd kill him someday."

Solina. Queen of Tiranor. My love and fire.

"We don't know that yet," Bayrin said softly. "Mori is still sleeping; she's hurt and in shock, and might not wake for a while. We'll have answers in time. But come now, El. A fire burns in the south and the sky turns red. The city needs you."

Elethor nodded, eyes lowered, and they walked across the tomb to its towering doors. The weight of the sky seemed to hang on Elethor's shoulders. He forced himself to walk straight, to hold his head high, to square his shoulders, to be a prince of Requiem. Inside, however, he felt ready to collapse.

My sister is hurt. My brother is dead. My father flew to war. He clenched his jaw, eyes stinging and throat burning. *Be strong, Elethor. Keep walking. The city needs you. There will be time for grief later.*

They stepped under a towering archway, its keystone embossed with golden dragons, and exited Gloriae's Tomb. From atop the marble staircase, Elethor saw the city roll across hills below. Domes and towers rose from the birch forest, glittering with icicles. Towering walls circled the city, rising from among the snowy trees like a crown of stone resting in white hair. Lord Deramon's dragons perched upon the towers and walls, watching the south where red light glowed.

The fire of Tiranor flies there, Elethor knew. *Stars protect you, Father.*

Elethor had been born after the war with Tiranor. Orin had been only a babe. But he had heard the tales countless times. In his mind, he could see that old war as if he himself had fought it. Father, then a young brash king, had flown against the deserts of Tiranor, howling with rage and vowing to avenge the death of his brother, whom Tiran soldiers had slain with arrows. The Tirans had no dragon forms; theirs was a doomed battle. They fought in caves, in forts, in mountains, firing arrows and spears against the wrath of Requiem's dragons. They died. Their palace fell. Father himself slew the king and queen of Tiranor.

But he spared the young princess, Elethor thought, heart wrenching. Father had spared Solina. He returned to Requiem with scars, dark eyes, and a girl who grew to bring fire, passion, and unending sweet pain to Elethor's life.

Standing upon the stairs of Gloriae's Tomb, Elethor shifted, growing and hardening into a brass dragon. Bayrin shifted at his side, becoming a green dragon with white horns. The two took flight, fire flickering between their teeth, and dived over temples, cobblestone squares, copses of birches, and marble homes. Soon they reached the southern wall, a curving battlement fifty feet tall. They landed upon its crenulations between dragons of Deramon's City Guard. Before them in the south, firelight rose over King's Forest, and smoke billowed to paint the sky dark red.

"A forest fire?" Bayrin asked, frowning. His own fire danced in his maw. Scales clinking, he clutched the battlements so tight his claws dug grooves into the stone.

Elethor shook his head, scattering the smoke that rose from his nostrils. "It is the fire of Tiranor herself." He clenched his jaw, remembering the fire that had burned Solina, and how she trembled and cried in his arms.

A distant blue glimmer caught his eye. He stared. A dragon was flying from the south, a speck fleeing a wall of fire.

"Blue dragon," Elethor whispered. "Lyana?"

Bayrin stared, squinting. With a grunt, the young guard took flight from the wall, wings thudding. His tail snaked behind him, and his green scales turned red in the firelight. With a curse and icy fear twisting his gut, Elethor flew too. The wind tasted like smoke, too hot for winter. The two dragons, brass and green, flew toward their distant comrade. The farms of Requiem rolled beneath them: fields of wheat and barley, rows of apple trees, pastures of sheep and cattle. Fifty thousand Vir Requis lived off this land; in his mind, Elethor already saw it burning.

They reached the blue dragon two leagues from the walls of Nova Vita. It was Lyana, and she was hurt.

"Sister!" Bayrin cried and circled around her.

Blood splashed Lyana's scales. A burn mark ran across her belly and leg. Her eyes, large emerald orbs, were haunted.

"Bayrin," she whispered, voice trembling. Her wings shook. "Elethor. Help me to the city. Quick! The phoenixes. They're coming. Faster!"

Elethor stared into the southern horizon. From here, he could see the flames rising, thrashing the sky and racing across the land. When he squinted, he thought that the fire took the form of great eagles, dragon-sized, their wings like fountains of sunfire. The fire crackled and he could hear their shrieks.

"Where are the others?" Elethor demanded. "Where is my father, his five thousand dragons?" Horror pounded through him, shaking his limbs. Were they all gone like his brother?

But Lyana was already flying back to the city.

"To Nova Vita!" she called. "Hurry!"

Elethor cursed and followed. Bayrin flew at his side.

As they flew, Elethor watched the city grow closer. Its walls rose, white and craggy, defending temples, homes, and workshops. Three hundred years since the Destruction when the tyrant Dies Irae had razed this land, Requiem's dragons were recovering. Trees grew where once fire and war had raged. Vir Requis sang and prayed where once skeletons had lain burnt. A million dragons had once flown here; Dies Irae had killed all but seven, but now myriads lived behind these walls, a renaissance for their race.

I will not let Requiem fall again, Elethor vowed.

When they landed on the walls, they shifted back into human forms. When their wings and scales vanished, they stood panting on the parapets. Lyana faltered, and Elethor caught her.

"Lyana!" he said. "What happened?"

Ash covered her face and darkened her hair. Her armor was singed and bloody. Pain filled her eyes, and something else... a haunting fear.

"They're coming," she whispered through pale lips. "The phoenixes. Great birds of flame." She clutched his shoulders. "We must get everyone into the tunnels. Everyone! And barricade the entrances. They will be here soon."

Bayrin stared at her, slack-jawed. The gangly young man rubbed his eyes.

"Sister, who is coming? What are these phoenixes?"

She glared at him, five years his junior and nearly a foot shorter, but twice as commanding. "I'll explain later. Now fly over the city, both of you! Sound the alarm. Roar the call. I'll run between the houses. Go, you blockheads!"

With that, she ran down the wall's stairs, dashed across a street, and began pounding on house doors.

Elethor looked back south. He could see them clearly now--countless firebirds, huge eagles blazing with fury, flying their way. With a growl, he shifted back into a dragon and began circling over the city.

"People of Requiem!" he roared. The city streets and houses spun beneath him. "This is Elethor, son of King Olasar. On my command, leave your homes and head to the tunnels. Now! Everyone must enter the tunnels at once!"

Bayrin was flying too, wings churning the hot air, roars shattering the night. "Enemies at the gates! Into the tunnels! Into the tunnels!"

Below them, Lyana was banging on doors and helping people outside. Soon thousands crowded the streets, shouting and weeping.

Three entrances led to Nova Vita's tunnels. Originally a network of natural caves, the tunnels now held stairways, cobbled floors, archways, and bridges--masonry added over centuries. In those underground chambers, Requiem stored its winter food, its ancient books, its magical artifacts. They were secret places for kings, priests, and scholars. Today thousands raced toward them.

As Elethor flew, sounding the alarm, fear pounded through him. Nobody else was flying back from the inferno. Was Lyana the only survivor? Was his father... *No.* Elethor swallowed the thought. *Do not panic,* he told himself. *Not now. Not until everyone is safe.*

When he looked back south, he saw them closer. The phoenixes were only a league away. The farms outside the city kindled, and their fire raced toward the walls. Smoke unfurled like demons. The farmers were shifting into dragons, taking flight, and heading toward the city.

"Everyone move calmly!" Lyana shouted below, still in human form, herding the people into lines. "That's right, form lines, head into the tunnels one by one. Stay calm and move quickly."

Father, Elethor thought. *Where are you? Why don't you fly here too?*

Shrieks sounded behind him, and Elethor turned to see the phoenix army fly over the walls.

The inferno stormed with heat, sound, and fury. It felt like a sun exploding over Nova Vita. Fire howled around Elethor. He reared and flapped his wings to blow back the flames. He only fanned them. The phoenixes swooped, larger than him, wings crackling and beaks flowing with fire. Their claws reached toward him, shards of lightning.

Below him, the people screamed. They ran through the streets, blazing. Cries of pain and fear rose across the city, muffled under the crackle and shrieks of the firebirds.

Elethor blew fire. The jet spun and slammed into a phoenix. The great firebird screeched, unharmed; the dragonfire only seemed to enlarge it, as if it sucked up the fire's strength. It dived and slammed its claws into Elethor.

He screamed. It felt like hot irons pressed against him. He soared, spun, and swooped. His claws tore into the phoenix's head, and he cried in pain. Its fire blazed across his legs; he thought his scales might crack from heat.

"Elethor!" rose Bayrin's voice somewhere in the distance. "Elethor, come, into the tunnels!"

The phoenixes swarmed everywhere. Houses cracked in the heat. People fell burning. Some Vir Requis became dragons and tried to fly, only to crash into the phoenixes. A young girl ran from her house, shifted into a lavender dragon, and took flight. Before she could fly ten feet, phoenix claws tore her apart. She crashed back onto the cobblestones as a girl, her neck and chest slashed open.

Smoke unfurled and flames filled the night. Elethor flew, dodging phoenix claws and beaks. He crashed through one's flaming wings, and the heat seared him. His eyes and throat burned with smoke.

"Bayrin, where are you?" he shouted. He could see nothing but fire. "Lyana! Mori!"

He heard Bayrin's voice again; it rose from the flames below. "Elethor, down here, into the tunnels!"

Elethor dived through flames and flew down the streets, wings beating back fire. People were still running toward the tunnels, some of them burning. Many lay dead; Elethor could see their seared bodies through the fire. The phoenixes were swooping, burning the fleeing people. Some Vir Requis were shifting, taking flight, and fleeing into the night. The phoenixes flew at them, caught them in their talons, and bit with fiery beaks.

One phoenix surged between buildings toward Elethor and slammed into him. It felt like a furnace door opened and the flames knocked him back. He hit a building, cracked the stone wall, and howled. He clawed and blew fire, but could not hold back the phoenix. Could nothing kill these beasts? Around him, dragons soared, only to be slammed down and burned. Bodies littered the streets.

"Into the tunnels, go!" Elethor shouted to the people. "Don't try to fight, just run!"

A long, green dragon soared from the inferno, howling. Leathern wings beat back the flames. Bayrin roared and grabbed Elethor's shoulders.

"El, we must go!" he shouted. "Now!"

Elethor shook himself free. "There are still people in the houses! We must get them into the tunnels. We must find Mori!"

"We can't help anyone if we're dead!" The flames burned around Bayrin; his scales blazed red. "The phoenixes are--"

Three firebirds dived and slammed into them. Elethor shut his eyes under the flame. He felt weight and heat pushing him down. He crashed against a road, cracking the cobblestones. When he opened his eyes, he saw bodies everywhere. No more people ran through the smoke. Bayrin was gone. The phoenixes screeched above him, beaks and claws lashing him. Elethor leaped aside, dodging the flames, and soared.

"Mori!" he called. "Mori, do you hear me?"

Was his sister still alive? Had she managed to flee the temple where Mother Adia had taken her? He'd already lost a brother; if he lost his sister too, there would be no meaning to his life.

Elethor looked around, but saw only phoenixes, an endless swarm of them, and smoke, and fire, and bodies burning into bones. Nova Vita flamed. The smoke was so thick, and the light was so bright, he could barely see.

"Elethor!" rose a voice from the distance.

"Lyana!" he cried.

"Elethor, we're sealing the tunnels! Come on!"

Ten phoenixes soared toward him. Elethor cursed, snarled, and swooped. He shot through walls of fire. He crashed against a temple's column, cracking it. Bricks rained. The body of a child burned below.

"Lyana, where are you!"

"Elethor, here! In Benedictus Square!"

He could just make out the columns surrounding the cobbled square. Only yesterday, philosophers, priests, and scribes would wander this square between the birches, praying and singing and studying the stars. Today bodies and smoke filled it. Elethor dived toward it, the forge of phoenixes in pursuit. He barely discerned Lyana standing at an archway; beyond it, stairs led underground. Elethor hit the cobblestones and shifted into a human. He leaped into the stairwell with Lyana, then spun to face the archway.

Phoenixes landed outside, screeching. Their flames shot into the tunnel, forcing Elethor and Lyana to leap back several steps. The craggy staircase led into darkness below. Hundreds of people crowded the stairs, weeping and moaning and screaming.

"Quick, seal the doors!" cried a burly man in armor, his red beard singed.

Elethor recognized Lord Deramon, father to Lyana and Bayrin. He had never liked the man. A harsh soldier with a face like a craggy cliff, Deramon seemed to always scowl and mutter around him. Elethor's hatred had only grown seven years ago, after Deramon caught him kissing Solina in the forest. The lord had marched to the king, revealed the secret love, and doomed Solina to exile.

"There are still people out there, Deramon!" he shouted. "They're dying!"

The phoenixes scratched at the archway but were too large to enter.

"They're dead already!" Deramon shouted back. His face flushed as red as his beard.

Elethor wanted to run outside, to find and save whoever he could. Had Bayrin made it into the tunnels? What of his father and sister; where were they?

"You don't know that, Deramon!" he shouted and drew his sword.

He watched the tunnel entrance and grimaced. Before his eyes, the phoenixes shrank, twisted, and took human forms. Soon they stood as warriors in bright armor, golden suns upon their breastplates. *The sun of Tiranor,* Elethor knew. The Tirans drew sabres. The Vir Requis in the tunnel shrieked in fear.

Lord Deramon drew his own sword--a thick, heavy blade of northern steel. Lyana already held her blade before her; it was bloodied and darkened with ash. Flickers of fire still clinging to them, the Tirans ran onto the staircase and blades clashed.

Elethor parried a thrust, grunted, and riposted. He was no great warrior; his father and Orin were the fighters. Today everything his swordmasters had taught him vanished, and he swung his blade with blind fear and fury.

"You will die, weredragons," said a Tiran, a tall man with blazing blue eyes. A crystal hung around his neck, a flame trapped inside it. His sword swung, and Elethor parried, raising sparks. Deramon fought at his side, his thick sword slamming at the enemy's thin, curved sabres. The tunnel was only wide enough for two men to fight side by side.

A dagger flew over Elethor's head and slammed into a Tiran's neck. Blood spurted and the man pitched forward, hit the stairs, and crashed down between Elethor and Deramon. Standing behind them, Lyana slammed down her sword, finishing the job. Vir Requis guards were racing up from the shadows below, drawing their own swords.

"Get down into the tunnels, boy!" Deramon howled at Elethor, swinging his sword. "We'll hold them back."

Elethor cursed and grumbled. "You will not call me 'boy'. I am still your prince, Deramon."

The man growled. "You are a boy, and you will enter the tunnels. Make room for men to fight by my side."

As he parried blows from Tiran sabres, Elethor fumed. He was no warrior, but he was still these people's prince; how could he run and cower among the women and children?

"I'm staying here to fight and die, old man!" he shouted, parried a blow, and thrust his blade.

Deramon slew a man. The body crashed down the stairs into darkness. "I'm not risking your life, not until I know if your father is alive. We're not losing another prince. Down, into the tunnels! Take my daughter with you."

A blade flashed. Elethor parried. Blood spurted and the enemies crowded at the doorway; there seemed no end to them. Nova Vita's survivors wept and shouted behind in the darkness.

"You think I'll run and hide instead of fight?"

"You will do what I tell you!" Deramon shouted, still swinging his blade. "As you like to remind me, you're our prince... not our champion."

Lyana rushed up behind him and grabbed Elethor's shoulder. "Come on, El. He's right. With me, down into the darkness. We have to protect you."

A Tiran broke past Deramon, leaped three steps, and lunged at Elethor. Blades clashed. Elethor grunted in pain. The Tiran's sword sliced his shoulder. Lyana's blade thrust, the Tiran leaped back, and Elethor drove his sword into the man's neck. He stared, gritting his teeth, at the blood dripping down his blade. It was the first man he'd killed.

More Vir Requis warriors, clad in the armor of the City Guard, raced upstairs from the shadows. Their heavy longswords clashed with the Tirans' sabres. Blood flowed down the stairs.

"Come with me, El," Lyana said, voice soft. "You're hurt."

He stared at the tunnel entrance. Deramon and three of his men now fought there. Thousands of Tirans seemed to fill the night outside. With a curse, Elethor tore his gaze away and took several steps down into the shadows. Survivors crowded around him, reaching out to touch him.

"Our prince," whispered an old woman, hands patting his shoulder.

"My lord," said a child, bowing his head.

They filled the darkness around him, burnt, bloodied, and weeping. Their arms reached to him and their eyes shone. The stench of burning flesh and blood and fear filled the tunnels.

Lyana held Elethor's arm and led him deeper into the darkness. "This is where the people need you, Elethor. They need to see you, to know that you lead them. You need to be their leader, not their soldier. You will be our king."

He froze, grabbed her arms, and stared at her. "What do you mean, Lyana?" he said through clenched teeth. "My father is king." His voice shook. "King Olasar, son of Amarin, descended from Queen Gloriae herself." His fingers shook around her arms.

Lyana lowered her head. "Elethor," she said softly. "Oh, Elethor."

She embraced him, this girl who would steal his toy swords when they were little, who once peeked into the bathing chambers as he undressed, who always looked down her nose at him and Bayrin and scolded them for being immature, good-for-nothing layabouts. Today this girl, now a woman stained with the blood and fire of war, placed her head against his shoulder, shed tears, and whispered into his ear.

"I'm sorry, Elethor. I'm so sorry. He fell." She touched his cheek. "Your father is dead."

The flames roared outside. Steel rang and the screams of dying echoed. Elethor closed his eyes. A tremble took him and he could not breathe. It felt like a vise clutched his head, twisting and cracking his skull. He forced himself to breathe. His head spun and he had to hold the tunnel wall for support.

Calm down, he told himself. *Don't panic yet. Not when these people need you... when Lyana needs you.*

Breathing through clenched teeth, he opened his eyes, still holding Lyana. She looked at him with huge, damp eyes.

"I'm sorry too, Lyana," he said. He tried to sound strong, comforting, a powerful man who could protect her--but his voice cracked. It sounded to him like the voice of a frightened child. He took another deep breath.

The survivors in the tunnel jostled and moved aside. Bayrin walked through the crowd, heading upstairs toward Elethor and Lyana. Burn marks covered his arms, and his face was damp and red. He stared with cold eyes.

"I found Mori," he said. "She's in the wine cellars. She's banged up and a little singed, but she's alive."

Elethor inhaled shakily--a breath of such relief that his knees shook and he nearly collapsed. *Thank the stars.* His eyes stung. *My sister is alive. Not all our family is dead.*

"Thank you, Bay," he said, voice choked.

Bayrin stared back solemnly. "And El... my mother is waiting for you. Come with me. She's going to crown you."

Elethor couldn't help it; he made a sound halfway between gasp and guffaw. He stared over Lyana's head at her brother, his best friend since childhood.

"You've gone mad, Bay," he said. "Adia wants to crown me? Now, here?" He shook his head wildly.

Lyana held him and stared at him. A fire blazed in her eyes.

"Yes, now and here," she said, voice stern. Curls of her red hair clung to her face with sweat and blood. "The people need a king, Elethor. They need a leader." She sighed. "You might be a blockhead, but you're all we've got now."

He laughed mirthlessly. "You've both gone mad! Both of you. My father... my brother..." His voice cracked. "Oh stars, we haven't even buried them. I don't want a crown. I never wanted to be king. Find somebody else." He looked back over his shoulder at the fighting. "Get your father down here! Crown him; the people love Deramon."

He sounded like a child, he realized and cursed himself. But what else could he say? He had never served in the army like Orin. He had never dreamed of the throne like Orin. He had never gone to countless ceremonies and feasts and met with foreign kings. He was just Elethor, the younger brother who'd count the stars, or sculpt, or walk for hours through the forest with Solina, or...

But those days are gone now, Elethor, he told himself. He clenched his fists. *You must do this. They're right. You can't abandon your people. They need you.*

As soldiers raced up the stairs and blood spilled down, his friends pulled him deeper into the tunnels. The shadows spun around him. Everywhere hands reached to him, the wounded lay moaning, and the stench of death spun his head. He moved in a daze, eyes burning.

My father. My brother. Gone.

Mother Adia, Priestess of Requiem, rose from the darkness toward him. A tall woman, she looked nothing like her red-headed, light-eyed children. Adia's hair was black and smooth as the night sky. Her eyes were pools of darkness. She could have been one of Elethor's statues--pale, beautiful, her skin like marble. Ash and blood stained her white robes.

"Elethor," she said, voice as deep and solemn as her eyes, and took his hands.

She whispered prayers to the stars in a shaky voice. Around them the people answered her prayers, reaching to the ceiling. Elethor did not know if starlight could ever glow here--or in the world again--but he answered the prayers in a hoarse, low voice.

They had no crown to place upon his head, no holy oil to anoint him with. There were no lords and ladies, no songs, only this stench of burnt flesh and sweat and nightsoil and death.

"Requiem!" Adia called, voice rising and shaking. "May our wings forever find your sky."

The words of their fathers, their people, their life. Those were the words the first kings had spoken when building temples in King's Forest. Those were the words the legendary Queen Gloriae had shouted in battle against Dies Irae the Destructor. The survivors in the tunnels repeated the prayer. Elethor spoke with them, his voice finally finding some strength.

"Requiem! May our wings forever find your sky."

Mother Adia turned to the crowd in the tunnels. Voice trembling, she said, "Kneel before King Elethor Aeternum, Son of Olasar."

Those who could, knelt, and Elethor looked over the survivors, his eyes dry. They filled the narrow tunnels, disappearing far into the darkness. Lyana knelt before him, holding her sword drawn, her eyes lowered. As Elethor looked at her mane of curls, he realized that by the law of the land, he had inherited not only his father's throne, but his brother's betrothed. If they survived this war, Lyana and he would be wed.

"Rise," he said to the people. They rose and wept, blessing his name.

Lyana looked at him, eyes huge and haunted. "My lord," she whispered, the first time she had ever called him that. "There is something more you must know."

Elethor stared at her, silent. His father and brother were dead. He had inherited the throne, and he was now betrothed to the girl who would torment him throughout his childhood. His city burned above him, and hundreds--likely thousands--were dead. What more news could she give him?

"Speak," he said.

She stared at him steadily, holding his arm. "Elethor... the leader of the phoenixes, and the one who killed your father and brother, is Solina."

He stared at her. The memories of Solina pounded through him: her kisses, her naked body against his, their forbidden love in secret forests and chambers. His world burned. He saw nothing but fire.

He spun around and began marching upstairs to the tunnels' exit.

"I will speak to her," he said, voice strained, fists clenched to stop them from trembling.

For the first time in seven long, aching, lonely years, he would see her again. He had dreamed of this moment. Today it chilled his belly and filled his throat with bile.

SOLINA

The city of Nova Vita, fair capital of Requiem, burned below her.

Solina flew above the carnage, woven of fire. The marble columns and towers undulated in the heat waves. With every thud of her wings, sparks flew and light flared like the beat of her flaming heart. The sound and fury pounded through her, crackling, buzzing, roaring for eternal pain and glory. She had been burned. She had lain for days in a temple, bandaged and crying for vengeance. She had tamed her fire, and now she soared through it, a goddess of inferno.

Bodies littered the streets below, the fire stripping flesh from bones, leaving blackened skulls that gaped. A scattering of dragons still flew, only for her phoenixes to hunt them, tear them down, and feast upon them. The rest huddled in the tunnels below, but Solina knew she would burn them too. She knew every twist and cavern in those tunnels. She had spent so many hours in their darkness, stoking her fire with Elethor.

Do you hide there now, my prince of tears? she wondered. *Will we meet again this night, after all these years?*

Elethor. The very name sent pulsing memory through her. She still remembered his birth. She had been only five, an orphan raised in the king's court, a timid girl still so scared of the world. When King Olasar let her hold the babe, she vowed to forever love him.

And I love you, Elethor, she thought. *I loved you when I held you as a babe. I loved you in our youth, when our lips touched, and our hands felt, and our naked bodies pressed together. And I still love you now, even as I burn your home.*

She dived toward the palace. It shimmered between the flames, its columns like bones. Her claws hit the cobblestones, splashing fire. She shifted, sucking the flames into her. Her wings drew in, forming arms. Her fire twisted, formed flesh and bones, and soon she stood upon human feet. The last tongues of fire pulled into the firegem around her neck, where they danced. She clutched the amulet and smiled, looking around at her old prison.

Requiem's palace. The place where they raised me... and where they burned me. She ran her finger across her line of fire, the scar that snaked down her face, between her breasts, and along her thigh. *But their fire can no longer hurt me.*

The columns rose around her, two hundred feet tall, carved of white marble. Between them, the birches blazed and crackled. When Solina was young, these columns had seemed so large to her, colossal monuments kissed with starlight that would never bless her. Orin and Elethor, like brothers to her, could become dragons, fly above them, soar so high the columns were as mere twigs to them. They had offered to carry her upon their backs, but Solina had always refused.

To ride you would mean I'm a cripple, she would think, fists clenched. *I am a proud Tiran, a desert daughter, a princess of the ancient Phoebus Dynasty. We do not ride dragons.*

"We kill them," she whispered.

Several phoenixes landed beside her, flaming and shrieking, their fire pounding the cobblestones. They shifted, flames pulling into their firegems, and soon stood before her as men clad in pale armor. They saluted, slamming their fists against their breastplates. Acribus stood among them, chief of her warriors, his armor bloody and his arm bandaged.

"My lady Solina," he said and bowed his head.

She stared at his blood. "The wound Princess Mori gave you is still bleeding. You need it stitched."

He bared his chipped, yellow teeth. "Princess? You mean a lizard whore. She will bleed worse when I catch her."

Solina shrugged. "Call her what you like. Hurt her how you like. You can cut off her freak finger, if it pleases you. Just don't bleed to death first."

Seven years had passed since she'd set foot in Requiem, but Solina had never forgotten Princess Mori, or the Lady Lyana, or any of the other girls who would torment her.

Mori was only a child then, Solina thought, *but I remember how she'd pity me, a mere Tiran who could not become a dragon.*

Lyana, meanwhile, had been only a snotty youth, a bookish girl whose nose was always upturned and whose father--Captain of the City Guard--would pamper her. *Lyana too always looked down upon me,* Solina thought. *She saw only an orphan, an outcast, a cripple.*

She clenched her jaw. *Acribus will hurt them well. They will hurt like I hurt. We'll see how they pity me when Acribus thrusts inside them, when he cuts them, when he feeds their fingers to the dogs.*

As if he could read her thoughts, Acribus licked his lips with that ridiculous white tongue of his. It always looked to Solina like a snake nested in his mouth.

"My lady," he said, "the weredragons have crowned a new king. He fights at the entrance of a nearby tunnel, and he wishes to treat with you." He laughed, a sound like snapping bones. "Would you like to hear this boy king beg for life before we kill him, or shall I gut him now?"

Solina felt like a bellows blasted hot air against her. She froze, fingers tingling, sweat dripping down her forehead.

"Elethor," she whispered.

Acribus barked a laugh. "Yes, that was his name. A soft boy; looks like he never swung a sword in battle until today. I will break him. I will shatter his spine. I will crush his limbs with a hammer, sling them through the spokes of a wheel, and hang him to die upon the palace walls."

She glared at him, baring her teeth. "You will not touch him, Acribus. If you do, you will be the one broken. Show me to the weredragons' new king. I will speak to him."

They marched down the streets, leaving the palace behind. Ash swirled around their boots. Trees and bodies burned at their sides, raising black smoke. Phoenixes soared and screeched above; the sky itself seemed to burn. The sounds of battle came from ahead: swords clanging, battle cries, and the shouts of dying men calling for mothers, lovers, or the mercy of death.

Soon Solina saw an entrance to a tunnel. The stone archway rose ten feet tall, its keystone engraved with dragon reliefs. The bodies of Tirans and weredragons littered the cobblestones around it. Living soldiers fought above the bodies, clanging swords. Blood puddled and flowed toward Solina's boots.

A memory thudded through Solina, aching in her chest. *Come on, Elethor!* she had cried, laughing, and pulled him down the streets. She had been twenty, maybe twenty-one, a young woman blooming into her beauty. He had still been a youth, awkward and gangly, but she was determined to make him a man. They explored the tunnels that day, moving between wine cellars, libraries, silos, and finally finding a nook full of rugs where they made love--fiery, passionate love that made her scream and scratch her fingernails down his back. *We returned to these tunnels most nights after that,* she remembered.

"Tirans!" she shouted. "To me. Form rank. Leave the weredragons to cower in their burrow."

With a few last sword swings, the men fell back and formed rank around her. Blood splashed their armor, and they glared at the tunnel archway. Weredragon warriors stood there, panting over the bodies of their fallen. One man clutched a hole where his ear had been, and another sat against a wall, cradling an arm that ended with a stump. The place seemed strangely silent without the clash of steel and cries of battle; Solina heard only the fire of phoenixes above and the moans of the dying.

"Elethor," she said, speaking to the gaping shadow of the tunnel. "Elethor. Come see me."

Flames crackled. Smoke unfurled. From the blood and shadows, the pain and hope of her youth emerged. All that sweet pain--the secret kisses, the forbidden taste of love--flooded her, made her fingers tingle, and she stared in silence.

He had been only eighteen when she last saw him, a tall and gaunt youth; she would poke him and laugh at how thin he was. He had grown into adulthood since then, a man of twenty-five with dark, haunted eyes and brown hair that fell over his brow, caked with blood and ash. And yet those were the same lips she would kiss, the same eyes she would gaze into--hound dog eyes, she would call them.

"Solina," he said softly.

Her eyes stung. She had not expected this to be so difficult. She had not expected to still feel so much, hurt so badly. She remembered him speaking her name so many times--as a child growing up in her arms, a lover in her bed, and that last time he called her name, shouting it from the walls of Nova Vita as she fled into exile, her line of fire burning down her body.

"Elethor," she whispered. She beckoned him closer. "Come. We will speak." She snapped her fingers, and her men formed lines around her. "Follow me; we will find someplace quiet."

He stood still, staring at her between strands of damp hair. "We will speak here."

She couldn't help it; she laughed, tears stinging her eyes. "I won't harm you, Elethor. And my men will not hurt yours until we've spoken. You have my word." She stepped toward him and took his hands. They were bloody and hot. "Come with me, Elethor. Let's work out this mess."

He stared into her eyes, scrutinizing her, and she saw the same memories and pain pound through him. He still loved her, she knew then. That soothed her. *This will make things easier.* She did not want to hurt him. Finally he nodded and took a step forward.

At once, two more wereragons emerged from the tunnels, making to follow him. Both held drawn, bloodied swords. Solina recognized them. One was Lord Deramon, Captain of the Guard, a burly man with a red beard now grizzled. *He is the man who caught me with Elethor,* she remembered, a deep rage simmering inside her. *The man who doomed me to exile.* The second weredragon was his daughter, the Lady Lyana. The girl Solina knew had been overbearing, an imperious brat. Today Solina saw a woman with fear and grief in her eyes. *We hurt her. Good.*

Solina held up her hand. "No. You two stay here. Elethor and I speak alone. Just me and him."

They began to object.

"She'll kill you, Elethor," Deramon said, eyes dark.

"We go with you," said Lyana and bared her teeth at Solina.

Elethor's eyes never left Solina; they were narrowed, seeking answers, reliving old years. He hushed his companions with a raised hand.

"Just me and her," he repeated softly. "They won't touch me. Deramon. Lyana. Stay and tend to the wounded. I'll be back soon."

They walked through the streets, she and Elethor. Her men snaked around them, forming a hallway of steel. Phoenixes circled above, bodies lay scorched, trees burned, and columns lay smashed. The battle had surged; for now it simmered.

The smell of burnt flesh filled Solina's nostrils. She remembered that smell from seven years ago; she had smelled it on herself. She felt her line of fire tingle across her body. She clenched her teeth and smiled.

"Here," she said to Elethor, gesturing at a gazebo rising from a stone square. "We will talk here."

He stared at the gazebo, eyes dark. *He knows why I chose this place.* The gazebo rose upon a dais, fifty steps leading toward it. Its columns were white marble engraved with dragon reliefs. The roof was domed and set with frosted glass panes. Solina remembered sitting here with Elethor at night, watching the stars and moon glimmer through that glass, a shower of fireflies. It was the first place she had kissed him.

He nodded. "We will talk."

She left her men below in the square. They stood at attention upon the flagstones, fists against their breastplates. She climbed the stairs toward the gazebo, Elethor at her side. When they stepped inside, she could see firelight through the frosted glass roof--countless phoenixes diving through the night, casting orange dapples upon her and Elethor.

She turned toward him, placed her hands in his hair, and pressed her body against his. She kissed his lips, and for a moment, their heat mingled like in the old days.

"Elethor," she whispered, eyes stinging. "I missed you. I love you."

He turned his head away, breaking their kiss, and pushed her back. His bloodied hands stained her breastplate.

"Solina, did you bring me here for that? You killed my father. You killed my brother." His voice shook. "How dare you kiss me now?"

She glared at him, teeth bared. Her line of fire blazed. "Your father?" She snorted. "He banished me, El. You remember. He banished me because of our love, cast me out into the desert." She clenched her fists. "Your brother? Orin burned me. He blew his fire upon me and left me scarred, deformed." She ran her finger along her scar, from her forehead, across her face, and down her neck. "But I tamed fire, El. I told you I would." She clutched his arms. "They can no longer banish me, no longer burn me. I did this for you. So we can be together, with no fear, no pain. No more hiding." She tried to kiss him again. "I've returned to kill those who hurt us and to be with you again. I love you."

He stared at her, and something filled his eyes... something dark, shocked, frightened. He shook his head. "Solina... what have you done?" He clenched his fists and looked aside. "Stars, Solina, how could you do this?"

She snarled and slapped his face, hard, driving all her strength into the blow. "How dare you speak of your stars here? Your stars are worthless." She laughed bitterly. "Starlight never blessed us, Elethor. It never protected Requiem. But fire..." She breathed heavily. "Fire is strong. Fire burned me. Fire is now my ally." She felt it burn inside her, and she dug her fingers into his shoulders. "You do not know the power of the Sun God, Elethor. He cured me from Orin's flames." She grabbed her firegem. "He gave me his power, so that I could become a phoenix, a deity woven of his flame. He has given me so much. He can give this fire to you too."

He shoved her back again, more roughly this time. "Do not speak to me of this Sun God. I know of him. I know that he destroyed Requiem once, driving the evil of Dies Irae the Tyrant. I know that his flame will burn everything it can consume."

"It will not consume those who serve it." She was panting now, and she touched his cheek. "Elethor. Oh, my Elethor; you were the fire of my youth. Now join your flames to mine. I will grant you a firegem; you will become a phoenix, a great firebird, no longer a lizard of scales. Join me in Tiranor and worship my lord at my side. We will rule together. We will cast our flames across the world and watch it burn." She held him, pressed her lips against his ear, and whispered. "Elethor, don't you love me? Don't you remember all those nights we spent here?"

He let out his breath slowly, and his head lowered; suddenly he felt so sad to her, the weight of the world upon his shoulders.

"I remember," he said softly. "Solina, I loved you more than anything--so much that it ached. For seven years since you left, I thought of you every day." He laughed bitterly. "Every minute of every day. I never loved another woman since you. I don't know if I ever will."

She held him tight, eyes stinging. "So come with me, El. Come south with me. They can no longer hurt us, no longer drive us apart. I will kill anyone who comes between us again."

She trembled, remembering those years so long ago, her life in the courts of Requiem. The pain flooded her, memories like rivers, streams of faces and words and feelings.

She had been only three years old when the dragons of Requiem burned her home. Their claws toppled the white towers of Tiranor, and their flames burned their oases in the desert. Solina had been too small to understand why the war raged. She did not understand why her parents would not wake, why their blood covered her. The dragon who slew them, the vile King Olasar, pitied her that day. He kidnapped her from her home, brought her to his cold realm of snow and birches, far from the warmth and light of Tiranor.

She grew in his court. A freak. An outsider. A Tiran girl not blessed by Requiem's stars. She could not shift into a dragon like Prince Orin, like King Olasar, like all the Vir Requis she grew up among.

Deformed, the children of the court would call her. *Freak. Cripple.* They would shift into dragons, slap her with their tails, and blast fire at her feet and make her dance. How she tried to shift too! How she dreamed of becoming a dragon! Yet she was a southerner, a desert child, doomed to be weak, scared, tormented.

And then... then her life changed. Then Elethor was born. A pure baby, younger brother to Orin and like a brother to her. Solina vowed to protect this soft, beautiful child, to make sure he never felt loneliness or pain like she did. She watched Elethor grow. He was her treasure, her foster brother, her reason to live. Even when he grew old enough to become a dragon, she still loved him. She would run her fingers over his brass scales and kiss him, and he was *her* dragon, her protector.

He was only fifteen when she kissed him in this gazebo. She was twenty, but still clinging to all the fear and rage of youth; in her mind, she felt no older than him. They conquered their fear together. For three years, they would hide in this gazebo, or in the forests, or in the tunnels beneath Nova Vita, and they would love each other. A forbidden, secret, wonderful, horrible love. For three years Solina felt pure joy... until Lord Deramon caught them in the forest, and told his king, and Requiem's rage rained down upon them.

"Solina of Tiranor!" King Olasar shouted in his court. She stood before him, head lowered, tears on her cheeks. "Despite the crime of your parents, who attacked our borders and sacked our temples, I raised you as a daughter. I sheltered you, taught you, protected you. And yet you cast your sin upon my son." His fists trembled at his sides. "Elethor is like a brother to you. How dared you seduce him? He is only a youth, five years younger than you. How dared you bring such perversion into my hall?" He pointed a shaky finger at her. "You are banished from Requiem! Leave this place now, and wander whatever lands you may please; if you are caught within our borders, your life is forfeit."

Rage bloomed within her. She drew her dagger and screamed.

"You will not speak of my parents!" Her voice was hoarse, torn with years of pain. "I know what you did to them. I know that you killed them, framed them for stealing jewels from your temples. Liar!" She ran toward him, knife raised. "You cannot know how Elethor and I love each other. You will not tear us apart!"

She almost killed him that night. A few steps more, and she could have plunged her blade into his heart. Yet Orin-- brutish, cruel Prince Orin--stood as a dragon by the throne. Like a coward, he did not face her as a man, but blew fire upon her. The flames shot toward her, a screaming inferno.

Elethor shouted and pulled her aside. He saved her life, she knew... but dragonfire burned bright, and tongues of its flames still seared her. She screamed, ablaze, and fell. Welts and smoke rose across her. Never had such pain filled her. It made her weep, roll on the ground, and claw the air.

For days she lay abed in a temple, bandaged and feverish. The priestesses tended to her in darkness. She cried for Elethor, but they would not let her see him. When finally she rose from her bed, and her bandages were removed, she bore her line of fire. The scar split her face, snaked down her torso, and crawled down her leg. *A reminder,* she knew. *A pledge. A battle scar.*

"Solina!" he shouted from the walls as they cast her out, goading her with spears, sending her into the wilderness with nothing but a waterskin and loaf of bread.

She dared not look back at him. She walked, barefoot, leaving the city behind. She heard his dragon roars calling her name, but she did not want to remember him this way. She would remember the Elethor who held her in the tunnels, laughed with her, whispered with her. She walked south for days, leaving Requiem, heading into the swamps of Gilnor. All of autumn she walked, until in winter she reached a land where no snow fell, and heat rose from sand.

Tiranor. Land of her parents. Land of the Sun God, of flame, of power. Her people welcomed her with joy--the last, lost

daughter of the great Phoebus Dynasty. They crowned her with
ivory and raised her to be their queen. In desert temples of stone,
she worshipped her new lord the Sun God. She swore that if he
gave her the strength, she would kill his enemies in Requiem.

"He gave me so much."

A chest of firegems, crystals that held flames from the sun
itself. With them, she could become the phoenix. With them, her
followers could soar as beasts woven of sunfire. Soon all the
temples of Tiranor praised her name, flew with her to battle, and
vowed to destroy the weredragons who worshipped night and
stars.

"But you, Elethor," she whispered in the gazebo as
Requiem burned, "you don't need to die. Come south and rule
with me. We will be together again... like we were born to be."

She saw in his eyes that he had relived their lost years too.
He removed her hands from his shoulders, took a step back, and
stared at her.

"You come with fire," he said. "You come with death.
You murdered my family and you burned my home. How can
you now ask me for love? Did you do all this from some... some
mad notion that if you destroyed everything I have, I would be
with you?" Pain cracked his voice. "I loved you so much, but I
don't understand this."

She shook her head sadly. "Elethor, oh Elethor, how to
make you understand? I did not kill and burn for you alone." She
touched her scar. "I killed for this. For how they hurt me, and
how they hurt you. I killed for my lord, the Sun God, and all that
he's given me. But I do not wish to kill you." She took a step
toward him, breathing heavily. "But if you refuse me, Elethor... if
you fight me, I will hurt you. Turn me down and I will kill you. I
will kill everyone who huddles in your tunnels."

He stared away from her, watching Requiem burn
between the gazebo columns. "I am king of this land now. I

never wanted the crown. I never imagined that I'd wear it. But I am King of Requiem, and I cannot abandon her. I cannot abandon all those who still live here."

"You will abandon them." She grabbed his shoulder, digging her fingernails into it, and spun him around. She snarled. "You will surrender this land to me, Elethor. You will return with me to Tiranor. Do this, and I will spare your life, and I will spare those of your people who still live. Refuse me, Elethor... and you will all die. You will die in fire."

He stared aside, jaw tight, fists clenched at his sides. She saw the turmoil on his face.

"You know my answer," he said.

She pulled his face to her and stared into his eyes. "You are loyal to your friends. That is admirable. How would you serve them by refusing me? Would you watch me burn them? Because I would make you watch, Elethor. You would watch them die in agony before I killed you." She turned her back to him and spoke through clenched teeth. "Go to your tunnel, weredragon, and think. Think of those you love. Return here at sunrise to surrender to me. If you still choose to fight me, my fire will consume the world."

With that, she left him and walked downstairs to the courtyard. Her fingers tingled and a trembling smile found her lips.

I love you, Elethor, she thought, breathing hard. *But if I cannot have you, I will destroy you.*

MORI

She stood in the corner, hugging herself, and listened to the adults argue. Elethor had returned with the news: They had until dawn to surrender. Everyone seemed to have an opinion, which they were shouting. Bayrin Eleison, who would tug her pigtails in childhood, shouted that he'd charge through the Tirans and kill Solina himself. Lord Deramon grumbled that surrender might be the only option they had. Others stood around them--the Lady Lyana, a priest, two wounded lords, a group of guards--calling for war, for prayer, or for surrender.

Only Mori was silent. She stood in the back, cloaked in shadows, and dared not speak. She worried that if she opened her mouth, her voice would tremble, and tears would fill her eyes. An iciness lived in her belly, twisting and growing. Her shame still ached, a deep pain she worried would never leave her.

She remembered his tongue, a wet serpent, licking her cheek. She remembered his stale breath, his hands crushing her, his body above her, her mouse dying under her chest. She remembered the pain, and she closed her eyes and forced herself to take deep breaths. Before, in the battle, she had found no time for shame. Now it flooded her.

"Stars, I've heard enough!" Bayrin shouted, so loud that Mori's ears ached. "You can't be serious, Father. To let Elethor go with this... this creature of fire back to her lair?"

Lord Deramon was glaring at everyone and everything. "How do you suggest we fight the phoenixes? Dragonfire only feeds them. Claws cannot cut them. Even if we could stop them from entering the tunnels, we'd eventually die of starvation and thirst."

Bayrin crossed his arms. "Our water reservoirs and our silos are here underground. We have enough to last all winter."

"And what then?" Lady Lyana interjected, clutching her sword so tightly her knuckles were white. "Will you have us linger underground all winter, only to starve in spring? That's assuming we can even hold back the Tirans that long."

For a moment everyone shouted together, and Mori felt like a mouse herself, a small thing that made its home in shadows, unseen and frightened. She looked at her brother Elethor. He stood between her and the others, eyes dark. Only he seemed to notice Mori; he looked toward her, and his eyes softened. His chest rose and fell, and such sadness seemed to fill him that Mori wanted to embrace him.

Our father is dead. Our older brother is dead. Elethor and I are all that's left of our family. We're all we have. Tears filled her eyes and her lip trembled.

"What do you think, Mori?" he asked softly, his voice barely heard over the shouts of the others. It was not a plea for advice, she knew. Elethor was not asking for help. What he was really asking was: *How are you holding on?*

She looked away. His eyes were too much like Orin's. Gazing into them hurt too much.

"I don't know," she whispered, and that pain between her legs flared, and the shame inside her cried to her, calling her a harlot, a disgrace, a soiled thing.

Bayrin, her brother's gangly oaf of a friend, laughed mirthlessly. "Finally, an honest one among us. The Princess Mori doesn't know what to do. Neither do I. Neither do any of us. At least the girl is honest." He guffawed; it sounded close to tears, close to panic, a last attempt at humor to hold back the horror.

"So tell me, Mori, maybe you know this: Will we die from starvation, fire, or the thrusts of Tiran swords?"

Bayrin would always tug her braids in childhood, stuff frogs down her dress, and mock her mercilessly for having one finger too many. Today Mori missed the trickster Bayrin; the frightened and bitter Bayrin seemed infinitely worse. She clutched her hands behind her back, twisting her fingers. She felt her eleventh finger there, her luck finger, the plucky pinky itself as she sometimes called it. *Bring me luck today,* she thought.

"I need to learn more," she said softly. "About the Sun God. About this magic of phoenixes." She turned and began walking away. "I'll visit the library; it's not far from here. I'll learn what I can and return."

She felt their eyes on her back. Their argument died, and an odd silence filled the tunnels. The wounded lay around her feet, moaning and clutching wounds. Other survivors stood along the walls, rows of them leading into the darkness below. These tunnels delved deep, Mori knew, eventually leading to the Abyss itself, a realm of hidden horrors.

She heard her brother speak softly behind her. "Mori. Mori, are you all right?"

What could she tell him? *A man with yellow teeth and a white tongue broke me, Elethor. He shoved my legs open and thrust himself inside me, and I'm a princess of Requiem, a daughter of starlight, but I cried like a child and could not fight him. I could not even kill him. I watched my brother tortured to death, and my father is gone, and I'm so scared, and I'm so hurt, and I can't get rid of this iceberg inside my belly.* She smiled bitterly and said nothing. She kept walking, leaving them all behind, and plunged deep into the tunnels of Requiem.

The craggy stairs led to a rough, sloping tunnel. Candles filled alcoves in the walls, their wax dripping like the faces of burnt men. These tunnels wound for miles under Requiem, Mori knew; she would often explore them as a child. The great elders of Requiem had placed their scrolls here underground. The legendary King Benedictus had fought the Destroyer, Dies Irae, in these tunnels. *And today once more Requiem's fate will be written here,* she thought.

As she kept walking, she saw no end to the survivors. Hands reached out to her in the darkness. Mothers held crying children to their breasts. The elderly stared with teary eyes. Most people were burnt. Most whispered prayers to the Draco Constellation, the stars of Requiem.

"Our princess," they whispered, kneeling, tears in their eyes.

"Princess Mori, thank the stars."

"The stars bless you, our princess."

Their hands reached out, touching her, and she shivered. *His hands touched me too, and his tongue, and...* She closed her eyes, trembling.

One old woman began to chant the Old Words, the whispers of Requiem since time immemorial. The others whispered with her, their voices chanting together, and Mori added her voice to the song.

"As the leaves fall upon our marble tiles, as the breeze rustles the birches beyond our columns, as the sun gilds the mountains above our halls--know, young child of the woods, you are home, you are home." Tears filled Mori's eyes, the holy words soothing her. "Requiem! May our wings forever find your sky."

She looked above her and saw only cold stone. She had never understood the meaning of those words until now, trapped under rock and grief. *Requiem. May I find your sky again.*

She walked for a long time, hugging herself, passing by silos, pantries, wine cellars, and reservoirs. Sunrise couldn't be more than two hours away. *I must find a way to defeat the phoenixes before then... or we'll have to surrender and live forever under the bane of Solina.*

"And under his bane," she whispered, remembering his fingers gripping her. How many more times would he hurt her, if they could not defeat the Tirans? Would he claim her as his own, take her to his chambers, chain her and invade her every night?

"We must defeat them." Mori's lips trembled. "We must."

Soon she reached the Library of Requiem. Its doors rose tall above her, set into the stone walls of the tunnel. Mori carried the old, filigreed key around her neck on a chain. This library was ancient, and its books were priceless; each codex of parchment and leather was worth more than a chest of gold. Only the royal family bore the keys to this chamber of secrets. With trembling fingers, Mori unlocked the doors, stepped inside, and found herself in a world of books.

Thousands of years ago, before the Vir Requis had built columns of marble, they lived in these tunnels. Before they wrote books, they wrote upon scrolls of parchment and kept them here in alcoves, safe from the dangers of rain and snow and war. None of those original scrolls remained; they had all burned in the Great War three hundred years ago, when King Benedictus fought Dies Irae underground. But today the library was rebuilt, and new knowledge filled the alcoves and shelves that lined the walls. A hundred thousand books, leather-bound and beautiful, rose all around Mori.

It was a lot to read within two hours.

For the first time since the phoenixes had invaded Castellum Luna, Mori felt peace flow over her. There was some solace here, some goodness hidden from fire. So many hours of her childhood had been spent here. While Orin would go hunting with Father, and while Bayrin and Elethor were drinking in alehouses, Mori would come to this place. She had read her first book here at age five, and she kept returning every day for more. She would devour poems of epic adventure; codices full of delicate illustrations of birds; tomes of herbalism, astrology, history; and more. More than anything--the softness of her gowns, the beauty of Nova Vita's gardens, or the warmth of her quilt--Mori drew comfort from books. As she stood here today, a hurt and damaged woman, she could still feel that comfort, that wonder of childhood. Centuries of knowledge surrounded her. The wisdom of thousands of poets and philosophers filled this one place.

"It's the best place in the world," she whispered. "May today it bring us salvation."

She walked across the tiled floor, approached a ladder, and climbed to a high shelf. She ran her hand across the books, caressing their smoothed leather spines, and smiled softly. *There is still some goodness in the world.* She knew the library well; this shelf held her favorite books, ancient tomes about creatures and monsters of legend.

She remembered one book, a heavy codex her father had claimed was a thousand years old, and between its pages dwelled a hundred monsters. The book was so old, Father claimed that even the legendary Queen Gloriae had read it, and the book had been ancient then too. Mori had always feared that codex and never dared read it; when Father would try to read it to her, she would run and he would laugh softly.

He thought me scared of the monsters inside, Mori remembered. But it was not the monsters that would scare her; it was the book's age. So many generations had passed since its author scribed its words and pictures, so many ages of men who lived and fought and died. So many generations read the book, laughed, whispered, loved and hated. It was a thing of ghosts, of ancient life that spun Mori's head. But how could she have told Father that? So she had pretended to fear its pictures of griffins and serpents, and she would instead read poems of love and heroes.

Today she sought this old tome. Today was all about conquering fears. Would the book tell her of birds woven from fire? She let her fingers dance across the spines, and soon her fingertips rested upon a large codex wrapped in leather so old, the binding formed a landscape of crevices, canyons, and valleys. Words of gold crawled along the spine, written in the tongue of Osanna, the realm of men to the east. Mori did not read that ancient language well, but she knew enough to read these words. It was the book she sought: *Mythical Creatures of the Gray Age.*

Perhaps it was the fear inside her, or perhaps the solace of this place after the storm of battle, but Mori felt like the book's wisdom crept into her fingers, pulsed through her, whispered comfort into her soul. Smiling softly, she pulled the book off the shelf, and dust rained.

She blinked, coughed, and clung to the ladder. She struggled for long moments to pull the book free, stuff it under her arm, and hold it tight. The tome was large, over a foot long, and its spine was wider than her palm. Clinging to the ladder with one hand, Mori descended to the floor, placed the book down, and sat crossed-legged before it.

A digging pain thrust through her, and she closed her eyes. Her pulse quickened. His eyes blazed, and his lip curled, baring yellow teeth. His breath blasted her, scented of rot, and she screamed as he invaded her, hand around her throat, and she shook and wept and--

No. She forced her eyes open, forced herself to take slow breaths. Cold sweat drenched her, and slowly as she breathed, the flaring pain faded to a dull throb. She wiped tears from her eyes. *Don't think of him, Mori,* she told herself. *Think of saving Elethor. He is the only family you have left. You must save him from Solina... and you must save yourself.*

She leaned forward and blew dust off the book. It flew in a cloud, covering the tiles, and Mori sneezed. She opened the book, revealing crinkly pages of parchment. The first page sported an illustration of a griffin, and Mori shuddered, remembering the stories she'd heard of griffins attacking Requiem long ago. Small letters covered the page, written in the tongue of Osanna, speaking of the beasts. Mori began to leaf through the pages. The parchment was so old, she worried it would crumble in her hands. As the pages flipped, they revealed and hid creatures great and small: the mythical salvanae, true dragons of the west, who had no human forms; the nightshades, demons of smoke and shadow; the cruel mimics, undead warriors sewn from dismembered corpses; and even a page about the Vir Requis themselves, warriors of Requiem who could become dragons.

Mori laughed, eyes still stinging with tears. She didn't feel like a mythical creature, only a girl--scared, alone in darkness, seeking answers. She sniffed, knuckled her eyes, and flipped the page. Her eyes widened and her breath died.

"The phoenixes."

The page seemed to stare back at her, screaming from years beyond counting, and Mori hugged herself. The scribe had drawn an eagle woven of fire in red and orange, its claws outstretched, its beak wide, its eyes of fire incensed. Mori could imagine that she heard its shriek, and she shivered. The phoenix seemed to move upon the page; Mori almost saw its flames crackle, almost felt its heat. Suddenly she feared that the drawing could burn the book, that the phoenix could rise from the page and turn into Acribus, grab her and toss her over a table, and she would scream and her pain would never leave her. The fire and the screams engulfed her, and her head spun.

She gritted her teeth, clenched her fists, and closed her eyes. She forced herself to breathe deeply, like Mother Adia had taught her. She inhaled through her nose, slowly, counting to five, until she filled her lungs from top to bottom. She held her breath, counted to five again, and exhaled slowly. Hugging herself, Mori forced herself to keep breathing, again and again--into her lungs, into her limbs, into every part of her that trembled, until the fear passed. When she was ready, she opened her eyes again, and found that the book was silent and cold, the library only a place of shadows and solitude.

It's only a book, Mori, she told herself. *It's only a drawing. It can't hurt you.*

She leaned down so that her nose almost touched the parchment and squinted. The letters were old and small, faded in places, and Mori had never found it easy to read the tongue of Osanna. She mumbled to herself, reading aloud:

"In the days of Chaos, the lights of the heavens fought a great war, casting light and fire upon the earth. The Sun God, lord of heat and flame, birthed the phoenixes to champion his cause. Great birds of sunfire, they flew upon the earth, burning forests and boiling lakes, and men died between their talons. The stars, guardians of Requiem, and the moon, goddess of the northern children, held council and forged weapons to fight the Sun God. The stars granted their children a Starlit Demon, a creature of rock and light, a devourer of fire. The moon crafted a Moondisk of stone and light, and its beams could douse all sunfire. The Starlit Demon consumed the phoenixes, and the Moondisk stripped them of their fire, until the Sun God returned to the heavens, and peace reigned upon the earth."

Her fingers tingled, and Mori rose to her feet so fast, her head spun. Was this the answer? A Moondisk? A Starlit Demon? Those sounded like fairytales to her, no different from the stories of knights, princesses, and unicorns she'd read as a child. But Mori was a woman now, eighteen years old; she had watched fire rain upon the world, and she had watched her brother die, and she had lain with a man, and...

Tears stung her eyes, and she wrapped her arms around her stomach, and suddenly she was trembling so violently that the library spun around her. That is what had happened, she realized; for the first time, she fully understood what he had done. She had lain with a man, with the cruel lord with the white tongue, like the princesses with the knights in her stories. Did his child grow within her now, a demon babe with a white tongue, and yellow teeth, and fingernails that could cut her? She felt evil inside her, shame and filth, and she fell. She curled up, hugged her knees, and lowered her head. Her tears claimed her, and she could not stop seeing it--Orin burnt, his entrails spilling, and how he gazed at her as Acribus stifled her screams, thrusting inside her, grunting, and she had let him do it, she *let* him. She could not shift into a dragon, not in a chamber so small, not with him choking her... but she could have fought him somehow, and she hadn't. *I let him do it. It's my fault. What kind of creature am I now?*

"Mori," whispered a voice, and a hand touched her hair.

She screamed and cowered.

"No! Don't touch me, please, don't. Please..."

Through her tears, she saw a figure lean above her, and Mori was sure it was him again, come to hurt her, come to place a demon child inside her, but the voice that spoke again was soft, soothing.

"Mori, it's all right. It's me, Lyana. You're safe."

Mori blinked, still cowering on the ground, and saw a head of red curls, a freckled face, and soft green eyes. *Lyana. My friend.* Mori sniffed, rose to her knees, and found herself caught in Lyana's embrace. She held her friend close, her tears wetting Lyana's shoulder. She could not stop trembling.

"Hold me," she whispered. "Don't let me go."

Lyana held her tight and stroked her hair. Her friend's armor was cold against Mori's cheek, but she didn't care. Lyana was a great warrior--a real bellator, a member of Requiem's ancient order of knighthood. There were only a few bellators in the whole kingdom, Mori knew. More than anyone, Lyana could protect her, hold the horror at bay.

Growing up, Mori had always wanted to be like Lady Lyana. *I've always been too thin, too frightened*, Mori thought, *a meek child running from shadows.* Lyana was two years older, a heroine to Mori. While Mori was afraid of swords, Lyana was a deadly fencer. While Mori cowered from spiders, Lyana dreamed of slaying griffins and nightshades. While Mori could charm the lords of the court with her needlework and poetry, Lyana could discuss warfare, politics, and governing.

I've always wanted to be brave like you, Lyana, she thought, holding her friend tight. *Especially now, give me some of your strength, some of your courage.*

"I'm with you, Mori," Lyana whispered and kissed her forehead. "We're safe here underground, and I'll watch over you."

Mori looked up at her, eyes blurred with tears. "Do you promise?"

Lyana nodded. "I promise. No one will hurt you while I'm with you."

Unless they kill you, Mori thought. *Unless they burn you, and gut you like a fish, and rape me as you lie dying.*

She shivered, her insides throbbing, and pressed her cheek against Lyana's breastplate. She closed her eyes but only saw yellow teeth, a white tongue, and never-ending fire.

LYANA

As Lyana held her princess, a chill ran through her, trickling down her spine and along her limbs. She did not know what Mori had seen at Castellum Luna. She did not know how Solina and her men had hurt her. But she saw Mori hug her belly and shiver, and Lyana knew enough of men at war to know what that meant.

They raped her, Lyana thought, *to fulfill their desire and to send us a message. They come to hurt us. They come to conquer us. If they break into these tunnels, they will rape Mori again, and me, and all the women they can capture. They will slay the men and children.*

Gently, Lyana kissed Mori's forehead, smoothed her hair, and whispered soft comforts. It had been thirteen years since little Noela had died in her cradle, leaving Lyana without a sister; since then Mori had become like a sister to her.

I won't let Mori die too, she thought. *I won't let her leave me like Noela did. We will stop the Tirans. We will fight.*

Huddled in her arms, Mori sniffed and pointed at the book. It lay open on the floor, showing a drawing of a phoenix.

"I found this about the phoenixes," the princess said, her voice small. "It talks about a Moondisk and a Starlit Demon. Do you know of these things?"

Lyana sat by her, arm around her waist, and the two young women leaned forward to read the book. Lyana scrunched her lips and tapped her chin.

"I remember hearing stories of the Starlit Demon," she said. "My mother would tell me of it. I don't remember much, only tales of Requiem's old kings trapping the beast, burying it deep underground in the Abyss itself, and placing many guardians around it. Does the book have an entry about it? Let's look."

They began flipping the pages, skipping entries about various beasts: undead skeletons from Fidelium, a northern land of ruins; the snowbeasts, gangly creatures of many limbs; the Poisoned, deformed men and women with webbed hands and eyeballs on stalks; the Dividers, hairy beasts who guarded the western borders; and many other creatures, each more hideous than the last.

Finally they found a page titled "The Starlit Demon" and Mori shuddered. An illustration appeared of a creature that seemed hewn from craggy stone. Its claws, spiky tail, and teeth glimmered like obsidian, and its eyes shone like stars.

"It eats fire," Mori whispered, pointing at words on the next page. "Look, Lyana."

The book spoke of the Draco Constellation, holy stars of Requiem, weaving the creature of stone and starlight to fight the phoenixes.

Lyana nodded and read aloud: "The Starlit Demon, ancient and powerful deity of wrath, feasted upon the sunfire of the phoenix and drank from the lava of the Sun God's fury."

Mori gasped and clutched Lyana's arm. Her damp eyes shone. "That's it! The Starlit Demon can defeat them. But where is it? Does the book say?"

She's still a child, Lyana thought, *and she's hopeful, and she's afraid, and she will believe anything that can hold her terror at bay.* Sadness ran through Lyana, like water dripping through her bones. There was pain in Mori, pain that would perhaps always fill her... but life and hope still flickered in those teary gray eyes. *Will I live to see joy return to her or those last flickers extinguished?*

She shook her head and sighed. "This book is ancient, Mori, written in the early days when many beasts roamed the earth. Who knows if any still live?"

"The phoenixes still live," Mori whispered and clung to her, pressing her face against Lyana's armor.

"Yes," Lyana whispered. "They do." She stroked the girl's hair and tried to remember the stories her mother would tell her. "In my bedtime stories, the Starlit Demon was wild, dangerous, a creature too powerful to tame. It would topple columns and eat dragons when it found no phoenixes; it was a menace as often as an ally. An old queen--Queen Luna the Traveler, I think, daughter of Gloriae--buried the Starlit Demon leagues under Requiem. It's said only Requiem's monarch can free the Starlit Demon and tame him; all others would die in his starlight."

Mori shivered and clutched Lyana's arms. "Is the demon buried here in these tunnels?" She looked around, as if seeking the demon between the book shelves.

"Deeper," Lyana said. "Many leagues underground, down in the Abyss itself." She shuddered to remember stories of that nightmarish realm. "Around its lair, Queen Luna placed many riddles and ancient guardians that would not die. Mother would tell me that it still lives underground, locked behind a Crimson Archway. When I'd misbehave, she'd tell me that the Starlit Demon ate bad children."

"But that's not true, is it?" Mori asked, eyes pleading. "It eats phoenixes. It *has* to. The book says so. Right, Lyana?"

Lyana sighed. She had never believed in Starlit Demons, or Moondisks, or old stories of legendary magic. But then again, until today she had not believed in phoenixes either. If stories of an old demon gave Mori hope, well, they were real enough. She stroked the girl's chestnut hair, again and again, until her shivering stopped.

"That's right, my princess," she said and kissed Mori's head. "If we can find the Starlit Demon, he'll help us. He'll eat all the phoenixes."

Mori nodded, closed her eyes, and mumbled, "Eat all the phoenixes..."

I wish I could turn back time, Lyana thought, a lump in her throat. *I wish I could have kept you here in Nova Vita, my princess, you and Orin my love. I wish I could have saved Orin's life, saved your innocence, saved everyone who died tonight. I will keep fighting for you, Mori, and for the memory of your brother, and for our home.*

Suddenly Mori rose to her feet, freeing herself from Lyana's arms. She bounded across the chamber, scurried up a ladder to a shelf, and pulled out another book. This too was an ancient tome, its leather old and cracked, its pages dusty. Holding it to her breast with both arms--the book was a good foot long-- she walked back to Lyana and placed the codex down with a shower of dust. Its cover read: *Artifacts of Wizardry and Power.*

"I used to love this book as a child," Mori said. "It has pictures of magical rings, and amulets, and bracelets, and all sorts of jewels with special powers. When I was little, I liked to pretend that I owned these jewels, that I had magic that could stop Bayrin from tugging my braids, turn my hair red like yours, or save me from the spiders that crawled in my room." She opened the book and began leafing through it. "But the book has pages about other artifacts too, not just jewelery." She gasped and slapped a page. "Here! The Moondisk."

Lyana leaned down and examined the book. The page showed an illustration of a green disk, chipped and dented; it seemed made of bronze. Golden symbols were worked into the bronze: a crescent moon, a full moon, and a cluster of three stars.

Mori tapped the page. "See? The Moondisk that can extinguish phoenix fire!"

Lyana read from the book: "In the Days of Mist, the Children of the Moon sailed upon ships to the Crescent Isle, built rings of stones among the pines, and danced in the moonlight. A Moondisk they forged of bronze inlaid with gold, and upon it the moon turns, and the Three Sisters glow, and its light can extinguish all sunfire, so that the Sun God may never burn them."

Mori nodded emphatically. "See, Lyana? See?" Her eyes lit up. "We can defeat them! We can kill the phoenixes! I'll find the Moondisk so we can put out their fire. You can find the Starlit Demon, who will eat them." She clutched Lyana's shoulders, panting, eyes desperate. "We can do this, Lyana. I know it. I believe."

Lyana sighed. Magical disks of moonlight? Ancient demons of stars? Were these but myths, fairytales for children? Lyana was a warrior. She believed in the heat of her dragonfire, the sharpness of her claws, the steel of her blade. She knew nothing of ancient magic and enchanted beasts.

"Come, Mori," she said. "Let's take these books to my mother. She knows much of old lore and can interpret these words better than we can."

The young princess shivered. "Do we have to? Adia is near the tunnel entrance, where the phoenixes are, and..." She gulped, nodded, and knuckled her eyes. "But we must, yes. I'm not afraid. Not with you by my side. Let's go."

Each holding a book, the two young women left the library. They walked through the tunnels. As the wounded moaned and prayed, and as the shadows swirled, Lyana's throat constricted.

They had until sunrise, Solina had said. *We can surrender and live under their yoke, let them torture us, rule over us with fire and steel...* She clutched the book tight to her chest. *Or we can go chasing a dream from old books.*

She did not know which path led to greater darkness, and the book seemed so heavy in her arms, Lyana wanted to lie down, to place her head against the floor, and to sleep until this nightmare ended. But she kept walking--for Mori's eyes full of grief and hope, for the memory of Orin, for her family, for all those who prayed and wept around her.

I am a soldier, she told herself. *Whatever horror dawn brings, I will face it.* She walked through blood, fear, and pain, head high and heart trembling.

ELETHOR

He stood in the wine cellar, arms crossed and head lowered, staring at the cobbled floor where centuries of boots had trodden. Dozen of oak caskets rose around him, holding wine from Requiem's vineyards. *If we go to siege,* he thought, *at least we can get royally drunk before the Tirans break down our doors.*

He had chosen this cellar as his war room. *My father ruled among columns of marble and gold; I think caskets of wine are a far wiser choice for a king.* He did not know how long he'd live to rule. Perhaps future poets would sing of the Drunk King--Elethor Aeternum who was crowned in darkness, reigned from a wine cellar, and died the next day.

He sighed and turned around. Lyana and Mori stood there, staring at him with solemn eyes. Their ancient codices lay on a scarred table between rolled-up maps, mugs of wine, daggers, and a helmet. Around them stood the rest of his inner council: Lord Deramon, a bloody bandage covering his neck; Mother Adia, her eyes solemn and her white robes splashed with blood; and their son, Bayrin, ash in his red hair and fire in his green eyes.

They want me to fight, Elethor thought. *Even Mori.* He couldn't help it; he laughed bitterly.

"You can't be serious," he said and slapped the old books. "A magical disk that can extinguish sunfire? A Starlit Demon? My nurse told me such stories at bedtime--until I was about nine and stopped believing them."

Bayrin raised an eyebrow and whistled. "Well, there's a trick. I never believed in phoenixes either, until about ten thousand of them nearly burned my backside to a crisp." He clutched the hilt of his sword. "I don't know if this Stardisk or Moonlight Demon are real, but I'd rather go find a fairytale than surrender to your old flame, El--literally an old flame, in this case."

Face still ashy from the battle, Lyana glared at her brother. "It's the *Moon*disk and the *Starlit* Demon, you dolt. And it's not about what you'd rather do. It's about our best chance of saving lives. You might want to go on some adventure in the great outdoors, not caring if the Tirans kill us all in the meanwhile, but I'm sure Elethor cares." She looked at him and sighed. "At least I hope you do, El."

He looked into her green eyes and saw the fear in them. They were all afraid, he knew, even grizzled Lord Deramon.

What would my father do? Elethor thought. *What would Orin do? They would rally the troops. They would never surrender. They would fight at all costs.* He closed his eyes. *And they are dead, while I survived.*

He dug his fingernails into his palms. It wasn't fair. He didn't want to be king. He didn't want to make these decisions. He had never asked for this, for any of this! He was only Elethor, the young prince, the sculptor. How did he end up here, bearing the yoke of monarchy, his people depending on him, waiting for his decree? He opened his eyes and looked at them, one by one. A gruff warrior. A priestess. A friend. A betrothed. A sister.

He let his eyes linger on Mori, his dearest love, the last living member of his family. She stared back at him, eyes soft and damp, face so pale. She was a frail, pretty thing, and more than anything Elethor wanted to protect her. *If I surrender to Solina, what would become of my sister? Of Lyana and Adia? Of the other women who hide in these tunnels?* Elethor was no soldier, but he knew enough of war and conquest. *Solina's men would plunder our halls, eat our food, ravage our women. They would spare our lives, but they would make those lives miserable.*

And what of him? If he accepted Solina's offer, he would need travel south with her, rule by her side in Tiranor. She still loved him; he'd seen that in her eyes, felt it in her kiss. He could rule there with her, feel those kisses a million times, make love to her like in the old days, forever be with the woman he'd spent seven years sculpting and missing and craving.

And meanwhile, my people would suffer in chains. He shook his head. No. He could not allow it. Even if it tore his soul, even if meant giving up Solina forever, he would fight for Mori. For Lyana. For his people.

"What do you choose, my king?" Mother Adia asked. She stared at him, her eyes deep and penetrating. "Sunrise looms and you must decree."

Elethor stared back at her, though her eyes felt deep as midnight sky, stronger than steel, as wise as the true dragons of old. More than ever, he was struck by how different Adia was from her daughter. Lyana was free and fast as fire, while Adia was like an ancient forest, wise and full of secrets.

He spoke softly. "Solina and her men wore crystals around their necks. When they shifted into humans, their phoenix fire seemed to flow into those amulets. I've heard stories of the Griffin Heart, the magical amulet that once tamed the griffins. I've heard stories of the Animating Stones, glowing gems that let the tyrant Dies Irae animate corpses and send them to war. I thought those only stories, legends, but... if Solina found amulets of fire, perhaps all those legends are true. Magic is real. Who's to say the Moondisk or the Starlit Demon are not?" He took a deep breath, struggling to calm the turmoil inside him. *For the memory of the dead. For the living. For Requiem.* "Let us find these weapons... and let us fight."

Bayrin slammed his fist into his palm. "Stars yeah! We fight."

Lyana stared at him solemnly, hand on her sword. "We fight," she whispered.

"We fight," whispered Mori, face pale but eyes staring steadily.

Lord Deramon nodded and clenched his fists around his weapons. "For blood and war."

"For peace and starlight," said Mother Adia and raised her eyes to the ceiling, as if gazing upon the stars. "Requiem! May our wings forever find your sky."

They all repeated the prayer, and a tremble ran through Elethor. *Be strong,* he told himself. *Be strong like your father, like your brother, like the great kings and queens of old.*

In the silence that followed, Bayrin cleared his throat.

"There is, ahem... one small problem." He sucked his teeth. "How the stars do we find this Moondisk and Starlit Demon? I can't find my socks most days, and Lyana once couldn't find a dagger she'd already strapped to her belt. And as for you, Elethor, I saw you get lost in the palace once, and you're our bloody prince. Well... king now, but the point stands. Finding these things won't be easy."

"Nothing's ever easy," Elethor said. He unrolled a parchment map across the table, then pinned it open with mugs. "Mori's book says the Moondisk belongs to the Children of the Moon on the Crescent Isle. Well, I only see two groups of islands on this map. One is far in the east, where the griffins live, and I've never heard them called Children of the Moon. And then there's this place." He tapped a cluster of islands in a northern sea, many leagues away, northwest of Requiem above distant realms of myth. "I don't know much about this place. I don't know if anyone alive today does; these maps predate Requiem's fall three hundred years ago, when most other maps were burned."

Bayrin frowned at the map. "Crescent Isle? Never heard of it. You reckon our Moondisk is there?"

"I don't know," Elethor said. "But look here. One island is shaped like a crescent moon. Three smaller islands surround it. Does this remind of you of anything?"

For a moment everyone stared at the map, silent. Mori understood first and gasped.

"They're shaped like the moon and stars on the Moondisk!" She tapped the page in *Ancient Artifacts* where the Moondisk was drawn in delicate ink. Indeed, it seemed like the golden stars adorning the bronze disk formed the shape of the smaller islands, rising above the larger Crescent Isle. Tears filled Mori's eyes. "It's true. I knew it."

Bayrin raised his eyebrows and bit his lip. "Well, seems like a long chance--literally, since these islands are a long, very long flight away. But... I'm up for a flight. In fact, flying hundreds of leagues away from Solina sounds just about perfect now. Who's going with me?"

"Mori is," Elethor said.

As he expected, the room erupted with raised voices. Mother Adia glared and spoke of Mori needing time to recover from her flight and wounds. Lyana cried that she was a warrior of Requiem, and sworn to defend her princess, and would keep her here under guard. Even Bayrin objected, shouting that Mori would only slow him down, and that he couldn't drag along the princess if he were to find the Moondisk and bring it back for war. Even Lord Deramon spoke up, claiming that he'd send a squad of tough, battle-hardened warriors to find the Moondisk, letting the princess remain in shadow.

Elethor waited for the voices to die down. When they were all silent and staring at him, he said, "Mori needs time to heal. That will not be in underground tunnels, under siege, under constant threat of violence. If I fall, she is the last member of

House Aeternum. I will not have her here, in a burrow, with the wrath of Tiranor outside our doors. Let her fly north! She will be safer in the wilderness, a single dragon in a wide world, while we fight here in a few chambers and halls. You say she would slow you down, Bayrin? Mori is the fastest dragon in Requiem. She's won every flying race she's ever flown. She flew from Castellum Luna to Nova Vita in only two days. As for sending strong warriors north, Deramon? We need them here, every last man, to protect our people. We don't know if anyone survived the battle over King's Forest other than Lyana. All those soldiers might be dead now, five thousand of them; those we have left cannot be spared." He stared into Bayrin's eyes. "Bay. You are my oldest, dearest friend. Fly north to the Crescent Isle with Mori. Protect her."

Bayrin stared back in silence for long moments, lips tight and eyes fiery. Elethor stared back at his friend, refusing to look away. He knew Bayrin; the man would grumble and quip as easily as he breathed, but he was also an honest man and a good friend, and Elethor trusted him. He could think of no one better to protect his sister.

Finally Bayrin's eyes softened and he heaved a sigh. "Oh bloody stars," he said, "I'm going to regret this, but all right." He walked toward Mori, slung his arm around her waist, and pulled her close. "Looks like it's me and you, Mors. I am sworn to protect you, my princess, and all of that."

Mori looked so slim and frail, pulled against Bayrin's gangly frame.

"Just try to keep up, Bayrin," she said in a small voice.

He snorted. "Just try not to fly into any cobwebs, little one." He turned to Elethor. "Of course, there is one small, tiny flaw in the plan--more a quibble than a flaw, really, but hear me out. How are we to, well..." He cleared his throat and raised his voice. "...leave these tunnels with about a million phoenixes and their mothers outside? I mean, I reckon Mors and I could just walk outside, wave, and say, 'Sorry, old friends, but we'd really like to fly off and fetch a weapon that could kill you all, how about you be good phoenixes and let us pass?' Yes, I think that'll work well."

Lyana groaned, rolled her eyes, and punched her brother. "Bayrin, you go do that, and spare the world your stupidity. Mori will escape the sensible way--using the Portal Scrolls."

Bayrin scratched his head of red curls. "The porta-what-now?"

Lyana groaned even louder. "You really are an idiot, aren't you? Are you sure we're related?" She slapped his head. "The Portal Scrolls! You should have spent less time chasing girls with Elethor, and more time listening to your teachers' lectures."

"I sense another lecture coming on," Bayrin muttered.

Lyana seemed not to hear him; she kept speaking, nose raised. "King Elaras, son of Queen Luna the Traveler, crafted the Portal Scrolls in the year 3318. That's 232 years ago; don't break anything trying to do the numbers in your head. Each Portal Scroll has a map with a star on it. When you read a scroll, it will magically whisk you away to that place on the map."

Bayrin whistled. "Some magic! So, you don't happen to have any Portal Scrolls leading to the Crescent Isle, do you?"

Lyana glared at him. "Bayrin! If you had ever listened to anything your teachers told you, or even bothered to visit the Chamber of Artifacts, you would know. But of course, the Chamber of Artifacts is next to the library, and I forgot that you avoid being within a league of any book." She sighed. "King Elaras and his descendents used most of the Portal Scrolls, visiting many distant realms. Only two scrolls remain in the chamber, both pointing to Lacrimosa Hill."

"But...." Bayrin rubbed his eyes. "Lyana! Lacrimosa Hill is only about a league from here. You can bloody walk that far in an hour, or fly in a second. Why would Elaras even bother crafting a magical scroll leading to a hill just outside the city?"

The groan that escaped Lyana's mouth was so loud, it echoed in the chamber. "My stars, you really are the dumbest man in Requiem, aren't you? He crafted those scrolls to get *back home*. A scroll leading to Salvandos isn't very useful unless you can get home, right?"

"Me, I'd stay in Salvandos if it meant escaping a know-it-all sister," he muttered.

Lyana placed her hands on her hips. "That's as may be. In any case, the Chamber of Artifacts has two scrolls; they will take you and Mori into the forest." She glared at her brother. "Do you understand now, Bayrin, or do I need to get some puppets?"

"All right, all right, I get it!" Bayrin said. He rolled his eyes. "Do you see what I have to put up with, El? The real reason I volunteered to grab the Moondisk is to get away from the constant history lessons. So, Mors and I visit the Chamber of Artifacts, find those Portal Scrolls, and zoom into the forest, nice and far from all those phoenixes. Then it's off to the magical lands of moonlight."

Elethor stared down at *Mythical Creatures of the Gray Age*. The illustrated Starlit Demon stared back up at him, carved of stone, its eyes two stars. Did this ancient being still live below Requiem, entombed in the Abyss, the mythical caverns far below these tunnels? Like everyone, Elethor had heard stories of the Abyss. As youths, he and Solina would even creep down to the Abyss Gates--a towering archway of stone and iron. Solina had once wanted to enter them, to make love in the Abyss itself, but Elethor had become frightened and hurried back to the surface. *Do I dare approach these doors again... and this time step through them?*

He spoke softly, still staring at the book. "Only the King of Requiem can wake the Starlit Demon, if the stories are true." He took a deep breath. "It seems I am the king now, so this task falls to me. I've been to the Gates of the Abyss, though I don't know what lies beyond them. They say that beyond those doors, evil dwells, and tunnels plunge for leagues into shadow and fire." He looked up from the book and found Lyana staring at him. He stared into her eyes. "I don't know if this demon is real. I don't know what awaits in the Abyss; none have entered that evil place for centuries. But if more hope lies there, I will go on this journey. If the Starlit Demon truly lives and truly sleeps in the dark deep, I will tame him and bring him to Nova Vita to slay whatever enemies the Moondisk cannot."

Lyana stared at him steadily, cheeks flushed, and nodded. "And I will go with you."

Her parents began to protest at once. Deramon spoke of needing her here, by his side, to help him defend the tunnels. Mother Adia spoke of Lyana being only a child, of the dark depths being too dangerous for her. Lyana shook her head.

"Elethor needs my sword," she said. "And he needs my knowledge. According to this book, many traps and riddles guard the way to the demon's lair." She smiled crookedly. "I've always been good at riddles. Mori might be the fastest dragon, my father the strongest, my brother, well... I'm sure he has *some* talents somebody will discover someday. As for me, I like to think I'm the smartest of the group. Elethor will need my knowledge."

Elethor was about to say more when the room shook. The mugs rattled on the table, and shrieks echoed outside in the tunnels. The cries of men and ringing blades filled the cellar. Deramon and Lyana drew their swords.

"It's sunrise," Elethor said softly, his insides chilling. "And Solina's wrath is upon us again." He looked at them all, one by one. "We know our tasks. Deramon, lead the men. Defend these tunnels. Adia--heal the wounded, and pray for us."

Deramon approached him, axe in hand, and gave him a hard look.

"You better not let any harm befall my daughter," Deramon said, eyes narrowed. "If you do anything stupid down there, Elethor... if you let any harm come to Lyana... I will hunt you down with more wrath than ten thousand phoenixes." He growled. "It's your lover who burns our city. I don't forget that. You find a way to extinguish her flames, or by the stars, it won't be a phoenix who kills you. It will be my axe."

Elethor stared back at the gruff, grizzled face. "You keep these tunnels safe until I return, old man. Swing your axe at the Tirans, not at me. I will extinguish Solina's fire."

Deramon spat onto the floor, gave Elethor a last glower, then turned toward his daughter. When his eyes fell upon her, they softened. The gruff warrior suddenly looked like a mother bear. He pulled Lyana into his embrace and held her tight. She clung to him.

"Take care, daughter," Deramon said. "Come back to me. Don't let the boy do anything stupid."

She nodded, tears in her eyes, and kissed his cheek.

"Goodbye, Father," she whispered.

Lyana turned to her mother next. The stately priestess stared at the young knight, tall and proud as ever, but then her eyes filled with tears, and she seemed no longer a great figure of starlight, but a mother overwhelmed with grief and worry. She hugged her daughter close, and their tears fell.

"I love you, child," Adia whispered. "I will pray for you."

Elethor turned away from them, his own eyes stinging, and found Mori and Bayrin staring at him, silent. *My best friend. And my sister. I'm sending them both into danger, and I don't know if they'll return.* A lump filled his throat, and he could not curb his tears. He approached them hurriedly, so they would not see his turmoil, and pulled them into an embrace.

"Goodbye, Bay," he whispered to his friend. The young man's shaggy head pressed against his cheek. Mori clung to his other side, her face pressed against his chest. He kissed her head, and she looked up at him with huge, damp eyes. "Goodbye, Mori. I love you, sister. Be careful out there. Fly fast and return to me."

She nodded, lips trembling, and held him tight. "Goodbye, El. Please be safe. *Please.* Listen to Lyana and don't do anything stupid, okay? And if you see anything dangerous, don't be brave, just run. *Promise* me."

He laughed softly through his tears and mussed her hair. "Okay, Mori, I promise."

He wiped his eyes and pulled away from the embrace. The sounds of battle echoed through the chambers. Deramon and Adia were gone already, off to fight and heal. Swallowing a lump in his throat, Elethor approached Lyana and smiled thinly.

"Are you ready?" he asked quietly.

"No," she said. "I was never ready for this. Nobody was. But let's go." She tightened her lips, nodded, and her eyes flared with rage. "Let's find this Starlit Demon and kill Solina."

SOLINA

The statue of King Benedictus--the vile weredragon who had
fought the griffins three hundred years ago--lay fallen and cracked
in the square. Solina stood upon it, her boots smearing mud
across its marble face. Hands on her hips, she stared at the
archway before her, which led into the tunnels. Her men fought
there, slamming sword and spear against defenders who lurked in
shadow. The sun rose around them, painting the ruins red, and
smoke unfurled like dark phoenixes. It stung Solina's eyes.

He did not return to me, she thought, pain pounding through
her. *He did not surrender. He wants to kill me.*

Watching the fight, she clenched her fists and snarled. Her
rage bloomed inside her like the fire of her amulet. She had given
everything for him! She had raised an army for him. She had
killed a cruel king and a vain prince for him. In her palace in
Tiranor, she had built chambers for his sculptures, dreaming of
the day he ruled by her side.

"You could have ruled in luxury," she whispered through
clenched teeth. "You could have ruled me, my body, my soul. I
would have given myself to you. I would have made love to you
every night, kissed you until you cried with the sweet pain of it."
She pounded her fist into her palm, growling. "But you choose to
fight for the reptiles. You choose their love over mine. You will
die for this, Elethor. You will die in more agony than any
weredragon ever knew."

As she watched the blood sluice the street, she imagined
Elethor's blood washing her. She swore that she would break
him. She would shatter him with hammers. She would gut him

alive. She would let him linger in life, deformed and begging for death. And finally, when he could bear it no more, she would burn him with her phoenix fire, then watch his ashes rise into the wind and scatter over the desert she ruled.

"That will be your fate, Elethor," she whispered. She shook her head, eyes burning and throat tight. "You will regret this. You will beg me to love you again, and I will laugh."

She drew her twin sabres with a hiss, leaped off the fallen statue, and marched toward the tunnel entrance. Her men fought around her, stabbing spears and sabres at the shadows. Solina saw weredragons fighting inside in their human forms, eyes dark and blades bloodied.

"Move aside!" Solina said to her men, snarling. "My blades thirst for blood."

Her men stepped aside, and Solina stepped toward the archway. Its stones, once white and carved with golden reliefs, were now slick with blood. Three weredragons stood at the entrance, hiding their lizard forms in facades of gruff men in armor. They raised the thick, double-edged longswords of the north--hacking weapons so crude compared to Tiranor's curved steel. More weredragons spread behind them into the shadows.

"Where is Elethor Aeternum?" Solina demanded, rushing toward the weredragons. "I will kill you instead, if he is too cowardly to die at my blades."

They thrust their swords at her, graceless hunks of metal. Grinning savagely, Solina swung both her blades. She parried two blows and swung again, slicing a man's face. Blood showered. Solina snarled, sabres whirring, shards of sunlight. Steel clanged and blood splashed. She parried more blows, sliced into a man's mail, and opened another's neck. He fell, blood spurting, and another replaced him only for Solina to slash his face.

She smirked. These were no warriors. They were brutes, their armor heavy, their legs stiff and their muscles slow. She was a dancer. She was wildfire. Her feet were quick, her sabres like striking asps, her teeth bared in a grin.

"We killed you in the sky," she said and growled. "We will kill you underground."

She swung her blades, reveling at the taste of splashing blood. She severed a man's leg, snarled, and swung her sword down so hard, she cut through another man's helmet. A sword hit her breastplate, knocking the breath out of her, but she only growled and kept fighting.

"Come face me, Elethor!" she shouted into the darkness. "Come taste my steel."

She kicked a soldier, cut down another, and forced her way into the archway. She found herself on a staircase that plunged into darkness. Her men cried for the Sun God and ran to fight with her; one stood at each side, and a hundred shouted for blood behind her. She swung her blades, kicked, sliced, and pushed her way down a step. Bodies fell before her. A hundred weredragons cried below upon the stairs, awaiting her steel. She slew three, suffered a cut on her arm, but pushed forward and descended another step.

"I will find you, Elethor. Step by step, I will descend into your lair."

Cries of war filled the darkness. Solina smiled and licked blood off her lips.

Time vanished. She fought for hours--maybe for days. Her sabres were parts of her, extensions of her arms, demons of her wrath. Soon her face, armor, and helmet were covered with blood; she was a red devil of death, blades always whirring, throat always growling. Her men shouted at her sides, dying, killing. A blade cut Solina's leg. She fell, pushed herself up, and drove her sword into a man's throat. Snarling, she pulled her sword back with a red shower, swung it again, and cut down another man.

She fought in darkness. The archway was far above her now, and she had descended many steps into this den of evil.

"You pitied me, weredragons!" she called, the blood of her enemies in her mouth. "You saw me as an orphan, a cripple, a sinner to burn and banish. Now you die at my feet, reptiles."

She swung her blades, cutting down more weredragons, and took another step into the darkness. Soon she saw the end of the staircase where a tunnel sloped into shadow. Corpses piled up there, a hill of her victory. A burly man emerged from the shadows and stood above the bodies, a sword in one hand, an axe in the other.

Solina grinned. "Deramon!" she cried to him and bared her bloody teeth. "Do you remember me, weredragon? Will you come die at my feet too?"

The memories filled her like fire in an oven. Deramon, cruel Captain of the City Guard, had always loathed her. He had once accused her of stealing from a temple--she had only taken one gem!--and twisted her arm, and would have beaten her had she not kicked him and escaped. Today she would do more than kick him. Today she would twist his arm too, until flesh ripped and bone snapped, and she would laugh as he screamed.

"Come to me, weredragon! You would torment me as a child, but I've grown. Come die."

He stood below, bodies around him, and stared at her. His eyes were narrowed and cruel. A cut ran down his face, dripping blood. For a moment the battle died, and the only movement was the thrashing of the wounded, the only sound their moans. Solina and Deramon stared at each other, and she grinned, prepared to dance.

Deramon nodded and stepped back.

Solina snarled and ran down toward him.

A dozen weredragons emerged from the shadows, shoving boulders.

Solina screamed. "Cowards! Fight me!"

They shoved the boulders and cried, and Solina slammed into the stone. She tried to climb above a boulder, but more piled up. She growled and punched the stone, bloodying her knuckles. Her men ran down to join her and pushed against the boulders, shoving them back.

"Break down their barricade!" Solina cried. "Kill them all."

But the weredragons were cowards. They piled up more stones, and she could not break through. She shouted to them.

"Deramon! Deramon, you coward! Fight me like a man. Or will you hide like a rat? Do you think your stones can hold me back for long?"

Soon she was forced to stop. She stood panting before the pile of boulders. Sweat and blood covered her. She spat, licked blood off her blade, and screamed. Her voice echoed like a hundred demons. Her men crowded around her, breathing heavily, swords drawn.

"Get hammers," she told them when she'd caught her breath. "We're breaking through."

Not waiting for a reply, she shoved her way through them so roughly she knocked one man down. She stormed upstairs, teeth gritting, until she emerged back onto the surface. She stood in the courtyard, dizzy with the heady smell of death.

Lord Acribus came marching across the courtyard, armor and sword bloody. He nodded his head at her.

"My queen." His voice was like crackling gravel.

"How are the other tunnel entrances?" she asked him, holding her blades crossed.

Acribus spat out a tooth. "They blocked them," he said. He uncorked his flask, took a draft of spirits, and swished it. When he spat it out, it was bloody. "Bastards put up walls of rock. My men are hammering at them. We will break them down soon."

Solina shook her head. None of this made sense. Did Elethor truly think he could win this way? Did he expect to survive, locked in darkness behind rock, forever buried underground?

"He'll die down there," she said. "He has enough food for winter, maybe. When spring comes, they will all starve. Unless..."

She thought back to the days she'd enter those tunnels with Elethor. Years ago, they would sneak underground most nights, undress in darkness, kiss each other across their bodies, make love in shadow where none could find them. She would scream in the darkness with nobody to hear, nobody to hurt her, pity her, judge her. One midnight, they had made love in the Chamber of Artifacts, their bodies pressed together as the wonder and secrets of the world covered shelves around them. Elethor had pressed her against a cold stone wall. She dug her fingers into his shoulders, head tossed back, and gasped at amulets, crystals, and...

She snarled.

"The Portal Scrolls," she said.

Acribus grumbled and scrunched his face, as if seeking more loose teeth with his tongue. "My queen?"

She growled and clenched her fists. "They have two Portal Scrolls down there, magical artifacts that can send two weredragons into the forest." She nodded. "Elethor will try to flee that way, or send his sister to safety. Come, Acribus." She started walking across the square. "We head into King's Forest."

Acribus snarled and followed. "If Mori the weredragon whore tries to escape, I will catch her." He clutched his wounded arm where the princess had stabbed him. "I will make her envy her dead brother. I will make her beg for death."

As they walked through the streets, Solina remembered the sight of Acribus thrusting into the princess as Orin lay dead, and she smiled.

BAYRIN

Soldiers rushed around them, shouting and drawing weapons.
Survivors huddled in shadows, some weeping, others nursing
wounds, all pale and trembling. Priests ran from wounded to
wounded, praying, healing, comforting the dying. As Bayrin
walked down the tunnel, stepping over and around survivors, he
kept looking at Mori. The princess, he thought, looked just as
hurt, pale, and haunted as any one of the dying souls on the floor.
Her eyes were rimmed with red. She kept sniffing and looked
close to bursting into tears.

"Hey, Mors," he said hesitantly and tapped her arm. "Chin
up, huh? We're going to find those scrolls, find the Moondisk,
and kick Solina's backside."

She only sniffed, twisted her fingers, and a tear rolled down
her cheek. Bayrin touched her shoulder awkwardly, not knowing
what to do. She flinched and shied away. How could he comfort
her? Would she be like this the entire journey, trembling and
weeping? He would go mad within a day!

"I know," she whispered, and her lips wobbled. She dared
not meet his eyes, only twisted her fingers behind her back and
stared at the floor.

Bayrin looked away from her and stared forward into the
darkness. He held a tin lamp, but its wick cast only soft light; he
could barely see three feet ahead. He kept walking, stepping
between the crowds of survivors.

Why couldn't somebody else have gone on this quest with
him--if not Elethor, then maybe Janith the blacksmith, or one of
Father's men... or really anyone other than the weepy, frightened

princess. Even his sister Lyana, for all her lectures and scoldings, would have made a better companion; though Bayrin hated to admit it, at least Lyana was brave and strong. But Mori? All his life, Bayrin knew Mori as the girl who screamed when spiders crept into her room, who cowered when dogs barked, who always stared at her toes shyly whenever he tried talking to her. The king had thought sending her south to Castellum Luna would toughen her up, but now Mori seemed even *more* timid and weepy. Bayrin sighed.

"Here we are, Mors," he said and pointed at a doorway in the tunnel ahead. "The Chamber of Artifacts."

The archway loomed above them, its keystone engraved with the Draco constellation. Its doors were thick oak clasped with a heavy lock. The archway only seemed to scare Mori further, and she hugged herself. She glanced longingly at the entrance to the library, which lay across the tunnel, then gulped and looked back the Chamber of Artifacts.

"I have the key," she whispered.

The Chamber of Artifacts, like the library, was locked to most people; the treasures within were too valuable. Only the royal family carried the old, filigreed keys to these tombs of secrets. Mori produced hers--she wore it around her neck on a chain--and unlocked the door with trembling fingers. She closed her eyes, whispered a prayer, and tugged the doors. They creaked open, revealing a room of shadows.

"After you," Bayrin said, but Mori only trembled.

Bayrin sighed. He considered holding her arm to guide her into the chamber, but knew she'd only cringe at his touch. Instead he stepped into the chamber alone and beckoned her to follow. With a shiver, she took small steps into the darkness.

Bayrin raised his lantern... and his breath died.

He was no prince; he had never been in this chamber, one of the holiest places in Requiem. All the magic, power, and history of the realm filled this place. On one shelf, he saw three golden skulls, twice the size of human skulls. *The Beams*, he knew; in countless bedtime stories, he'd heard how the old heroes of Requiem shone their light against the nightshades. In a chest on the floor, a thousand red gemstones glowed. *Animating Stones*, Bayrin thought--the magical gems that had given life to Dies Irae's monsters of rotting bodies. On other shelves he saw the Summoning Stick, an enchanted candlestick that could call griffins for aid; a jar of shards labeled "The Griffin Heart"; and dozens of jewels, statuettes, quills, and... two parchment scrolls.

"Look, Mors, some scrolls," he said, hoping that at least would cheer her up. "You reckon those are the Portal Scrolls, or some naughty drawings your brother hid here? Either way, we're winners!"

She only sniffed, and Bayrin groaned inwardly. *This is going to be a long quest.* He stepped around a few golden vases, reached up, and grabbed the two scrolls. Tied with blue ribbons, they felt unnaturally cold. He tossed one to Mori, untied the ribbon on his scroll, and began unrolling it.

"Wait," Mori whispered.

Bayrin paused, the scroll half-unrolled in his hands. "What is it?"

She shivered, the scroll rolled up in her hand. "What if... what if there are phoenixes out there? In the forest." She sniffed. "Lacrimosa Hill is only a league away. What if he sees us?"

Bayrin frowned. The princess was trembling and pale; Bayrin had never seen anyone look so frightened.

"Who is *he*, Mori?" he said, scrutinizing her.

She knuckled tears from her eyes, bit her lip, and clutched the sixth finger on her left hand.

"I mean... the phoenixes." Her voice was so quiet he barely heard.

Bayrin patted her shoulder, but she flinched and lowered her eyes. He sighed and said, "Mori, the phoenixes want to kill us. And they think we're all in these tunnels. They won't waste time searching a bleak forest a league away. Once we magically appear there, we'll find a nice, empty hill far from any phoenixes. And if they *are* there? Well, you're the fastest dragon in Requiem, right? You escaped thousands of those phoenixes before. If any lurk in the forest, just fly away, fast as you can. I'll be right behind you."

That seemed only to terrify her further. For the first time, she met his eyes. Tears rolled down her cheeks. "But I don't want to flee them! I want to hide here." She clutched his sleeve. "Please, Bayrin, please let's not go. *Please!* Let's just find a place to hide here underground, or... or look for a different, better magical artifact."

"Mori!" Bayrin groaned inwardly, and he felt his anger rise. "You're the one who wanted to find the Moondisk in the first place, remember? You can't back out now! I know you're scared, but... stars, Mori. Crying and trembling won't help us defeat the phoenixes, will it?" She began to sob, and Bayrin rolled his eyes and softened his voice. "Look, Mors, I know you can do this. I believe in you. So chin up. Stand straight. Be brave. I'm with you, remember?"

She nodded, sniffing and rubbing her eyes. "All right." Her voice was so soft, he barely heard.

He helped her untie the ribbon binding her map. "On the count of three, all right?"

She nodded, face white and lips trembling, but she met his gaze. Her voice was but a whisper. "All right."

Just to be safe, Bayrin clutched the hilt of his sword. "One... two... three..."

They unrolled their Portal Scrolls, and Bayrin looked at his. It showed an ancient map, torn in one place, its ink faded. He recognized Nova Vita in the north and the ruins of Draco

Murus in the east. And in the center, between small ink trees, a red star was drawn above Lacrimosa Hill.

The star began to spin and glow.

Bayrin looked over the map at Mori. She stood before him in the Chamber of Artifacts, staring at her map. She looked up to meet his gaze...

...and the world swirled.

The chamber twisted like a whirlpool. Mori's face stretched, ten feet long and curving. Light pulsed. Bayrin felt nausea rise in him. He winced and raised his hands, but his fingers extended across the room, and the shelves coiled, and shadows leaped. Then the room bulged and rippled, like a reflection in a pond under rain, and sparks rained. With a pulse of light, branches rustled, smoke filled his nostrils, and black streaks settled into the forms of burnt birches. The shadows faded, and Bayrin found himself standing in puddles of melted snow in a smoldering forest.

Mori was nowhere to be seen.

Frowning, Bayrin drew his sword and looked around. Something had gone wrong. The smell of smoke filled his nostrils. He was in the right place--this was the hill where, according to legend, the tyrant Dies Irae slew Lacrimosa, Queen of Requiem. But shouldn't Mori's scroll have pointed here too?

"Mori!" he whispered, belly churning.

Figures stepped out from behind the trees.

Bayrin cursed.

There were six of them. They wore breastplates over chain mail, the steel so bright it was almost white. Their hair was platinum, their skin golden, their eyes blue. Their sabres bore pommels shaped as rising suns.

Tirans, Bayrin knew. *These are their human forms.*

One of them--a tall and slim woman, her breastplate snug against her body--wore a golden mask. She removed it slowly and smiled at him.

"Hello again, Bayrin."

It was Solina.

Still clutching his sword, Bayrin raised his eyebrows and clucked his tongue. "Well hullo, Soli old friend. Been what, seven years? Time does fly. You must be looking for your old lover, El. Sorry to say he's not here at the moment, but if you'd like a roll in the hay--you know, for old time's sake--I'm more than happy to fill in."

She sighed. "Time has not made you any wiser." She turned to one of her men, a beefy warrior who looked like a rabid bear with yellow teeth. "Acribus, kill him."

The man snarled, drooled, and burst into flames.

Bayrin caught his breath.

The fire raced across Acribus. The man's flaming arms outstretched, and he rose into the air, ballooning and crackling, until he soared as a phoenix.

With a growl, Bayrin shifted into a dragon, flapped leathern wings, and shot into the sky.

He crashed between burnt branches, scattering chips of wood. Flames crackled and phoenix screeches rose. Bayrin growled and flew higher, as high and fast as he could. Below him, the other Tirans combusted into phoenixes. Their inferno rose, and heat blasted Bayrin.

"Stars damn it!" he shouted and flew forward, circling the hill. Phoenixes rose around him, their flames reaching toward him. One firebird shrieked behind him, and talons blazed against Bayrin's tail. He howled, spun around, and blew his own fire. The jet slammed into the phoenix, its beak lashed, and Bayrin screamed.

I can't fight it, he knew. *Fang or fire can't kill it.* He cursed and swooped, crashed between branches, and soared again.

"Mori!" he shouted. "Mori, where the stars are you?"

A phoenix swooped from above. Two more took flight from each side. Bayrin cursed, dived, and flew between trees. Smashed branches flew around him. He soared again, covered with ash, his scales blazing.

"Mori!" he shouted. "Stars damn it, Mori!"

He saw a flash of blue below. He dodged a phoenix, suffered a blast of fire, and dived. He saw the color again--a girl in a blue cloak, huddling between the trees.

"Mori! Mori, fly!"

She looked up at him, shivered, and seemed ready to faint. The phoenixes swooped toward Bayrin, and the trees below crackled. The snow melted.

"Mori, shift into a dragon! We're getting out of here!"

With a cry of fear, Mori became a slim golden dragon and took flight. A phoenix dived toward her, lashing fire. So fast Bayrin gasped, Mori skirted around the phoenix and soared higher. She flew toward him.

"Bayrin, behind you! Fly!"

He spun in time to see the phoenix shoot toward him, a blazing comet. The firebird crashed into him, and flames engulfed Bayrin. He howled in pain. Golden scales flashed, and Mori flew toward them. Her wings beat and her claws slammed into the phoenix, kicking it off. She cried in pain.

"Come on, Mori, we're out of here!" Bayrin shouted.

He began flying west. She flew at his side. When Bayrin looked over his shoulder, he saw five phoenixes following.

"Catch them!" Solina cried below, the only Tiran still in human form. "Bring me their heads, Acribus, or I will content myself with yours!"

Bayrin flew as fast as he could. Mori flew at his side, panting. The flames howled behind them, the heat bathed them, and ten thousand more phoenixes flamed a league north above the city. Bayrin cursed, narrowed his eyes, and flew.

LYANA

"Well, here it is," she said quietly and couldn't suppress a shudder. "The Gates of the Abyss."

Lyana raised her tin lamp, shining its light against the archway. It rose fifty feet tall, dwarfing her; she could have walked through this archway even in dragon form. Its keystone was shaped as a dragon's skull, horns blood red. Its remaining stones bore engravings of screaming mouths full of shattered teeth. Heavy doors filled the archway, wrought of iron that had not rusted in two thousand years. Cold air blew from beneath those doors, sneaking under Lyana's armor to chill her flesh. She clutched her sword's hilt like she would clutch Mother's hand as a child.

Standing at her side, Elethor drew a silver key from his tunic; it hung around his neck on a chain. All members of royal House Aeternum owned these keys, Lyana knew, even the young Princess Mori. They unlocked all forbidden places here in the underground: the library of ancient codices, the Chamber of Artifacts... and these dark doors to the Abyss.

"Are you ready, Lyana?" he said. "Are you afraid?"

Lyana shuddered to remember the stories her nurse would tell her of this place. The old woman whispered of horrors that dwelled below--rotting bodies that walked, naked moles the size of horses, ancient demons that could shrivel your body with a glance. Lyana had never believed those stories, not even as a child, but then again, she had never believed in phoenixes either. She had never believed she would lose her beloved. She had never believed she would see her friend and princess, the dear

Mori, broken and ravaged and left a trembling shell of a girl. Who was to say what horrors truly existed in the world, and what were the whispers of old wives?

Yet she only glared at Elethor. She would show him no fear.

"I'm not afraid," she said. "I am a knight of Requiem. We will find this Starlit Demon, and we will tame him."

Elethor looked at her strangely, as if trying to read her mind.

"But I am afraid." His voice was soft. "This is a dark place, and I wonder if, on our quest to defeat the phoenixes, we unleash more beasts whose evil we cannot expect." He lowered his head, took a deep breath, and looked back up at her. Compassion softened the fear in his eyes. "It's okay to fear this darkness. Even great warriors feel fear; Orin would too."

Her insides trembled, cold sweat trickled down her back, and her head spun. But Lyana only raised her chin, tightened her jaw, and whispered, "I don't."

Slowly, Elethor placed his key in the heavy lock. It scraped against the metal, a sound like a banshee. Suddenly Lyana wanted to stop him. *Don't!* she wanted to cry. *Don't unleash what horror dwells there! There must be another way!* Yet she only tightened her lips, clutched her sword, and took a deep breath. *Be brave, Lyana,* she told herself. *You are a bellator. You are a warrior. Whatever waits behind these doors, you can slay it.*

Elethor paused, key in lock, and looked at her. She stared back, silent. He took a deep breath and shut his mouth. He seemed to be considering his words, then spoke again in a low voice.

"Lyana, I don't know what lurks beyond these doors. I don't know how long we will live once we walk past them, or if we'll even live long enough to enter. Before I unlock these doors, I want to tell you how sorry I am for your loss."

A deep sadness seeped into Lyana, like an underground river of ice. She sighed and lowered her eyes. Suddenly thoughts of demons and skeletons paled in her mind, overcome with this sadness, the tragedy of all this death.

"I know," she said softly. "I'm sorry too, Elethor."

Pain filled his eyes like ghosts in old castles. He placed a hand on her shoulder. His voice was hoarse.

"Lyana, I know this might not mean much now, in these tunnels, in the cold dark. And I know that you're a strong, capable woman, and I know you're not afraid. But however I can, I swear to you: I will look after you. I..." He swallowed. "I'm not a warrior like Orin was. I'm not strong as he was, nor as wise. But I promise you, Lyana. I will protect you however I can--in the Abyss, and if we return from it. For whatever it's worth, you have my sword, and you have my loyalty."

She couldn't stop a sad smile from touching her lips. She stood on tiptoes and kissed his cheek.

"Thank you, Elethor," she said. "But for now, focus less on protecting me and more on finding this Starlit Demon. All right?"

His eyelids flinched, as if her words stabbed him, and Lyana sighed inwardly. What did he want her to do? To throw her arms around him, weep and kiss him, and vow her eternal love? He was her betrothed now; his older brother had died, so he had inherited all of Orin's claims, his titles, and his woman. Lyana was a daughter of Requiem, and she accepted her laws. That did not mean her grief left her. That did not mean she could forget how Elethor had spent years shunning the court, yearning for the woman who now burned it. He confessed that he lacked Orin's strength and wisdom. Did he want her to deny it? She could not. He was her king now. She would respect that. But love him... love him like she loved Orin? Accept him as a hero, a protector? She could not.

"All right, Lyana," he said softly, and pain lived in his voice. "We enter the darkness."

He turned back to the lock, took a deep breath... and twisted the key.

The lock clanked.

The doors to the Abyss, this dark lair of secrets deep below Requiem, began to creak open.

Lyana shuddered and gritted her teeth. Iciness stung her fingertips and roiled her belly. She would never admit it, of course. She was a soldier. A heroine of Requiem. She must show strength, especially now, especially to Elethor. And yet as the doors creaked open, revealing mist and shadow, cold sweat washed her.

She did not know what she was expecting. Demons to attack? Rotting bodies to lunge at all? Soon the doors were opened wide, and she saw nothing but shadow, smoke, the glimmer of smooth stone walls. That was all. Just a tunnel. And yet this darkness filled her with more fear than skeletons or demons would. She could kill skeletons or demons, smash them with her sword, beat them down, defeat them with all her skills of war. It was the darkness she feared. The secrets. The unknown.

"Are you sure you're all right, Lyana?" Elethor asked, standing at the doorway. "You're pale, and your fingers are trembling."

She snorted and shoved by him.

"Out of my way, Elethor." She drew her sword. "I'm going in."

She walked through the archway, sword drawn in one hand, tin lamp in the other. She delved into the darkness.

The chill filled her bones. Mist swirled around her legs. As she walked, her boots clanked, echoing like the laughter of demons. Her lamplight flickered against smooth walls carved by old streams. The floor curved steeply, forcing her to move slowly. The tunnel plunged into darkness like a giant's gullet. She kept listening for enemies, but heard nothing--no grunts of beasts, no scuttling feet, no screeches of ghosts.

There is nothing here, she told herself. *No demons. No skeletons.* She clenched her jaw and held her sword high.

Bring me strength, Levitas, she prayed to her sword as she walked. It was an ancient weapon, its blade engraved with coiling dragons, its pommel shaped as a claw. Her father traced its lineage back to Terra Eleison, a knight of Requiem who'd survived the griffin war, helped found Nova Vita, and restored their house to glory. Many Vir Requis today carried longswords, heavy weapons for both hands; Elethor carried one at her side, the old blade Ferus. Lyana's sword was shorter, faster, easy to wield in one hand; the weapon of a knight.

Your sword was ancient even then, Father had said when giving her the blade five years ago. It had defended Requiem for centuries and slain many of her foes. Lyana tightened her fingers around the leather grip. Under the sky, she fought with claw and fire, a dragon roaring her fury. Here she would wield this ancient shard of steel.

May Levitas defend me underground, she thought, *in darkness, far from the sky of Requiem. Shine bright, Levitas. Shine bright, for the world is full of more darkness than I can bear.*

They kept walking down the tunnel. Lumps rose upon the walls like warts. When Lyana touched one, she found it clammy. She imagined herself walking through the veins of some great beast of stone, and she shuddered. She held her lamp out at arm's length, but could see only several feet ahead.

A screech filled the darkness.

Lyana froze, panting. She raised her sword.

"What was it?" she whispered. A shiver ran through her.

Elethor stood frozen by her side, his own sword raised. He stared ahead, but the darkness nearly swallowed their lamplight. They saw nothing. Silence filled the tunnels.

"I don't know," he whispered. "Was it the Starlit Demon?"

Lyana squared her jaw. "If it is, we will tame the beast. Come, we go farther."

They walked five more steps before the screech sounded again.

It was so loud, Lyana grimaced. She nearly dropped her sword and lamp to cover her ears. The tunnels shook and a crack ran along a wall. Many feet pattered in the distance, clanking, scratching. The screech went on and on, rising and falling, a banshee cry. Lyana's insides trembled and she could barely breathe. A ghostly light glowed ahead and shadows scurried.

"Stay by me, Lyana," Elethor said, hand clutching his sword. Sweat beaded on his brow.

Keeping her eyes on the tunnel ahead, Lyana laid down her lamp and drew her dagger. She held both blades before her, ready to fight whatever enemy approached.

A shadow lurched.

A creature emerged from the darkness.

Lyana grimaced. Her heart burst into a gallop, and cold sweat flooded her.

With a screech, the creature scuttled forward on many legs. It looked like a great centipede, many feet long and wide as a tree trunk. Its body was made of segments, each bloated and furry like the body of a spider. Its curved legs looked sharp as blades. Worst of all, however, was not the body that snaked behind, but the front of the creature.

It had the head, torso, and arms of a human girl, no older than ten. Her flesh was pale, her red eyes rimmed in black, her hair scraggly. Her bloated belly was slashed open, revealing cockroaches that nested and bred inside her. The girl grinned, showing rotting teeth, and raised her arms. Her hands ended with curving, yellow claws that dripped sizzling liquid. Below her belly, her centipede body pulsed black and hairy, coiling into the shadows behind her.

"Stars," Elethor whispered.

"What are you?" Lyana shouted at the beast, baring her teeth. "Why do you dwell in Requiem?"

The creature stared at her, eyes dripping pus, and tilted her head. She opened her mouth wide, and her tongue rolled out, a foot long and covered in ants. She screeched, a deafening sound that made Lyana grimace and scream.

"This is... not... Requiem!" the creature said, voice like shattering glass. Blood dripped from her eyes down her cheeks. "This is the Abyss. I am Nedath, guardian of this realm. Turn back, creatures of sunlight! Leave our... world..."

Her voice turned to wind that howled, blowing back Lyana's hair. The creature thrust herself up, rising ten feet tall upon her bloated segments. Her spider legs stretched out like black blades. Blood spurted between the demon's sharpened teeth, spraying Lyana's face. The droplets stung like acid.

"Turn back, Nedath, guard of the Abyss!" Elethor cried. He waved his lamp, as if light could cow this creature of darkness. "I am King Elethor Aeternum. My forefathers sealed you here. Now obey me."

The creature cackled, hair rustling with maggots. With a screech, she spat a glob of blood and mucus at Elethor. He swung his blade, blocking the discharge. What droplets sprayed him sizzled, and he cried in pain.

"Turn back, creature!" Lyana cried, waving her sword. "I am Lyana Eleison, daughter of Lord Deramon, knight of Requiem! You will kneel before me."

She swung her sword, but Nedath pulled her body back, and the blade whistled through air. The creature cackled and spat a glob of bloody mucus. Lyana had no time to parry, and the glob hit her face.

Her eyes blazed with pain. She could not breathe or see. She screamed; it felt like her face was being ripped off.

"Elethor!" she tried to shout, but the mucus entered her mouth, choking her, running down her throat like a living thing.

"Back, creature!" Elethor cried, voice muffled, a million leagues away. "Turn back into the darkness."

Lyana could not see him. She swung her sword blindly, not knowing if she hit anything. The creature screeched again, but she could barely hear.

She fell. She hit the ground. She dropped her weapons, clawed at her face, tried to tear the slime off her eyes, her nose, her mouth. Her head hit the ground, and she heard only a distant screech, a cry of horror, and then nothing but cruel cackling.

ADIA

She moved between the wounded, her robes soaked with blood. Her fingers stitched wounds, her eyes shed no more tears, and her heart felt no more pain. Around her the wounded shivered, wept, and screamed; she healed them. The dying lay feverish; she comforted them. The dead lay stinking; she prayed for them. She was a healer, a priestess, and a mother grieving.

Come back to me from your wilderness, Bayrin, she prayed silently as she bandaged a burnt, trembling man. *Come back from the darkness, Lyana. I love you, my children.*

The man groaned, his face melted away, his hands burned to stumps. If he died, Adia thought, it would be a blessing for him, and yet she fought for him, gave him the nectar of silverweed to dull his pain, and she refused to surrender his life. He was somebody's son, and Adia too had a son. What if Bayrin returned to her like this, burned into red, twisted flesh and pain? She moved to a young girl, her legs shattered, her hand severed, and she prayed for her, bandaged her, set her bones as best she could. What if Lyana returned to her broken and bleeding too?

Stars, please. I already lost one of my children. I already lost my sweet Noela. Don't let me lose Bayrin and Lyana too.

Her worry seemed too great for Adia to bear, and yet she bore it. She was High Priestess of Requiem. All these bleeding, broken, burnt souls were her children too. They lay in rows upon the floor, dozens of them filling the armory. The swords and shields were gone from this place, taken to battle; the wounded were returned. Every few moments they were carried in: men whose legs ended with stumps, men with entrails spilling from sliced bellies, men burnt and cut, men crying for wives and mothers. In battle they were brave warriors, heroes of Requiem. Here in her chamber, they were sons and husbands, afraid, the terror of battle too real.

"Mother Adia... Mo..." A wounded man reached out to her. Skin hung from his hands, the flesh of his fingers blackened, falling to show the bone. "Mother, a prayer, please..."

She turned to him, placed her hand on his forehead, and prayed for him. She prayed to the stars to comfort him, to heal him or lead him peacefully to the halls of afterlife. And yet Adia did not know if starlight could reach these tunnels. All her life, she had prayed in temples between columns and birches, watching the sky. Now that sky burned, and here they hid, in darkness and pain. *The world has become fire and shadow, and all starlight is washed away.*

But still she prayed. Still she believed, forced herself to. If her stars had abandoned her, what purpose did her life hold? So she prayed for this burnt man, kissed his bloodied forehead, and bandaged his wounds. She gave him the nectar of silverweed, until he slept, feverish and dying.

"As the leaves fall upon our marble tiles," she whispered, lips sticky with blood, "as the breeze rustles the birches beyond our columns, as the sun gilds the mountains above our halls-- know, young child of the woods, you are home, you are home." She held him as his breath stilled and his face smoothed. "Requiem! May our wings forever find your sky."

She closed his eyes, covered him with his cloak, and stood up. She pulled him to the corner and placed him among the piles of bodies. There he would stink, decay, lie as rotting flesh until they found room to bury the dead. Adia needed men to dig graves underground, or soon the disease of bodies would claim them all. She needed healers to help her. She needed her husband by her side, and she needed her children back, and she

needed this war and death to end. But all she had were her hands
that could stitch a wound and hold a dying man, her bandages and
nectar, and whatever faith still remained in her heart. And she
used them all as the blood flowed, the stench of bodies wafted,
and soldiers kept dragging new death into her chamber.

Stay safe, Bayrin and Lyana. Stay alive. Return to me.

She did not know how many hours or days passed as she
worked, healing and praying. She did not know night from day.
When her husband appeared at the doorway, armor splashed in
blood and eyes dark, her fingers were sore, her eyes stinging, her
head light. She walked to him, embraced him, and kissed his
bristly cheek.

"Adia," Deramon said to her, voice deep as these tunnels,
rough as his hands and hair and body. "You need sleep. You
need food and drink. Come, we will rest. Sister Caela will take
over."

The young healer stood by his side, a girl no older than
Lyana, her hair braided tight behind her head, her eyes haunted
but strong. She held bandages, towels, and vials of herbs and
silverweed.

Adia shook her head. "Sister Caela is too young. She is
only a healer in training. She... come, sister. Work with me. Help
me."

A man wept at her left, crying for his mother. His hands
clutched a wound on his stomach; it gaped open, glistening and
red, gutting him.

"I want to go home," he whispered, lips pale, eyes deathly.
"Please. Please, I want to go home."

Adia realized that he was just a boy, younger than her own
children, and she turned to him, to heal him, to pray for him, but
Deramon held her fast.

"Let Sister Caela tend to him," he said, voice low, touched
by a softness Adia rarely heard in him.

He held Adia's arm, gently but firmly. His hands were bloody and rough, and Adia wanted to break free, but she was so tired. Her head felt so light. His second hand held the small of her back, keeping her standing.

Sister Caela moved forward, lips tight, and knelt by the dying man. With sure fingers, she uncorked her vials, then poured silverweed nectar into the man's mouth.

"Sister," he whispered, shaking now. "Hold me. Hold me as I leave."

The young woman held the dying man, praying for him, until he lay still in her arms. Adia watched, eyes moist, and she shed tears, all those tears she had not cried for hours, maybe days. Her body shook with them.

"Come, my love," Deramon said softly. "You've not slept in three days. Sister Caela will tend to these men for a few hours."

They left the armory, this place of death and blood and screams. They walked down a tunnel, moving between soldiers who ran and survivors who huddled and prayed. Darkness, stench, and whispers of fear swirled around them. Adia's head spun. Three days. Had it truly been that long? Only several lamps lined the tunnels, casting shadows like dark phoenixes. From above came hammering and cries of battle.

"How are the defenses?" she asked.

Deramon clenched his jaw. "Holding. Barely. The Tirans broke through one blockade--the entrance at the temple. Many died. We raised more boulders and are holding them back. For now." He looked at her. "We will not hold out for long, Adia. But we will hold out for the night."

She realized that Deramon too had not slept for three days. His face was haggard. New lines creased his face, and more white streaked his red beard. His clothes and armor were covered in dust and blood.

"You look like you've been to the Abyss and back," Adia
said. She shivered, realizing the grimness of the phrase she'd
chosen. *No, he had not been to the Abyss, but Lyana now delves into that
place. Our daughter. Our sweet, brave light.*

Deramon seemed to read her thoughts. He held her hand
tight.

"I trust Lyana," he said, voice a low growl. "She is the
finest swordswoman I know. She is wise and strong and fast. If
anyone can survive down there, it's our girl. She'll return to us
with the Starlit Demon. I promise you."

Adia looked at him, and she wanted to believe, but she
saw the fear in his eyes. She knew that he himself did not believe
those words.

Lyana will die, she thought. *We will die. Requiem will fall.
But if we are doomed, we will go down fighting, and we will not give up until
death's grasp pulls us to the stars. Does my Noela wait for me there?*

Survivors covered every corner of these tunnels, sleeping
on the floors, standing against the walls, huddling into nooks.
Adia made her way between them, until she entered the wine
cellar which had become their war room. She and Deramon
stepped in, and the chamber seemed so bare to her. This was
Requiem's new center of power, but where was their king? He
was gone into darkness. Where was their princess? She had
flown into the night. Where were Olasar and Orin? Their bodies
lay burnt in the inferno of the world.

Who will lead us now? Adia thought. How could this lost,
hunted people survive underground with no father or mother?
She would be that mother, she knew. She was a priestess, a
leader, a healer. *Let me lead and heal as best I can until my king returns.*

Deramon moved about the room and found them mugs
of wine, old cheese, and bread, but Adia could not eat nor drink.
She huddled on the floor by a casket, pulled her knees to her
chest, and wept.

"My love," Deramon whispered. He sat by her, wrapped his arms around her, and held her. She trembled against him. He was all cold steel and rough flesh; he seemed so strong to her, forever her lord and soldier.

"I'm so scared," she whispered to him. "I'm so scared, Deramon. I'm so scared for Bayrin, for Lyana, for everyone." Her tears claimed her.

He kissed her head and held her close, his arms so wide and strong; when she was younger, Adia used to think he could lift the world with those arms.

Finally she slept, held in his embrace, her cheek against his shoulder. She dreamed of gaping wounds and burning flesh and haunted, bloody eyes.

MORI

She could not breathe. She could see nothing but clouds and stinging snow. Her fear gushed through her, she blew fire, her wings beat madly, and it was all she could do to keep flying.

I'm suffocating, she thought. Her head spun and her lungs ached. *I can't breathe. Help, stars, help.*

The shrieks rose behind them, cries like great eagles, like crashing flame, like the pain that still dug through her. The phoenixes soared, chasing suns of fury, crackling and howling.

It's him, Mori thought, eyes burning and wings trembling. The clouds streamed around her. *He flies there as a firebird. The man who... who...*

Once more she lay upon that oak table, staring into Orin's dead eyes. Once more his hand clutched her throat, and his pain drove into her, and her mouse fluttered in her pocket like a heart, until her weight crushed him. Once more Solina stood above her, watching, laughing.

"Mori!" rose a shout, distant and muffled, as from leagues away. "Mori, *fly!*"

She blew fire, clearing the haze, and saw Bayrin flying at her side. His green scales flashed between the clouds, and his tail nudged her, steadying her flight. The fire of the pursuing phoenixes gilded the clouds.

"Mori, fly!" Bayrin shouted. "Faster!"

She flew, neck outstretched, tail straight, wings churning the clouds. She sliced the sky, wind blowing around her.

Orin always said I was the fastest dragon in Requiem.

Bayrin flew at her side, flames seeping between his teeth. Soon he was falling behind, and Mori forced herself to slow down, though all her horrors blazed behind. She could not see them clearly--the clouds still hid them--but their shrieks tore the sky, and their fire blazed like sunset.

If he catches us, he will kill Bayrin, she thought. *But he will not show me that mercy. He will chain me, and rape me again and again, and force me to watch Solina kill Elethor.*

A growl found her throat, surprising her. She had not thought any anger remained in her, only fear, and yet her rage now blazed.

So I will not let him catch me.

"Bayrin!" she cried, flying at this side. "Keep your neck and tail straight! Keep your body smooth! Cut through the wind, like this."

She was slim and small; he was long and gangly. She shot forward, as straight and flat as she could, until she flew before him. The wind flowed around her.

"Fly in my slipstream, Bay!" she shouted. "I'll shield you from the wind."

They drove forward, the shrieks rising behind them, the wind howling. The clouds parted, and Mori found herself under blue sky. Mountains rolled below, their slopes golden, the peaks white with snow. Between them, silver strings of frozen rivers snaked through forests of evergreens. Red light blazed against the landscape, and when Mori turned her head, she saw the phoenixes emerge from the clouds.

There were five. Their flames twisted and rained sparks. Their beaks like molten steel cried in fury. One phoenix led the pack, larger than his brethren, his wings a hundred feet wide. He was Lord Acribus. Mori knew it was him; she knew the cruelty in those white eyes.

"Bayrin, fly!" she shouted.

He was lagging behind, tongue lolling, chest rising and falling. He stared at her, eyes glazed; he had reached the end of his strength.

Again she saw Solina in her mind, scarred face cold, blue eyes staring. Again she heard that voice.

Have your treat, dog.

The fingers dug into her, and she could not breathe, not even scream.

"No," she told herself, wings flapping. *I won't let them catch us.* Her breath ached in her lungs. *Never. Never again.*

She looked around madly, over mountain and river and forest, seeking a place to hide. When she saw the fallen tower, she gasped. It lay upon a mountaintop, jagged and crumbling. These were the ruins of Draco Vallum, she knew. She had always loved books of maps and histories; she had spent so many hours poring over them in the library. She remembered reading about these ruins--the crumbling remains of proud, ancient forts from Requiem's Golden Age before the griffins destroyed the land.

"Bay, fly to the ruins!" Mori shouted into the wind. "Do you see them?"

She slapped him with her tail, nudging him in the right direction. He panted and his eyes rolled, but he managed to nod. The two dragons, gold and green, began diving down toward the mountains. Wind howled and Mori's belly twisted. She swooped so fast that she nearly fainted, and the tug of the world pulled her stomach and skull. She gritted her teeth and kept diving.

"We'll have to fight them in the ruins!" she said.

Memories pounded through her, and she saw herself again in Castellum Luna, slamming the doors shut, racing into darkness. *That is where he killed Orin, hurt me, and spat on my bleeding body.* Suddenly Mori wanted to turn away from these ruins. She wanted to fly to the phoenixes, to die in their fire, to fall burnt upon the forests of her homeland. Anything seemed better than hiding underground, waiting for him to shove her down, clutch her throat, grunt above her as she wept.

But she growled and kept swooping.

I'm stronger now. Bayrin is with me, and we both bear swords. This time I will fight him... and I will kill him.

She looked over her shoulder. The phoenixes swooped behind her, talons outstretched. Fire rained from them, and their wings crackled like crashing pyres. Mori stared into his eyes-- white orbs of swirling flame. There was so much hatred there. Mori had never known such hatred and madness could exist. Though the phoenixes drenched the world with searing heat, she felt cold.

"Mori, come on!" Bayrin shouted.

The dragons were near the ruins now. Little remained of Draco Vallum, this old fortress of fallen heroes. Only one wall still stood, craggy like the gums of an old stone giant. The rest of the fortress lay as fallen bricks. Mori discerned half of an archway leading into a cellar, and she dived toward it.

"We'll kill them in shadow," she shouted and swooped.

The ruins rushed up to meet her. She landed, claws digging into snow. At once she shifted, becoming a girl again, and drew her sword. She ran, blade in hand, and leaped through the archway. She found herself upon a staircase plunging underground.

"Bayrin, in here!"

She turned to see him land in the snow outside. The lanky green dragon shifted, and Bayrin ran forward in human form, drawing his sword. He leaped onto the staircase to join her.

Mori had time to see the phoenixes land too, melting the snow, before she turned and ran downstairs into darkness.

The steps were narrow and craggy. She tripped, pitched forward, and just barely righted herself and kept running. Bayrin ran behind her, boots thudding and scabbard banging against the walls. He cursed as he ran, such foul words that Mori had never heard. She cursed too, repeating words she had never dreamed a princess would utter.

Soon she heard other voices--calling for her blood, calling for her flesh. When she glanced over her shoulder, she saw the Tirans, and she saw *him*.

In human forms they were no less frightening than phoenixes. The Tiran soldiers wore armor darkened with soot, and their sabres were bloody. Her tormentor walked at their lead, the Lord Acribus, his face like beaten leather and his eyes cruel, blue chips. He opened his mouth, revealing his yellow teeth, and his tongue licked his lips, serpentine.

"Mori!" he called to her. He grinned like a rabid animal, drooling. "Are you ready for more, weredragon? Are you ready to scream?"

Fear pounded through Mori, nearly freezing her. Her heart thudded, tears leaped into her eyes, and she whimpered. But then she saw that his arm was bandaged. She had cut him there with Orin's dagger. *He can be hurt. He's just a man now, not a phoenix, not a demon, and I can kill him.*

She and Bayrin reached the end of the staircase. They found themselves in a dusty, ancient cellar, too narrow for shifting into a dragon or phoenix. Rusted blades lay upon the floor between fallen bricks, the wood and leather of their hilts rotted away. The back of the chamber lay in shadow. Mori raced into the darkness, seeking a tunnel, a doorway, somewhere to flee, but found herself facing a brick wall.

She spun toward the Tirans, her back to the wall. Bayrin stood by her, panting and holding his sword before him.

"Bayrin," Mori whispered. She reached out and clutched his hand. "Bayrin, we will fight them."

He nodded and spoke with a choked voice. "Be brave, Mori. I won't let them hurt you."

At that moment, she loved him--loved him like she loved Orin, her fallen hero, like she loved Elethor, her new king. Bayrin was no warrior, she knew. To her he'd always been a fool, a jokester, Elethor's gangly friend whom she always thought looked like a grasshopper. Yet now he stood by her, sword raised, sworn to defend her... and in the darkness of this chamber and her fears, she loved him.

Acribus came walking toward them, a half snarl, half smile on his lips. His firegem blazed around his neck, painting his face red. Drool dripped down his chin. He was tall, even taller than Bayrin, and twice as wide. He cracked his knuckles and stripped Mori naked with his eyes. His tongue licked his chops, dropping as far as his chin. Lust for her body and blood filled his eyes.

"Men," he said to his four companions. "Kill the boy. Keep the girl alive. We'll have our fun with her."

The four soldiers eyed her, no less hunger in their eyes, and raised their swords. They approached Bayrin, their firegems crackling; in the flickering light, they looked like demons of shadow and fire.

Mori raised her sword and prayed.

BAYRIN

Cold sweat washed him, and his fingers shook, but he forced
himself to grin--a terrified, trembling grin.

"So, dear friends." He forced the words through stiff lips.
"Thank you so much for visiting Requiem. We do love visitors up
here in the north. I hope you enjoyed our tour, but now we really
must be on our way."

The Tirans kept advancing toward him, sabres raised. They
bared their teeth. Their faces became demonic masks in the light
of the firegems.

Bayrin gulped, his own sword raised. His limbs throbbed.
His every instinct called for him to retreat into the corner, to press
his back against the wall, to move as far as he could from these
men--even if that meant retreating only a foot. He forced himself
to step forward instead, feet numb. With his left hand, he pushed
Mori behind him, shielding her with his body.

Stars, he thought. What had that rabid, leathery-faced
Acribus meant? *Are you ready for more, weredragon?* he had asked.
Nausea filled Bayrin. Had he meant that... had this man met Mori
before... and hurt her? Even now the Tiran eyed her with lust,
that white tongue of his licking his lips and dripping drool.

"Well," he said to the five Tiran soldiers. He forced a laugh,
sweat dripping down his forehead. "I suppose now is the time
that you try to stab me, and I try to stab you, and swords clang
and blood pours. I do love swordplay--I'm quite good at it too--
but I suppose I'll show some mercy, and I'll offer you a chance to
settle this over a nice game of dice. What do you say?"

The Tirans laughed.

One lashed his sword at him.

Bayrin parried, and steel clanged, and he couldn't help but yelp. That drew more laughter from the Tirans. They formed a semicircle around him, like vultures over prey.

His heart hammered so powerfully, Bayrin thought it would burst from his mouth. His belly roiled. How had he come to this? He was no warrior like his father. He knew no swordplay like his sister. He... he was only Bayrin the prankster, the fool, the young man nobody expected anything of. And yet here he was, in a dark dungeon, defending his princess against five soldiers.

A Tiran swiped his sabre, and Bayrin parried madly, holding his sword with two hands. The Tirans laughed again, and Bayrin realized they were toying with him. They knew he was no fighter.

"The boy wants to play dice!" one said and laughed, a hoarse sound, almost inhuman. "Maybe we'll carve dice from his bones."

His comrades laughed, and one swung his sabre so fast, Bayrin could not parry. The blade sliced his shoulder, blood sprayed, and Mori screamed.

"We'll play with his bones after we play with the girl," said another Tiran, voice a deep growl. "I haven't had a girl since we left home."

Two more swords flew. Bayrin parried left and right. He thrust his weapon, trying to kill a man, but the Tiran parried and nearly yanked the sword from Bayrin's hand.

None of this should have happened, he thought. The scrolls should have taken them to safety. They should have been on their way to find the Moondisk now.   It should have been King Olasar fighting, or Prince Orin, or...

He gritted his teeth. *But they're dead, Bay. They're dead, and you're alive, so man up and defend your princess.*

With a wordless cry, he thrust his blade at Lord Acribus.

The Tiran swung his sword, blocking the blow. His left hand drove forward, and his fist slammed into Bayrin's face.

"Bayrin!" Mori screamed behind him.

White light flooded him. He fell back, hit Mori, and she screamed. He swung his sword blindly, pain suffusing him. A blade bit his left arm, and a chill washed him. Another blade flashed, and Bayrin raised his sword, blocking most of the blow. But the sabre still sliced along his arm, cutting his sleeve and skin. Another sword slashed. Bayrin parried and tripped on a fallen brick. He fell down hard, knocking the breath out of him.

He spat out a glob of blood, coughed, and said, "Do you..." He coughed again. "Do you give up yet?"

The Tirans stared silently for a moment, then laughed--cruel laughter like crashing stones. Bayrin chuckled through the blood in his mouth. He nodded, raised his eyebrows, and laughed harder until the Tirans' laughter grew too. *This is what I've always known how to do... make people laugh.* As his bloody laughter roared, he grabbed the fallen brick and hurled it.

It smashed into Acribus's firegem.

The laughter died when the gem shattered. Acribus howled. Fire burst from the shattered gem like demons escaping a tomb. It raced across him, until Acribus blazed, a creature of fire.

He's turning into a phoenix, here, underground, Bayrin thought. He leaped to his feet and grabbed Mori's hand.

"Come on, Mori!" he screamed. "Run!"

He pulled her forward, sword swinging. Fire blazed. He could barely see. He knocked aside a Tiran's sword, plowed forward, and drove his shoulder into the man. The soldier crashed down, flames roared, and Bayrin and Mori whipped around him.

Firelight filled the chamber. Behind Bayrin, a phoenix shriek rose, deafening. It was a small chamber; the phoenix would be crushed, he knew. It would burn everything alive inside. He leaped onto the staircase. He ran, pulling Mori behind him.

"Mori, run, faster!" he shouted.

Smoke and flames blasted their backs. They raced upstairs into the fort's courtyard. Tirans shouted and cursed behind them, running upstairs too.

Bayrin spun around and shoved Mori aside. He shifted into a dragon, so fast that his head spun, and blew a jet of fire into the dungeon.

His flames roared, spinning and blazing down the stairway. Tiran soldiers burned and fell back, dragonfire before them, phoenix fire in the dungeon behind. They screamed. Their screams filled Bayrin's ears, cries of such agony, that he knew he would forever hear them. He kept blowing fire. He could make out one Tiran, his skin bubbling, his flesh burning away, until the blackened thing fell back into the inferno and vanished in fire.

"Bayrin, fly!" Mori cried. She shifted into a dragon and panted. Firelight blazed against her golden scales. "Acribus is a phoenix down there, he's still alive!"

Bayrin let his flames die. He growled, spun, and slammed his tail against the entrance to the dungeon. The crumbly archway collapsed, raining stones. He slammed his tail again, shoving down more bricks and dirt.

"So we'll bury the bastard," he said. "Help me."

The slim golden dragon trembled but began lashing her own tail and claws, shoving dirt and stones into the dungeon. Soon the fire was contained. Smoke rose between cracks and fissures. Inside the tomb, the phoenix was screeching.

Bayrin surveyed the ruins, seeking more bricks. He found only a few pieces of shattered columns. He began shoving them. With Mori's help, he placed them over the dungeon. The phoenix inside was slamming against the blocked entrance, and the bricks and stones jostled. Searing heat rose from below, almost intolerable against his claws.

"This won't hold him for long," he said and heard the grimness in his voice. "Let's get out of here."

The two dragons took flight. They soared over the ruins, smoke and heat rising around them. They righted themselves and began flying north, the scent of fire in their nostrils. The frozen valleys of pines blurred beneath them. The shrieks of the phoenix, and the screams of the burning men, still echoed in Bayrin's ears. Most of all, he kept seeing Acribus lick his chops and heard the man's voice again: *Are you ready for more, weredragon?*

Bayrin growled, belly cold. He began to descend toward the evergreens.

"Bayrin, fly, come on!" Mori cried above him. "We have to fly fast before he escapes."

Bayrin shook his head. Fire caressed the inside of his mouth.

"We're not flying anymore," he said. He spiraled down toward a valley. "We're too easy to spot in the air. We're a beacon up there. Tirans might still crawl this land. We go on foot from here."

He crashed between branches and landed by a frozen stream. His claws dug into snow, and when he shifted into human form, he shivered. The pines creaked in the wind and sap covered him. Blood dampened his clothes and his wounds blazed. He sniffed the air and could still smell the phoenix fire, and when he looked south, he saw a plume of smoke rising between the trees.

Golden scales glimmered and Mori landed by him. She shifted into human form and stood trembling, hugging herself. She stared at him, her eyes huge and haunted, and for a moment, Bayrin could only stare at her. So much pain lived in those gray eyes that his chest ached.

At home, he always knew what to say--he could spout countless jokes, bawdy lyrics, taunting puns. Now he was speechless. He took three steps toward her, reached out his arms, and embraced her. She flinched and trembled like a bird caught in his palm, but soon her trembling eased and she laid her head against his chest.

"Oh Mori," he said softly, remembering those rabid teeth, that lolling tongue, those lustful eyes. "Did..."

Did he hurt you? he wanted to ask. *What did he do to you?* But the words caught in his throat. He feared that if he spoke them, her heart would shatter. So he only held her, kissed her forehead, and smoothed her hair.

"You did well," he said instead. "But damn it, Mors, you make me look bad! Flying fast like that... I'm going to tie some weights onto you next time so I can keep up."

A soft smile touched her lips, and Bayrin couldn't help it. He grinned, a huge grin that made his cheeks hurt. It was the first time he'd seen her smile since the Tiran invasion.

Her eyes were lowered. She spoke, her voice so soft, he could barely hear.

"I bet I walk faster than you too."

He snorted. "No way. You walk like a turtle, I've seen it."

Still staring at her feet, she whispered, "You walk like a snail."

"Oh that does it!" he said, still holding her. Mockingly, he pushed her back and started stomping through the snow. "It's a race, turtle girl. See if you can catch up."

The Crescent Isle lay countless leagues away. They walked between the trees, smoke and phoenix screeches rising behind them.

ELETHOR

He ran down the tunnel, eyes stinging, heart pounding, searching for Lyana in the darkness. He saw nothing but black mist, craggy walls, and shadows. His boots thudded against soft ground, as if running over moss. *Or over corpses*, he thought.

"Lyana!" he cried, and his voice echoed, taunting him, twisting through endless caverns. His heartbeat pounded in his ears, and his clothes clung to him, damp with sweat.

The image still burned against his eyes--Nedath the Guardian, a rotting girl with the body of a centipede, lifting Lyana in her arms. Licking her. Biting her. Elethor had tried to stop the demon, but Nedath moved too quickly. She had vanished into the bowels of the Abyss with her meal--with Lyana.

"Lyana!" he called again, and again his voice echoed like a hundred ghosts. Was she still alive?

As he ran, shadows swirled. Feet clattered all around. He could not tell if they moved near him or echoed from a distance. Cobwebs hung from the ceiling, slapping against him.

"Elllethorrrrr..."

The voice rose ahead, high-pitched as wind between canyons, mocking him. Laughter rolled.

"Nedath, come and face your king!" he cried again. "Bring back Lyana or I will kill you."

Somewhere ahead, Nedath laughed and sang. Her voice echoed from countless tunnels, a symphony of chaos. "Again the humans run... again their sweet stench rises... again Nedath shall feed!"

Elethor ran, slapping cobwebs aside, trying to find the demon. The tunnels branched, a labyrinth of them. Whenever he thought he heard footsteps or laughter, he headed that way, but then heard the sounds from behind him.

The cobwebs flapped against him, heavy and thick. Moans and pleading whispers rose from them. Elethor raised his lamp... and felt nausea swell.

Some cobwebs held severed arms with fingers that still moved. Others held ruined bodies stripped down to bones; the spines ended with withered heads whose mouths gasped, whose eyes spun, whose voices begged for death.

"Boy... boy, are you a skeley, are you skeley yet?" whispered one creature, an upside down, mummified thing, no thicker than Elethor's arm, its head shrunken and its lips smacking, its gums toothless. "Boy, it's skeley good, do you think?"

Elethor screamed and shoved past the hanging, mummified creatures. They gasped around him, eyes spinning and fingers twitching, swinging wildly on the cobwebs that bound them. *Stars, what are these things?* Elethor's head spun and he tasted bile. *Were they humans once? Will Nedath turn Lyana into one of them?*

In the shadows, the demon's laughter rolled.

"Poor poor humans, yes, Nedath. See how they cower! See how their fear fills the air, so sweet. Soon they will rot, and shrink, and hang, and lick, and smack, and whisper, and weep, and beg, and we will eat them slowly, yes Nedath, we will suck their juices dry, and the marrow from their bones, and their eyeballs, and their sweet innards, as they rot, and shrink, and hang, and..."

"Silence!" Elethor shouted, spinning around, seeking her, seeing only mist and cobwebs. He wanted to rage, to find this creature and fight, to be strong and proud and a warrior like Orin. But he felt close to tears. His legs shook. He gritted his teeth, and would have crumbled and wept had Lyana not needed him.

Around him the withered, hanging creatures swung on their cobwebs, sucking the air and whispering madness.

Be strong, Elethor told himself. *For Lyana. You must find her. You can't let her turn into one of these hanging things.*

"Nedath!" he shouted, hoarse, close to panic. He swung his sword, cutting cobwebs. "Nedath, come and face me!"

Mist rose, cobwebs parted, and the demon emerged.

She was more hideous than Elethor remembered. Her centipede body rose, each segment bristling with black fur. Mounted atop the last segment, the torso, arms, and head of the rotting girl were slick with drool and blood. The girl's mouth opened, revealing chewed flesh. With a screech, she vomited, spraying meat and broken bones and fingers.

"Elethor!" she screamed, a sound that shook the tunnels. "King Elethor of Requiem, fell lord of lizards!"

With a shout, Elethor swung his sword.

The blade sliced Nedath's top half, cutting into the rotten girl's belly. Snakes spilled like entrails, bloody and hissing.

Nedath screeched, a sound like shattering bones. Cobwebs tore and the bodies within them burst, spraying white ooze.

Elethor swung his sword again, aiming for Nedath's head, the head of a rotting girl. The demon raised her arm, and the blade halved her hand, cutting down to the wrist. Her spider legs lashed. Two slammed into Elethor, cutting him, shoving him down. He struggled to rise, but more legs hit him.

Nedath leaned over him, snarling. Drool dripped down her chin. Her eyes shed blood. Three tongues slipped from her mouth, fell onto Elethor, and squirmed across him like snakes. Around them, the hanging creatures twisted and smacked their withered, pursed lips, gasping for air and mumbling.

"The numbers don't line, the numbers don't line, they say, I heard them line it!" said one creature, a spine with clinging skin, its head a mere mouth with two eyeballs on stalks.

"Into my lair, boy, into my lair, we will drink somebody, boy, in here I say, listen, yes," said another, a twisting stem of a thing, its head a wilting cloth bound in iron wire.

They spun around him and Elethor screamed. He swung his blade, cutting at Nedath, but she pinned him down with her legs. She laughed, blood bubbling in her mouth.

"The new Boy King of Requiem," said the demon, voice twisting and rising. "You will be king of my withered things, and you will hurt more than them all."

He drove his fist up and shattered her face. Her skull cracked and cockroaches fled from it, the insects' faces almost human. Nedath laughed. She leaned down and bit Elethor's shoulder, and pain blazed--more pain than he'd ever felt. He writhed and screamed.

Darkness spread across his eyes, closing in until the world was black, and all pain dulled to throbbing cold. In the shadows he saw blue eyes, cruel and mocking, lips that kissed him, a golden face.

"Solina," he whispered hoarsely.

She leaned over him, her naked body pressed against him, and kissed him with the kisses of her mouth, and he ran his fingers through her hair of molten gold. She whispered into his ear, laughing softly, and he held her close.

"I love you, El," she whispered and laughed. "My secret prince."

He wept, clinging to her. "Don't leave, Solina, don't leave, stay here, don't go into fire, don't go into fire..."

But she burned. She burned atop him, screaming, her flesh peeling and melting, until he saw her skull, and still she screamed and clung to him.

No, he thought, shaking. *No, I can't let her burn. I can't let this happen. I can't turn into one of these things, these hanging twisting things of memory and pain and madness.*

He shouted Solina's name as he drove his blade upward.

Ferus, his sword forged in dragonfire, shone with starlight. It pierced through the burning apparition of his love. Blazing, it drove into the rotting, mad Guardian of the Abyss. With the howl of collapsing stars, the steel blazed into darkness, and Nedath howled too, and the world seemed to explode.

The demon's head shattered. Fragments of bone and gore flew. Behind her, her snaking body of black, furry segments burst, showering the tunnel with blood. Her scream echoed and the hanging things swung, eyes spinning and mouths gasping.

Elethor rose to his feet, breathing raggedly. He looked around him. It looked like the innards of a dead whale. Blood and entrails covered the tunnel. His lamp had fallen and set fire to cobwebs. He stamped out the flames, lifted the lamp, and surveyed the darkness.

"Lyana!" he shouted.

The withered bodies cackled around him, swinging on the cobwebs. They cried out in a mocking cacophony. "Lyana! Lyana! Lyana!"

Elethor began shoving his way between them, knocking them aside. They careened around him, some only spines and skin, others pale creatures whose hearts beat red behind transparent skin. Was Lyana hanging here too? Had she become one of them?

"Lyana, answer me!" he cried. His eyes stung. Stars, he couldn't leave her here. He couldn't let her become a creature. "Lyana!"

Coughing sounded in the distance. A muffled voice cried out. "Elethor!"

His heart leaped. He ran, boots sucking at blood, sword swinging at hanging creatures. His lamp swung and shadows swirled. Down a tunnel and around a bend, he saw a figure cloaked in webs, hanging from the ceiling.

"Lyana!"

Tears stung his eyes. He ran to her and began tearing the cobwebs off. She hung upside down, coughing and blinking. He kept ripping off webs, not knowing what he'd find. Would her body be withered, her skin clinging to bones, her heart beating behind clear skin? When the cobwebs were torn and he pulled her free, he breathed in relief. Blood covered her armor, and black ooze covered her face, but she was whole. Her drawn sword clattered to the floor.

"Lyana, talk to me, are you all right?" He wiped her face, revealing her pale skin.

She coughed, gasped for breath, looked at him silently... then crashed into his embrace. She clung to him.

"I... saw him," she whispered. "I saw Orin. He was here, Elethor!" She looked at him pleadingly. "He was hanging here from the webs, and I could see his spine, and his head looked like, like... it was just a flat piece of leather, but his eyes moved."

"It was a dream, Lyana," he said softly. He picked webs from her hair. "I saw Solina too. We see the ones we love here, I think."

She gulped and lifted her sword. Blade raised, she looked around her: at the blood on the walls, at the creatures who still hung and stared at them, at the torn segments of Nedath's body. With a sigh, she closed her eyes and leaned her head against Elethor's chest.

"Thank you," she whispered. "You killed the guardian. You did what I could not."

They stood silently for long moments, holding each other in the darkness. Lyana's mane of curls tickled Elethor's nose, and as he held her, he too thought of Orin. In the old days, some claimed that the souls of dead sinners landed in this place, while the pious glowed among the stars.

Elethor clenched his jaw. *No. Orin was a hero. A noble son of Requiem. He dines now in our starlit halls, and his soul will never see this cursed place.*

"Elethor, look!" Lyana said. She gasped and fear filled her eyes. Slowly, she stepped away from him and raised her left hand. Her fingertips were gray and withered, thinned to sticks.

Elethor's stomach churned. Cold sweat dripped down his back. He forced his fear down and spoke through a tight throat. "Adia can heal them, Lyana. She is a great healer."

Her chest rose and fell as she panted. "Stars, Elethor, stars, am... am I turning into one of them?" She gestured around her at the chamber. The shrunken, withered creatures snorted and cackled and licked their toothless gums.

"No," Elethor said and clenched his fists. "Nedath is dead now. She can no longer harm you. And your mother will heal your fingertips, I promise you." He reached out, held her good hand, and squeezed it. "Now come, Lyana. We go find the Starlit Demon. The faster we leave the Abyss, the better."

She nodded and wiped a tear off her cheek.

"Let's go," she said and raised her sword. "We delve deeper... and I pray that the worst is behind us."

As they walked deeper into the darkness, Elethor prayed too. But he knew in the pit of his stomach: The worst still lay ahead.

SOLINA

With a trembling heart and the whispers of old pain, she walked toward his home.

Solina had told herself she would be strong this day. She was a queen of Tiranor, a great warrior clad in steel and gold. Her twin blades were sharp, her army was vast, her power endless. She was hardened by fire, then by sand, finally by blood. She had not thought this place could hurt her.

Yet some pain drove past armor, and some memories haunted even great queens of cruel desert lands. As Solina walked toward Elethor's old home upon the hill, that pain clutched her heart and twisted.

It was a small home for a prince--a narrow hall, its walls lined with columns, their capitals shaped as dragons. It rose upon a hill where grass had once rustled, pines rose like sentinels, and birds always sang. Solina remembered the old smell of the place, the sweetness of lilac in the gardens, the wine that forever poured here, the musk of him as they made love between these walls. Now the grass was burnt, the pines fallen, and she only smelled smoke and blood. The columns still stood, but while they were once snowy white, soot now stained them.

"This was a good place," Solina whispered as she walked uphill. "This was the only place we found peace, away from the court of the cruel king."

She stepped between columns toward the hall's doors. Once carved with dragons and stars, they were now charred and cracked; the phoenix fire had reached even this place, the doors to her chamber of old secrets. When she shoved them, the doors opened, showering ash. Solina stepped inside, heart like a bird caught in her ribcage.

She saw the chambers as they had been, lush with flowers from the gardens, warm with pillows and divans, sweet with the secrets of forbidden love. She would lie naked here by his side, holding him, and they would talk and kiss and laugh until dawn rose. She remembered the wooden turtle with emerald eyes he had carved her, and his songbirds in their golden cage, and the tears she cried here when the pain of exile was too strong.

The room now lay in ruin. The fire had burned those pillows, divans, and flowers. All that remained were seven marble statues, life-sized, and Solina's breath caught.

They were her.

She stepped toward one, tears stinging her eyes, and touched its cheek. The statue stared back, a girl blossoming into womanhood, pure and beautiful, her eyes soft and her lips smiling. She was draped in cascading robes that revealed her left breast, and her hands were held out as in offering.

"Oh, Elethor," she whispered.

He had not forgotten. He still loved her, had missed her like she missed him, and suddenly Solina was trembling. She wanted those days back, if only for a respite from this pain and fire. She wanted to see the wooden turtle again, and hear the birds sing, and lie with him and kiss him with all those forbidden kisses.

She looked away.

"But those days are gone," she said and clenched her fists. "I was an exile then. I was afraid. I was weak. I was burned. I returned to my southern land, and now I come here as a queen."

Sudden rage exploded in her. Who was that smiling, beautiful woman carved of marble? That was not her. Not anymore. The dragons had burned her, ruined her beauty, scarred her face and soul. With a snarl, Solina drew her dagger and pulled it down the statue's face. The marble chipped, and she kept hacking at it, until a rut halved the statue's face.

"There," Solina said and touched the scar that rent her own face. "Now you are Solina of Tiranor, burned with fire, seeking revenge."

She moved between the other statues, hacking at them, until scars snaked down their faces, torsos, and legs. She would allow no more memories of pureness to fill this chamber. Those memories were lies.

"My power is truth," she whispered.

She opened her leather pack and looked inside. Nestled between rations, sharpening stones, and bandages lay a box carved of olive wood, a foot long and half as wide. Golden runes of suns and flames lined the wood, twisting and glowing. When Solina touched the box, it nearly seared her hand. The weapons within buzzed as if begging for release.

"Soon your fire will be unleashed," Solina whispered. With an angry jerk, she sealed her pack, spun around, and marched out of Elethor's house. She walked downhill between charred pines and birches, jaw clenched, refusing to look back. She would never return.

"I will scar you too, Elethor," she whispered as ash blew around her boots and phoenixes shrieked in the sky. "I will destroy all memories of this place. I will fill it with only my strength and majesty."

She made her way through the ruined city of Nova Vita. The birches still smoldered, charred sticks rising from mounds of ash. The palace rose ahead, its proud columns blackened, its lush gardens now crackling with scattered flames. The city amphitheater dipped into a hillside, a bowl cut into the earth, its tiers of seats holding charred bones, its stage splashed with blood. A hill of bodies burned between the columns of a temple, an offering of death for the cruel stars of Requiem.

No more weredragons filled this place--their vile, shapeshifting bodies now cowered underground. Her troops of Tiranor lined the roads, tall and proud men and women, their skin golden and pure, their hair shimmering platinum, their eyes sapphire jewels. They were as noble a race as weredragons were foul. Even as smoke rose across the city, their armor glimmered, and the firegems around their necks cast ten thousand lights. They stood with swords drawn, the blades curved like the beaks of sacred ibises, their pommels carved as sunbursts. Above them a hundred phoenixes circled in patrol of the skies. Ash rained and smoke rose in pillars.

Solina called out as she walked. "Sandfire Phalanx, fall in behind me! Jade Phalanx, follow! Deserthawk, follow!"

Her troops slammed blades against shields and cried for blood. They marched down the road behind her, boots thudding as one. As they moved between the ruins, Solina summoned more troops, and soon a thousand marched behind her. A snarling grin twisted her lips.

"It is time," she said, "for a fire in the deep."

This would be no long siege. She would not wait here for moons, even years, until the weredragons' food and water dwindled. She would break through their defenses. She would burn them all, and her men would take their women, and her blades would cut her old love.

"For your glory, Sun God," she whispered and looked to the heavens. The sun burned there behind smoke and cloud; it was smaller here in the north, and colder, but Solina would bring all its wrath to this place. She would serve her lord with the flames he'd given her. Her hand clutched the firegem around her neck and its heat shot through her, rivers of flame in her veins.

Soon they reached the tunnel entrance, where a hundred Tirans stood with drawn steel. The archway rose around the darkness, stained with fire and blood. The stairs plunged into shadow.

Elethor waits down there.

Lord Deramon had raised barricades of stone, sealing her outside. He would find that no rock could face the flame of Tiranor.

As her troops stood behind her, swords raised, Solina opened her pack. Delicately, as if handling a holy artifact, Solina withdrew the long box of olive wood. It thrummed and its runes blazed, nearly blinding her.

She whispered a prayer to the Sun God. "May your light forever cast out the darkness. May your fire forever burn out the cold."

She caught her breath and opened the box.

Six clay balls lay there, placed into holes lined with cloth. They nearly burned her hand when she touched them. Decorative red lines, shaped as flames, ran across them.

"Tiran Fire," she whispered. A hungry smile touched her lips.

Her priests had labored for moons to produce these weapons. Each clay container had taken many nights of work and prayer. One alone could destroy a phalanx of troops. Six would destroy Requiem.

She raised the box over her head, ignoring the heat that ran down her arms, and faced her troops. Firelight blazed in their eyes.

"For the glory of the Sun God!" she called. "We cast out the darkness!"

Her troops howled and waved their weapons. Their roar shook the ground. Snarling, Solina turned back toward the tunnel, thrust the box forward, and sent the six balls of Tiran Fire tumbling into darkness.

She stood facing the stairway, panting, teeth bared. She let the empty wooden box thud to the ground. The clay balls clanked down the stairs, and Solina snarled and waited... one breath, two, three...

An explosion rocked the city.

Fire and wind blasted from the darkness, and Solina turned aside, gritting her teeth. Dust flew and coated her. Rocks fell. The ground shook beneath her boots. The flames roared so loudly she could hear nothing else.

Soon she heard more sounds--screams from below.

A smile spread across her face, becoming a grin.

When the dust settled, she found the staircase coated with debris, some stained with blood. Black lines stretched along the walls. Solina drew her twin blades, Aknur and Raem, and the golden runes upon them blazed. She would lead the charge.

"For the Sun God!" she shouted. "And for Tiranor!"

Her army answered the call behind her, shouting so loudly, the ruins shook. "For the Sun God! For Tiranor! For Queen Solina!"

Solina charged into the darkness with her light and heat. She raced down stairs covered with dust and rock. Her men charged behind her, shouting for sun and glory. The walls rushed at her sides, stained with blood and ash and weredragon stench. Her blades blazed like the sun, casting out the shadows.

This is my purpose, Solina thought with a snarl. *This is my glory. I will banish the darkness of reptiles with my lord's light.*

At the bottom of the staircase, the barricade Deramon had raised was gone. The boulders were smashed to shards. Grooves dug into the walls. Blood, dust, and chunks of flesh covered everything. Blades raised, Solina stepped over the debris... and crashed against an army of weredragons.

Dozens of them filled the darkness, thrusting their straight, heavy blades of the north. The stains of fire and blood coated them. Stubble covered their faces and pain filled their eyes. They were desperate men, pushed into a corner, and wild; but Solina was glorious and strong and she would defeat them.

Her twin sabres lashed. Aknur, her left blade of nightfire, parried a blow from a weredragon's sword. Raem, her right blade of dawn, sliced into a man's neck. Blood sprayed like sunrise. Her troops roared behind her and burst into the chamber, sabres clashed against longswords, blood spilled, men fell. They fought over the bodies of the fallen, boots snapping bones and crushing faces.

She fought for hours. Aknur and Raem spun like disks of light. Blood coated her armor when she finally drove into the deeper chambers, where tunnels snaked wide and tall, lined with doors. The women and children of Requiem cowered here, wailing. They began to flee, a mad rout into darkness.

"Kill the reptiles!" Solina cried hoarsely. "Kill them all."

She marched through the tunnels, swinging her blades. Soldiers still hacked at her. A child ran to her left, wailing. Solina swung Aknur and cut him down. More soldiers raced up from the darkness, blades lashing. She parried and thrust, shedding their blood upon the fleeing survivors.

"Solina of Tiranor!" howled a deep voice, and Lord Deramon himself marched toward her. He bore a sword in one hand, an axe in the other. His armor was thick, his arms wide, his face cold.

She smiled at him and raised her sabres in salute. "Come die at my feet."

They circled each other, blades raised, and blood pounded in Solina's ears. It was Deramon who had caught her making love to Elethor. It was Deramon who had told her secrets to the king--who had her burned, exiled, torn apart from her lover. It was Deramon who would now die in pain and fear.

Her sabres lashed. He parried. His axe flew and she blocked, riposted, shouted in rage. Steel rang and pain thrust up her arms. Men fought around them, but Solina would not remove her eyes from her foe. He was a tall, broad man--almost twice her size--and his blades were heavier than hers. But she was younger and faster. Aknur blocked a thrust of his sword, and Raem, her blade of dawn, slammed against his breastplate.

Steel dented and Deramon grunted. His axe thrust, and Solina fell to one knee as she parried. Aknur, blade of nightfire, clanged against his axe. Raem swung against his leg, steel sparked against steel, and Deramon grunted. She leaped up and swung both blades down.

He blocked one. The other hit his shoulder, cleaving his pauldron, and blood seeped.

She lashed again at once. This was her chance to slay him. But despite his wound, he did not miss a step of the dance. His sword rose, blocked her blow, and his axe slammed against her breastplate.

Steel bent. Pain blazed. She gasped for breath and found none. His sword clanged against her pauldron, and she thought her arm would dislocate. She fell, armor dented, by the body of the child she'd slain.

Deramon stood above her and stared down, eyes cold, blood seeping. A lesser warrior might have given her some last words, spoken some poetry of farewell or justice. Deramon wasted no time on dramatic partings; he lusted for nothing more than the kill itself. His axe swung down.

On her knees, Solina raised her blades and crossed them. The axe slammed down, chipping Aknur and shooting pain down her arms. Keeping Raem raised, Solina dropped Aknur, snarled, and grabbed the dead child's hair. She tugged the head up and tossed the small, lacerated body at Deramon.

The child slammed against him, and Deramon fell back a step. Solina leaped up, swung her blade, and hit Deramon's helmet. He staggered.

She would have killed him then. She would have ended this. Yet Deramon had no honor; he would not even duel her to the death. Five of his men rushed forward from the shadows, blades lashing. With a snarl, Solina grabbed the fallen Aknur, parried a blow, and stepped under an archway. Here she could slay them one by one.

Men lashed at her. Moans and wails rose behind her. Solina glanced at the reflection in her blades. A wild smile tingled across her face. *Perfect.*

As men thrust blades at her, Solina retreated through the archway and into the chamber of wails. She found herself fighting in Requiem's old armory, now a hospital crowded with dying weredragons. They lay around her on the floor, bandaged, burnt, some with severed limbs, others with gaping wounds. A hundred filled this place. A single healer, a young woman with a stern braid of dark hair, huddled over the wounded.

Soldiers of Requiem came spilling into the chamber, and Solina fought alone. The hospital was wide, fifty feet deep, its ceiling twenty feet tall. She licked her lips. *It is large enough. It is time for fire.*

She parried a blow, clutched the firegem around her neck, and smiled.

She summoned her lord's gift.

At once, she burst into flames. They raced across her, scorching, intoxicating. She reached out her arms, and flaming feathers grew from them. She howled, and her voice became the shriek of an eagle. Men cowered before her. The wounded burst into flame. The young healer screamed and ran, a living torch. Solina grew in size until she was a great phoenix, dragon-sized, an inferno of flame and smoke and wind.

The hundred wounded weredragons blazed. A few were well enough to run, but none made it to the doors. They fell, burning into charred bones. The fire filled the chamber until it was a furnace, a pyre for her glory. The weredragons at the door howled. Some brought crossbows but their darts only passed through her flames, and Solina screeched, a great bird of sunfire.

She was a queen. She was a goddess. Soon she would destroy these tunnels, find her cowering Elethor, and she would burn him too until he screamed and begged and knew her glory.

MORI

She huddled under the trees, cloak pulled over her, and prayed.

"Please, stars, please *please* don't let him see us, please stars, send him away."

Above in the clouds, the phoenix dived and shrieked. Its wake of fire spread behind it like a comet's tail. Mori pushed herself against the tree, as close as she could. Bayrin huddled at her side, also covered in cloak and hood. They had strung branches and leaves over their cloaks, but would that fool the phoenix? It circled the veiled sun, crackling.

Mori did not know if Acribus could still take human form. Bayrin had smashed that crystal he wore around his neck, the one with the fire inside. She knew little of southern magic, but thought that the firegem let the Tirans turn into phoenixes. Solina had worn one too, which she never had back in those days in Requiem. With his firegem smashed, could he still turn into a man? A man who could choke her with cracked hands, tear off her clothes, thrust into her with such blazing pain that she wanted to die? Or would he remain forever a phoenix, a questing demon of fire that would forever hunt her?

"Bayrin," she whispered. She wanted to ask him about the firegem, but he hushed her.

They huddled together, frozen in the cold. The wind cut through their cloaks, icy but scented of fire. It seemed ages before the phoenix turned east and flew away, and its shrieks faded in the distance. Mori shivered and rose to her feet. She clasped the hilt of her sword, that sword she had never wielded in battle, and watched the wake of fire disperse above.

Daniel Arenson

Bayrin too stood up. He spat. "Good riddance. I
thought the damn bird would never fly away. Peskier than bees in
your underpants, these phoenixes are." He squinted and watched
the skies for a while. "We might be fine for flying soon. The
phoenix is heading east, and we're going north."

"No!" Mori clutched his sleeve. "Please, Bayrin, please
don't make me fly. He'll see us. I know he will. Phoenix eyes are
sharp, and if we fly, he'll see us, and he'll burn us." She trembled
and tugged on his cloak, as if that could convince him. "Please,
Bayrin, I don't want to fly. Not yet."

He sighed. Circles hung under his eyes. "All right, Mors.
We'll walk for a while under the trees. But sooner or later we'll
have to fly again. Walking all the way to the sea can take moons;
flying would take days. And once we reach the sea, we'd *have* to
fly, unless you know how to build a boat with your bare hands."

"We'll walk for today," she said and drew her sword,
wondering if she'd ever dare swing it at an enemy. She lowered
her head, remembering how even in the dungeon of Draco
Vallum, she had only cowered, and dared not fight like Bayrin did.
She took a shaky breath. "We'll fly tomorrow."

They walked through the forest in silence. The pines rose
around them, frosted with snow, their branches snagging at their
cloaks and smearing them with sap. Soon snow began to fall.
The cold air drove into her bones. Mori pulled her cloak tight,
but the wind kept creeping under her clothes to caress her skin.
She missed home. She missed sitting by the fireplace with a good
book, maybe one with maps, or one about adventure. She missed
drinking mulled wine and talking to Lyana about what gowns the
ladies of the court wore, or talking to Elethor about the stars, or
even just cuddling with her pet mouse and whispering her secrets
to him. Would that world ever return? So many had died. So
much of the city had fallen.

178

Mori lowered her head. For the first time, she realized that she was an orphan now. True, she had not stopped thinking about her dead father, not for an instant. And even now, years after her mother's death, she still thought about the queen every day. But that word--*orphan*--only now filled her mind. To Mori, orphans had always been poor children with shabby clothes and hungry bellies, figures from books and stories. She had never thought she would one day tread in the wilderness, her own clothes torn, her own belly twisting with hunger, her own two parents gone.

But I have Elethor, she thought. *He's still alive, and he'll protect me. And I have my friend Lyana.* She shivered and wrapped her cloak as tight as she could. *Unless they're dead too. Unless some creature in the Abyss killed them.*

"Mori, you're shivering," Bayrin said. He looked at her, his black cloak now white with snow. Snow even coated his eyebrows. And yet he began to doff his cloak. "Here, wear this too."

She held up her hands. "No, Bay. You're cold too. Keep your cloak, I'm all right."

His words, if not his cloak, warmed her. She wasn't sure why, but since battling Acribus underground, Bayrin had seemed much nicer. He sighed and rolled his eyes less often. He made fewer quips. He even held her hand when they stepped over ice-- the hand with six fingers, which he would mock so much back at home. Had something happened underground to change him? Maybe he was only scared too... scared that the other Vir Requis were all dead, that the city of Nova Vita had fallen, that they would die out here.

Mori did something she never thought she would dare, something that a moon ago would terrify her. She stood on her tiptoes, leaned forward, and kissed Bayrin's cheek. His red stubble tickled her lips.

"But thank you, Bay."

He raised his eyebrows and whistled. "Oh my." He made to remove his boots. "Here, take my boots too! And my pants and shirt. Would you like some nice warm socks?" He wiggled his eyebrows. "Does that get me a kiss on the lips?"

Mori couldn't help but giggle. She shoved him back. "It'll get you frostbite, that's what."

As they kept walking, Mori hugged herself and wondered: What would it be like... to truly kiss Bayrin on the lips? Mori was eighteen already, but she had never kissed a boy. Her mother had been married at her age, and Lyana had kissed her first boy at age fourteen, but Mori had always feared it. Would it be painful and cold like... like when...?

She shook her head wildly, scattering snow. *No. Don't think about that, Mori. Love isn't like that night, and if I ever kiss a boy, it will be for love. He would love me, and I would love him, and it will feel like those old days, when I'd sit by the fireplace and read books with maps.*

She slipped on some ice, and Bayrin caught her hand to steady her, and she let him hold it as they kept walking. The forest spread cold ahead, as far as she could see. In the distance, upon the eastern wind, she thought she could hear a phoenix shriek.

LYANA

They walked down a twisting tunnel. Its floor was rubbery like skin and strewn with eyeballs like pebbles. Shattered spines rose in ridges along the walls, seeping blood. Fingers rose in tufts from nooks and crevices, nails cracked, snagging at them.

Lyana could see only several feet in each direction; shadows pushed deep around her, swirling and cackling, red eyes blazing in their depths. When the tunnels forked, Elethor did not hesitate, but always chose the path that sloped deeper down.

"Do you know where we're going?" she asked him.

He stared ahead, holding his tin lamp high. The flames flickered. They had oil enough for another day, two days at most.

"This tunnel is steeper," he said. "So that's where we go. Deeper into the darkness."

"You don't know that'll take us to the Starlit Demon," Lyana said. "This labyrinth is vast, Elethor. It might be larger than Requiem itself, larger than the world. According to the stories, the Starlit Demon is locked behind the Crimson Archway, and I haven't seen a single archway here. We need to find a map, or a source of knowledge, or--"

He spun toward her and glared. "Lyana, what map? What 'source of knowledge'? The last creatures we met who could talk were dangling on cobwebs, mumbling nonsense about numbers not lining up, and hairs that grew too slowly, or stars know what else."

"So your answer is to just walk blindly?" she demanded, voice rising now. She swept her sword around her. "Elethor, we are getting lost down here. You have no idea where to go. No idea what to do. No idea how to get back home. You--"

"Well, do you?" He raised his eyebrows. "Do you have answers? You're just as much in the dark. So unless you have suggestions, keep walking."

"Well, I..." She searched for words but found none and fumed. All her life, she had always had an answer to any question. She knew everything about geography, heraldry, warfare, swordplay, history, astronomy. She was the smartest person in Requiem, she was sure of it; yet now she felt so lost, so afraid.

She raised her left hand and shivered. Bandages covered her fingers, hiding the gray, withered flesh. A day ago, only her fingertips had been shriveled and pale. Now lines of rot stretched from under the bandage, spreading across her palm to her wrist. The skin looked old, spotted and wrinkled, the bones beneath it brittle.

Elethor looked at her, his eyes softened, and he sighed.

"Does it hurt?" he asked quietly.

She shook her head. "I can't feel my hand anymore. At least there's no pain."

She shivered and lowered her eyes, remembering the withered creatures back at Nedath's lair. She had hung among them for hours. Most were no wider than snakes, nothing but spines with loose skin, their limbs wilted stalks. Their skulls had long crumbled to dust, leaving loose faces like old rags.

"We are the Shrivels," one had told her, swinging on its cobwebs. "We are the lost ones, the cursed, the counters of the numbers... or maybe the numbers themselves." It grinned, showing toothless gums. "Soon you will be one of us, soon you will help us count, we will count all the numbers, we will line them, or she will hurt us, she will eat us, she will feed upon our sweetest meat."

How long will it be? Lyana wondered. She no longer doubted that their curse infected her. How long until her palm withered completely and the disease spread to her arm, then her body, and finally left her a shrunken creature that could not die? Would she remain here in the Abyss, mumbling of shattered teeth that must be found, screws to turn, and more ramblings of the dark? Or would they hang her on a post in Requiem, a thing to pity, and she would linger there as seasons turned, unable to die?

Suddenly she laughed. She couldn't help it.

"Imagine it, Elethor!" she said, tears in her eyes. Laughter shook her. "Me, only a piece of shriveled skin on a hook! Would you hang me by your throne so I could still watch the court?"

She laughed so hard that she didn't realize she was crying, that her laughter was becoming a panicked pant. She jerked when Elethor touched her shoulder, sure for an instant that it was her, Nedath, the demon who had bitten her shoulder and spoken of sucking her bones. She found herself wrapped in Elethor's arms, like the cobwebs had wrapped her, and she wept against him.

"I won't let that happen," he said softly, stroking her hair.

She shivered, unable to stop her tears from falling. "I'm so scared, Elethor. I saw things in there, in the darkness she showed me. I saw... there was a black hill, and a black rose on it, and horror filled the air, as if fear were a physical thing. And... Elethor, I have to stop the bones from lining up! I have to *count* them, Elethor. I have to count the hairs that are growing sideways."

He shook his head, eyes narrowed. "What, Lyana? What do you mean? There are no bones. There's nothing to count."

She sobbed, body shaking. "I don't know! I don't know, Elethor. But..." She sniffed. "If my teeth fall from my gums, I..." She gritted those teeth and rubbed her eyes. "No! No. I can't think like them. I can't talk like them." She clung to his clothes with her good hand, staring into his eyes through her tears. "I won't turn into a Shrivel. Promise me that, Elethor. Promise you won't let me go."

He held her. "I promise you, Lyana. As King of Requiem, I will do whatever I can to cure you; I will summon healers from across the world, from Salvandos in the west to Leonis in the east. I won't let you turn into anything." He touched her hair. "Do you remember how, when we were children, we'd go to Lacrimosa Hill, eat walnuts from a pouch, and look at the stars? You and Mori would whisper, and Bayrin and Orin would laugh, and I'd try to tell you all about the stars, but you'd never listen." He smiled softly. "We'll do that again, Lyana. We'll go stargazing, and eat walnuts, and laugh..."

He fell silent. They stood holding each other, and Lyana tried to remember those days of her youth, the glow of the stars, the warmth of the breeze, the sound of her laughter, and she knew those days could never return. Orin was gone now. Mori was hurt, maybe too much to ever recover. As for herself... could she ever be the woman she had been? When fire rained, and darkness clutched her, was there still a path home?

"Let's keep going," she said and pulled back from his embrace. She raised her lamp, casting its light upon a dead, dark land. "Let's find this Starlit Demon and go home."

They walked across the grass of fingers, crushing them. They moved through darkness, lashing their swords at red eyes that blazed around them. Shadows swirled, taking the shapes of bloated dragons that burst, shedding bodies of smoke from their bellies. Ribs rose around them, framing the tunnels, columns of dead cathedrals. Bodies hung from the walls on meat hooks, their faces burnt. Some bodies looked almost like Orin, others like Lyana's parents, some like herself. Their bellies were split, revealing nests of transparent eggs, snakes moving inside the shells. Hatched snakes squirmed along the tunnel floor, bloated, screeching, laughing, mocking them.

"Walk deeper, weredragons!" spoke the bodies on the hooks. "Enter our darkness. You will hang here too! You will rot and burst and feed our hatchlings."

The bodies' faces twisted, mouths gasping. They screamed, begged for death, and wept tears of blood.

"Don't look at them," Elethor said, jaw clenched. "It's not real, Lyana. It's just a dream. It's just a nightmare they're showing us."

Lyana nodded, desperate to believe him. When bodies rubbed against her, she shoved them aside and stabbed them, shedding blood and pus and maggots. Their stench filled her nostrils. Their flesh against her felt hot, sticky, too real to be a vision. Yet she kept walking, forcing herself to stare forward, to ignore them.

"They're just a dream," she repeated through stiff lips. "Just a dream."

"Are we just a dream?" asked a hanging body, speaking through a gaping wound in its rotted face.

"You have been kissed by Nedath!" said another, the skinned body of a man with a bull's head.

A snake coiled toward her, spine peeking through rents in its skin. It hissed and stared with blazing red eyes. "The Guardian of the Darkness bit her, children! She will soon be a Withered One. Look at her arm!"

The bodies on the hooks stared and hissed. Tongues thrust out from their wounds and licked their blood. Lyana looked at her arm and saw that Nedath's disease had spread to her elbow. Her forearm was now thin as bone, her flesh gone, her skin dangling.

"Can you cure her?" Elethor said, raising his voice over their cries and laughter. "How can we stop the curse?"

The bodies on the walls growled, revealing fangs. "Feed us! Feed us and we will tell you. We know of a cure. Feed us and we will help."

Fingers trembling, Lyana opened her pack. She had brought food from Requiem: sweet apples, grainy rolls of bread, cheese, oranges, and dried fish. Maggots filled the food now, and Lyana grimaced.

"I have food for you!" she shouted. The bodies were twitching around her, legs kicking, as if trying to escape the meat hooks.

"We do not want your food of sunlight and soil!" one said.

"Feed us ourselves!" cried another. "Let us feast upon our comrades, upon our sweet hands and feet!"

They opened their maws wide, drooling, begging for meat. Those with arms reached out and pawed at her. Their bellies bloated, pulsing with eggs.

"Stars, they're cannibals," Elethor whispered. He was pale and his sword wavered in his hand.

Lyana wanted to gag, to weep, to run. How could she do this? To take a squirming body from the wall, hack it apart, feed it to its comrades?

"It would be like cutting meat, just like cutting meat!" they begged. "Feed us, feed us our comrades!"

"Tell me of a cure first!" Lyana shouted. Their voices rose so loudly, her ears hurt. "Tell me how to cure Nedath's curse and I will feed you then!"

A halved body, ribs white and twisting, hissed at her. "You must find the Feasting Table!" it said. "You must eat there from the sweet meats. Then you will be cured. Then you will be a Withered One no more. Then you must feed us!"

Elethor shouted, swinging his sword to hold back the groping arms. "Where is this Feasting Table?"

The bodies pulled aside, like sweeping curtains of flesh, and revealed a gaping doorway. Lyana could see nothing but shadows through it, but scents hit her nose. She could smell... food, *real* food! Fresh bread, and cakes, and fruits. The scents mingled with the stench of the hanging bodies, a sickening mix of the delicious and rotting.

"Enter and feast, child of starlight," said the bodies. "But choose wisely, so we may feast too."

Lyana looked at her arm. The disease was spreading up to her shoulder. Through her hanging skin, she could see the bones of her elbow, pale and full of worms. She no longer cared for danger. She rushed past the bodies into the dark chamber of scents. Behind her, she heard Elethor follow.

They walked for a moment in darkness until they saw candles burn ahead. The craggy walls widened, revealing a chamber with a tiled floor, white walls, and a chandelier.

A table stood in the room, and upon it lay a feast--such a feast as Lyana had never seen, not even in the courts of Requiem. Golden platters, bowls, and plates held roast ducks on beds of mushrooms, glazed hams, grapes and apples and peaches, thick gravy, bread still steaming from the oven, stewed vegetables, and every other delight Lyana could imagine. She realized that she was famished. Her mouth watered.

She would have leaped toward the food, were it not for the figures that sat around the table.

Seven chairs surrounded the feast. In all but one sat a Shrivel. Their limbs had atrophied into mere twigs wrapped in loose skin. Their spines were slung across the chairs, and their heads dangled over the backrests, forever looking at the walls behind them. Their faces gasped and sucked at their toothless gums. Dark liquid dripped from them, forming pools below their heads. The last chair, the one at the head of the table, was empty.

That chair is for me, Lyana knew.

A portrait of King Olasar of Requiem hung upon the wall, framed in giltwood. Somebody had smeared blood across it, giving the king horns and a forked tongue. The eyes had been gouged out. Words were scratched across the canvas, and Lyana read them, a shiver running through her.

At the table of lost souls
A feast awaits the withering
Nedath's cursed seek a cure
For skin, flesh, and bones decaying
Feed upon our sweetest meats
Your tainted blood again shall bloom
Crave and eat the lesser treats
And rot forever in our room

"What does it mean?" Elethor asked, standing beside her. He was pale, and his dark hair clung to his damp forehead.

Lyana looked back at the feast covering the table: roast ducks, fresh fruit, pastries, breads... Would one of these heal her?

"What is the sweetest meat?" she asked. "Feast upon our sweetest meats, and your tainted blood again shall bloom. Does that mean that if I eat the right food, I'll be cured?"

Elethor shivered. "Eat the lesser treats, and rot forever in our room." He gestured at the Shrivels who gasped upon the chairs. "That must be what happened to them. They ate the wrong dish."

Heart hammering, Lyana walked to the table. The scents of the feast filled her nostrils. Her left arm dangled at her side, a flap of useless skin, its bones so brittle now, no wider than a porcupine's quill. When she looked at a golden bowl, she saw her reflection. Already her left cheek sagged, the skin gray.

"What should I eat?" she called, turning to the Shrivels on

the seats. She grabbed one and shook it. Its skin was clammy, and its spine rattled. "What did you eat?"

The creature's head flapped from side to side. It gasped and sucked its gums. "Eat, child, eat the treats, join us, count with us..."

Tears stinging her eyes, Lyana tossed the creature aside. It slapped against the floor and squirmed. She grabbed another Shrivel. She shook it, and its heart pulsed behind its clear skin, shooting black blood down a single vein.

"What do I eat here?" she demanded, tears on her cheeks. "Tell me!"

The Shrivel whispered, and its eyes shed black tears. "Please, light one, please, tell him, tell him to turn, he has to turn it, he has to turn the *screws*, please tell him!"

She tossed this creature aside too and spun toward the table, trembling. Her left leg shook, and when she took a step, her foot pulled out from her boot.

"Lyana!" Elethor cried. He ran toward her and held her, and she gasped, clinging to him. Her sock fell off, revealing a shriveled foot, no larger than the foot of a baby. Her toes curled inward, white and brittle.

"Oh stars, Elethor, stars," she whispered.

"Eat something!" Elethor said. He pulled her toward the table. "Eat... what is the sweetest meat? Duck? Veal? Ham?"

Lyana looked at the feast. For the first time, she saw that drool covered the dishes. The marks of toothless gums filled the geese, the ham, the fruit.

The Shrivels had tried eating these foods, she knew. *They all chose wrong.* She raised her head and looked at the empty seat. She trembled, wept, and held Elethor tight.

"Please, Elethor," she whispered. "Please, don't let him turn the screws, please, tell him, *tell him.*"

She tried to say more, but felt a tooth come loose. She spat it out, and she wanted to sink her gums into the meat, to feed, to count, to line things up, to...

No! No, not yet. You are not a Shrivel yet. She fumbled toward the table, tossed her sword down, and lifted an apple with her good hand. Even that hand was shrivelling; it looked like the hand of an old woman. She raised the apple to her lips. Was this the fruit? Was this the sweetest meat?

I will feast upon you... I will feast upon your sweet meat...

The words echoed in her mind, and Lyana gasped. She had heard this before! She had hung in cobwebs in Nedath's lair. The great demon had bitten her shoulder, wrapped her webs around her, and whispered and cackled in her ear. *You will be my sweet meat, child, I will feed upon you....*

"It's the Shrivels!" she shouted. She turned toward them, trembling. "It's not the food. Those are just lesser treats. This is Nedath's Feast, and she eats what lies on the chairs, not the table."

She stepped toward one seat, where lay a Shrivel with hairy tufts on its hanging skin. Her right foot pulled out from her boot, skin and bones twisting and rotting, and Lyana fell to the floor. She reached out her right arm, which was now thin as a twig, and grabbed the Shrivel on the seat. She pulled it down to the floor, like pulling down a wet cloth. Ignoring the nausea that twisted her belly, she bit into the creature.

It was stringy and cold, like biting into raw chicken skin. She forced herself to bite, though her teeth were loose, and she chewed, swallowed, bit some more.

"Lyana, don't!" Elethor cried, and she heard the terror in his voice, but she ignored him. She had to keep eating. She dug her teeth deeper, and liquid exploded in her mouth. The Shrivel flapped, screaming and squirming, and she kept biting and chewing, eating it alive.

It is the sweetest meat, she thought. *I am a huntress, a feeder, a creature of darkness, and--*

Starlight blazed.

Above her shone the Draco Constellation, the stars of Requiem, her homeland. Hot tears flowed down her cheeks, and she gasped, shook, blood on her fingers, blood on her lips.

I am a creature of starlight, she knew. *I am... I am Lyana! I am a knight of Requiem. I am a daughter, a sister, a warrior.*

She rose to her feet, the dead Shrivel hanging from her mouth. She spat it to the floor and cried for her betrothed.

"Elethor! Elethor, where are you?"

He ran toward her. He held her, shook her, touched her cheek. Tears filled his eyes.

"Lyana, I'm here! You're changing. You're healing. Can you see me, Lyana?"

She kept gasping for air, and the chamber swirled around her. She saw the hanging things move and laugh and swing, and Nedath's fangs, and that black hill with the black rose, but... she also saw marble columns rising from a forest of birches, and she heard harpists play, and she saw--

"Dragons!" she said, digging her fingers into Elethor's shoulders. "I see dragons, Elethor, herds of them. They fly over our home." She wept. "We are from Requiem. I am Lyana. You are Elethor. Don't forget that, *never* forget."

She trembled so violently, and he held her so tight, not letting her fall, not letting her forget herself, drown in that dark place.

"You are Lyana Eleison, daughter of Deramon and Adia," he said, stroking her hair. "You will not forget. You will see dragons again. We will return to Requiem." He held her tight. "We will return, and we will save our home, and we will destroy this place with fire." He kissed her forehead and touched her cheek. "You are healed, Lyana."

She turned to face the golden dishes and saw her reflection. Her red curls fell around her shoulders in a mane. Her skin was once more white, young, and strewn with freckles. Her limbs were strong again. She pulled her boots back on, lifted her sword, and marched toward the doorway.

"Let's go, Elethor," she said, her voice cold. "Back to the bodies outside."

She walked through the darkness. Soon she stepped back into the tunnel where bodies hung on meat hooks, snake eggs in their bellies. They howled and smacked their lips, drooling.

"Feed us!" they cried. "Feed us, child of starlight! You promised."

Lyana took several steps to where the tunnel widened, ten feet between the walls. It would be a tight squeeze, but Lyana narrowed her eyes. She would do this.

"Stand behind me, Elethor," she said softly. She pushed him behind her. "Go farther back. Fifty steps. Go."

"Lyana, are you sure?" he said, and from the softness in his voice, she knew that he understood.

She nodded and looked into his eyes. She saw something new there, something she had never seen when he looked upon her: warmth, caring... even love. It made her eyes sting, and she couldn't help it. As the bodies shrieked around them, she touched his cheek and kissed his lips.

"I'm sure, El," she whispered. "I'll do this. Now go."

He nodded and walked down the tunnel into the darkness. The bodies lined the tunnel in front of Lyana, screaming on their hooks, thrashing their limbs.

"Feed us ourselves!" they demanded. Some began to eat their own limbs, coating their teeth with blood. The eggs inside them squirmed. "You promised! You promised!"

Lyana took a deep breath, lay down on her stomach... and shifted into a dragon.

Wings burst from her back and slammed against the tunnel ceiling. She pulled them close to her body. That body grew scales and ballooned until it pushed against the tunnel walls. Her tail flapped behind her. Fangs grew from her mouth, fire filled her maw, and with a howl, she shot a stream of flame.

The jet blasted the bodies. They screeched. The tunnel shook and rocks fell from the ceiling. They screamed and screamed as they burned, and the eggs inside them popped, and small snakes fled only to burn too. Lyana could not believe how long they screamed. They screamed as their flesh charred, until nothing was left but bones, and still they screamed and thrashed. She thought that they would never die, and she blew all the fire inside her, until finally their screams faded to whimpers.

"You promised," the charred remains begged. "You promised to feed us. You are cursed, daughter of Requiem! Your kingdom is cursed! We will seek our vengeance. Your land will turn to our darkness! We will find your kingdom and we will twist it!"

With a last howl, their bones shattered, and they fell to black dust.

Lyana crawled forward, craned her neck around, and blew flames through the doorway. The dragonfire crackled into the white banquet room. Inside, the Shrivels screeched, voices high and twisting.

"She burns us!" they called. "Black! Pain! She turns the screws, skeleys. She counts the pain. Count the hairs that burn sideways, Withered Ones!"

A few Shrivels came crawling from the room. They squirmed until the fire consumed them and they collapsed. They lay as crisp, blackened things, stared up with melting eyes, then crumbled to ash.

Lyana let her fire die, and silence filled the tunnels.

She shifted back into a human. She lay in the ash, shaking, smoke rising around her. Elethor rushed toward her, helped her up, and she embraced him. She stood for long moments, her head against his shoulder, his arms around her.

"Elethor," she said softly.

He pushed back a curl of her hair. "Lyana."

She swallowed and stared at him. "It's time to find that Starlit Demon. I want to leave this place."

He nodded. They walked into the darkness, swords raised, smoke curling around their boots.

ADIA

She tried to run past her husband's soldiers. They held her--broad men in armor, their eyes hard. She tried to push them aside, but they stood firm.

"Let me through!" she demanded, glaring at them. "I am High Priestess of Requiem, and I command you move aside."

Adia was a tall woman, and she knew that men often whispered of her stern eyes, her cold face, her commanding voice that could wither flowers. Yet none of that held sway in these tunnels, as men clashed and cried and died ahead in the darkness. She looked over the men's shoulders and saw their comrades pile rocks and wood, sealing the chambers above--the library, the wine cellar that had become their war room, the armory where Solina had burned all those Adia had labored to heal.

"I'm sorry, Mother Adia," one of the soldiers said, eyes lowered. "Your lord husband commands it. The upper tunnels have fallen, from the library to the armory."

"It is no longer an armory!" Adia said. "It ceased being an armory once you donned your armor, and once we started moving the wounded in. It's a hospital now, and I'm a healer, and you will let me through."

She was about to shove them again when she felt a hand on her shoulder. She spun around, glaring, to see her husband. Dust covered Deramon, painting him gray. Blood trickled from a wound on his shoulder, thick with dirt. Dents and scratches covered his armor, and welts ran down his cheek.

"The upper chambers have fallen," he said, voice low and gruff, but tinged with softness. "They're dead, Adia. They're gone."

She spun back to the soldiers, then back again to Deramon, and felt close to panic. She forced herself to stand still, to take deep breaths, to ease the hammering of her heart. Her eyes stung and her belly felt so cold and heavy, as if ice filled it.

I swore to heal them, she thought. *They depended on me. I shouldn't have left them. I shouldn't have gone to sleep while they burned. Now the hurt are gone, while I, the healer, linger.*

She turned and faced the other direction, staring into the darkness. Survivors huddled before her, lining the walls. There were so few of them. So many had not managed to escape the upper chambers. From behind her, she heard the cries of the Tirans, clashing steel, and a scream. A voice cried out the words of Requiem--"May our wings forever find your sky!"--torn with pain.

"There are still Vir Requis alive up there," she whispered, a tremble running through her.

Deramon nodded, grim. "They're beyond our help now."

The voice behind her rose in a scream--a cry of more anguish than Adia had ever heard, even in her hospital.

"They're torturing our men," she whispered.

Deramon held her shoulder and began leading her away. "We can no longer help them, only pray. Come with me, Adia."

How could she just leave this place? How could she abandon those Vir Requis who still lived beyond the line of battle, cut and broken and tortured by Tiran steel? And yet she walked, head raised, eyes staring ahead. She would pray for those still left behind... pray that death found them quickly.

They walked deeper into darkness and found a corner to huddle in. She sat on the cold ground, Deramon's great arms holding her, and Adia closed her eyes. She could still hear the screams, even down here, and she clenched her jaw so tight, her teeth ached.

Did her children scream like this too? Had the phoenixes caught Bayrin, her firstborn, the son she loved with all her heart? Did the terrors of the Abyss now torture her daughter, the brave and beautiful Lyana, the light of her life? Would her children leave her like Noela?

I should not have let them go! Adia thought, fingernails digging into her palms. *I should never have let them leave me! They need me now. They need me to protect them.*

"Mother Adia," spoke a soft voice. "Mother Adia, I beg you. My wife, she's... she's giving birth, and... the midwife is in the upper chambers. Please, Mother, can you help?"

Still held in Deramon's arms, Adia opened her eyes. She saw a young man with a wide, pale face. Sweat soaked him and his left arm was wrapped in bloody bandages. Adia stared at him in silence, and for a moment she only thought: *What of my children? What of those I gave birth to? Leave me. Your child will die with the rest of them.*

She wanted him to leave, and she hated herself for it, and her thoughts scared her more than anything in this darkness.

She rose to her feet.

"Lead me to her," she said. She was still Mother of Requiem, and all the survivors were her children. She would protect them, heal them, comfort them... until the fire consumed them all.

BAYRIN

Dawn rose cold and bleak. Bayrin lay under his cloak, his head on a rolled-up blanket. Mori lay at his side, her cheek upon her hands. She still slept, face pale in the dawn, her hair spread out like a halo. Even in sleep, she seemed fearful; her lips were scrunched, her eyelids were closed tight, and she occasionally winced. Bayrin lay watching her as the sun rose. Her thigh pressed against him, a hint of warmth in the icy forest.

"No, please," she whispered in her sleep, and her legs kicked. "Please, Solina, please, please don't."

Bayrin sighed. He raised his hand, hesitated for a moment, then stroked her hair. It felt soft and smooth, like running his hand over silk. She calmed, her face smoothed, and her breathing deepened.

A deep anger filled Bayrin as he watched her. She was only a thin, pale thing, the last petal of a flower in snow. Bayrin knew of the shame she carried. She had spoken in her sleep of that night, begging for Acribus to release her, begging for the stars to forgive her for her shame.

She's only a child, he thought. *Eighteen years old, but so much younger in spirit. How could anyone have done this to her?*

With a pain like a dagger in his gut, Bayrin regretted all those years he had taunted Mori, all those times he'd mock her extra finger, tug her hair, and joke of her tears and trembles. It had been easy to roll his eyes at Mori back in Nova Vita, when walls and guards surrounded them, when wars were merely the words of old stories. Here in the wilderness, the phoenix on their trail, he felt ashamed. Careful not to wake her, he kissed her pale cheek. It was cold against his lips.

She mumbled and her brow furrowed.

"Mmmm... Bayrin?" She opened her eyes and blinked. "Did I kick you?"

"You damned near cracked my ribs," he said. "Horse kicks are weaker than yours."

She blinked and kicked his leg. "How's that?"

He feigned a look of pain and let out a long, exaggerated groan. "Oww... my bones are shattered!"

When she smiled sheepishly, eyes lowered, Bayrin couldn't help but feel warmth inside him, like butter melting.

You are my princess, he thought. *I might only be a lowly guard, the lesser son of a great house, but I will serve you as best I can.*

They rose in the cold morning, breath frosting before them, and wrapped themselves in their cloaks. Snow filled Bayrin's hair and his boots were soggy. Clouds glided across the sky and flurries fell. In their packs they found only some bread, cheese, and dried fruit. They shared the breakfast, eating with numb fingers.

"Mori," he said, "we should fly today."

She bit her lip and shook her head silently.

"It's been two days since we saw the phoenix," Bayrin continued. "If he's still hunting us, he's hunting us leagues away. We should shift into dragons and fly to the sea. It still lies hundreds of leagues away; walking is too slow."

She lowered her head, and a tear ran down her cheek. "But Bayrin, if we fly, he'll *see* us. I know it." She raised her eyes; they glimmered with tears. "Can't we walk for just another day, to be sure he's gone?"

Bayrin placed an awkward hand on her shoulder. "Mori, Requiem needs us. My sister needs us. Your brother needs us. Solina is still attacking them, and if we can't bring the Moondisk back soon, more will die. We can't dally any longer."

She hugged herself. "But... but what if he *sees* us, Bayrin? What if he's flying up there? We're little as humans. But dragons are too large, our scales are too bright, and..."

"We'll have to take that risk. For Requiem. We'll have to be brave. We'll be brave together, all right? I know you can do this."

She looked at her feet, trembling, then looked up at him again. Her eyes were so large, so haunted, so full of pain, that Bayrin felt his chest twinge. Without breaking her stare, she shifted.

Wings sprouted from her back, a pale gold like honey. Scales clanked across her, fangs and claws sprouted from her, and soon she stood before him, thirty feet long, a golden dragon with sad eyes. Bayrin shifted too and stood before her, a long green dragon, fifty feet from snout to tail's tip. Snow fell around them, their breath plumed, and their scales frosted.

They leaped, scattering snow, and flapped their wings. With a shower of twigs and snow, they crashed through the treetops into the sky. Snow flurried and wind howled in Bayrin's ears. Their wings thudded, bending the trees, and they soared until they flew among the clouds. Hidden among them, they leveled off and dived north. Wind and snow flowed around them.

As they flew, Bayrin kept looking around him, seeking phoenix fire. Once he thought he saw the beast, and his heart leaped, but it was only the sun glowing dimly through the clouds.

He's leagues away, he told himself. *Stars, I hope we never see that bastard again.*

They flew for several leagues before the clouds parted, revealing a rolling landscape. Cliffs and mountains rose like battlements, their eastern facades gilded with sunlight, their western slopes melting into mist and purple shadow. Evergreens rose tall and frosted, and a frozen lake glimmered like beaten silver. Herds of deer swept across valleys, while eagles soared from mountainous nests. The two dragons' shadows raced across the land. Even this high up, the smells of pine filled Bayrin's nostrils.

He saw no towns, no farms, no sign of civilization. Mori was better at maps, but Bayrin thought they flew beyond the Old Kingdom's borders, heading toward the distant Terius Bay. This was a cold hinterland north of Requiem, west of the fallen kingdom of Fidelium, and east of the mythical land of Salvandos. Few bards ever sang of these lands. Few scrolls told their tales. In most maps, they were empty spaces of canvas. It was a realm untouched by man or dragon, wild and beautiful.

As he flew, Mori at his side, his thoughts kept returning to Requiem, to his family and friends. While he flew here, the cold air in his nostrils, they huddled underground. While he fled one phoenix, they fought an army. Suddenly he wished Elethor had not chosen him for this task. He was no explorer, no hero, no warrior. He should be back home, helping his family and friends. Even if he couldn't fight well, he could still comfort them, make them laugh, bring some light to the darkness. But here... was he truly helping Requiem here? Was there truly a Moondisk beyond mountain and sea, or did Elethor merely send him here to spare his life, to save the princess from death underground? Bayrin didn't know. If all should die and he lived, the shame would be too great to bear, he thought.

They should have sent my sister. Lyana would know where to fly, what to do, how to fight. They should have sent my father; he's a great warrior and would have killed Acribus in the fort. They should have sent my mother; she's a healer, and could have healed the pain inside of Mori. But they sent me... Bayrin. A lowly guard. A jokester. A fool. Why should they fight and die, while I flee over wild country?

He ground his teeth. He had to believe. He had to find this Moondisk, if it truly existed, or die seeking it. He would not be a coward, hiding beyond map and measure as his kingdom fell.

"We will return, Requiem," he whispered into the wind. "Fight. Stay alive. We will bring aid."

Mori looked at him, wings churning the clouds, smoke seeping from her nostrils. He could see the same thought in her eyes.

They glided over mountain and forest. In the afternoon, they spotted goats upon a mountain and swooped to hunt. They flew again with bellies full, soaring over an icy lake, a frozen waterfall, and cliffs bristly with pines. At night they slept as dragons, curled up in the snow, coiled together for warmth. At dawn they flew again, frost on their scales, blowing fire to warm them.

For three days they flew--over ancient forests, plains of snow, and mountains that rose around them as jagged walls. On the fourth morning, the sun cold in an iron sky, they saw Terius Sea ahead.

It stretched beyond Bayrin's sight, curving to span the horizon. Lines of foam ran across it. The water was deep iron, stained cobalt where hidden valleys plunged. Jagged boulders rose from the depths like the hands of drowning gods. Bayrin had once flown east to Altus Mare, a port city in the kingdom of Osanna. There the waters had been green and bright, but here they spread like oil, dark and foreboding. He hovered before the sea, wings flapping.

"I'm scared," Mori said, flying beside him. There was no wind, and he could hear her words clearly, even above the thud of their wings.

He gestured with his head toward the rocky beach, snorted a blast of fire, and spiraled down. Soon he felt the spray of crashing waves. He filled his wings with air, reached out his claws, and landed, smoke rising from between his teeth. Mori landed beside him, claws nearly silent against the rocks, and folded her wings. The sea grumbled before them, spraying them with salt.

"Mori," he said, "you used to love books of maps. How far is the Crescent Isle from this shore?"

She stared into the sea. "Hundreds of leagues," she said. "A distance as wide as Requiem. But... those maps are very old, and the Crescent Isle appears only in ancient myths. I don't know what the true distance is." Her claws dug into pebbles. "Maybe the island doesn't exist at all."

Bayrin shot a jet of flame over the waves. Was this a fool's errand? They could perhaps navigate by the stars--he knew some of the skill--but how far could they possibly fly at once? Fifty leagues? A hundred? Soon or later, they would need rest. What if they found no island; were they doomed to drown?

Despite his earlier vows of heroism, he was tempted to turn around, find a quiet forest, and spend the rest of his days there with Mori. They could live forever here in the hinterlands, far from any phoenix or war. They would hunt goats, and sleep in their cloaks, and Mori would kick him at night, and he would smooth her hair, and kiss her cheek, and never have to feel like a failure again, the lowly son of a great father.

So don't act like a lowly son, whispered a voice in his head. *All your life, you've watched men praise your father, worship your mother, admire your sister for her courage and knighthood. So you would mock them, and run off with Elethor to alehouses, and forget the world. But now Requiem needs you--not the great Lord Deramon, or the beloved priestess Adia, or the brave knight Lyana, but you... Bayrin. Now is your time to be the hero.*

Bayrin didn't know who spoke to him. Was it a part of his own mind? The stars of Requiem? Was it the voice of Elethor, his best friend and now his king?

"Bay, are you all right?" Mori asked. She touched him with her snout, her breath warm against his scales.

He shrugged his wings. "I could use a ship. And a night's rest in a soft bed. And some tavern wenches with big eyes and bigger mugs of ale. But otherwise I'm fine. Are you ready for the longest flight of your life?"

She lowered her head and whispered. "I flew from Castellum Luna in the south to Nova Vita, and it took me two days with no rest." She raised her head and stared at him, her eyes haunted with the death of her brother, the death of her father, and her own tragedy. "I am ready to fly as far as it takes."

Bayrin briefly considered waiting, resting, spending the day here on the beach, then flying tomorrow. But Solina would not wait; she would be slaughtering his people as he stood here on the shore. With a blast of fire, he kicked off the beach, his wings flapped, and he soared into the sky.

Mori flew beside him and they streamed forward, shooting so low the sea sprayed their bellies. Their reflections raced along the water beneath them, and Bayrin saw the shapes of submerged boulders, valleys, and hills. When he looked behind him, he could see distant forests under mist. Soon they too were gone, and they flew over endless water.

The sea stretched into the horizon, cold and cruel as a grave.

ELETHOR

He flew, a brass dragon with white claws, wings roiling ash, flames trickling from his mouth like the tails of comets. Lyana flew at his side, squinting. The sea of lava below painted her blue scales a deep purple. The liquid fire gurgled, whirled, and shot up fountains. The dragons flew side to side, dodging them. A stone ceiling rose above them, embedded with countless skulls of dragons, spiders nesting in the eye sockets.

"We must be close now!" Lyana cried, voice dim under the roar of lava and wind. "In the books of Requiem, the Abyss is said to end where rock turns to fire. We will find the Starlit Demon here."

Elethor was less hopeful. They had been flying for hours-- since the tunnels had given way to this sea of fire. He had seen no sign of a demon, no sign of life but for the spiders that crawled in the skulls. This place could be vast, larger than the world aboveground. And yet what other hope did they have? And so he flew, wings aching, the heat baking his belly, the smoke stinging his lungs.

A fountain of lava gushed from the sea. Elethor cursed, banked, and knocked into Lyana. They tumbled aside, nearly hit the burning sea, and soared. The stream of liquid fire crashed into the ceiling and boulders fell. One knocked Elethor's tail, and he shouted a curse but kept flying. Drops of lava fell like rain.

"Are you all right?" he asked Lyana.

She nodded, but weariness filled her eyes, and a burn spread across her wing.

Damn this place, Elethor thought. His tail ached and droplets of lava sizzled on his wings. He was tired, so tired that he could barely flap his wings, barely breathe the smoky air.

"I see a rock ahead!" he shouted to Lyana. "Let's rest for a bit."

The boulder rose from the lava, fifty feet tall, black and craggy. Elethor flew toward it, narrowly dodging another shower of lava. He landed on the rock with a grunt, claws clacking against stone. Lyana landed beside him.

Elethor perched upon the rock, tail curled around it, as fire rained from the stone ceiling like falling fireflies. Lyana lay beside him, her head against his neck, and he folded his wing over her. He dared not return to human form, not as lava still boiled around him, spreading for leagues.

"Are you all right?" he asked Lyana, voice soft.

She nodded, smoke rising from her nostrils. The firelight danced on her scales. "A few burns, that's all. I'll be fine."

"I don't mean the burns."

She looked up at him, eyes like sapphires the size of apples.

"I don't know," she whispered. She lowered her head and nestled against his neck. "I miss him, Elethor. I miss him all the time. I keep thinking how... if Orin were still alive, he'd know what to do. He'd rally the troops, tell me how to fight, and..." A tear streamed from her eye. "And I wouldn't feel so lost, so alone."

Her words dug into him, a shard of ice. *Orin would know what to do. Orin would fight. Orin would save us.* But how could he, Elethor, the younger son, the lesser prince--how could he inspire such love from his people... from Lyana? How could he be a good king to Requiem, and a good husband to Lyana, if he too felt so lost, so afraid?

"I miss him too," he said, voice cracking. "But... it's up to us now. We must know what to do, how to fight, how save our home. And we will, Lyana. We will save Requiem."

His words sounded trite to him. As a king, he would have to inspire, to lead, to galvanize. He wanted to sound as wise as the ancient leaders of Requiem from the stories--the legendary King Benedictus who fought the griffins, or the great Queen Gloriae who slew the tyrant Dies Irae, or Queen Lacrimosa who led Requiem in the Battle of King's Forest.

But I'm not like them, he thought. *I'm just a sculptor. And I still miss and love Solina, the very enemy who attacks us.*

Lyana nestled closer to him, her breath hot against his cheek.

"I... I think I now know how you felt," she whispered. "When Solina left, I mean. You loved her. And you lost her. The pain must have been so great, tearing inside you. I cannot think of greater pain." She lowered her eyes. "I'm sorry, Elethor. When Solina left, I was glad. I scolded you for loving her. I mocked you for your pain." Her eyes glistened with tears. "I'm sorry."

They huddled in darkness as lava gurgled around them, fire rained, and the stone walls shook and cracked. A fountain gushed by the boulder, nearly spraying them with lava, then crashed back into the sea. They huddled closer, scales clanking, and wrapped their wings around them as a tent.

"Yes," Elethor whispered. "I hurt when she left. And I hurt when she returned. I loved her for so long, it's hard to switch to hating her, even now, even when I know that she killed my father, my brother, and so many of our people. I... I hate myself for it, that I once kissed her, wanted to marry her, spent years pining for her." He closed his eyes. "I'm the one who should be sorry. You were right, Lyana. You were right all along about her, and about me."

How had he come to this place? A moon ago, he would never have thought it possible. Solina, the love of his life, was now his greatest enemy. Lyana, the girl who always scorned him, now huddled at his side, his betrothed and future queen consort. Requiem lay leagues above them, past tunnels of terrors he had never imagined could exist. His life seemed so mad now that his head spun, and he could only cling to this rock and to Lyana, and he felt lost.

"Come, Lyana," he finally said. "We'll fly again. Maybe we'll find the Crimson Archway today... and the Starlit Demon who's locked behind it."

They flew over the fire. They flew for hours through the great caverns of the Abyss, down tunnels where lava rushed, over great forests of bones, through chambers where smoke blinded them and the howls of ghosts filled the darkness. Finally, when their lungs burned and their wings could barely flap, they emerged from a tunnel into a great cavern the size of a city.

"Stars," Elethor whispered, feeling sickness rise inside him.

The cavern was a league wide and tall, carved of craggy rock. Pillars of stone stood like ribs, and rivers of lava coiled. A mountain rose in the chamber's center, pale pink and knobby. When Elethor squinted, he saw that the mountain was made of bodies--thousands of them, maybe millions, naked and interwoven.

"Who are they?" Lyana whispered, flying at his side.

Elethor didn't know. He saw the bodies of men, women, and children, skin pale and hairless, eyes staring, mouths gaping. Were they dead Vir Requis? Were they but a nightmare? Nausea rose inside him, and the stench of death filled his nostrils, spinning his head. Suddenly he was sure he would see his father and brother there, dead and naked, eyes staring. He gritted his teeth, forcing down his sickness.

"Look, El, on top of the mountain!" Lyana said.

An archway rose atop the mountain of bodies, carved of craggy stones. When they flew closer, Elethor saw that blood seeped from between the bricks, painting them red. Mist and shadows swirled inside the archway, casting black light, like a portal to a storm.

"The Crimson Archway," Elethor whispered. "The path to the Starlit Demon."

They flew up the mountain. Countless bodies lay below them, famished and limp like discarded chicken skins. Elethor narrowed his eyes and soared toward the archway. It looked just wide enough that, if he pulled his wings close, he could shoot through it. Whatever shadowy land it led to, and whatever enemy waited there, he would face it.

He was only seconds from flying through the archway when a creature rose from the pile of bodies.

At first, Elethor thought that the bodies themselves were rising upon the mountaintop. Then he realized that the creature had lain there all along, but was as naked, fleshy, and famished as the bodies. Fifty feet long, its skin hung loose on knobby bones. It had the body of a great cat, furless and starving. Its head was the head of a woman, but much larger, the size of a carriage. Her face was pale and stoic, her eyes golden and feline. Her torso, nude and stitched from collarbone to navel, rose to block the archway.

Elethor thrust his claws forward, beat his wings mightily, and slowed to hover in midair. He growled. Lyana flew and hovered by him, fire flickering between her teeth. Elethor's heart beat against his ribs.

"Who are you?" he demanded of the creature. "Name yourself."

The beast watched them, a soft smile on her lips. Her eyes glimmered gold, and a trickle of blood dripped from her pale lips.

"I am Herathia," she said, voice hissing like wind, "the Guardian of Crimson, the Sphinx of the Abyss, the Protector of the Starlit Demon. You cannot enter, King Elethor Aeternum of Requiem, Son of Olasar. The way is forbidden to you."

Elethor flapped his stiff wings, refusing to land upon the mountain of bodies. The thrusts of air sent the smallest bodies, mere babes, tumbling down the mountain.

"Stand aside, or we will burn you," he said to the sphinx. "The Starlit Demon is a servant of Requiem; you will not block our way to him."

The sphinx tilted her head. The stitches running up her torso shifted, and blood seeped from them, trickling between her breasts to her feline paws. She snarled, baring sharp teeth stained with blood. Human heads filled her mouth, rotting, faces twisting in anguish.

"The old kings of Requiem placed the Starlit Demon here, long before the griffins attacked your halls, before your ancestors raised columns of marble, back in the days when your people lived feral, digging underground for shelter and knowledge. It was as a behemoth, devouring all, bringing evil upon the world; its starlight seared flesh and its wrath tormented and broke the minds of those who fought it. I am the Guardian of Crimson! I protect the evil of the beast. I move for none, not even for the spawn of those who placed me here. Leave this place of shadow. Return to your land and leave the darkness to rustle below the earth you till."

Lyana growled deep in her throat. "I know of you, Herathia! You lie. You are a riddler. We keep scrolls of your trickery in Requiem. You guard the way with riddles. I've read of them."

The sphinx turned her feline eyes to the blue dragon. "Lyana Eleison, daughter of Deramon, I do not merely ask riddles. I *kill* with riddles. If I ask you my questions, you will fail to answer. You will die. You will join the bodies at my feet, a million souls who thought they could answer me. They now form my bed. Turn back, Lyana and Elethor. Leave this place and do not tempt me; my words are poison and will cost you your souls."

Elethor stared at the bodies in disgust, still not daring to land upon them. "Do you mean... you asked these people riddles?"

The sphinx nodded. One of her stitches tore, and pus dripped from her. "They failed to answer."

Elethor growled. He had no time for this. His people languished underground while Solina attacked; he could wait no longer. He let fire grow in his belly.

"They did not have dragonfire," he said, roared, and blew a jet of flame.

The fire spun and slammed against the sphinx. Lyana howled and added her fire to Elethor's. The inferno roared, white hot. The bodies on the mountaintop burned. The heat blazed against Elethor's eyes, blinding him. He kept spewing his fire, wings fanning it, as much as he could muster.

Finally, after long moments, the flames died.

The sphinx stood upon seared bodies, unharmed. The stitches along her torso had melted, revealing a gaping cavern full of severed hands. The skin around her wound, however, was as pale and sagging as before.

"Do you think mortal fire can burn me?" she asked. She narrowed her feline eyes, bared her teeth, and raised her claws.

Black lightning blazed from them. A bolt slammed into Lyana. She gasped and fell. A second bolt crashed against Elethor's chest, and pain suffused him. He opened his maw to roar, but found no breath. Agony spread across him, clutching at his throat, crushing his innards. The pain was so great, he lost his magic. His wings and scales vanished, and he thudded onto the mountain in human form. Black lightning raced across him, raising smoke, and finally he found his voice. He screamed in anguish. Lyana twisted on the bodies beside him, also back in human form, sparks twisting around her like serpents. She wept and screamed.

"Enough!" Elethor shouted, tears streaming down his cheeks, and with a flash, the lightning vanished. He doubled over, gasping for breath and trembling. Lyana coughed beside him, on hands and knees, head lowered and hair dangling in a red curtain. He crawled toward her over the bodies, his knees digging into their flesh, and raised a trembling hand to touch her hair.

"Lyana," he said, voice hoarse.

She coughed, struggled to her feet, and stood atop the bodies. Legs shaking, Elethor stood up beside her. The sphinx dwarfed their human forms. She towered over them, an implacable sentinel of bone and skin and stench. Her golden orbs, each the size of a human head, glimmered down at them.

"Turn back, children of starlight," the sphinx said, voice deep as the sky. "You will not pass my door."

"We will pass!" Lyana shouted up to her. "Ask us your riddles, Herathia, Crimson Guardian. We will answer them. We will not fail."

The sphinx bared her fangs. Blood rained from her mouth. "Very well. I will ask you my riddles. And you will ask me yours. We will take turns like the great riddle masters of old. If I cannot answer your riddles, I will let you pass." She licked the blood off her lips. "And if you cannot answer mine... your bodies will lie forever at my feet."

DERAMON

He stood, stiff and aching, and lowered his head. The smoke
stung his eyes and his gut felt colder than the heart of winter. His
men stood at his sides, staring at the ground. His wife stood
ahead, eyes raised, praying to the ceiling as if stars could still shine
upon them.

"May the Draco constellation bless their spirits. May their
souls find their way to our starlit halls."

Adia closed her eyes, whispered last words, and nodded.
Ten of Deramon's men began shoveling dirt into the ditch,
covering the dozens of bodies. They had dug this crevice into the
floor of a narrow, earthy tunnel, using makeshift shovels from
broken axes and helmets.

This is no proper burial for warriors of Requiem, Deramon
thought, jaw clenched. They deserved to be buried in a field of
grass and flowers, or burned in a pyre like the great warriors of
ancient days. Not this. He looked away, grimacing. And yet he
knew they had to bury them somehow, and fast. If they began to
rot, disease would spread, and more in these tunnels would die.

Adia sang softly as the dirt mounted, covering the bodies'
limbs, then torsos, leaving the faces for last. Deramon had seen
too many young men buried in his life, and they always buried the
faces last. A bitterness caught in his throat, half a laugh, half a
moan. *It's as if we hope that, as we shovel on the dirt, the dead might still
awake and cry for salvation.*

His throat constricted. *Noela was wrapped in a shroud when I
buried her,* he remembered. *At least I never had to see her face--the soft,
innocent face of a babe--covered in dirt.* It had been thirteen years since

his daughter's death, but the pain never lessened. If Noela truly waited among the stars, Deramon prayed that his fallen men would find her, protect her, and comfort her until the day they buried him too.

When the bodies were buried, Adia whispered, eyes damp. "As the leaves fall upon our marble tiles, as the breeze rustles the birches beyond our columns, as the sun gilds the mountains above our halls--know, young child of the woods, you are home, you are home. Requiem! May our wings forever find your sky."

Deramon mumbled the prayer with the rest of his men. Would they ever see sky again? He did not know. Did the souls of the fallen truly rise to the Draco constellation, dine in ghostly halls among the great kings of old? Deramon did not know that either. *When darkness surrounds you, belief in light comes hard.*

An image flashed through his mind, churning his gut: his eldest children lying dead in a mass grave, earth piling up upon them. Bayrin's face was pale, a gash running down his cheek. Lyana was as beautiful as ever, as beautiful as the day she'd been born. Finally earth would cover their faces too, leaving them to rot underground. Deramon gritted his teeth and clenched his fists, banishing the image.

They're still alive, he told himself. Bayrin was brave and clever; not as hardened as some guardsmen, but quick-witted, resourceful. He would know how to survive, how to protect the princess. Lyana was just as clever, and swift with the blade; if anyone could survive in the Abyss, that shadowy world beneath these tunnels, it was her.

Deramon rubbed his shoulder; it still blazed from where Solina had cut him. Worse was the shame of failing to kill her. *She was mine,* he thought, stomach roiling. He had only to swing his axe one more time, and he could have slain the Queen of Tiranor, ended this war, and sent the invaders fleeing. And yet he had failed. He had let her wound him, let her reach the armory, burn the wounded, claim the upper chambers. He lowered his head, eyes narrowed to slits.

"Deramon," came a soft voice. Adia approached and placed a hand on his shoulder. She stared at him, eyes soft. "You should rest. When is the last time you've slept?"

He sighed and held her hand. "Time? It has no meaning in the dark. It might have been a day, maybe three days, maybe a week." He turned away from her and nodded at two of his men. "Baras, Ilvar, follow. We will inspect the lines."

They walked through a narrow, clammy labyrinth. The tunnels were darker and rougher down here. In the upper levels, passageways were wide and sturdy, their floors cobbled, their walls smoothed, their ceilings held with columns. Up there, archways led into fine chambers: the library, the armory, the wine cellars, and more. All these had fallen to Solina. Here, in the deeper levels, only crude burrows wound. Some were natural caves. Others were abandoned mines where the ancients had dug for iron and gold. All were as cold and dark as wormholes.

His men lined the walls, holding spears and swords; most were bandaged, burnt, and bloody. Survivors sat and lay at their feet: frightened children, mothers holding babes, and old men and women who whispered and wept. Every Vir Requis over age thirteen now stood as a soldier, even those who'd never swung a sword. They bore the steel of their fallen comrades. As Deramon walked down the lines, inspecting them, they stared back with solemn, deep-set eyes. Many were mere youths--boys who had never shaved, kissed a girl, or dreamed of war.

So many gone, Deramon thought as they walked. Once, he had commanded a thousand men of the City Guard, warriors to defend Nova Vita. Two hundred of those men now stood here; the Tirans had killed the rest. Once, five thousand more warriors, King Olasar's Royal Army, had fought for Requiem; they had burned over King's Forest. Once, fifty knights had defended the realm; now only one remained, his daughter.

So many burnt. So many dead. Even if Bayrin finds the Moondisk, and even if Lyana wakes the Starlit Demon, how can we recover from such loss?

Soon Deramon turned around a bend and reached the barricade, a pile of boulders and pikes blocking the upper chambers. Fifty men stood here, clad in plate armor, swords drawn; they were as many as could fill this tunnel. Silence blanketed the darkness. No more screams rose from above.

Good, Deramon thought. *May our men who fell captive find some peace in death.*

"Garvon," he said to one of his captains--a gaunt man with one eye, a white beard, and a splintered shield. "How is the guard?"

The man bowed his head. A cut ran down his cheek, freshly stitched. "Quiet, my lord. The Tirans have made no attempt to break the barricade for hours. They're regrouping; many of them are wounded too."

"They will attack soon," Deramon said, voice hoarse. *Stars, if they have more of that dark magic that broke our first barricade, how will we hold back the tide?*

Garvon nodded, gripping his sword. "We are ready for them, my lord. We will hold them back. And if they break through, we will fight them in the tunnels and cut them down in darkness." He raised his chin. "The upper chambers are wide; they could burn us there. Here in the narrow depths, they will fall."

No, Deramon thought. *We cannot defeat them, even here. Not with so few men. Not against the wrath and fire of these southern demons.* They needed aid; Deramon knew that. They needed his children back.

Boots thumped behind him, running up from the deeper tunnels, and a man called out, "Lord Deramon!"

He turned to see Silas, a young soldier who had once guarded the eastern wing of Olasar's palace. Today half his face was burnt and bandaged, but he still carried a sword and shield. His eyes were wide and blood splashed his dented armor.

"What is it, Silas?" said Deramon. "Speak."

The young soldier reached him and bowed his head. "My lord Deramon, men are fighting at the silo. One stabbed another. Others are trying to grab the sacks of grain."

Deramon began marching at once, fists clenched. Silas followed. What guards lined the walls stood at attention, chins raised, hands grasping swords and spears.

Children of Requiem squabbling over grain like hens, Deramon thought in disgust. *I will have them flayed.* His anger bubbled in him. His king had fallen. The new Boy King had plunged into darkness. He, Deramon Eleison, was caretaker of Requiem now, an ancient and proud kingdom. He would not let it descend into madness on his watch.

He marched down sloping, twisting tunnels like the veins of a stone giant. Soon he reached the lower silos. The main pantries were higher up, in the chambers Solina had claimed; there Requiem stored its dried fruit, vegetables, smoked meats, salted fish, barley, and sacks of golden grain. Here in the depths was only what grain the upper chambers could not hold--a meager supply that Deramon doubted could feed the survivors for a moon. Ten guards stood at the silo's gateway, holding back a crowd of men who were trying to push through. One man lay dead in the corner, a knife in his heart.

"My daughter is starving to death!" a man was shouting, shoving a guard. "Starving! She has not eaten in three days. She is only four years old. How could you stand here like this, letting us die?"

Another man began shoving a second guard. "There is grain behind you! You are a man of Requiem, or do you serve the Tirans? Let us through."

The guards were scowling and shoving the men back. "The grain is rationed. Your children are not starving; they received grain like everyone else."

The first man had tears on his cheeks. "What grain? She hasn't eaten in three days! Where are these rations? Not all received them." He grabbed the guard's spear and tried to wrench it free. "I will hand out the grain."

Deramon stormed toward them, howling. "Cease this!"

His guards bowed their heads. The men who'd tried to break through cried of hunger, of famished children, of youths eating double rations, leaving others to starve. Deramon listened and scowled. He was a fighter; he knew how to kill an enemy with steel, claw, and dragonfire. Hunger was a foe he had never known, and it might be the foe that slew them here.

How long before this grain is gone? How long until we turn to eating one another? Two moons? One?

"Silas," he said to his guard, "organize another round of rations--one cup of grain per person. Take what men you need to make sure everyone eats. If you see anyone eating double rations, depriving another of food, I want them clamped in irons and brought before me."

Silas bowed. "Yes, my lord."

Sacks of grain were opened and gourds being filled when shouts rose from the tunnels behind. Steel clanged and cries echoed. A soldier came racing from around the corner, face red.

"My lord Deramon! Tirans are breaking through the barricade. They have a battering ram."

Deramon cursed, drew his sword, and ran. His soldiers ran with him. He raced up the tunnels, heart hammering.

Maybe it won't be hunger that kills us after all, he thought. He rounded a corner and beheld the barricade collapsing, sending boulders tumbling and dust flying. Through the wreckage, he glimpsed a battering ram slam into the rocks. Tiran troops stood around it, blades drawn and eyes full of bloodlust.

It is a blessing, Deramon thought and snarled. *We'll die of steel and fire. We'll go down fighting after all.*

A dozen Tiran troops broke through the wreckage, leaped over the boulders, and ran toward him. Deramon howled, swung his sword, and leaped into battle.

MORI

Her pain had faded into a daze. Her wings blazed with agony; she knew that, but could barely feel it. Her lungs burned, her muscles cramped, her heart thudded. The agony drove through her, but exhaustion drowned it like a gag muffling screams. She and Bayrin had been flying for a day and a night. Dawn rose around her, and still she saw no island, only endless leagues of sea.

She wanted to ask Bayrin how he was, but could find no breath. He flew by her, tongue lolling. Her wings felt like they could fall off. She could almost imagine it--one more flap, and they'd disconnect like sails torn from a ship, fly alone into the horizon, and she would tumble. Despite herself she laughed weakly.

"Bayrin," she managed. "Let's... let's swim for a while."

If she could no longer fly, perhaps she could swim, let her wings rest and her legs propel her onward. She began spiraling down, wings billowing, the smell of salt in her nostrils. When she reached the water, she nearly crashed into it. It stung her belly, ice cold, shocking her. She lost her breath and wanted to take flight again, but could not. Her wings hurt too much. Lashing her tail, she managed to flip onto her back, stretch out her wings, and float.

Bayrin spiraled down above her. He crashed into the water by her side, howled, and cursed.

"Stars, this water's cold!" He flipped onto his back and floated beside her. He panted, smoke rising between his teeth. "Gone is the hope for any future little Bayrins."

Mori smiled wanly, not sure she understood the jest, but thankful that Bayrin's spirit was high enough to attempt one. Though she shivered in the water, she was thankful for a break from flight; her wings cramped and blazed in pain. She lay upon the water, watching the clouds roil. They formed gray and blue shapes like swooping dragons which soon began to weep. The sleet pattered against her belly. Suddenly she found that she too was weeping.

"Mori!" Bayrin said. "I know you were hoping for little Bayrins, but... what's wrong?"

What was wrong? How could he ask that? Her world had fallen. Orin was dead and so was Father. Her city lay in ruin, Elethor was in the Abyss, and she lay here, a dirty and impure thing, floating in a sea that could never wash her shame. She wept for her fallen brother and father, for her soul that too felt dead. But how could she tell Bayrin that? How could she speak to anyone of the twisting guilt, grief, and agony inside her? How could she tell them that she still saw Orin's eyes, lifeless, staring at her from his burnt face as Acribus choked her?

Instead she only said, "Bayrin... I want to go home."

He sighed and his eyes softened. He reached out his wing and touched her shoulder.

"We will go home," he promised. "We'll fly over Requiem again, Mori. You and I, and Elethor and Lyana. We'll hunt in King's Forest, stargaze from Lacrimosa Hill, and lie in the palace gardens and watch the birds. We'll sit by the fireplace in Alin's Alehouse, drink sweet ice wine, and listen to minstrels play. You'll read your books with maps, and Elethor will whittle those little wooden animals of his, do you remember them? We will rebuild our city. We will go home again."

But was there a home? she wondered. Was there still a forest, and a garden, and an alehouse, or had they burned? Was there still a city to rebuild, or mere piles of ash and bodies? Did

Elethor and Lyana lie dead underground, or twisted by black magic?

"I have to believe," she whispered. "Or otherwise let the sea claim me." She stared into Bayrin's eyes. "We will find the Moondisk. We have to."

Or else all this pain, this death, was for nothing.

Bayrin opened his mouth, as if about to speak, when suddenly his eyes widened. A cry of pain tore from his maw.

"Bayrin!" Mori cried.

He kicked and floundered. His wings fluttered, spilling water, and he rose from the sea.

Mori screamed.

A twisting lamprey clung to Bayrin's back, its mouth locked onto his scales. The creature looked like a great, writhing worm, tall and wide as an oak. Its tail lashed in the water. Hovering above the water, Bayrin tried to soar. His wings fanned the sea, sending ripples across it, but he was upside down, legs kicking uselessly at the air. He could not rise. The lamprey tugged, holding him down like a chain.

"Get it off!" Bayrin cried.

Mori flipped onto her belly, craned her neck forward, and blew fire.

The jet slammed against the lamprey, roaring hot. The creature opened its mouth, detaching itself from Bayrin, and screamed. Its mouth was a perfect circle, a foot in diameter, and ringed with several rows of teeth. Blood filled it.

Bayrin soared, teeth marks on his back. Below, the burnt lamprey crashed into the water and began swimming toward Mori.

Heart pounding, she leaped from the water, wings flapping. Waves rippled. She soared, dripping wet, and the lamprey leaped, soaring after her. It was massive--easily the length of her tail--its body slick and undulating. Its mouth opened wide. Wings thudding madly, Mori screamed, swiped her tail, and knocked it aside. It crashed into the water, writhing and screeching.

"What the stars was that?" Bayrin shouted, blood on his scales. He looked from side to side, as if seeking it.

Water rose in curtains. Two lampreys leaped from the sea and flew toward them. They had no wings, but they soared as if shot from geysers. Their maws opened wide, and their teeth glimmered.

Mori screamed and blew fire at one. The other slammed against her tail, and its teeth sank into her flesh. She cried in pain, lashed her tail, and began to fall. It tugged her down--she could barely believe its weight. She flapped her wings madly, struggling to rise.

"Bayrin!"

He swooped, leveled off, and shot forward. His flames baked the creature. It screeched and fell.

Three lampreys leaped from the sea.

Mori shouted, batted one aside with her tail, and flew high. A lamprey shot up to her right, dripping water and screeching. She flamed it and kept soaring, and soon the sea was distant below her. Ten more lampreys leaped from the water, and Mori was sure that she flew high enough. But the lampreys kept flying upward, as if they were mere fountains of water. Their mouths opened wide.

Bayrin blew fire at one. Mori blasted her flames at another. One flew up directly beneath her, mouth wide, tongue reaching out. She swerved, and the lamprey knocked against her side, mouth sucking the air. She tumbled, flapped her wings, and knocked into another lamprey. She clawed at it, beat it back, and flew higher.

"Bayrin, higher!" she shouted.

They climbed the sky. Soon they flew so high, the waves were mere ripples, and the air was cold and thin. When the lampreys crashed back into the sea below, they seemed small as earthworms. Mori blew out her breath in relief.

"Bayrin," she said, "you're hurt, I--"

Screeches rose below. She looked down to see a hundred lampreys, maybe more, shoot up from the water. *They must be mad,* she thought. *We're hundreds of feet in the air.*

And yet they kept soaring, tails flapping, propelling themselves through the air as if swimming underwater. Mori growled and flew even higher, but the lampreys were faster. Soon they were feet away, and she bathed them with fire. They kept shooting up, aflame. Several shot around her, so fast that she felt the whoosh of air. Another slammed into her belly, and she shouted, clawed at it, and knocked it off.

The lampreys who overshot her turned in midair and began to fall. One slammed onto her back, its teeth dug into her shoulder, and she screamed.

A growl pierced the air. Bayrin swooped, a lamprey clinging to his tail, and slashed his claws. He dug into the lamprey on Mori's back, and when it opened its mouth to screech, it detached from her flesh and fell.

"Bay!" Mori cried and blew flame, hitting the lamprey that tugged on his tail. It burned, writhed madly, and tumbled.

Dozens more came shooting up from the sea.

"Damn it!" Bayrin said. "These things could probably fly to the stars themselves. If flying up won't stop them, fly north! Come on!"

The lampreys soon soared around them, mouths sucking air, tongues seeking. The dragons flew forward on the wind, blasting fire at the creatures. They seemed endless. Whenever one crashed back into the water, three more shot up. The wounds on Mori's shoulder blazed; the lamprey's teeth had chipped her scales and dug down to the flesh. Blood trickled from her leg. She blew fire in all directions, but soon her flames dwindled to mere sparks; she would need rest and food to replenish them, and she would find neither in this sea.

"Mori, look, ahead!" Bayrin shouted. He slammed a lamprey with his tail and clawed another.

Mori stared ahead and gasped. Her heart leaped. Tears sprang into her eyes, and she howled.

"The island! The Crescent Isle!"

It still lay leagues away, but her eyes were sharp, and she knew this was the place. Green and misty, it formed the shape of a crescent moon. From here, it seemed as small and distant as the moon itself. She had never felt such hope, such joy and relief. Her body shook with it. She blazed toward her salvation.

A volley of lampreys flew at her. Several slammed into her belly, knocking her into a spin. Teeth dug into her. For a moment she saw only spinning sky and clouds.

She clawed the lamprey on her belly, but it wouldn't release her. More of the beasts flew around her, mouths peeling back, revealing their many teeth. They leaped from all sides, flew in arcs, and rained above her. One more slammed into her side and bit. Soon they were sucking her blood as she screamed.

"Bayrin!"

Three of the beasts clung to him, writhing as they fed. Bayrin howled. He tried to roast them with fire, but only sparks left his maw; he too was too tired, too famished, too weak. He clawed at the beasts, and one fell, but two others slammed into him and bit.

"Fly, Mori, to the island!"

She coughed and gasped for breath. Two lampreys clung to her, and dozens more leaped all around. She lashed her claws and tail, knocking them aside. She couldn't even claw the ones attached to her without letting ten more bite.

"Mori, fly!"

She flew. Her wings blazed. She howled in pain. She shot forward, dipping, rising again, tumbling. She managed to slash the lamprey on her belly, and it fell, but two more leaped. One attached its maw onto her leg, and the other replaced the one on her belly. She screamed and clawed but kept flying.

She dipped. Soon she flew a hundred feet over the water, then fifty. The lampreys kept tugging her down, drinking her blood, and she howled as she flew.

Please, stars, give me strength, let me reach the land alive.

She did not know how long she flew. Minutes seemed like hours. Her eyes blurred. She could barely hear Bayrin roar at her side, barely see him. Mist swirled around her. Pines rose ahead.

The island.

It lay a league away, maybe closer, its trees towering, dark green columns rising from fog. She flapped her wings with every last drop of her strength. Just to reach that island. Just to land. To rest. To sleep.

A lamprey leaped from the water, slammed into her, and bit her neck.

Her eyes rolled back, she tumbled, and icy water crashed around her.

Her head went under. Water filled her nostrils. She kicked, dazed, pain pounding through her. She screamed and bubbles rose around her, white orbs in the deep blue. Her blood rose like red ghosts. Weakly, she lashed her claws, pierced one lamprey, and saw ten more swim toward her.

Goodbye, Bayrin, she thought. *Goodbye, Requiem. I go now to the starlit halls... to Father and Mother. To Orin.*

Claws slashed. A tail swung. Fangs bit. Lampreys screeched and fled, and Bayrin grabbed her under her wings, pulled her up, and her head rose from the water. She gasped for air.

"Mori, fly! Fly, Mori, we're almost there. Fly!"

He tugged her, raising her from the water. Boulders jutted around them. A rocky beach rose ahead, appearing and disappearing as waves crashed. She flapped her wings once, rose from the water, flapped again. Pines rose ahead like the columns of Requiem. She growled and flew, a lamprey still on her shoulder. She knocked her feet against a boulder, flapped her wings again, and drove a dozen feet forward. She hit another boulder, flew again, leaped and soared and crashed onto a beach.

Bayrin landed beside her, three lampreys on his body. He thrashed and knocked them off. Mori leaped onto them and bit, digging her fangs into their flesh. They opened their bloody maws to screech, and the dragons scurried up the shore, coughing and hacking. Bayrin slammed his tail against the last lamprey clinging to Mori, and it too fell, wriggled down the beach, and disappeared back into the water.

The wet, wounded dragons pulled themselves forward, too weak to fly, until they crawled beneath the pines. There they crashed down upon fallen pine needles, panting, blood seeping.

"We made it," Mori whispered, staring up at mist that swirled between the evergreens. "We reached the Crescent Isle."

Bayrin coughed and smoke rose from his mouth. Their tails reached out, seeking each other, and braided together. Soft rain began to fall. Mori closed her eyes and slept.

SOLINA

She walked down the tunnel, sabres drawn, and entered the
library. Her lips peeled back in a smile.

The chamber was as she remembered. Its ceiling curved
high above, high enough that if she wanted, she could shift into a
phoenix here too, burn all the books and scrolls upon the shelves.
But she was no brute, no mindless killer. Unlike most of her men,
she knew how to read and write--both Old and Common Tiran,
the Dragontongue of Requiem, and the High Speech of eastern
Osanna. She knew that books held power--a power greater than
steel, as great as magic itself. She would empty these shelves. She
would take these books and scrolls back to the desert, place them
in her temples, and learn from their lore.

Requiem will remain bare of knowledge, she thought, *a wasteland of
skeletons and dried blood.*

"My queen!" said one of her men, a captain with a bloody
sunburst on his breastplate. He bowed before her, fist against his
chest. "The prisoners await your inspection."

She nodded curtly and walked deeper into the library. At
the back wall, twenty weredragons stood in chains. Solina snarled.
When she had lived in Requiem, the weredragons would taunt
her. They would shift into dragons, fly above, blow fire, and she
would watch from below, a scared and weak girl with no magic.
In chains, they were as helpless as she had been. They had been
stripped naked. Their bodies were lashed, bloody, and broken.
Three were men, supposed warriors; the rest were women and
children.

"Reptiles," she said to them, voice dripping with disgust.
"Look at you. Naked. Filthy. Weak." She laughed bitterly.

"You call yourself a noble race, an ancient and proud people." She spat. "I see only wretches."

A few of the weredragons stared back, defiance in their eyes. Others moaned, blood seeping from their wounds. The chains chafed their wrists and ankles, digging into the flesh. One, a girl no older than the princess Mori, was trying to shift. She grimaced, and scales appeared and disappeared on her body, and wings sprouted and vanished from her back. When her limbs began to grow, the chains dug deeper, shedding blood, keeping her in her filthy human form. Tears ran down her cheeks.

Solina approached the girl, a soft smile on her lips. "Precious," she said softly. "Do you still try to fight?"

The girl looked up with teary eyes, opened her mouth to speak, and Solina swung her sword. Raem, her blade of dawn, sliced the weredragon's neck as easily as a fisherman gutting his catch. Blood gushed, the girl gasped and choked, and her head slumped back. She lay still, blood spilling down her body to pool around her.

Solina grinned, teeth clenched, as the other weredragons howled.

Five years ago, this girl would have taunted me, she thought. *She would have shifted, soared in the sky, mocked my lack of magic. She would have burned me too, burned me like Orin did.* She snarled. *They all would burn me if they could.*

She ran her fingers along her line of fire, the scar that split her face and body. It still burned sometimes. She could still feel the screaming agony of fire. The rage and pain pounded through her, spinning her head. She turned to another chained weredragon, an old man with one eye, and she lashed her blade across his stomach. She stared with cold eyes as he screamed, as his innards spilled.

She turned to the next one. Her blades swung. She moved from weredragon to weredragon, ridding the world of their evil, banishing their shadow with her light.

"For the Sun God!" she cried as she plunged her blades into the last one, a child clinging to the corpse of his mother. "For your glory, Lord of Light! I banish the weredragon curse for you."

Blood washed the floor, rivers of it, intoxicating with its scent. Blood had splashed her face, Solina realized. She wiped it with her fingers and licked them eagerly.

Soon I will drink Elethor's blood too, she thought. *Soon we will meet again, my love.*

"Clean this mess," she said to her men. "If the blood dirties the books, I will replace the parchment with your hides."

She turned and left the library, grinning savagely, boots sloshing.

ELETHOR

He stood upon the mountain of bodies, still in human form, and faced the sphinx. Herathia's feline body rose taller than him, draped in wrinkly skin. Her torso and head towered, a pale woman as large as a dragon. The Crimson Archway rose above her, leading into shadow and mist.

"Ask us your riddles," Elethor said to her, heart pounding. He reached out and clasped Lyana's hand. She squeezed back.

Behind that archway waits the Starlit Demon, he thought. *Behind that archway is the hope for my people, for Lyana, for my sister. I must pass.*

He swallowed a lump in his throat, remembering the pain of the sphinx's curse. If he failed to answer her riddles, how long would she torment him before letting him die? A minute? Hours? Moons or years? Eventually he and Lyana would join these bodies, a new peak for the mountain of them, and Requiem would fall. Everybody he knew would die.

No, he told himself and drew sharp breaths. *Don't think about that now. You will answer the riddles. You will pass through the archway.*

The sphinx regarded him, a soft smile on her lips, as if she could read his mind. A trickle of blood ran from her lips and trailed down her body, snakelike. She opened her mouth, revealing bloody fangs and chewed human heads, and spoke in a deep voice like wind through tunnels.

"All love me with full hearts
They visit me by day
Yet they cry around me
At night they stay away"

Elethor raised his eyebrows, considering. He turned to look at Lyana. She stared at the sphinx, frowning, lips scrunched together. She turned and met his gaze, thought a moment, then nodded.

"Seems easy enough," she said.

Elethor couldn't help it. Even here, wounded and famished, leagues underground upon a pile of bodies, he rolled his eyes.

"Of course it's easy for you," he muttered. "Everything always is."

She glared at him, fire blazing in her green eyes. "If it were up to you, Elethor, I think we'd grow old trying to solve it." She turned to look up at the sphinx. "I have the answer!"

The towering creature gazed down upon them, stars glimmering in her feline eyes. Her tongue licked her lips. "Answer! But if you answer wrong, your souls will be my prize."

Elethor winced, remembering the pain of her black lightning.

"Lyana, wait," he began. "What are you--"

But she ignored him and called up to the sphinx, "The answer is: a beloved's grave."

Herathia's lips curled back, showing teeth and gums. Elethor's heart pounded as if trying to escape his chest, and his palms dampened. A beloved's grave? He wished Lyana had consulted with him first, but by the stars, the answer did fit.

"Well?" he demanded of the sphinx. "Is that the answer?"

She shifted her claws, each one as long as his body. They dug into the corpses she sat upon, tearing through the pale flesh into bloodless cavities. Her tongue darted out and a hiss left her throat, a sound like steam. She was laughing, Elethor realized.

"You have," she said, "answered correctly."

Elethor breathed out a shaky sigh of relief. His hands tingled and he turned to Lyana. She looked at him, gasping and smiling. She hesitated an instant, then stepped over a body and embraced him. She clung to him, and Elethor realized that she was trembling and that tears filled her eyes.

"I was right," she whispered, voice shaky. "Thank the stars, I was right."

He tried to snort derisively, but only a weak puff of air left his nostrils. "Of course you were right. You always are, remember?" He turned to the sphinx. "Herathia! We answered your riddle. Will you let us pass?"

Her lips pulled back further, past the gums, showing veins and red flesh clinging to her skull. "You will not pass, child of stars. You answered one riddle, but did not ask one of your own. Ask me a riddle, Boy King. If I cannot answer, then you may pass my door."

He groaned. Ask her a riddle of his own? He knew no riddles. He was a sculptor, a stargazer, a reluctant king. He squeezed Lyana's hand.

"Any riddles under that mop of red curls?" he asked her.

She scrunched her lips, a line appearing between her eyebrows. She spoke in a low whisper into his ear. "The answer would have to be something Herathia wouldn't know. Something of sunlight, or sky, or trees... something foreign to this dark place."

Elethor looked around him. The mountain of bodies sloped into valleys of stone. Rocky walls surrounded the place, rising to form a dome above their heads. Rivers of lava flowed and clouds of smoke danced like demons.

"That pretty much includes everything other than fire, rock, and death," he whispered back.

They thought in silence for long moments. Elethor tried to remember riddles he had heard in childhood. He vaguely recalled reading a book of them in the library--he had shared a few with Mori--but could remember none.

Mori would have remembered, he thought. *She loves that library.*

His sister was always so sad, so frightened, but when reading in the library, she would smile, laugh, and her eyes would sparkle. She would run to him with a new book, show him a word that she loved, or a tale that moved her, and life and joy would overcome her shyness. At the memory of her eyes and smile, a lump filled Elethor's throat, and tears stung his eyes.

"El, how's this?" Lyana said. She leaned forward, hid her mouth with her hand, and whispered into his ear.

He thought about her riddle but could not guess the answer until she revealed it. Nodding slowly, he helped her fine-tune the wording, praying that Herathia could not hear whispers behind palms. Finally, when they were happy with their riddle, Lyana turned to face the sphinx.

"Herathia!" she cried. "We have a riddle."

The sphinx gazed down at them, eyes blazing, tongue licking the air. She seemed eager like a cat toying with a mouse.

"Ask," she said.

Lyana raised her chin, thrust out her chest, and called out her riddle.

> *"I sing as fairly as a bird*
> *I glide as gently too*
> *I comfort the most aching soul*
> *With a voice so clear and true*
> *I live on branches and windowsills*
> *Relishing the breeze*
> *Yet I don't live*
> *Just place me down*
> *You'll silence me with ease"*

The sphinx did not miss a beat. An instant after Lyana fell silent, Herathia calmly spoke: "Wind chimes."

Elethor's heart sank. She had solved it! She hadn't even thought for a second! Had the sphinx heard them whispering? Had she cheated?

"You heard us whisper the answer!" he shouted at her. "Your ears must be sharper than ours. Will you cheat at our game?"

She snickered, a bubble of blood bursting on her lips. "I cheat not, shapeshifter. Insult me again, and our game will end, and you will die. I would like that." She snarled. "Prepare for my second riddle, children of stars. If you cannot answer, you will join my nest of corpses."

Elethor steeled himself with a deep breath and waited. After a moment of silence, the sphinx spoke her second riddle.

"I sadden the sun
High in heaven
And the night's moon too
I follow the eagle in his flight
I lived wherever he flew
At a ball I slide away
In a crowd I'm shy
I'll sneak up when you're alone
I'll make you shake and cry"

Lyana frowned and tapped her cheek. Elethor thought long and hard, but his mind was blank. He tapped his thigh, pursed his lips, and ran a dozen answers through his mind, but none fit. When he looked at Lyana, she was pale and her lips trembled.

She doesn't know either, he realized.

"Answer, shapeshifters!" the sphinx demanded and her eyes reddened. A growl left her throat, stinking of rot. "Solve my riddle or my light will sear you." She raised her claws.

Cold sweat washed Elethor. Lyana gasped and clutched her sword.

"Wait!" Elethor said to the sphinx. "I will answer, I..."

What riddles would he read with Mori in the library? He summoned back the memory, seeing his sister again; she would huddle in the shadows between books, a single candle lighting the library, smiling to herself softly, fleeing the world that scared her into the realms of imagination.

He breathed out shakily. He knew the answer.

"Loneliness," he said softly.

Lyana gasped at his side and whispered, "Of course."

The sphinx's eyes sparkled with amusement and hunger. She leaned forward, sending bodies rolling down the mountain. Elethor nearly fell, and Lyana clung to him. A gutted child rolled by him, disappearing down the mountain into shadow.

"This game is getting interesting," Herathia said. "You have answered true. Now ask me a riddle." She licked her lips, cutting her tongue on her teeth, then sucked the blood. "Make it hard."

Elethor turned to look at Lyana. Her eyes were solemn as she stared at him.

"We'll think silently," she said. "No more whispering."

He nodded. He tried to think of riddles, brow furrowed. Lyana covered her eyes and her lips moved silently. The sphinx leaned forward, drooling and hissing.

"Ask!" she shrieked. "Ask me your riddle or die!"

Elethor clenched his fists, shut his eyes, and thought until his head hurt. Suddenly, in a flash, it came to him. He remembered! Mori had asked him the riddle two years ago, laughing when he could not answer.

"I have a riddle for you," he said. He opened his eyes and looked at Lyana. She nodded, and he looked back at the sphinx and recited from memory.

"Never leaves home
Walks alone
When in danger
Turns to stone"

The sphinx sighed, rot on her breath. "A turtle," she said, "entering its shell for safety."

Lyana stared at him, mouth open, eyebrows raised and head tilted.

"It was a tough riddle," he answered in a small voice. "I couldn't answer when Mori asked me."

Lyana's face turned red, and she looked ready to throttle him. She gritted her teeth as if stifling rage, breathed in heavily, and turned away.

"I will ask you a third riddle," said the sphinx. "Are you ready, children of stars?"

Elethor and Lyana looked at each other, took deep breaths, and nodded. The sphinx raised her head and spoke, voice echoing across the mountain.

"Young princess of sand
Sad prince of snow
Turned to queen and king
From the desert
With heat and blood
The birds of fire sing
When father falls and brother dies
When flesh and fire burn
When an ancient kingdom falls to ruin
Why does our king still yearn?"

Elethor clenched his fists and lowered his head. Rage and shame coursed through him. This was not fair. This was no riddle; it was an accusation, a cheat, a trick. He raised his burning eyes and stared at the sphinx.

"You speak of me," he said, voice raw. "And of Solina."

He did not know how the sphinx knew of life aboveground. Could she see through leagues of rock and flame? Was she a goddess like the stars of Requiem?

Lyana clenched her fists and howled. "You are cheating!" she said. "This is not a true riddle. I've read books of riddles before." She panted with rage, cheeks red. "Riddles follow a format. Their answer is simple, their hints obscure. The answer always snaps into place and seems obvious when you know it. This is just a question, not a riddle!"

The sphinx raised her brow. "This is the greatest riddle of his life. He must answer."

Elethor gritted his teeth and looked away. Did the sphinx want to cheat? Fine. He would answer. He would play her game.

"Because she was *mine*!" he said, digging his fingernails into his palms.

The sphinx growled and raised her claws. "That is no answer, Boy King."

"It is the only answer!" he shouted, eyes burning. "I'm not ashamed of it. You want to know why I still love Solina? Why, even after she butchered my family, toppled my city, and murdered my people, I still love her?"

His breath came heavy. He was aware of Lyana gaping at him, but paid her no mind. Blood pounded in his ears, and his heart thrashed as if trying to break his ribs. His head spun, and the sphinx eyes stared at him, boring into him, peeling his soul.

"Yes," he whispered. "I still love her, Herathia. When I think of her eyes, her hands in mine, the sunlit days when we lay upon grass, yes... I still love her, even now. Because she was mine." Tears burned in his eyes. "Orin had his inheritance, his sword, his betrothed. My father had his throne. Mori was adored

by the court. But I had no room there; I was a lesser prince, a
mere sculptor, no warrior or leader. But Solina..." He could
barely breathe; his lungs ached. "She was beautiful, and strong,
and wise, and from another world. She was a princess, a great
light in her homeland. And she loved me. Me, the younger
prince--not Orin, not my father, but me. She was mine, and
proud, and beautiful, and I would share her with none. Earning
her love was the greatest thing I could do; she was my crown, my
throne, my golden pride."

He realized that tears ran down his cheeks, his chest rose
and fell, and his fingers shook. Vaguely, he was aware of Lyana
placing her hand on his shoulder.

"So yes," he whispered, "I still love her, and I hate her. The
heart will still love those that broke it, like a drunkard loves the
wine that ruined him, like a poor gambler still loves his favorite
game." He looked up at the sphinx and smirked through his pain.
"Does that answer your riddle, Crimson Guardian?"

The sphinx was grinning--a cruel, feline grin, the grin of a
huntress.

"Yessss," she hissed. "That answered it well. I like this
game. Ask me another riddle."

Rage flared in Elethor, turning the world red. This was all a
game to her! He had spilled out his innermost secrets, secrets he
had spoken to no one. His people were dying. Lyana probably
hated him now, and always would, as much as he hated himself.
And all this demon could do was grin! Anger made him tremble.
If she would cheat, he could cheat too. If she could ask questions
to trap him, he could do the same to her.

Without even looking at Lyana, he shouted out his next
riddle. It was an old riddle Mori and he would laugh about as
children. A trick. A game of words. A *cheat*.

"Why don't donkeys drink dawn's delicious dew?"

Beside him, Lyana gasped and spun toward him. Her face reddened, and she looked ready to shout, attack him, or faint. Elethor ignored her. He stared at the sphinx, chin raised.

Herathia hissed and glared. "That is no riddle." Her voice crinkled like old parchment. "What game do you play?"

"Answer me, Herathia!" he shouted. "Answer, or can you not? If you fail to solve my riddle, let us pass. These are the terms you agreed to, that the elders of Requiem bound you to. Answer!"

She tossed back her head and screamed, a sound so loud that Lyana covered her ears, and Elethor nearly fainted. Blood spouted from her mouth like a volcano. Her claws thrust, knocking down bodies.

Elethor refused to cow. "Can you not answer?"

She whipped her head down, spraying blood. "I should kill you, mortal. I should rip your head off and chew upon it for a thousand years as you scream in my mouth. Donkeys? Dew? What riddle is this?"

He took a step toward her. Blood filled her eyes, and he stared into them levelly. "That is my riddle. My sister told me this riddle years ago, when we were children. I could not solve it then. Can you?" He shouted over her screeches. "Why don't donkeys drink dawn's delicious dew?"

The wound along her torso split wider. Bodies spilled out, teeming with maggots. Skinned and bloody and headless, the bodies writhed, still alive, fingers groping.

"I asked for a riddle, not a trick, not a cheat!" cried the sphinx. Her voice rose like a storm. "Donkeys drink no dew, mortal! Donkeys in a field? They drink water, mortal. They drink water from a bucket or a stream. What trick is this? I do not accept your riddle. You cheat."

He stood firmly, even as she screamed so loudly, he thought his eardrums would burst. The bodies from her torso convulsed around him, nearly tripping him, but he managed to stay standing, to stare at her, to shout.

"Is that your answer? That donkeys drink from buckets and streams?"

Her skin peeled back, revealing rotten flesh crawling with centipedes. Her head caught flame and ballooned, boils growing across it.

"This is no riddle! He cheats, he tricks us! What is the answer? What is the trick?"

"Elethor!" Lyana cried. "We have to fly! She's going to kill us!"

No, Elethor thought. No, he would not flee. He had fled for too long. He had solved her riddle; he would answer this one too.

"Dawn's dew," he said, "drips from drunken dragons drooling." He smiled mirthlessly. "It's not much of a riddle. But it was enough to stump you."

Her head grew grotesquely, five times its previous size. Segments burst, revealing the skull within. Still she screamed, voice so high-pitched, it tore at Elethor's ears.

"Dawn's dew drips from drunken dragons drooling!" she cried. Her voice rose like steam. "He cheats! A joke! A trick!" Her eyes burst into flame. "You will suffer, Elethor of Requiem. You will suffer for this trickery. Requiem will fall! Her columns will crack and her skeletons will litter the earth. You will watch as she burns! You will watch as your people die. This I curse you with. This I vow to you. Your land will crumble as I do!"

The sphinx burst, shattering into a thousand pieces of flesh. They fell, chunks of meat, onto the bodies, turned to liquid, and seeped into the mountain like rain into soil. The screeching echoed through the chamber, then too fell silent.

She was gone.

The Crimson Archway loomed before Elethor, unblocked.

Slowly, blood on his face, he turned to Lyana. She gaped at him, wet and red. She opened and closed her mouth three times before she could speak.

"That was incredibly, inconceivably stupid!" she said. "Woolhead!"

He nodded. "That's the beauty of it."

She howled and hopped. "How dared you not consult with me first? How could you ask her a... a stupid tongue twister, not even a riddle?"

He shrugged. "It worked, didn't it?" He grasped her arms. "Lyana, that was the idea. The sphinx would have solved any real riddle. She lived here for thousands of years. She had heard them all, and if she hadn't, she'd heard enough to figure out any new ones. But a dumb tongue twister Mori invented? There was no chance she could have answered it." He swept his arm around them. "And it worked. It blew her apart." He sighed and looked into Lyana's eyes. "I do know what I'm doing sometimes, Lyana. I'm not always a woolhead."

She sighed, looked away, and blinked silently for long moments. Finally she looked back at him, leaned up, and kissed him on the lips.

"That," she said, "is the last kiss you'll ever get from me, so I hope you enjoyed it." She grabbed his hand and pulled him. "Now let's enter this archway and wake this Starlit Demon of yours."

They walked toward the bleeding archway. Shadows and mist swirled within it. With deep breaths and drawn swords, they stepped into the darkness.

BAYRIN

They slept through the night, holding each other as rain pattered against their scales. Dawn rose cold and so misty, Bayrin could only see several feet ahead: pines behind him, a rocky beach at his sides, whispering waves ahead. When he rolled onto his side, his scales clinked and his wounds blazed.

Mori stirred, smoke rising from her nostrils like more mist. Her eyes cracked open and gleamed. Dew glimmered on her golden scales, and lamprey bites dug red and raw on her shoulder, belly, and tail.

"Are we... are we on the island?" she whispered. "Or was it a dream?"

Bayrin struggled onto his feet, wincing as the bites across him burned. He unfurled his wings, flapped once, and tossed his head. His neck creaked. He was a lanky dragon, bones longer than most. And yet the island's pines dwarfed him; they must have stood two hundred feet tall, maybe more, as tall as Requiem's palace. Birds chirped, hooted, and cawed within them, and mist floated between the branches like ghosts. The piny scent filled the air, thick and heady. He breathed it deeply.

Mori rose to her feet, craned her neck back, and gasped. Her eyes lit up.

"Look at the size of them!" she whispered. "I've never seen trees so large." She turned to Bayrin, a smile showing her teeth. "These must be Mist Pines. Luna the Traveler wrote about them in her books. She said they're the largest trees in the world, and some are ancient, five thousand years old; that's older than Requiem itself."

Bayrin looked around at the mist. "How are we going to find the Moondisk here? Would it just be lying on the ground, hidden in a cave, stuck in a tree?" He snorted smoke. "Did Luna the Traveler write about that?"

Mori shook her head, scattering raindrops. "No. All I know is what I read in the book *Artifacts of Wizardry and Power.*" She quoted from it, chin raised. "In the Days of Mist, the Children of the Moon sailed upon ships to the Crescent Isle, built rings of stones among the pines, and danced in the moonlight. A Moondisk they forged of bronze inlaid with gold, and upon it the moon turns, and the Three Sisters glow, and its light can extinguish all sunfire, so that the Sun God may never burn them."

Bayrin watched a snowy owl glide between the trees. He flapped his wings, rose in the air, and tried to grab it for breakfast, but it hooted and flew away. He landed back on the shore, claws digging ruts into the pebbly sand.

"So, we look for rings of stone," he said. "And we look for these Children of the Moon, whoever they are. That seems like a good start. Flying won't help us; the whole place is cloaked in mist and treetops." With a deep breath, he shifted into human form. When he stood upon his human feet, the trees seemed even larger, towering monoliths. "Let's walk and explore and find these Children of the Moon, if they're still around."

Mori shifted back into human form too. Her dress was tattered and damp, and tangles filled her hair. Her cheeks were pink and crusted with salt from the sea. Her eyes, however, still shone with hope, and Bayrin felt a jolt run through him, like a shot of strong rye on a cold night.

Stars, she's so beautiful when she's happy, he thought, and the thought surprised him. Mori--beautiful? How could Elethor's baby sister, a frightened girl who'd cry and run from him in childhood, seem so fair and kind and gentle?

He noticed that he was staring and looked away toward the trees.

"Let's go," he said and began to walk, leaving the beach and entering the forest. Mori walked at his side, head tilted back, gaping at the distant treetops.

They walked for a long time, though Bayrin could not judge how long. He couldn't see the sun; when he looked up, he saw only mist, branches, and leaves. His stomach twisted with hunger, but he found no food in this forest; birds hooted and cawed but remained hidden, and he saw no other animals. He rummaged through his pack, but found only moldy cheese and a soggy bread roll. As they walked, he scraped off the mold and shared the paltry meal with Mori.

A glimmer of white flashed between the trees.

"Bayrin, look!" Mori whispered.

He narrowed his eyes and stared. "I saw it."

Whatever it was, it was gone. Only mist remained between the branches, undisturbed. Bayrin cocked his head, listening, but heard only the distant sea, the wind in the pines, and the hooting owls.

"What was it?" Mori whispered. "Did you get a look? I saw only something white and flowing, like a silk scarf."

Bayrin sighed. "That's all I saw too. It was just another owl."

She shook her head. "No, it was larger than an owl. Let's go look for it."

They walked across a carpet of leaves, trunks rising around them. A stream gurgled ahead between mossy boulders. Across the stream, a boulder rose white and sharp upon a knoll, drenched in a sunbeam. On its craggy surface glowed a rune of three stars around a crescent moon. The moon glowed soft blue, while the stars glowed golden.

Bayrin and Mori approached the boulder silently, boots sinking into pine needles and crumbly earth. When Bayrin touched the stone, it felt unnaturally warm, like touching a mug of mulled wine.

"Bay!" Mori whispered and pointed.

He whipped his head around and saw the white flash again. It glowed a hundred yards away; it indeed looked like a silk scarf. In an instant, it was gone between the trees. Bayrin began to run, boots kicking up needles. Mori ran at his side.

"Come back here!" he called. "We're friends. Show yourself!"

He heard no reply, and after long moments of running, he stopped and breathed heavily. Mori panted at his side.

"I saw it!" she said. "It looked like an animal, a deer or a horse." Her eyes shone.

Bayrin rubbed his belly. "I could use a deer. I'd settle for a horse too."

He sighed and sat down heavily. His feet and back ached, and hunger gnawed at his belly. The lamprey bites had shrunk when he shifted into human form, but still burned. He wanted nothing more than to sleep, but how could he? It had been long days since they left Requiem. The survivors back home needed him, if they still lived. He placed his head in his hands.

"Bayrin, are you all right?" Mori sat down beside him and touched his shoulder.

He looked up at her soft, pale face, her gray eyes that melted with concern, her smooth brown hair full of leaves and salt. Could she be the last Vir Requis other than him? Were they doomed to be lone survivors from the slaughter?

"I don't know, Mori," he said and held her hand. "I don't know if we can find the Moondisk, or if it even exists. I don't know if anyone is alive back in Requiem. What if they're all dead already?"

A moon ago, he thought, Mori would have shivered and wept to hear his words. Today she stared back steadily, chin raised.

"Then they are dead," she said softly, "and we're the last ones. But I don't believe that, Bayrin. I can't believe it. Not yet." Her hand tightened around his. "When I was a child, I read stories of the great heroines who fought Dies Irae. I would dream of being brave like them--like wise Queen Lacrimosa, or like the warrior Gloriae the Gilded, or like the great Agnus Dei who burned her enemies with fire. I... I always felt so scared and weak compared to them. They were great fighters, and I... I was just a girl in a library, reading adventures to escape the world." A tear rolled down her cheek. "But now *we* face a war, Bayrin. We must be like those great warriors of old. It is our time to be brave, to believe, to fight for Requiem, to defeat the Sun God who burns us. Those heroes in the old stories... they never gave up. Even when things seemed hopeless, even when everyone died around them, they kept going. This is what courage means: to keep fighting even in the darkness, even when all but a sliver of hope is lost. An enemy can take your treasure, your land, even your life, but one thing he cannot take: your choice to fight back." She sniffed, tears in her eyes. "And I will fight back, Bayrin. I won't give up. Ever. Not so long as any of our people live, even if only you and I are left."

She trembled, and her tears fell, and when Bayrin reached out to wipe those tears, he found himself embracing her. Her eyelashes fluttered against his cheek, and his lips touched her forehead, and without knowing how, he was kissing her. Her lips were soft, warm, salty with her tears but sweet too. He cupped her cheek and kissed her for long moments, as if melting into her; he knew nothing but her softness, her scent, her hair around his fingers, and her body trembling against his.

Suddenly she gasped, pulled back, and gaped over his shoulder. A white figure, like a snowy animal, reflected in her eyes. Bayrin spun his head around and saw it there. The breath left his lungs.

It was no deer or horse, but a great white lion. Its mane seemed woven of moonlight, long and white, and its eyes shone silver, narrowed like two crescent moons. Its breath plumed and its tongue lolled, blood red. It met his gaze and held it for long moments, then turned and began loping away.

"It wants us to follow," Mori whispered. She rose to her feet and pulled Bayrin up too.

"She's scared of spiders," he muttered, "but vicious predators with dagger-like teeth? Those we follow."

They walked through the mist, following the white lion along palisades of pines. Its mane glowed like a beacon. When they fell behind, it would turn its head, stare, and wait. They followed for what seemed like leagues--over a cliff that overlooked the sea, along a fallen log that bridged a river, and into a valley like a bowl of mist. Dusk fell. Fireflies emerged to float through the mist, little moons behind clouds. The lion glowed ahead, and Bayrin and Mori followed in the shadows, crickets chirping around them.

As he walked, Bayrin touched his lips, still feeling Mori's kiss. Though Requiem burned in the south, and an island of magic rolled around him, he couldn't stop thinking of her lips against his, the softness of her hair, how her body had trembled against him. Bayrin had kissed girls before--Tiana, the kitchen maid in Requiem's palace, and Piri, the daughter of a winemaker, and a third girl who'd visited from the east and whose name he never learned. But none of them had felt so delicate in his arms, a flower he wanted to protect from the frost. He glanced at Mori as he walked, and when he saw her soft smile, again he felt it, that warm melting of his heart, like butter over fresh bread.

Mori... the girl he used to taunt, whose braids he would
tug, whose tears he would mock. The girl who'd always tag along
when he'd go hunting with Elethor, then cry whenever he caught
a deer. The girl he'd scare at nights by squawking and pretending
to be a griffin. How could he now feel this way toward her, the
way he felt toward Tiana or Piri, but a hundred times stronger?

He realized that the lion had stopped walking, and Bayrin
stopped too and looked ahead. In the darkness, a mountain rose
from the pines, black against the stars. The lion stood at its feet,
gazing up toward the peak, then turned toward him and Mori.
Fireflies haloed around its head. Owls hooted in the darkness,
crickets chirped, and wind rustled the trees, a night music like soft
pipes in the temples of Requiem.

"Child of the Moon," Mori whispered, silver in the night's
glow. She approached the lion and touched its head, gingerly at
first, then warmly. She stroked it with a soft smile. "I am Mori
Aeternum of Requiem, a child of starlight. I come seeking your
help."

The lion's glow blazed, like a moon emerging from clouds.
Mori pulled her hand back and gasped. The light coiled around
the lion, a hundred fairies of silver, and it stood upon its back legs.
Its back straightened, its front legs became arms, and soon it
stood as a man. His skin was milky, his beard long and white. A
broach, shaped as a crescent moon, glowed upon his silver robes.
He seemed ageless, his face unlined, his eyes wise.

"You... you're a shapeshifter too!" Mori said, her breath
catching. "Are you related to us Vir Requis?"

The man nodded and spoke with a deep, soft voice like
waves and mist and the sound of light. "I am Aeras of the
Crescent Isle, a child of moonlight." He smiled softly. "We have
heard of Requiem, our sister land, whose children dance in the
light of stars. We watched you fly over our sea, then become a

man and woman upon our shore." He reached out his hands.
"Welcome to our land, friends of the night."

Bayrin took a step forward, frowning. "If you saw us fly,
why didn't you help us? Why did you wait and only show yourself
now, when you knew we were hurt?" He looked around him, but
saw only shadows. "And where are the rest of you?"

Aeras bowed his head. "We did not know if you were
friends or foes; we have never met the children of Requiem's
stars. Our only knowledge of your people comes from old songs
and older whispers." His face darkened. "When we heard you
speak of fighting the Sun God, we knew that we share a foe.
Once our people covered many islands, but the cruel deity of
sunfire burned us." He sighed and his eyes softened. "As for the
others, you will meet them. We will give you food and healing
herbs."

Bayrin had many questions. He wanted to ask about the
Moondisk, and how many other lions lived here, and how they
had managed to survive the Sun God's attacks. But before he
could ask, Aeras turned and walked into the mist, robes gliding
around him.

Mori took his hand. "Come, Bay, let's follow him." She
smiled. "He'll help us."

They walked in darkness over fallen pine needles until they
reached a gateway cut into the mountainside. Two statues flanked
the opening, twenty feet tall, carved as owls. Their silver wings
spread above them, forming a lintel. Aeras led the two Vir Requis
under the wings and into a tunnel carved into the mountain.

Silver arches supported the tunnel, carved with runes of
moons and stars. Jars of fireflies glowed in alcoves, lighting the
way, and the air smelled of soil, deep water, and pines. They
walked for long moments. Mori tilted her head back, gaping at
the silver columns, the fireflies, and the glowing runes. A soft

smile touched her lips, and on a whim, Bayrin reached out and
held her hand. She squeezed his palm.

I used to mock her hand for its extra finger, he remembered.
Now the feel of her hand in his felt warmer than mulled wine.

The tunnel began to widen, and cold air flowed from ahead,
scented of wine and fur. Silver light fell upon them, like
moonlight between summer clouds. A few more steps, and the
tunnel opened into a vast, glittering chamber.

Mori gasped and tears filled her eyes.

"Beautiful," she whispered. "It's so beautiful, Bay."

Bayrin whistled softly.

"Stars," he said. "Now this is something."

He had been in caves before, but this was more like a
palace. The chamber loomed, larger than Requiem's royal hall.
Stalagmites and stalactites coiled and glittered, a hundred feet tall,
like the melting candles of gods. Some formed shapes like
dragons, others like knobby people, and some like trees.

These columns surrounded a silvery pool large enough to
bathe ten dragons. Upon its water rippled the reflection of the
moon, larger than Bayrin had ever seen it; he could see craters,
valleys, and hills upon it. The moonlight filled the chamber.
Bayrin looked up, expecting to see the true moon shining through
a hole in the ceiling, but saw only a rocky dome glowing with
runes.

Hundreds of white lions filled the chamber, he realized.
Some lay between the stalagmites, eyes shut. Others whispered in
nooks. Some stood around the pool of moonlight, drinking from
its waters. When they saw Bayrin and Mori, the lions looked
upon them, nodded, and whispered blessings.

"Welcome," said Aeras, "to the Chamber of Moonlight.
Welcome to the heart of our realm."

He walked between the stalagmites, silks billowing. Bayrin and Mori followed, gaping at the melting stones, the glittering pool, and the lions who followed them with silvery eyes.

Aeras approached an alcove in the wall. The stone here was smooth, forming a rounded nook like a basket. Aeras gestured at it.

"Sit and rest," he said. "We will bring you food and song and healing."

Mori bit her lip and climbed into the nook. She leaned back against the smooth stone, pulled her knees to her chest, and smiled. She looked like a babe in a stone bassinet. Bayrin, however, remained standing. He ignored the ache in his muscles and wounds.

"Aeras," he said, "we can't rest. The Sun God attacks our home and we need your help. We seek the Moondisk--a weapon to defeat the phoenixes, great birds of fire that serve the Sun God and burn our people. Give us no food, no music, no healing--give us the Moondisk. We can't wait another hour."

The Children of the Moon looked at one another. Their eyes darkened and their glow dimmed.

Aeras sighed deeply. "The Moondisk will douse the fire of the phoenix; it has sent them fleeing from our island. But the disk has since been taken, and reclaiming it has failed us."

Bayrin felt the breath leave his lungs like air from a bellows. His shoulders stooped and his eyes stung. Ice seemed to wash his belly. Sitting in the nook, Mori gasped and her eyes dampened.

"So we failed," Bayrin said, voice choked. He felt like weeping, and it was all he could do to remain standing. "We've come all this way, and... the Moondisk is gone." He thought of his parents, his sister, and his friends, and his voice cracked.

Aeras raised his hands. "Not all hope is lost, child of stars! The Moondisk is not gone; it lies here upon this island, on the peak of this very mountain. Sit, child of starlight. Eat and drink, and we will tell you what you must know."

Warmth flickered inside Bayrin. The Moondisk, here on the mountain? What riddles was this man speaking? He wanted to throttle Aeras, to demand answers, but forced himself to sit by Mori. When more Children of the Moon brought him bowls of fruits, he ate, and when they served him jugs of water, he drank. Vaguely, he was aware that the fruit was fresh and sweet, the water pure and cool, but he could barely taste them. Famished as he was, he cared about no food, drink, or rest, only about one thing--getting the Moondisk.

"Speak, Aeras!" he demanded as two young women, pale Daughters of the Moon with silver eyes, bandaged his wounds. "I am thankful for your hospitality, truly I am, but our people are dying. They burn as we speak. We must bring them the Moondisk at once and cannot delay. How do we find it?"

Aeras stood before him, eyes dark. "It was five thousand years ago that we made the Moondisk, forging it from bronze and gold and the light of the moon. It protected us from the wrath of the Sun God for many generations, even as our people burned upon islands we could not reach. The Sun God sent many beasts and spies to steal our Moondisk, to cleave it with their axes of steel. As our numbers dwindled, we took the Moondisk to the mountaintop and raised there a champion, a great demon of wood and stone, and set him to guard our Moondisk."

Mori swallowed a bite of pear. "Is this demon still there?"

The Children of the Moon lowered their heads. Several shed tears.

"Yes," said Aeras, "he still lives upon the mountaintop, guarding the Moondisk from any who would claim it. We named him Ral Siyan, which means Beast of Wood and Stone in our tongue. He obeyed our ancestors, but many seasons of loneliness drove him mad, and he no longer serves us. He will not obey us.

He will not surrender the Moondisk we set him to guard, not even when threatened with spear and arrow."

Bayrin rose to his feet, clasped his head, and sighed deeply. "Great. Just great. First phoenixes on our tails. Then lampreys the size of my sister's vanity. And now this, a beast of wood and stone that no spear or arrow can kill." He groaned.

Mori stood up and placed a hand on his shoulder. "Don't despair, Bayrin," she whispered. "We've come this far. We'll find a way."

"There is only one way to claim the Moondisk, children of stars," said Aeras. "You must defeat Ral Siyan in battle. Our people are blessed with moonlight, and we can become the white lions, creatures of the moon; we are beings of magic, of meditation, of wisdom. But you..." His eyes shone. "You are of Requiem. You are blessed with starlight, the light of the Draco constellation. You can become dragons, creatures of wrath and ruin. You can fight Ral Siyan and reclaim the sacred Moondisk of our ancestors." He squared his shoulders and raised his chin. "Fight him, Bayrin and Mori of Requiem, and you may take the Moondisk to your land, and defeat the servants of the Sun God, for we are your brothers and share your enemy."

Bayrin swallowed, looked at Mori, and clasped her hands. "Are you up for a good old-fashioned fight, Mori my dear?"

She trembled but bit her lip, raised her chin, and nodded. "We fight," she whispered.

LYANA

Shadows and lightning swirled around her. Whispers rose like wind. She looked ahead but saw nothing, and her feet walked upon mist. Suddenly she was falling, tumbling through an endless storm, and she shouted and shifted. Wings burst from her back, and she flew, roaring fire. Wind and clouds whipped her.

"Elethor!" she called. She had stepped through the Crimson Archway holding his hand, but he was gone from her now. She whipped her head from side to side, blowing flames, but could not see him. Nothing but storm clouds flowed around her, charcoal and blue and deep purple like bruises. When she spun around, the Crimson Archway was gone; she saw only the endless storm.

"Lyana!" His voice rose somewhere in the distance; she could not tell from which direction. He seemed leagues away. She called for him again, but he did not answer.

Fly, Lyana, she told herself and tightened her lips. *Fly!*

Winds blasted her, billowing her wings like sails. She nearly tumbled. Shadows tugged her like chains, but she kept flying, one wing flap after the other. Stars streaked around her, countless lines of light. Lightning crashed. Thunderclaps deafened her. She blew fire and roared.

"Elethor, can you hear me?"

Rain of blood pattered against her. Faces of shadow and clouds swirled in the storm, mouths opening and closing, eyes appearing and disappearing. She saw Orin's face smiling, then screaming, then melting in lightning fire. She saw the face of her brother Bayrin, and of her young sister Noela who had died in her cradle. She saw her parents, Deramon and Adia, burning in a rain of acid and calling to her.

"Lyana!" they cried. "Lyana, why did you forsake us to die?"

She howled. *No. No, they cannot be dead! They cannot.* It was only a dream, a vision, a lie.

Her sister Noela wept in the clouds, a mere babe, crying to her. "Why did you not weep when they buried me? Why did you shed no tears?"

I wanted to! I wanted to cry like my parents, like Bayrin, but I couldn't, I couldn't, I had to be strong for them....

Her beloved Orin flew toward her, a dragon of cloud and lightning, bleeding and burnt. Half his face was a gaping wound, showing the crimson innards of the heavens.

"Why do you fly with Elethor?" he cried. "Why did you leave me to die and take my brother for your betrothed?"

He blew flames that washed her, red clouds that dispersed into rain.

"I should have been there," she whispered, wings roiling the clouds. "I should have gone with Orin to Castellum Luna, helped him fight the phoenixes, not stayed north and let him die... I let him die... Elethor, I let him die."

She tried to fly, to escape Orin's burnt face, his one eye that blazed, his dripping wounds. She beat her wings madly, shoving through the storm, but a gust of air caught her, and she tumbled through the sky. Lightning smashed into her scales, and they grabbed her, all of them--dead and burnt Orin, and her dying parents, and her dead sister Noela. They clung to her, begging.

"Don't fly, don't run, don't leave us, Lyana! Don't leave again. It's cold and dark in the Abyss, please save us, save us Lyana, don't leave us again...."

She wept and tried to flee, but could not; she knew that they would always follow her. She knew that no matter how far she flew, those eyes would haunt Her--across endless skies and into her grave. She saw herself years in the future, a great Queen of Requiem upon her throne, her king Elethor at her side. Gold and jewels and peace surrounded her, but still at night she would curl up, weep, and try to flee them but find no peace.

For there is no peace for you, child, whispered a deep voice, and Lyana screamed and saw the black hill with the black flower. It rose before her between the clouds, a towering monument, larger than Requiem herself, woven of her terror. A great black bowl, it rose from a landscape of ink. A single black rose grew atop it, and Lyana tried to reach it. She knew she had to save that rose, to heal it, to stop the terrible pain of it, the horror that pounded. She screamed, for this mountain was larger than the world, larger than her mind could grasp. Her soul left her body and spread across the landscape, twisting with its fear, and everywhere she saw those petals.

"I have to... I have to save it," she whispered. "I have to *count* them. I have to *line* them. You have to keep the *numbers.*"

The Shrivel she had eaten laughed inside her belly, a coiling worm, forever inside her, forever mocking, forever counting. Its teeth gnashed at her entrails, and its claws dug, her eternal child, a parasite of her womb.

I am here within you, it whispered, taunting. *You cannot flee me, and you cannot flee those you let die, not until you climb the mountain and heal the black rose... until then I will remain and feast upon you.*

"Lyana!" cried a desperate voice. "Lyana, listen to me! Lyana, do you hear?"

She shouted and blew fire. "Leave me! Leave me! I killed no one. Please..." Tears streamed down her cheeks. "I am a soldier! I am a knight of Requiem. I have to save him, Elethor. I have to save the king, and Orin, and Noela... oh stars, Noela..."

She wept. Her body convulsed as she tumbled from the sky. Sweet Noela, little Noela, only a moon old, and they buried her, and Lyana couldn't even weep, she couldn't be weak, but now she wept and shouted. *I have to save her... I have to save her from this place. I have to save all of them.*

"Lyana!" the voice cried. Claws dug into her shoulders and pulled her. "Fly, Lyana!"

She could see nothing but her tears, but she outstretched her wings, and the wind billowed them, tossing her higher. She leveled off, banked, and flew upon the wind. The sky. She had to find the sky. Elethor flew beside her, brass scales shimmering, and she saw it, a hint of dawn ahead, a smudge of blue.

Requiem! May our wings forever find your sky. She remembered those words. She soared, howling and blowing fire. Though the storm blasted her and lightning smashed against her, she flew, tearing free from the grip of the dead. Her tail lashed and her claws reached out.

"Elethor!" she cried. "Fly with me, Elethor!"

They soared, cutting through the storm, smashing through rain and rock, until Lyana saw it. Tears filled her eyes again, but now they were tears of joy. *I see it... stars, I see it.* They were the columns of Requiem, white marble rising from fire and blood into good, healing starlight. They beamed from death to hope, from firelight to starlight, and Lyana flew like she had never flown, tears on her cheeks. *I will find your sky, Requiem... forever.*

The two dragons dived through the lightning, streaming toward the ghostly columns that rose among the storm of the Abyss, and soon flew between them. The pillars gleamed around them, palisades guiding them home. Flames blazed against their bellies, and starlight kissed their backs, and wakes of red and white light trailed behind them. They shot between the columns, through the storm, and dived into a great cavern of stone and starlight.

The storm silenced.

Lyana gasped.

She flew. She heard nothing but the thud of wings. Elethor flew at her side, panting, fire rising between his teeth. The chamber rose around them, the size of a kingdom, its ceiling of stone lit with countless stars. Lyana's heart pounded.

We made it, she thought. *We passed through the storm.*

A great boulder rose ahead like an island rising from darkness, and she spiraled toward it. She landed upon its top, so weak, and shifted into a human. Elethor landed beside her, shifted too, and they lay holding each other. Tears wet their cheeks and their chests rose and fell.

She clung to him. "What was that storm?" she whispered. "Did you see them too? Did you see the dead?"

His face was pale. His arms held her close as the stars gleamed above. "I saw my dead brother, and my dead father, and..." His eyes dampened. "I saw Mori dead too. She cried for me to save her, and I tried to, but I couldn't." He blinked and whispered. "Are they all dead, Lyana?"

"No." She clenched her fists behind his back. "I will not believe it. The storm... it showed us our nightmares, I think. It isn't real." She laid her head against his shoulder. "It can't be."

A shiver ran across her. Did that Shrivel truly live inside her, a coiling worm in her belly? Or was that merely her fear that nested in her soul? She did not know.

"El," she said, "thank you... for holding me. For pulling me from the darkness. I was drowning."

He stroked her hair and kissed her forehead. "I told you, Lyana. I will always fly by your side. I will always look after you. You can repay me later by smashing those statues I carved of Solina." He sighed and laid his head down against the stone. "You were right. I was a fool." He shook his head, grimacing. "When the sphinx asked me about her, I couldn't lie... I had to tell her that I still love her, even now. Lyana, she killed my father and my brother." He looked at her with haunted eyes. "How could I still love her?"

She held him close. "Love me instead," she whispered, "and hold me for a while longer."

He kissed her cheek and held her, and stroked her hair, and their bodies pressed together until the pain and fear faded, until their whispers and warmth could drive away the memories.

Lights blazed from below.

Lyana and Elethor rose to their feet upon the pillar of stone. They gazed into the darkness below. Two eyes like stars cracked open, shooting pillars of light like the starlit columns of afterlife.

"Stars," Lyana whispered.

In the new light, she saw great shoulders of stone and a rising tail, and soon a creature unfurled in the shadows, larger than a palace, a being of rock and light.

The Starlit Demon rose before them in the darkness.

MORI

As they flew up the mountain, heading toward its granite peak, Mori wanted to think about the task ahead. She wanted to steel herself for battle, imagine seizing the Moondisk from its demon guardian, prepare for a long flight over the sea and back to Requiem. Yet as her wings stirred the cold air over mountainsides of pines, she only thought of Bayrin's kiss.

Stupid love-struck girl! she scolded herself. *You think of kisses and love and romance while your people burn, while your brother and father lie dead?*

She looked at Bayrin who flew beside her, his eyes narrowed, mist swirling around his green scales. Mori felt a chill invade her.

No, she knew. This was not how romance felt. Lyana had told her about love--she said how when Orin was near, she would tremble, her heart would flutter, how warmth would spread through her, how joy bloomed inside her. This felt different. Mori felt no flutter, no warmth, no joy.

She lowered her eyes. She felt shame. She felt unclean.

Would Bayrin love me if he knew my secret? she thought, soaring over mountainsides of chalk and leaf. *If he knew how I let Acribus claim me, and how I didn't even fight him, how I... how his filth still clings to me? He thinks I'm just sweet Mori, the young princess, like from the fairytales... but I'm not her anymore. Not now. Not ever again.* Her shame burned inside her like a demon child in her womb. Was that Acribus's child, a babe with cruel eyes and a white tongue, that festered inside her?

"Mori, are you ready?" Bayrin called to her.

No, she thought. *No, I'm not ready to kill a demon. I'm not ready to fly over the sea again, to return home and find more dead. I'm not ready to face this world and keep flying.* She growled, thought about the old heroines from her stories, and nodded. *But I will do these things nonetheless.*

She gave her wings three great flaps, filling them with air like sails, and soared toward the mountaintop. Bayrin soared beside her. Smoke streamed between his teeth, and the thud of his wings blasted her. They cleared the mountain's peak, and Mori found herself looking down upon an ancient ruin.

Pillars lay fallen and chipped. Their capitals were shaped as bucking elks, but smoothed with centuries of rain. An archway rose from a tangle of ivy and bushes, the wall around it long fallen. Bricks lay strewn. Shattered wood, snapped branches, and boulders littered the ruins. Wild grass grew from a smashed mosaic. Whatever structure had once stood here, nature was overgrowing it; the fallen bricks were more moss than stone.

"There was a temple here once," Mori said, circling above it. She had seen enough temples in Requiem to know them, even when ruined; she could feel the old holiness of the place. The Children of the Moon had worshipped the night here.

"Where is the Moondisk?" Bayrin said, flying beside her.

Mori flew above the ruins, fanning the grass and mist. She squinted, seeking the glint of bronze and gold. Did the Moondisk lie hidden among these tufts of grass, fallen trees, and ruin of an ancient temple?

"And where is the demon who guards it?" she whispered.

She saw no life here but for the plants; no call of birds, no chirp of crickets, nothing but the rustle of grass.

Bayrin grunted. "Maybe the demon left years ago, and the Children of the Moon had never bothered checking." He began spiraling down toward the ruins. "Come on, Mori, let's start overturning rocks, find this Moondisk, and get out of here."

Mori puffed out smoke, uncertain. This place was too quiet. Yet Bayrin was descending, and so she joined him, throat tight.

A moan shattered the silence.

The ruins shifted.

The fallen columns began to rise.

Mori screamed and banked, shot across the ruins, and soared. Rocks flew skyward. The fallen walls rose like a marionette on invisible strings. Columns formed legs and arms. The archway rose like shoulders, bedecked with a cloak of ivy and grass. The roots of fallen trees entwined, forming a great head with blazing eyes of blue crystal. Arms lashed out, ending with claws of leafy branches. Mori flew backward, gaping at the beast. The creature twisted and formed before her, and soon stood as a giant, three hundred feet tall, a behemoth woven of wood, leaf, and crumbled ruins.

Ral Siyan, Mori knew. *The demon of stone and wood.*

"Bay!" she screamed. She trembled and her heart thrashed. Where was Bayrin? She could no longer see him. Her wings thudded madly, billowing the demon's leaves. Its blue stare transfixed her, burning her eyes.

"Mori, it has the Moondisk!" came a cry, and Bayrin flew around the demon, eyes blazing.

He seemed so small compared to the creature, a mere bird flying around a tree. The demon of wood and stone howled, a sound like a collapsing dam. It lashed an arm at Bayrin. Its bricks creaked like joints, raining dust. Its branches twisted and groaned. Its fingers of wood missed Bayrin by a foot. The green dragon flapped his wings, blasting the beast with air, sending leaves flying.

When the demon turned toward her, Mori gasped. She saw the Moondisk! A circle of bronze, the size of a shield, it lay within the archway that formed the demon's torso. Vines and brambles held it like veins around a heart. Upon its dented and dulled surface, a golden moon and stars still glimmered.

Bayrin soared, turned, and swooped toward the beast.

"Time to burn," he said and blew fire.

"Bayrin, no!" Mori cried. She soared and slammed into Bayrin, pushing him aside. His flames rained upon the mountaintop, missing the demon. The beast of wood and stone roared, a sound like cracking boulders, and swung its arms. A log slammed into Mori, and she gasped for breath, head spinning.

"Mori, what are you doing?" Bayrin shouted, smoke billowing from his maw. He rose higher, dodging another blow from the demon. Mori flew beside him, panting. Her side blazed with pain where the beast had struck her.

"You'll burn the Moondisk!" she managed to say. "It's surrounded with branches. The bronze and gold would melt in dragonfire!"

Ral Siyan howled, a deep cry, the rage of forests and oceans and buried rock. The demon leaped, columns swinging. The two dragons scattered, and Mori found herself growling, anger pounding through her.

I won't let my family die, she thought. *I won't let Solina cut open Elethor too. I won't let Acribus rape Lyana like he raped me.* Her growl turned into a roar, and she swooped, claws outstretched. *I will grab the Moondisk.*

The demon spun toward her, all twisting roots and vines. Her claws glinted. She reached toward the Moondisk. Her claws almost closed around it... but the vines and brambles that encased the disk twisted. A branch lashed out, and its thorns slammed into her, each like an arrowhead. She screamed as they pierced her scales, fell, and her back hit the mountaintop.

The demon swung its arm like a hammer. The stone column came crashing down, as wide as an oak. Mori screamed and rolled aside, and the column smashed into the ground, shattering rock.

A roar pierced the air, and Bayrin swooped. His tail swung and slammed into Ral Siyan's head of root and leaf.

Wooden chips flew. A branch cracked. The demon turned. The stone archway--its torso--creaked and rained dust. The branches within the archway bound tighter together; Mori could barely see the Moondisk within them now, but she drove forward. Her howl rose. Her claws slashed at the brambles.

The Moondisk loosened. It fell a foot within the archway. Before Mori could grab the disk, the branches and vines wrapped around it again. The demon spun, arms lashing. One column slammed into a swooping Bayrin, knocking him to the ground. Another roared over Mori's head.

"Bayrin!" she cried. "Bayrin, get up!"

He lay on his back, wings flapping too feebly for flight. His tail flopped weakly and his eyes rolled back. The scales along his left side were cracked. Ral Siyan laughed--a grumble like an avalanche--and raised stony arms above the fallen green dragon.

Mori howled.

"You will not hurt him!" she cried and drove forward.

She slammed into the beast, cracking the stones of its archway. It tumbled forward and crashed down, and its leg--a column of stone and ivy--slammed into Bayrin.

Horror exploded inside Mori. *Stars, no, stars, please don't let Bayrin die, please please. I killed him, stars....*

Ral Siyan rose to its feet, the stones of its body shifting and rearranging themselves. The vines inside the archway coiled like a nest of snakes, wrapping tight around the Moondisk. The demon's mouth, a mere crack in wood, opened in a mocking grin.

Mori screamed with all her rage, all her pain, all her fear. It was the cry she could not utter when Orin died, when Acribus raped her, when her home burned and crashed around her. It was the cry of Requiem, of loss and wrath. She shot forward like an arrow, howling. Her claws reached out. Fire streamed from her maw, trailing behind her as a wake. A battering ram, she crashed into the demon, breaking through its archway. Roots and branches snapped against her. Her teeth closed around the Moondisk, and she shot out the archway's other side, scattering splinters of wood.

Howling, she spat the Moondisk into the air, where it spun and blazed in the sunlight. Before it could fall, Mori spun and blew her fire.

The stream of flame crashed into Ral Siyan. Its branches and leaves ignited. It howled, consumed with fire, a living torch the height of a palace. The mountain seemed to Mori like an erupting volcano.

"Bayrin!" she cried, tears in her eyes, and dived down. She saw him lying on his back, head drooping, wings limp.

Is he dead? Stars, please, let him live.

As the demon lashed its arms and howled, Mori grabbed Bayrin with her claws. She grunted with effort, pulling him back. Her feet dug into the mountainside. With a howl, she managed to drag Bayrin ten feet back, then twenty, until they were sliding down the mountainside. His eyes were still closed, and she wrapped her wings around them as they tumbled. Pebbles cascaded around them. With a thud, they slammed onto a rocky outcrop and lay still.

A hundred feet above her, Mori saw Ral Siyan still thrashing and burning. Smoke billowed from the demon. Its cry pierced the air, a cry of mourning, of endless pain. The cry was wordless, the cry of a wounded beast, but the more she listened, the more human it seemed to Mori. She thought she could hear words within it.

"Maaaa!" it seemed to cry. "Maaaa! Mother! Mother, please!"

It raised its hands to the sky, and Mori saw the moon there, a pale disk in the soft daylight. Blazing branches tore off the demon and fluttered, a thousand fireflies. It cried to the moon, its mother, a dying child. Mori wept for it; suddenly the creature was beautiful to her, a wonder she had slain.

With a great crack like snapping bones, Ral Siyan's archway crumbled. The stones crashed. Columns fell and shattered. Branches landed, crackling with fire. When the rocks settled, nothing remained of the demon but more ruins and scattered flames.

Tears in her eyes, Mori lowered her head toward Bayrin. He lay still, head tilted back and scales dented. Mori wept and shook him.

"Bayrin!" she whispered, throat tight. Her tears fell upon him. "Bay, wake up! Come on! Wake up, please!"

She cradled his head. He couldn't be dead. Couldn't! In death, Vir Requis returned to human forms. He was still a dragon. He had to live, *had to*, otherwise his magic would fail, he couldn't die like this, not in her arms, not like Orin had died. She sobbed and trembled.

"Bay?" she whispered.

As she held him, his scales melted. His wings pulled into his back.

He turned into a bloodied man.

Sobs racked Mori's body.

Dead...

She shifted into a human too. She sat upon the boulder, cradling him in her arms. Her hair covered his face, and she shook him.

"Bay, Bay, wake up!" she whispered, unable to speak any louder. "Please, Bay, please. I love you." She kissed his cold lips and held him tight. "I love you, Bay, please, don't leave me."

He moaned.

He moaned! Mori's heart leaped. Fresh tears fell and she shouted and shook him wildly.

"Bay!" She touched his cheek. "Bay, you're going to be all right. I'm going to take care of you."

His eyes fluttered and he moaned again. His lips moved, but only a hoarse whisper left his throat. Mori leaned closer to hear his words.

"What is it, Bay?" she whispered.

"I... I fell on my lamp." His face crinkled up. "Ouch."

Mori laughed as she cried, body shaking. She touched his cheek and kissed him again, a peck on his lips, and felt his hand in her hair.

She thought that they would kiss again, like last time, and she wanted to. She ached for it. But she pulled back, and once more her shame flooded her, ice inside her. But then his arms were around her, and she *was* kissing him, and she melted into it.

And it feels right, she thought. *It feels good.* Her tears streamed down her cheeks, mingling salty in their kiss. She lay down beside him, arms around him. When she looked up, she saw a glint. The Moondisk lay on the mountainside above them, a beacon of light for her home and her life.

DERAMON

He slew the Tiran with a downward swing, driving his axe into the man's head, through helmet into skull. Blood spilled and the man fell dead, joining his fallen comrades. When he hit the ground, his visor clanked open, revealing a young face.

A boy, Deramon thought. *Nothing but a stupid boy, fifteen if he was a day.*

He spat and gritted his teeth. He cursed under his breath, damning Solina for this slaughter, for killing his people, and for forcing him to kill hers.

"Bring the hammers!" he bellowed. "Break this tunnel upon them!"

The corpses of Tirans and Vir Requis rose in piles. They stank, blood and offal seeping from them. Severed limbs littered the floor. Years ago, Deramon used to read to his children stories of epic battle. In those books, the heroes smote the enemies with light and justice. *The books never mention the entrails and bones and human waste,* he thought. *They never mention the heroes cleaving the skulls of boys too young to shave.*

Men came running from deeper below, holding hammers still hot from the forge. As Deramon and ten soldiers swung swords at those Tirans who surged from above, the hammermen slammed at the ceiling and walls. Chips of stone rained. One Tiran leaped forward and slew a hammerman. The Tiran fell, face caved in like a red crater, when a second hammerman bashed his skull. Blood splashed and the screams of men echoed. The body of a slain child lay torn under the fighters' boots, limbs ripped off, her head a flattened ruin. Chunks of stone fell and cracks raced along the tunnel walls.

"Where are you, Solina?" Deramon grumbled as he swung his sword and axe. "Come and face me again."

Two more men died. Hammers swung. Stones rolled and cracks pierced the ceiling.

"Back, men!" Deramon shouted hoarsely. Dust flew. "Back!"

He slew another Tiran, cleaving his armor with an axe blow, and leaped back into the darkness.

Boulders tumbled. Men screamed and dust filled the air. The tunnel collapsed.

A boulder slammed down an inch from Deramon. A rock crashed against his helmet, another against his pauldron. He ran, leaped over a body, and fell. His men leaped around him. The sound roared like an army of dragons. For a moment Deramon thought that all the tunnels below Requiem would crumble, that every last survivor would die.

Bayrin and Mori will live, he thought as rocks pummeled him. *We've saved my son at least.*

For long moments, he lay on his stomach, rocks raining against him. The dust flew; he saw nothing but gray and black. It seemed the passing of ages before he realized that he could hear men moan. One cursed and spat, while another wept and prayed. The dust was settling, and soon Deramon could see again. Men shifted around them, coated in dust, their blood seeping through it.

His body ached and his head rang. Grimacing, Deramon sat up and turned around.

The tunnel had collapsed into a heap of boulders. He could neither see nor hear the Tirans. Blood seeped from under the wreckage.

"Good," he muttered. *May they all lie dead.*

He rose to his feet, leaning against the wall for support. His men rose around him. Behind them, the tunnel sloped deeper into darkness; the prayers and cries of survivors rose from the depth.

I've buried us alive, Deramon thought. *How long until we run out of air? How long until we all perish in the darkness? Will we ever find a way back to light?*

He did not know. But death was delayed. They had staved off fire, even if hunger, thirst, and suffocation still awaited.

"Their battering ram will not break this blockage as easily," said Garvon, the captain with the white beard and one eye. Dust filled a gash along his cheek, and a dent pressed into his breastplate, leaking blood.

"No," Deramon agreed and scratched his own beard, wondering if he'd live to see it as white as Garvon's. "Go see my wife, Garvon. Go see Adia. Get your wounds bandaged. Silas!" He turned to see the younger soldier struggle to his feet; blood seeped from under his helmet. "Silas, can you stand? Can you still swing a blade?"

The young man nodded, lips tight, and lifted his fallen sword. "My blade will always swing for Requiem."

He is younger than my son, Deramon thought. *But not as young as the boy whose skull I cleaved.*

"Good. Stay here and guard this pile of rubble." Deramon passed his eyes over the others who were rising from the dust. "Talin! Raion! Stay here with him. The rest of you too. I'll send up fresh men."

Leaving them there, he walked with Garvon down the tunnel. Soon they were stepping through crowds of women and children. If the survivors had been cramped before, they were now pressed together, a wall of flesh and tears and blood.

This place is a grave, Deramon thought. How much more of these tunnels could they lose? So much of the underground had fallen. All that remained was this--a few burrows, a few alcoves, thousands of survivors breathing and crowding together. How long until their air was gone? A day? An hour?

We cannot wait for you, Bayrin, he thought. *We cannot wait, Lyana. Return to us... or flee as far as you can, and never return to our tomb.*

Robes swirled, and Adia came walking toward them. The survivors around her bowed their heads and moved aside as best they could, letting her pass. She mumbled blessings to them. The priestess's face was pale, her eyes sunken, and blood stained her robes.

"Deramon," she whispered. She touched blood that trickled down his forehead.

"We held them back," he said, so hoarse he could barely speak at all. "We brought the tunnel down upon them."

And upon a dozen of my own men, he thought.

She stood for a moment, stern, the Mother of Requiem, the great Priestess of Stars... and then her lips trembled, and she embraced him and clung to him.

"Thank the stars," she whispered. "Deramon, I thought you had left me. Stars, so many are dead. So many I cannot heal."

He looked over her shoulder at the survivors. Here too people were dying. Some were sick, their wounds festering. The elderly huddled on the floor and babes wept.

Deramon wanted to comfort his wife. To be strong for her, to give her hope... but he knew that hope was gone. *We will die here. But we will die fighting.*

"Adia," he began... and his breath died.

Cracks raced along the ceiling, and with a crash and sound like crumbling mountains, boulders rained. A hole broke open above, and firelight blazed, like the sun breaking through clouds.

"Storm the tunnels!" rose Solina's voice above. "Slay them all!"

Tirans leaped from above, tossed down shovels, and drew swords. Solina landed like a cat, snarled, and swung her twin blades. Vir Requis screamed and tried to flee, but there was nowhere to run; they fell dead at the Tirans' blades.

"Garvon, with me!" Deramon shouted and ran forward, shoving men aside. Behind him, he heard more of his troops rushing into the tunnel. He saw Solina stab an old woman who gasped and fell. Then a Tiran man charged toward him, thrusting a spear, and Deramon parried with his sword.

The Tirans' torches filled the tunnels. There were dozens, maybe hundreds. They kept pouring in from above. Cold winter winds came with them, shrieking through the tunnels, tasting of flame and night.

Deramon swung his blades. As soldiers, women, and children fell dead around him, he grimaced and thought: *At least we now have air.*

MORI

She flew on the wind, the Moondisk clutched in her claws, clouds streaming beneath her. When she saw the mountains ahead, their snow golden in the dawn, tears filled her eyes. Those were the mountains of Requiem.

"We're home," she whispered into the wind.

When she looked at Bayrin, who flew at her side, she saw his eyes gleam. Flames crackled between his teeth.

"Home," he said, voice streaming into the wind like the smoke from his nostrils.

The clouds obscured all but the mountaintops, and fear filled Mori. What would she find beneath that cloud cover? Smoldering forests? Nothing but ruin and skeletons? The city of Nova Vita still lay many leagues away. When she arrived, would the Moondisk bring hope for her people, or would her gift be given to the dead?

"Remember, Mori!" Bayrin called to her. "When we see the phoenixes, you point the Moondisk at them. I'll burn them with fire."

Mori nodded, clutching the bronze disk in her claws. Would it work? The disk seemed so small, no larger than a shield. How could it defeat the flame of Tiranor? The Children of the Moon had claimed its rays would extinguish phoenix fire, but what if they were wrong? What if that was only a legend? It had been thousands of years since the Sun God had attacked the northern isles; tales from so long ago also spoke of golems of clay, fairies that snatched the teeth of errant children, and other stories that could not possibly be true. Was this Moondisk just another myth?

"Bay, are you sure that--"

She had no time to voice her concern. Before she could complete her sentence, a ball of light flared on the horizon, like a sun rising from the clouds.

Bayrin cursed and bared his fangs.

"Stay near me, Mori," he said. "There's only one. It's time to test the Moondisk."

Fear pounded through Mori. Her limbs shook and flames danced inside her maw. She growled and showed her fangs, and smoke streamed from her nostrils. She glided upon an air current, diving toward the orange ball of light ahead.

Be strong, Mori, she told herself. *Be brave. For Requiem. For Bayrin.*

The ball of fire burst from the cloud cover, and Mori couldn't help it. She screamed.

The phoenix shot forward. It screeched, a sound like shattering mountains and typhoons. Its wings outstretched, a hundred feet in span, crackling with fire. Its body coiled, woven of liquid fire, and its eyes blazed like two suns.

It was him. She would know him anywhere. Acribus.

Every instinct inside her screamed to flee. Her heart thrashed. Her wings shook. She could barely breathe. *Turn and fly, Mori! Fly away and hide!*

"With me, Mori!" Bayrin shouted at her side, roaring fire. "Fly!"

Mori howled and blew flame. Heart thrashing, she shot toward the phoenix.

The Moondisk thrummed in her claws, vibrating. Soon it shook so wildly, she nearly dropped it. It felt so hot, hotter than coals, its heat shooting up her limbs. She clutched it tighter and screamed, driving forward along the wind.

The phoenix howled and its eyes met hers. Its beak, white hot shards of molten steel, opened to screech, revealing a maw of lava. It came surging toward her, wings flapping, raising fountains of light.

A ring of silver light exploded in her claws.

A shock wave shot out, the color of sky, its hum deafening. A beam of light coalesced and blazed forward, faster than arrows, wider than the pillars of Requiem, consuming Mori. She screamed with pain. She wanted to die. The light and sound vibrated through her, claiming her; she could see and hear nothing else. And yet she kept flying. She held the Moondisk. She raised it in her claws.

Wings flapping madly, she pointed the beam forward and heard the phoenix howl. The light washed it. Mori could see nothing but blue, but she growled, forced herself to narrow her eyes, to stare, to see her enemy.

Caught in the beam, Acribus howled. His wings flapped and his claws lashed. No more fire covered him. He flew as a great, naked bird, his flesh pale and wrinkled, his eyes black and beady. He looked to Mori like some plucked, starving vulture, a weak and wizened thing.

"Burn it, Bayrin!" she screamed, voice nearly lost under the deafening howl of the light. "Burn it dead!"

Through the silver beam, a dragon swooped. Bayrin's scales blazed under the light, a bright white tinged with silver. His claws outstretched. His maw opened. A stream of fire shot from his maw, spinning and crackling, and crashed against the naked phoenix.

Acribus howled. The fire engulfed him. His flew back, wings pounding the air. He clawed and burned.

Growling, Mori dived forward, the Moondisk clutched in her claws. She swooped. Rage filled her. Keeping the Moondisk's light upon him, she showered Acribus with fire.

Her flames cascaded against the naked bird. Acribus howled. His wrinkled skin burned, burst, and peeled off. Welts rose across his flesh, swollen like rotten fruit. His eyes melted. Soon he looked like a phoenix again, covered in burning flames-- but this fire burned him.

He mewled, a high sound that chilled Mori, and she realized: *This is the sound I made when he hurt me.* She blasted him with fire again, tears in her eyes, a howl in her throat.

Her fire burst against him, and Acribus fell from the sky.

He tumbled, a burning bird, his skin crackling. Mori swooped above him, Moondisk in her claws, keeping the beam upon him. Wind and smoke stung her eyes. Acribus tumbled through clouds, a comet crashing toward the earth. Mori followed, screaming, holding him in the beam lest he became a phoenix again. Forests rushed up toward them. The earth spun. Mori screamed and dived.

The naked, burning bird crashed through the treetops and hit the ground.

His magic vanished. He shrank like a piece of meat crumbling under fire. Soon he lay upon the earth as a broken, charred man. Smoke rose from him.

Mori landed beside him and tossed the Moondisk aside. It thumped into dry leaves, its light dimmed, and its hum faded. Once more, it was nothing but a shield of bronze inlaid with gold. Mori turned her eyes toward Acribus, who lay at her feet.

He moaned and twitched, still alive. Burns covered him. His clothes stuck to his soft, red body, melted into his flesh. He gasped for breath and whimpered.

Mori shifted into a human, drew her sword, and held it above him.

She wanted to slay him, but her hand shook, and tears filled her eyes. She could only stand above this ruin of a man, this living piece of burnt meat. In the old books she read, stories of epic adventure, dragons always slew their enemies with fire and glory. But the books never told of this. They never told of flesh melting over bones and the stink of it.

This is what Orin looked like, she remembered. *It's how he looked when you raped me by his body.*

With the flap of wings, Bayrin landed beside her in smoke and fire. He shifted into a human too, came to stand beside her, and blanched. Shock and disgust suffused his face, and he gritted his teeth. When he drew his sword, his hand shook.

"Stars, Mori," he whispered. "Look away. I'll finish this."

He tried to turn her aside, but she would not move.

"No," she whispered. "I... I want to see him die. I have to."

She looked up at Bayrin. Ash and dirt covered his face. Blood still stained his clothes from the lamprey wounds. His red hair was now black with soot. Mori wanted to tell him, *needed* to tell him, to tell somebody the secret that burned inside her.

"Bayrin, he..." Tears caught in her throat, and her body trembled, but she had to do this, she had to speak now before her courage left her. "Bayrin, at Castellum Luna, after they killed Orin, he... Acribus, he grabbed me and..."

Bayrin winced. "Mori, it's all right. You don't have to speak of it. I think I know what happened. You don't have to tell me... if you don't want to."

A sob fled her lips, but she tightened her jaw and clutched her sword. *Stay strong.*

"I have to tell you," she said, "I have to, I have to speak to somebody. He raped me, Bayrin. He raped me by the body of my brother, and... I didn't even fight him. I let him do it. I'm sorry." Tears filled her eyes.

Bayrin shook his head, eyes damp and narrowed. "For what, Mori? Sorry for what?" He blew out a shaky breath. "Stars, Mori, it wasn't your fault. You didn't let him do anything."

Mori closed her eyes, sword wavering in her hand. She still felt so dirty, so ashamed, so impure. But a sliver of relief filled her, a dim ray of hope. She had told Bayrin, and he hadn't recoiled in disgust. He still stood at her side. For an instant fear swelled inside her, and she was terrified that he would try to embrace or kiss her, and she knew she would flinch at his touch, that the memories would flow through her. But he only stood at her side, sword in hand, and she loved him for it. It was all she wanted from him right now.

"Bayrin," she whispered and opened her eyes. "Can you... can you do it?"

He nodded, face pale, eyes haunted but determined.

Mori turned away and walked several feet, facing the trees. She clutched her sword so tight her fingers hurt. She closed her eyes. When she heard the cry behind her, a mewl like a kicked dog, she winced and a tear ran down her cheek.

She heard Acribus moan no more. It was over.

"He's gone," she whispered, trembling. "He's gone forever."

The sun began to set. They had flown for two days and a night, not resting, and Nova Vita still lay many leagues away.

That night they slept upon a bed of dry leaves, naked birches rising around them. Under their cloaks, Mori shifted until she lay against Bayrin, warm in his arms. She slept with her head against his chest, his hand stroking her hair, and for the first time in many nights, she did not dream.

Daniel Arenson

ELETHOR

The Starlit Demon rose before him from the shadow.

A beast of stone, it rose two hundred feet tall, nearly as tall as the cavern that held it. Fissures ran across its bulky form, leaking starlight. Its teeth were white boulders, its eyes swirling pools of starlight. Its body shook and clanked as it grumbled, a sound that shook the chamber.

Elethor and Lyana stood upon the pillar of stone, still in human forms. Holding hands, they gazed upon the rising beast.

"Demon of Starlight!" Elethor cried. "I am Elethor, Son of Olasar, King of Requiem! I come to free you from your lair and call upon your help."

The Starlit Demon's head thrust forward, as large as Elethor's house in Nova Vita. Its mouth cracked open, a canyon in rock, and it rumbled with a voice like cascading boulders. The chamber shook with it.

"I serve no king... return to your sunlight... and let me sleep."

The behemoth of stone began descending into the shadows again, a mountain sinking into night. Its eyes began to close, leaving but glowing slits like crescent moons. A ridge of boulders rose down its back like a spine, creaking and shifting.

Elethor tightened his jaw. After all this--walking through the Abyss itself--would this creature refuse to help them? Floaters of light filled his eyes. His breath shook in his lungs. Lyana's hand tightened around his, squeezing it like a drowning woman.

"You will not sleep!" Elethor called to the demon. "Wake, Starlit Demon, and serve those you are bound to! You served my

forefathers. You are still sworn to my house. Rise and serve
Requiem, the kingdom your stars shine upon."

The demon raised its great head again. Dust and pebbles
rained from its body. Its eyes opened again, blazing so bright
Elethor snarled and looked aside, his own eyes narrowing.

"Sworn to your house!" the demon bellowed, voice echoing
across the cavern, its waves thudding against Elethor's chest.
"Your fathers imprisoned me here. Your fathers stripped me of
fire to feast on." A growl left its maw, so powerful Elethor
swayed and nearly fell. "Leave this place, lest I feed upon your
flesh instead."

Clutching Elethor's hand, Lyana raised her chin and
shouted to the beast.

"If it's fire you crave, we will feed you fire!" Her cheeks
flushed and her eyes blazed. "Are you hungry, Starlit Demon?
For years you slumbered here, and your light is dim. Will fire fill
your belly?"

The Starlit Demon turned its head so quickly, its tail of
stone lashed and hit a wall. A crack ran along the chamber,
showering stones. The beast roared, baring its teeth. Its gullet
blazed like swirling, molten stars.

"I have craved fire for longer than your mind can grasp," it
said. "For two thousand turns of your seasons, I slumbered here,
craving heat and flame to devour. The hunger in my belly is a
forge you cannot fill."

Elethor and Lyana looked at one another and nodded.
They shifted as one, flapped their wings, and rose as dragons.
The Starlit Demon roared before them, maw open so wide,
Elethor knew it could swallow even his dragon form.

"Here is a taste of the fire you crave!" Elethor shouted and
blew his flames.

The stream of fire roared toward the Starlit Demon, and for
an instant, fear filled Elethor. What if his fire burned the beast?

What if it attacked them? But the Starlit Demon opened its maw wider, swallowing the flames. Lyana blew fire too, and the demon feasted.

The dragons let their flames die. The Starlit Demon roared.

"Is that all the fire you can kindle?" It made a deep sound like laughter, body shaking. "All the dragons of Requiem would not fill my belly. Ten thousand blew their fire upon me, but I knew no fill."

"If you follow us, we will grant you more fire!" Elethor shouted.

The demon's laughter deepened, cruel laughter that made the chamber shake. The pillar of stone upon which Elethor and Lyana had stood crumbled and fell. Cracks raced across the Starlit Demon's stone body, emitting beams of light.

"The armies of your fathers blew flames from their mouths into mine, but my craving was stronger." The Starlit Demon glared at Elethor, drenching him with light. "And so I toppled their halls, and feasted upon their children. Your kings were not pleased. How will you feed me when your fathers could not?"

Elethor hovered before the beast, his wings blowing rocks and dust off its body.

"I will not feed you dragonfire. I will feed you sunfire itself. Ten thousand phoenixes fly over Requiem, and each is woven from the Sun God's flame. Emerge from your lair, Starlit Demon! Follow me to Requiem, and you will feast."

The Starlit Demon rose, filling the chamber with its girth. Its claws emerged from the darkness below, raining earth; each seemed carved of flint, larger than a horse. It tossed back its head and roared, and the sound crashed against the chamber walls, cracking them. Lyana screamed in pain; the demon's howl knocked her back in the air. Elethor grimaced. He felt like that roar could crush his scales and snap his ribs.

A Dawn of Dragonfire

"Will you follow, Starlit Demon?" he cried. "Will you fly to Requiem and feast upon the phoenix fire?"

The demon leaped.

The chamber seemed to explode.

A fountain of stone and light, the Starlit Demon crashed into the ceiling, claws digging, maw biting. Boulders cascaded. Dust filled the air, blinding Elethor. He flew backward until his back hit a wall. He saw nothing but raining rock, clouds of dust, and beams of starlight.

"Lyana!" he shouted.

He could not see nor hear her. A boulder fell before him, grazing his tail. Elethor flattened himself against the wall. Rocks pummeled him. He tried to call for Lyana again, but dust and rocks filled his mouth.

The starlight dimmed, and Elethor managed to blow fire, lighting the darkness. Through the storm of debris, he discerned the Starlit Demon burrowing into a hole in the ceiling, tail lashing. Soon the beast disappeared into the tunnel it dug, driving upward like a great earthworm.

"Elethor!" came a cry from across the chamber, and Lyana flew toward him. Dust coated her blue scales, turning her gray. With three great flaps of her wings, she soared toward the hole in the ceiling. "Come on, Elethor, we follow!"

With that, she soared into the hole above, following the Starlit Demon. Heart hammering, Elethor pushed himself off the wall. Dust and rocks rained against his wings as he flapped them, but he gritted his teeth, narrowed his eyes, and forced himself to fly. The tunnel gaped above him, fifty feet wide. He saw Lyana's tail swish above and he followed.

Tunnel walls blurred at his sides. The light of the Starlit Demon fell in rays. Dirt and rocks cascaded, clanking against his scales.

He flew for what seemed like leagues. The Starlit Demon burrowed and roared, crashing through the stone and dirt. Elethor growled, slipstreaming in the beast's wake. If he swerved to the right or left, boulders would tumble against him, denting scales. Lyana flew above him, drafting behind the demon's tail. The behemoth dwarfed the two dragons, ten times their size.

The demon cut through the Abyss. The tunnel drove through craggy chambers, revealing the horrors of the underworld: nests of squirming eggs, rotten children coiled inside them; bloated worms, six feet long and bearing human faces; bodies that rotted, squirming with insects, yet still screamed in pain. But soon the tunnel grew colder, and Elethor saw bones, rocks, soil, and the buried ruins of old cities.

We are leaving the Abyss, he thought. *We are leaving this unholy underworld and entering the crust of the world.*

He exhaled a shaky breath of relief, and his eyes stung. How long would nightmares of this place haunt him? At once he knew the answer: for the rest of his life. He would not forget the sight of Nedath, a dead girl atop the body of a centipede. In the dark he would always see Lyana wrapped in cobwebs, turning into a shriveled creature. Every night, he knew that he would dream of the bodies upon the hooks, undying beasts that fed upon their own flesh.

He looked at Lyana, who flew above him, and his heart seemed so small, so cold, wrapped in ice.

Nobody else will ever know, he thought. *Only Lyana and I. We'll never be able to speak of what we saw... not to anyone above ground, maybe not even to each other.* He could barely see; his eyes blurred with tears. *But we still have each other. Lyana is saved... and I will always be with her, to hold her in the darkness when our nightmares swell.*

The thought of Lyana made his chest feel a little warmer. She kept the terror at bay. Elethor nodded as he flew, eyes damp.

We will live in peace again, together--we will save our people, we will stargaze on Lacrimosa Hill, and we will leave this darkness behind us. She and I.

All his life, Lyana had been a thorn in his side, the sanctimonious girl who'd endlessly scold and lecture him. But today as he flew, he saw above him a strong, wise woman... a woman he wanted to spend his life with. A woman, he knew, that he could learn to love.

The Starlit Demon burrowed for what seemed like hours, roaring in the dark, until it crashed through a slab of stone, and screams rose above.

Elethor gasped.

As he shot up, he saw burrows running alongside the tunnel the Starlit Demon carved. His people--thin, bloodied Vir Requis-- cowered there like ants underground. They covered their eyes in the demon's starlight and cried.

An instant later, the Starlit Demon crashed through the topsoil and shot into the night sky, a geyser bursting into the world. An army of phoenixes burned above, screeching and flapping wings of fire. The world spun. The sound deafened Elethor. Boulders cascaded and the tunnels began to crumble. Several Vir Requis fell into the darkness, tumbling past Elethor. They shifted into dragons below him, howled, and flew behind him.

"Elethor!" Lyana cried above. She soared out of the tunnel and into the night, crashing into the army of phoenixes.

Elethor howled and shot into the night. The phoenixes swooped. Dragons flew up below him. Vir Requis still in human forms ran deeper into tunnels. Sound and light crashed.

SOLINA

She was flying with her troops, a phoenix in the night, when the demon burst from underground.

It looked like a great scarab made of stone, larger than a whale. Its claws tore through the earth, and its eyes blazed, two stars shooting beams of light. The earth crumbled around it, a sinkhole falling into darkness. Vir Requis screamed and fell from their burrows, now revealed to the night.

It looks, Solina thought in a moment of incredulity, *like a gopher bursting from an anthill.*

She spread out her wings of fire and shrieked. Considering its girth, she had expected this stone demon to crawl upon the earth, but it came soaring into the sky. Wingless, it flew toward her and her phoenixes. Its eyes nearly blinded her, and its roars thudded against her, fanning her flames.

"Kill the beast!" she shrieked, her voice emerging from her beak like typhoons of sound. "Sunspear Phalanx! Dragonbone! Bring it down!"

The two phalanxes swooped in formation, each a terror of fifty phoenixes. One fell upon the stone demon from the right, the other from its left. Their beaks and talons thrashed its hide.

They crashed against the beast like flaming paper against a cliff.

Solina watched, shrieking, the flames crackling with fury across her. The phoenixes attacked the stone demon again, wave after wave of them, only to crash against it. The demon's eyes blazed with starlight. Its claws lashed and its teeth bit, tearing phoenixes apart. Their flames filled its maw, ran down its throat, and blazed through the fissures along its belly. The demon seemed like a great, flying furnace.

And my men are stoking its fire, Solina realized. She howled, a sound that could shatter walls. Elethor had found a demon in the depths, a creature to eat the flames of her wrath. As she flew above, she saw the beast swallow three phoenixes. Other firebirds slashed at its body, only to die at its claws and fall, shredded, like burning leaves.

Solina narrowed her eyes and swooped, claws outstretched.

You think yourself clever, Elethor. But you have only doomed yourself.

Where the stone demon had burst from the ground, a chasm loomed, its rims crumbling into darkness. Alongside the cavern walls, Solina saw openings to a dozen burrows. Inside each burrow the weredragons still cowered, fragile humans not daring to fly, even now. She saw only several dragons flying behind the stony demon; the rest were too cowardly to shift and emerge to battle.

But I will bring the battle to them, Solina thought. *I spent a moon trying to break into these places... and now, Elethor, you have opened a dozen doors.*

She snarled, skirted around the feasting demon of stone, and swooped into the gaping chasm. A dozen burrows surrounded her, running from the chasm walls into darkness. Weredragons wept in their human forms and tried to flee deeper, but their burrows were packed tight; they could either become dragons and fly into the phoenix sky, or die as humans underground.

Men with swords were rushing to each tunnel's entrance, pushing back the women and children. But in one tunnel, a crumbly burrow like a wormhole, only children wept, torn from their mothers' grasps when the demon had crashed through their hideout. Shrieking, her flames crackling, Solina flew toward that tunnel.

The children screamed. Across the crater, men howled inside their own tunnels. A ball of fire, Solina shifted in midair, becoming a woman again. As she flew, she drew her twin blades. She tumbled into the children's tunnel, swords swinging.

Aknur, her left blade of nightfire, halved a young boy's face. Raem, her right blade of dawn, cut a girl from collarbone to navel. The other children were fleeing deeper, tripping over one another, wailing in fear. Solina grinned and walked deeper, blades swinging, showering blood and cutting down the vermin.

I will not let these creatures grow and breed, she thought as she sliced two girls who embraced and wept. *I will clear the world of their darkness, Sun God, for your wrath and glory.*

She stepped deeper into the tunnel, over bodies and severed limbs, leaving a trail of blood and sunlight.

I will kill them all.

Howls rose behind her. Flames crackled. Solina spun to see a brass dragon fly toward the tunnel she stood in. Solina's grin widened, her heart pounded, and she licked blood off her lips.

"Elethor!" she cried and raised her dripping swords. "You have come to me at last."

ADIA

She stood in the tunnel, comforting a girl whose hands had
burned to stumps, when the world collapsed.

The floor cracked, and she watched children fall into the
chasm. Boulders fell from the ceiling, crushing people around
her. The tunnels shook, dirt rained, and a tower of stone jutted
up before her. Great claws, larger than Adia's body, sliced before
her. A creature as large as a temple, its eyes blazing beacons, rose
before her, leaving ruin and blood in its wake.

As people fell and screamed, Adia thought she glimpsed
two dragons--brass and blue--flying after the creature, following it
through the tunnel it carved.

The Starlit Demon, she knew. Tears sprang into her eyes.
Lyana is alive. My daughter is alive!

As dust flew and stones rolled, Adia clenched her jaw. She
wanted to run through the people, shift into a dragon, and fly to
Lyana. She forced herself to remain.

This is my station. These are my people to heal.

She moved from one to another, digging them from the
rubble. One old man wept, clutching a fractured arm. Beside him
a young boy lay, his leg buried under a boulder. How could she
heal them all? How could she choose between them--grant death
to one, life to the other?

Adia was kneeling over a pregnant woman whose head was
bleeding when fire screamed. She looked up and saw phoenixes
raining into the chasm the Starlit Demon had left. One phoenix
flew to a tunnel that gaped open across the chasm, shifted into
Solina, and leaped into a crowd of screaming children. Several

other phoenixes swooped toward the tunnel Adia huddled in, shifted into Tiran men with blades and armor, and ran into the throng of survivors.

Adia found herself snarling. The time to hide was over, she realized; they would find no more shelter underground, not with the tunnels collapsing around them. They had to flee. Her heart ached to leave the wounded woman... but Adia left her.

"Vir Requis!" she shouted, running toward the Tirans at the entrance. "Vir Requis, follow! We shift! We fly! To the sky, children of Requiem!"

As she ran, she grabbed a sword from a fallen soldier, drew it, and swung the blade. Around her, living soldiers of Requiem swung their own blades. One Tiran fell into the chasm. Adia ran and barreled into another, shoving him into the darkness.

"Find the sky!" Adia shouted, leaped from tunnel into chasm, and shifted into a dragon.

Wings sprouted from her back with a thud. White scales clanked across her. Fangs sprouted from her mouth. She tossed back her head and howled, blowing blue fire. It had been so long since she had shifted, so long since she had felt air under her wings, flames in her gullet, the magic of starlight in her veins.

Beneath her, the falling Tirans shifted into phoenixes and soared toward her. Behind her, Vir Requis were leaping from the tunnel, shifting into dragons, and soaring. Adia soared with them. She flew up the chasm, following the path of the Starlit Demon, and shot toward a night sky strewn with firebirds. More tunnels gaped open along the chasm's walls, and hundreds of Vir Requis were leaping from them, turning into dragons, and soaring after her.

Adia shot past layers of rock, soil, and frost, and finally burst out from the underground. The ruins of Nova Vita spread below her, walls and columns fallen. Thousands of phoenixes flew above her. Hundreds of dragons soared around her. The

Starlit Demon howled in the sky, a great slug of stone that flew with no wings. It crushed phoenixes between its teeth, and its belly bulged with their flame, a furnace in the sky like a sun.

"Rise, dragons of Requiem!" Adia cried. "Into the sky!"

Phoenixes came swooping toward her, crackling and raising sparks. More flew below. If death flowed underground, and death burned above, she would lead her people to die in the sky. The Starlit Demon could not consume all their enemies; its jaws bit many, but too many phoenixes flew. This creature of the underworld would not be their savior.

But maybe, Adia dared to hope... maybe in this chaos, a few dragons could escape. Maybe as the Starlit Demon devoured their enemies, some of her people could flee into the mountains, the forests, the southern swamps.

But I will stay, she thought. *I will stay until they are all fled or burned. I will die in the sky of my home under the light of my stars.*

Phoenixes dived toward her, lashing their talons. Adia shot between them, soaring through their wings of fire. The flames crackled against her, and she screamed but drove past them. More flew above. Around her, hundreds of dragons were rising.

"Fly to all directions of the wind!" she cried. "Fly to the mountains and forests. Flee into the wilderness, dragons of Requiem!"

Adia saw a group of young dragons, mere children barely old enough to fly, soaring into the air. They wailed, sparks left their throats, and their wings fluttered like the wings of hummingbirds. A crackling phoenix, thrice their size, began swooping toward them. Its howl tore the air and the young dragons wailed.

Narrowing her eyes, Adia surged. She flew straight up, roaring. She shot around the young dragons, spread her wings wide, and raised her front claws. The swooping phoenix crashed against her, and Adia screamed. The flames bathed her scales.

"Fly, children!" she shouted as the phoenix claws tore at her shoulders. "Fly north to the mountains."

She slammed her tail against the phoenix, but it was like clubbing a forest fire. Smoke filled her nostrils and she could barely see. She pulled her wings close, tumbled, and flew again. Welts covered her belly, where she had no scales to protect her. The scales on her back felt like stones in an oven, and lacerations covered her shoulders. She looked around madly, seeking the children, but could not see them, only countless firebirds. Had the young ones escaped?

The phoenix that had attacked her screeched above. It swooped, a comet of spinning fire. Adia closed her eyes, fearing the fire would melt them, and raised her claws. She prayed, ready to die.

A shadow fell upon her. A howl thudded in her ears. When she opened her eyes, Adia saw the Starlit Demon crash into the phoenixes above.

Stars, the size of him, she thought. She was a powerful dragon, her wings wide and her tail long, but beneath the Starlit Demon, she felt like a fish swimming under a ship. Flames crashed around the demon as dozens of phoenixes attacked it, but none could burn it. The creature's appetite knew no bounds; its jaws opened and closed, biting phoenixes like a wolf biting hens.

Blue scales flashed to her left.

A cry pierced the night.

"Mother!"

Adia looked and saw her daughter there. Lyana looked slimmer, the shine of her scales dimmed, but she was alive, she was flying, she was well. Tears filled Adia's eyes. *My daughter. My beloved.* She wanted to fly toward Lyana, hold her, never let her go again. But she steeled herself.

"Lyana!" she cried. "Lead the southern route!" Behind her daughter's shoulder, she saw a hundred dragons fly into a cloud of phoenixes. Many burned and fell. "Lead them to King's Forest and I will meet you there!"

Lyana looked behind her, saw the phoenixes swoop against the fleeing dragons, and nodded. With a growl, the sapphire dragon flew toward them.

"Dragons of Requiem, follow!" Lyana called. "We fly to the forests!"

Adia looked around her. Hundreds of dragons were fleeing to all directions of the wind. Thousands of phoenixes were swooping upon them or chasing them into the distance. Below, in the collapsed chasm, some Vir Requis still huddled in what shelter remained of the tunnels. The sounds of battle rose from the earth; Tirans and Vir Requis still fought there in human forms.

We are overrun, Adia realized. A chill ran through her. The Starlit Demon could not devour ten thousand phoenixes. It could not stop the fire that burned her people.

Our era ends here, she thought, tears in her eyes. *The Second Age of Requiem ends like the first... in blood and fire and destruction.*

Three phoenixes fell upon her. Their claws lashed, their beaks bit, and their fire blazed against her. Adia shouted and could barely hear her own voice. She called for the Starlit Demon, but could not see it. She saw nothing but fire.

No more pain filled her. Only warmth.

I die now, she thought. *I go to the starlit halls of my fathers. I will forever dine there with my parents, with the fallen men and women of my house. I am coming to you, stars of Requiem.*

She heard the glow of those celestial halls, a sound like harps. She saw their glow, silver and soft, bathing her with light. No more fire burned her, and Adia could smile, for she died as she had lived--fighting for the song of her people.

She raised her eyes, and looked to the stars, and saw the silver light blaze. Caught in the beam, the phoenixes still flew, but no more fire burned upon them. They were as naked vultures, black and wizened, exposed for their true ugliness and frailty.

Two dragons came coiling down from the light, tails whipping behind them, and Adia gasped.

"Bayrin!" she called. Her son flew there! She knew his great, lanky frame, his emerald scales, his bright eyes. Princess Mori flew by him, gripping a disk of silver light; she seemed to be holding the moon itself. Did they too die? Did they too now fly among the stars of Afterlife?

"Mother!" Bayrin called. He dived. His fire rained upon the naked vultures, and his claws slashed them. The beasts burned, bled, and fell.

Adia's heart thrashed, she gasped, and tears ran down her cheeks.

They were not dead, she knew. She laughed as she cried. *They found the Moondisk.*

She flapped her wings--three great thuds--and soared. Her fire roared, spun, and crashed against a naked phoenix that screeched in the Moondisk's glow.

The phoenix blazed. For a moment it looked like a firebird again, but this was dragonfire. This fire burned it. The creature squealed, cawed to the sky, and fell. As it tumbled by Adia, it became a man again... nothing but a burning man who thudded against the ruins of Nova Vita below.

Adia spread her wings wide, blew fire, and roared. Hope burned anew--hope of moonlight and dragonfire.

LYANA

She was rallying the fleeing dragons, driving them toward the southern forests, when the light blazed behind her. Lyana turned and saw her brother plunge through the light, blowing fire upon extinguished phoenixes. Princess Mori flew behind him, holding a disk like the moon, bathing the world with its glow.

Tears sprang into Lyana's eyes.

Bayrin and Mori are back. Hope is back.

"Fly to the forests!" she cried to the children who flew around her. "Wait for us there!"

As the small dragons flew off, Lyana turned, snarled, and soared into battle. Her fire bathed the sky.

Under the beam of Mori's Moondisk, the phoenixes lost their flames, only to ignite under dragonfire. Lyana saw her mother fly above, a great white dragon in the night, blowing her flame upon the enemy. Her father came soaring from below, a burly copper dragon, a hole in his right wing and fire in his maw.

Ten phoenixes flew toward Lyana from all sides. The Moondisk's beam blazed far in the north. The Starlit Demon howled and feasted to the west. Lyana flew alone against the enemy.

"Mori!" she shouted across the battle. "Mori, give me your light!"

Did the golden dragon hear? Phoenixes filled her vision. One crashed into Lyana, and she howled. Talons cut her. Wings of flame blazed against her. A second phoenix slammed into her right, and fire roared, and Lyana cried in agony, and--

Moonlight washed the world.

The flames vanished like a candle under a blanket. The light hummed. Caught in its glare, the phoenixes were nothing but naked birds, blinded and screeching.

Ignoring the pain of her wounds, Lyana howled and spun, blowing a ring of fire around her. The phoenixes kindled, welts rose across them, their skin cracked, and they crashed from the sky.

Howls of dying dragons rose to the north. The moonbeam left Lyana, its light rushing to extinguish a northern horde of phoenixes. Lyana looked around, panting. Hundreds of corpses rained upon the ruins of Nova Vita. Thousands of dragons were fleeing or fighting, and countless phoenixes still blazed. Above the battle, Mori was directing the Moondisk from left to right, pausing on each group of phoenixes just long enough for dragons to burn them. The Starlit Demon still moved across the sky, consuming phoenixes that fled from Mori's light.

"Yarin!" Lyana called to a red dragon who flew above. She remembered him well--a young man in the service of her father.

He turned toward her, fire between his teeth, a gash along his face. "My Lady Lyana!"

"Yarin, to me!" she called. "Bring your men. We follow that beam."

She shot under a swooping phoenix, soared above the Starlit Demon who dived by, and surged toward a group of young dragons. They were mere youths, no older than fifteen, but they would have to fight like men today. Welts covered them and one's wing was torn.

"Dragons of Requiem!" she called. "Follow--to blood and glory!"

They howled and blew flame, and Lyana soared, rallying more dragons as she flew. Phoenixes descended upon them. Three dragons fell, turned to humans, and crashed against houses below. Fire bathed her. Lyana narrowed her eyes and flew toward the light of the Moonbeam.

Silver light covered her. The phoenixes cried, naked. She burned them. Her dragons blew flames around her. They howled for death and glory, for Requiem, for their princess. The phoenixes fell dead.

The moonlight left them, shooting to the east. Lyana snarled, spun, and followed it.

"Stay in the beam!" she shouted. "Dragons of Requiem, behind me! Burn the enemy!"

They flew among the fire and moonlight, blood raining. As Lyana sounded her roar, she looked around the battle, seeking Elethor. Where was their king?

"Elethor!" she cried over the battle, but did not hear him. She gritted her teeth. Requiem needed their king, needed Elethor to rally them around his cry--not her, not Lyana, but King Elethor Aeternum.

"Elethor! Hear me!"

Rage boiled inside her. If he was not dead, she would kill him herself. He needed to lead his people, now more than ever. Where the stars was he?

She roared her dragonfire, bathing the phoenixes. They fell dead, thudded against the Starlit Demon as he dived below, then crashed to the city ruins. Requiem trembled with fire, blood, and light.

BAYRIN

A dozen phoenixes soared toward Mori.

Flying beside the princess, Bayrin roared.

"Mori, to your left!"

She spun in the sky, pointing the Moondisk to her left. The beam caught the phoenixes and they extinguished. Bayrin swooped upon them, bathing them with fire. They crackled and fell.

"Bay!" Mori shouted above him, fear twisting her voice.

The beam of moonlight left Bayrin, sweeping to the north. He turned his head and saw ten more phoenixes surge toward Mori. They shrieked, claws outstretched. When the beam hit them, they cried and lost their fire. Wings aching and wounds blazing, Bayrin soared toward them. He roared fire and burned them down.

He spared the battle below a glance. Phoenixes fell like rain. The dragons of Requiem were flying from side to side, staying within the moonbeam. He saw his sister, a sapphire dragon blowing fire. He saw his parents--Deramon flew as a burly copper dragon, crashing into phoenixes, while Adia soared as a white dragon, leaving a wake of flame. When Mori moved her Moondisk, those dragons too slow to follow burned in phoenix fire.

"Mori, phoenixes over the temple!" Bayrin shouted. A hundred of them were roaring from the marble roof, comets of fury.

Mori nodded and moved the Moondisk upon the enemy. The phoenixes screeched and Bayrin saw dozens of dragons swarm upon them, roaring fire.

More screeches sounded above. Bayrin looked up and cursed. Ten phoenixes had managed to flank the battle, fly over the clouds, and were now swooping upon Mori from above.

"Mori, fire above!" he shouted and soared. She banked, and Bayrin crashed upward. His wings brushed her, and he slammed against the phoenixes above.

Fire engulfed him. Talons tore him. Beaks of flame ripped his flesh. He howled and lashed his claws but cut only fire.

Silver light bathed him. Below, Mori was flying upside down, pointing the moonbeam toward him. He roared fire and the phoenixes fell.

"Point the Moondisk down!" Bayrin shouted to her. Welts blazed across him. He felt ready to fall from the sky, but forced himself to keep flying. "I've got your back. Protect the dragons below."

Mori looked as hurt and wounded as Bayrin felt. The lamprey bites still bled on her shoulders. Like him, she had not slept or eaten in two days. And yet she snarled and directed the Moondisk down, catching a formation of soaring phoenixes. Bayrin showered them with fire.

Three more phoenixes swooped from the clouds above Mori. Cursing, Bayrin drove toward them.

"Keep that moonbeam pointing down!" he shouted as he soared by her.

He crashed into the firebirds above. Their flames washed him. He screamed in agony. It felt like flying into a forge. He clawed blindly.

I will protect Mori. I won't let them burn her.

Moonlight bathed him. He roared fire. The phoenixes fell.

More flew at Mori's left. He drove forward and crashed into their fire. When she lit them with moonlight and he burned them, more flew from the right. Bayrin howled, scales blazing, and crashed into them.

Protect the princess. Don't let them burn her. Don't...

Fire washed him.

Talons ripped him.

Bayrin howled and blew flame, and his world was nothing but heat, screams, and pain.

ELETHOR

He flew toward the tunnel, shifted into human form, and rolled into the darkness. He leaped to his feet while drawing his sword. When his eyes adjusted to the shadows, his stomach churned. The sight was as sickening as anything from the Abyss.

Dead children covered the tunnel floor, cut with blades. One girl's face was slashed. A boy was missing his arm. A second boy lay in the corner, disemboweled. The sight and stench nearly made Elethor gag. He gritted his teeth and raised his sword.

Ahead in the darkness, before a crowd of weeping children, stood Solina.

Elethor's heart thudded. His head spun.

Solina. Flame of his life. Light of his soul. The woman he had loved with heat like dragonfire. Blood covered her armor, face, and blades. She stared at him, and he saw the same emotion swirl in her eyes. She gave him a sad, crooked smile.

"Elethor," she said softly.

He walked deeper into the tunnel, stepping over strewn limbs and corpses, his boots sloshing through blood. His eyes narrowed, he could barely breathe, and for a moment he only managed to shake his head and whisper.

"Solina... how could you do this?"

A snarl fled her lips, sounding almost like a sob. A shaky, toothy grin twisted her face; Elethor couldn't decide if she grinned like a wolf or a madwoman.

"They are vermin, Elethor," she said. "They are nothing but lizards. You saw how they taunted me." Her eyes blazed, narrowing to blue slits. "You saw how they would fly above me, mock me, roar fire down on me. They burned me." She took a step toward him. "I won't let them come between us again. I will kill every weredragon between you and me until you're mine again."

"I am one of them!" Elethor shouted. His eyes stung. "Solina, you have gone mad. You have lost your mind. This is not the woman I knew, that I loved. You were good once, Solina. You were--"

"I was weak!" she screamed. "I was scared." Tears fled her eyes. "I was an orphan, Elethor. Your father murdered my parents, slaughtered my brothers like animals, and made me live here, a prisoner, a cripple." She took another step toward him, tears rolling. She let one sabre clang to the ground and reached out to him. "But you made it bearable, Elethor. You loved me, even though I could not become a dragon, even as everyone else in this land loathed me, saw me as less than human. But *they* are less than human. They are creatures. They are dead now; I killed them. I burned them. I did this for us, Elethor. Don't you understand? For me and you."

He shook his head, looking at the blood that covered the tunnel. "Killing children?" His voice was barely a whisper. "Stars, Solina, how could you think this would bring us together?"

"Because I know that you still love me." She stared into his eyes. "Because I remember. I remember your kisses. Your whispers. I remember how we would come here, to this very tunnel, and speak of our dreams. We would speak about how cruel your father was to me, how one day we would fly away and be together in some faraway land." Her eyes shone. "That day has come, Elethor! I brought it here. I made it happen so our dream could come true." Her body shook. "Don't you see?" She clutched his shoulder. "We can be together now like we always wanted, like we knew would always happen. We'll fly to Tiranor, you a dragon and I a phoenix. I've built a palace where we will reign, king and queen of a desert land. It's that magical place we've always dreamed of, Elethor. It's what we've always wanted."

"I did not want this!" he shouted. His pulse pounded in his ears, and his head spun. "You will not cast this blood on me. You've gone mad in your southern land, with this... this Sun God who corrupted your mind." He swept his arms around him. "Dreams? Magical kingdoms? Love? You drenched the world in blood! You slaughtered children!"

"For you!" she shouted hoarsely. "For us!"

"Not for me!" His eyes burned. "I did not ask for this. You--"

A child tore free from the group of survivors behind Solina. He ran forward, skirted around Solina, and made toward the tunnel exit, maybe hoping to fly outside. Solina cut him down. Her blade flashed and sliced his leg, then swung down onto his shoulder, cleaving him. The child fell, gurgled, and died.

Elethor sucked in his breath. Head spinning and heart pounding, barely able to see through the sting of tears, he swung his sword at Solina.

She stood only three feet away, but it seemed the longest distance his sword had ever swung. It seemed the longest instant of his life. He was cutting the roots of that life, the old memories and meaning that had forever filled him, driven him, defined him. In that instant that lasted hours, he realized how much Solina had shaped him--he had grown up in her light, in her arms, almost a part of her. Without her, who was he?

A king, a voice whispered inside him. *A betrothed to Lyana. A leader of dragons.*

A whole man--no longer a boy in his brother's shadow, no longer a sculptor who shied away from the court his fathers had built. If he cut her down, he would cut himself free--free to become this man of his own right, to sit upon the throne with a whole heart.

He had always felt like half a soul; a night to Solina's day, starlight to her fire. Now he became one.

The instant passed. His sword reached her. Her blade rose and parried, and steel clanged.

She thrust her sabre at him, snarling, a wild animal, no longer human. He parried. He thrust again. And they danced.

It was a dance like they used to love--of passion and rage and hope. Her sword bit his shoulder, like her teeth would as they made love in this tunnel. He bled and thrust again, slamming his blade against her armor. Her sword flew at him, he parried, swung again.

He felt no rage. No more sadness. When he looked upon her, he no longer saw the old Solina--the girl of golden hair, of bright eyes, of secrets only he knew. He saw only the rot inside her, and he slammed at her until he cut her down. His blade shattered hers, and she fell. His sword slammed against her armor, denting it, and she gasped.

She knelt before him, head tossed back. Blood poured from a crack in her breastplate. Her mouth opened and closed.

"El," she whispered. "El..."

He stood above her, his sword raised. He could stab her now. He could slice her neck. He could--

"El," she whispered, "do you remember the wooden turtle?"

Blackness clutched him. He could not help but lower his head, close his eyes, and feel the breath leave him. She spoke with a trembling voice; she sounded so much like the Solina who would hold him years ago. Her every word shot arrows through him.

"El, you carved it for me. I remember... I said how I wanted a pet, a friend in Requiem, and you made me a wooden turtle. Remember how we'd imagine that, in the magical kingdom we would find, our turtle would come alive? How--"

Pain blazed on his thigh, not the throb of memory, but searing agony. Elethor gasped. His eyes snapped open to see Solina twisting a dagger in his leg.

Blood spurted and Solina leaped. She drove her fist into Elethor's chin, and his head snapped back, and he saw nothing but light and blood and stone. He fell, stars floating before his eyes. Solina pounced atop him, baring her teeth.

"I will spare your life this night," she hissed, "so you may see the death I bring to your land. But I will give you this first."

She pulled the dagger from his thigh. He raised his arms, but could not block her strength. She drove her blade down his face. Pain exploded. Blood filled his eyes and mouth.

"I will kill them all, Elethor!" she screamed. "I will burn them all with my fire. You will watch! And then you will crawl to me and beg to be mine!"

She leaped past him, tossed herself outside, and shifted into a phoenix. Her flames crackled, and when Elethor turned his head, he saw her soar into the night. Her scream carried on the wind, high-pitched, a storm of rage.

"You will beg, Elethor! You will beg!"

He struggled to his feet. Blood washed his face and leg. He made to leap after her, but his thigh twisted, and he fell. His elbows banged against the tunnel floor. He crawled to the exit, stared up, and saw the Moondisk bathe the world with light.

He tried to shift into a dragon. He let the magic fill him. Light and agony flooded him, his eyes closed, and his head fell.

BAYRIN

Time swirled like stars.

Darkness clutched him, pulling him into slumber, and Bayrin dreamed. In his dreams, he lay in human form upon bloody earth. Mori was kneeling above, also a human, cradling him in her arms.

"Bay!" she cried and shook him. "Bay, please..."

He dreamed of his sister there too, weeping over him, and his mother praying, and soldiers bearing him on a litter into a temple of marble and candles.

"Mori," he whispered. "I have to protect her... I have to fly...."

His voice died and he slept.

He felt like he slept for years.

When his eyes finally fluttered open, he thought he was dead. Soft light bathed him, and marble columns rose around him. He lay in a bed, a white blanket pulled over him. It was supposed to be night, but dawn's light fell from the windows.

"Mori?" he whispered, voice hoarse. He raised his arm and saw that bandages covered it.

"Do I look like Mori?" a voice answered him. "Bay, if I look like my sister, you look like a phoenix. Actually, for a while up there, you did look like one."

Bayrin pushed himself up in bed, pain blazing. He winced. A figure sat at his bedside, silhouetted in the dawn's light. Bayrin squinted, bringing the figure into focus. His breath caught.

"Elethor?" he whispered.

His friend nodded, smiling softly, though his eyes were sad.

"El!" Bayrin cried. He tried to leap up, to hug his friend, but his head spun, and he fell back into bed. Everything hurt; he felt like he'd been dipped into a bath of coals.

"Take it easy, Bay!" Elethor said and squeezed his shoulder. "You got banged up pretty badly there."

In a flash, Bayrin remembered. *The phoenixes!* They had swooped toward Mori, and...

He pushed himself back up, panting. "I have to save her, El. The battle! Mori is..."

"Mori is *fine*, Bay!" Elethor said. "Lie down, for stars' sake, or I'll tie you down." His voice softened. "You saved her life up there. You saved all of us."

Elethor himself was wounded, Bayrin saw. Bandages covered his shoulder and leg. Fresh stitches ran along his face, from forehead to chin. The young king looked like he'd been to the Abyss and back--which, Bayrin supposed, he had been. He couldn't help but laugh.

"Look at us, El--a pair of beaten up patients." Suddenly he found that tears filled his eyes. "Stars, Elethor, I missed you. What happened? Is the battle...?"

"The battle is over." Elethor sighed and lowered his head. "Solina fled. So have those phoenixes who survived. Not many of them did, but some managed to flee into the south. After the Starlit Demon ate his fill, he vanished back underground; I imagine he'll sleep for a good long while to digest his meal." He winced. "It was bad, Bay. Many Vir Requis died. Too many." His voice dropped to a pained whisper. "Thousands are gone."

Bayrin's breath caught and horror clumped in his throat. "Is... my sister? My parents?"

"They're alive. Your father looks like he was dropped into a nest of weasels, and your mother has seen better days. Lyana is bashed up like an old leather ball after a thousand kicks, but she wouldn't admit it." He smiled softly. "They're here in the temple, wounds tended to."

Relief swept over Bayrin, but grief too. *Many Vir Requis died. Too many.*

Eyes stinging, he looked outside the window. He watched the morning light fall upon ruins. Clear skies rolled outside, blue without a tinge of smoke. A lump filled his throat, and he swallowed.

"Where..." His voice caught, and he blinked for a moment, unable to speak. "Where is Mori? I want to see her."

Elethor helped him up. Bayrin slung his arm across the king's shoulder, and they walked slowly. Step by step, they left the chamber and moved down a hallway. Wounded filled the hall, lying on makeshift beds. When they passed by chambers, Bayrin saw more wounded inside. Healers rushed back and forth, robes swishing. Many were hurt themselves, faces and limbs bandaged, but they still bustled about, carrying herbs and bandages.

Most of the wounded were Vir Requis, Bayrin saw, but some were Tirans with platinum hair and pained blue eyes. For a moment rage filled Bayrin. Why should they tend to wounded Tirans, the men who had tried to slaughter them? But he only sighed, his rage soon dissipating. *Let the bastards live. Let them see the mercy and goodness of those they thought mere reptiles.*

Finally they reached a narrow hallway, its wall smashed and its floor strewn with bricks. Two guards in breastplates stood before a doorway, clutching spears. They bowed to Elethor and pulled the door open.

"Go and see her," Elethor said softly. "I'm needed at court, and you two have a lot to discuss." He clutched Bayrin's shoulder, then pulled him into an embrace. "It's good to have you back, friend."

When Bayrin stepped alone into the room, he found himself holding his breath, suddenly sheepish. Their quest north, the battle with the demon of wood and stone, the inferno over Nova Vita... it all seemed like a bad dream to him now. He had kissed Mori on the Crescent Isle, had vowed to protect her, but... back home, in Nova Vita, would she mock him for it? Would they be as before the war--he the ne'er-do-well guard, she the timid princess who shied away at every touch? It felt like waking from a dream, not knowing what the dawn would bring.

She lay in a bed, wrapped in embroidered blankets, her wounds bandaged. When she saw him enter, she smiled wanly and lowered her eyes. The dawn's light kissed her pale cheeks, pink lips, and chestnut hair. She was so beautiful.

Bayrin stepped toward her, hesitant. She looked up at him, then down again, and her eyes dampened. His breath caught, he froze... and then he took three great strides toward her. He found himself embracing her, nearly crushing her in his arms, as she wept against him, soaking his shirt. As the morning's light fell upon them, they kissed with tears and laughter. She touched his cheek, and he couldn't help but cry too; joy and relief swept over him.

"Hi there, Mors," he whispered.

She smiled tremulously, tears on her lips. "Hi there, Bay."

He laughed and pulled her back into his embrace. He rocked her gently in his arms.

"I told you we'd do it," she whispered.

Still holding her, Bayrin looked outside. Burnt trees rose between ashy walls. Buildings lay toppled. But he saw people move between those buildings, lifting fallen bricks, collecting shattered weapons, and sweeping the ash away. It would be a time of pain, he knew, of mourning and grief. *But we will rebuild.*

He knew then--things would not return to how they had been. He had changed too much. He remembered himself before the phoenix fire--a lowly guard with great parentage. He had watched his sister rise in the ranks of the court, his father lead

armies, his mother speak to the stars. And he would joke to hide
his pain, run off with Elethor to escape his failed life.

But he had purpose now. He had Mori.

*I may still be nothing but a lowly guard... but I guard the Princess of
Requiem, the woman I love.*

"I won't let anyone hurt you again," he whispered into her
hair. "I love you, Mori. I know that healing will be long and
painful--for you, for this city, for all of us. I know that some
battles only now begin. But you have me. We'll go through this
together."

She lowered her eyes, her lashes brushing his cheek, and
clung to him. "I miss them, Bay. My brother. My father. I miss
them so much, that... I don't know if the pain will ever end." She
looked up at him, eyes sparkling with tears. "I love you too,
Bayrin. Always. So much that it hurts, so much that... when you
fell from the sky, I thought I would die, that light could never
more shine in the world." She smiled shakily and nodded. "We
will heal together, Bay, you and I. It hurts so much, but... we have
each other. We'll do this together."

A robin took flight outside the window, rising into a clear
sky. *Spring is here,* Bayrin thought, Mori in his arms. They sat
together silently, embracing, watching the dawn rise.

ELETHOR

He stood above the twin graves, jaw tight, staring with dry eyes.

The stones rose tall and white, carved of marble and engraved with the Draco constellation. One bore the name of King Olasar. The second bore the name of Prince Orin.

My father. My brother.

Elethor lowered his head. Spring had come to Requiem, and grass grew where snow, blood, and ash had fallen. Bluebells bloomed upon the hill, and the air was sweet, but Elethor's heart was heavy. He found no peace here, only memories and grief.

He remembered the day of the funerals. His throat tightened to remember the coffins, their birch wood inlaid with golden leaves and stars. Elethor had looked upon them, unable to stop the horrible thoughts, the twisting imagination. Inside the coffin, was his father only a burnt skeleton? Was his brother just a severed head--the only part of him found? He had clenched his fists, praying to remember Father as the wise ruler, his brother as the handsome hero, to forget the blood and fire.

That had been a moon ago, but the blood and fire remained in Elethor's mind, and even the song of birds or the scent of flowers could not dull them.

How do you forget the sight of dead children, limbs severed and bellies slashed? How do you forget the demon Nedath, or the sphinx of the underground, or the shriveled bodies that lingered there?

He turned away from the graves, jaw clenched and eyes burning.

He walked that day through the city of Nova Vita, his guards at his sides. Requiem's crown, forged three hundred years ago by Queen Gloriae herself, rested on his head. He visited the temple and spoke to those who still lay wounded, healing or slowly dying. He visited buildings covered with scaffolding, where masons spoke of new walls, arches, and towers. He visited the barracks of soldiers, too many of them gone, and praised their courage and sacrifice.

The numbers spun through his head as he moved through the city. Fifty thousand Vir Requis had lived here under his father's reign. He now ruled thirty thousand haunted souls.

Everywhere he looked, he saw the wounds of battle. As he walked through the city, Elethor saw a child sitting upon a toppled wall, his face wrapped in bandages, his eyes peering and haunted. He saw a young woman sweeping her porch; her left arm ended with a stump. He saw a husband leading his wife down a street; a scarf covered her eyes, and a scar ran along her head.

Elethor greeted all those he passed, squeezed shoulders, whispered comforts. He tried to stand strong. To smile. To jest that wounded children were stronger than knights, that farmers missing limbs would be back plowing tomorrow, that women with burnt faces were still as beautiful as queens. His words tasted stale.

He turned to face a wall and shut his eyes. *Did I drive her to this?* he wondered, as he wondered every day, the guilt clawing inside him. He touched the scar along his face, a twin to the one Solina bore, her last gift to him. *Did I cause this death and pain?*

"My lord."

The gruff voice rose behind him. Elethor turned to see Lord Deramon. The burly man stood in burnished armor. His sword clanked at his side, and in his left hand, he held his axe. More white than ever filled his beard.

Elethor approached him, and the two stepped into a quiet, cobbled alley.

"So many lost limbs, eyes, faces." Elethor lowered his head. "Every wounded person mourns dead family and friends. Deramon, how do I give them strength? How do I comfort them?"

Deramon gave a low grumble like a bear disturbed in his cave. He blew out his breath and said, "Give them time to mourn. You walk among them. You stand tall. You smile rather than cry. This is well, Elethor. You are doing right."

Elethor nodded, eyes stinging. "I keep thinking... what would my father do?" He looked up at Deramon. "How would he lead today?"

Deramon's lips tightened and he clutched Elethor's shoulder. For a moment, Elethor was sure that the lord would admonish him, call him a callow boy, speak of how greater King Olasar had been.

But Deramon only stared at him steadily and said, "Your father watches from the stars, Elethor, and he's proud of you. *I* am proud of you. You will make a fine king, and a fine husband to my daughter." He growled and hefted his axe. "I'll be here to make sure of it."

Grumbling, the lord trundled out of the alley, barked orders at some wandering guards, and disappeared around a corner.

That evening, Elethor walked toward the gazebo in the city square, the place where she had asked him to surrender, and where he chose to lead Requiem to war. He stood staring at the columns and glass panes, then turned and looked south. Somewhere beyond forest, mountain, and desert, Solina waited.

Are you looking north now, Solina? Do our eyes meet across the endless leagues?

"Elethor."

Again a voice rose behind him, but this voice was high, fair, and soft. For a terrible instant, he was sure it was *her*, Solina. He spun around, saw Lyana, and slowly exhaled.

She stood in her silvery armor, the ancient armor of the bellators, the knights of Requiem; she was the only one of their number to survive. Her eyes were soft, and her sword hung from her waist. Her wounds had healed, the scabs peeling to show her pale skin strewn with freckles like stars. A year ago, the mere sight of Lyana would chafe him, like seeing a bee during a garden meal. Today she seemed so fair to him, so soothing, that his eyes stung.

This is how I let go of the ghosts, he thought. *With Lyana.*

"She offered me surrender here," he said to her, voice soft. "In this gazebo. If I had gone with her to Tiranor, how many would still live? How many lives would I have saved?" He shook his head. "Did I make a mistake, Lyana?"

She walked toward him, placed her hands on her hips, and glared at him. "Elethor, if you do not stop speaking utter nonsense, I will kick your backside across this square. If you had surrendered, she would have burned us all, and you know it." Her eyes flashed. "So will you please stop moping, and maybe grow some sense in your hollow head?"

He sighed. *Same old Lyana after all.*

"Would have saved me the lectures," he said and couldn't help but smile.

She shook her head, curls flouncing. "Just wait until we are wed, Elethor. If you think this is bad, you haven't seen nothing yet." She grabbed his hand and tugged him. "Now come *on*! Stars. We're meeting my parents in the court today, and the Prince of Osanna will be there, and if you are late again, I swear that I will..."

He stopped listening. He let her pull him across the square toward the palace, and as they walked, he looked at the flowers that grew in gardens, and the masons hauling bricks, and the doves that flew, and he felt something new, something he had never felt in his life.

He felt whole.

SOLINA

She stood upon the Tower of Akartum, a spire of sandstone and platinum. The wind billowed her hair, tasting of sand and palm oil. Tiranor rolled before her: the lush palms of her oasis, fluttering with cranes and ibises and falcons; the ships that sailed along the River Pallan, laden with spice and gems and treasures of distant lands; the towers of her city, shards of white capped with gold; and beyond them dunes kissed golden with her lord's light, rolling to distant yellow mountains.

"It is my realm," she whispered into the wind. "My magical world of secrets." She shook her head, hair billowing. "You could have been here with me. You could have stood here too."

She looked north past oasis, dune, and mountain. Did he stand there too upon a tower, looking south toward her? She caressed her shoulder where she bore a scar his sword had given her. And yet she loved him, even now.

She could have killed him, she knew. She had wanted to. In the tunnels of Requiem, the bloody dagger in hand, she could have plunged it into his heart. But no. Not yet. He had not suffered enough in life to escape her torment.

"I will bring you here, El," she said and licked the sand from her lips. "But first... first you will watch me slay your sister, and your betrothed Lyana, and all the people of your realm. You will stand and watch them die, and I will make you drink their blood." She nodded, a soft smile on her lips. "And then, El, then I will bring you here, a broken man. I will chain you to this tower, and let the vultures feed upon your living flesh and eyes. And then, El... then maybe I will grant you mercy. Then maybe I will kiss you and let you die."

Upon her tower, she turned around and faced south.

Her army spread across the desert.

A hundred thousand men stood in burnished breastplates, bearing spears, bows, and arrows tipped with poison. Ten thousand horses stood in armor, tethered to chariots of wood and iron. The sun fell upon them, and the golden suns upon her men's breastplates blazed. And behind her men...

Solina's smile widened.

Beyond the army, the dunes undulated, and grumbles rose from beneath. Something was buried there, something ancient and cruel. Beneath the sand waited her greatest champions, like the eggs of snakes waiting to hatch. Soon the desert was trembling, and a crack opened, a womb ready for birth. Sand fell into the crevice. The grumbles turned to roars that shook the city.

Solina raised her arms. Her heart thrashed and her blood thrummed in her ears.

"Arise, my children!" she cried. "Arise from the desert and serve your queen!"

As the beasts hatched from the sand, Solina snarled, tossed her head back, and howled at the sun and its glory.

The story continues in...

A DAY OF DRAGON BLOOD

Dragonlore, Book Two

NOVELS BY DANIEL ARENSON

Standalones:

Firefly Island (2007)
The Gods of Dream (2010)
Flaming Dove (2010)

Misfit Heroes:

Eye of the Wizard (2011)
Wand of the Witch (2012)

Song of Dragons:

Blood of Requiem (2011)
Tears of Requiem (2011)
Light of Requiem (2011)

Dragonlore:

A Dawn of Dragonfire (2012)
A Day of Dragon Blood (2012)
A Night of Dragon Wings (forthcoming)

KEEP IN TOUCH

www.DanielArenson.com
Daniel@DanielArenson.com
Facebook.com/DanielArenson
Twitter.com/DanielArenson

ACKNOWLEDGEMENTS

I could not have written *A Dawn of Dragonfire* without lots of help.

Thank you, Anne, for editing this book.

Thank you, Kerem, for your cover art.

Thank you, Janelle, for beta reading.

Thank you, Leticia, for helping me fight tax forms, spreadsheets, and other real world monsters; they can be as vicious as dragons.

And of course, thank you all the fantastic *Song of Dragons* fans--meeting you has been the best part of writing these books, and I could never have written this new one without your support.

Made in the USA
Lexington, KY
11 December 2012